This series is dedicated to all
US military veterans of all branches
who served in times of peace or war,
for your families who stood by you,
for all of you now serving our country,
for all now waiting for a loved one to return,
and for those whose wait has ended in tragedy.
God's love is for you.
The Homeland Heroes Series is for you.

★★★

**Also by Donna Fleisher**

*Wounded Healer* (Homeland Heroes—Book One)

HOMELAND HEROES
✭
Book Two

DONNA FLEISHER

# WARRIOR'S HEART

ZONDERVAN™

GRAND RAPIDS, MICHIGAN 49530 USA

We want to hear from you. Please send your comments about this book to us in care of zreview@zondervan.com. Thank you.

ZONDERVAN™

*Warrior's Heart*
Copyright © 2005 by Donna Fleisher

Requests for information should be addressed to:
Zondervan, *Grand Rapids, Michigan 49530*

**Library of Congress Cataloging-in-Publication Data**

Fleisher, Donna
    Warrior's heart / Donna Fleisher.
      p. cm.
    ISBN-10: 0-310-26395-6 (softcover)
    ISBN-13: 978-0-310-26395-1 (softcover)
    I. Title.
    PS3606.L454W68 2005
    813'.6—dc22
                             2005002987

All Scripture quotations, unless otherwise indicated, are taken from the *New King James Version*. Copyright © 1982 by Thomas Nelson. Used by permission. All rights reserved.

*Interior design by Michelle Espinoza*

*Printed in the United States of America*

05 06 07 08 09 10 11 12 /❖ DCI/ 10 9 8 7 6 5 4 3 2 1

*For Brooke*

*What made me think I could take five weeks off in the middle of
deadline to travel the entire western hemisphere? But sharing that trip
with you, and sharing each moment of the journey of this book with
you across the miles, has been incredible. Especially those last two
weeks of desperate overtime. You're not just a friend, you're a gift.*


*And for Margaret*

*What made me think I could take five weeks off in the middle
of deadline to travel the entire western hemisphere? But from
Philadelphia to Denver to the rolling Caribbean and back,
watching you sing, speak, laugh, and share so much of yourself
with all of us . . . it was incredible. What you do, how you do it,
for all these years, there are no words to describe how grateful I am
to you. Fro you. For all you are. Thanks, lady.*

# ACKNOWLEDGMENTS

Precious Lord God, here we are again! Thank You so much for this incredible journey. And thank You for all those who encouraged and strengthened me along the way. Especially . . .

Mom and Dad, Chris, Thess, Christine, and Mario. My precious family.

Karen Ball, Diane Noble, and positively everyone at Zondervan. I cannot thank them enough, Lord, so I'll leave it up to You to bless them in ways I can't even imagine. Please, again, accept our offering and use it to Your honor.

Thanks for everyone at the 2004 and 2005 Mount Hermon Christian Writers Conferences and everyone at Oregon Christian Writers. What can I say, Lord? So many sweet memories. So many sweet friends. Thank You for each and every one.

Thanks again for everyone at the Sandcastle, and for my little beachfront home.

Thanks for Shannon and Susie and Vickie and Heather and Melissa and Trish and Steph and June and their families. I love them all so much. Thank You for Jeanna. Thank You for Brooke and the Schwhew Crew. Thank You for Margaret Becker and Gayle Erwin, who minister Your Word straight to my soul. Thank You for Francine Rivers, who is my example in this crazy mixed-up industry.

And Lord? Thanks for Corinne at Ole's Gun Shop, who answered my questions about 9mm Berettas and .38 Specials while praise and worship music filtered through the speakers in her store. Of all the gun shops in Salem, Oregon, You sent me to Ole's to meet a sister. What an awesome God You are!

# WARRIOR'S HEART

# FEBRUARY 1996

# ONE

ERIN MATHIS PULLED OPEN ONE of the new glass double doors lead-ing into the hollowed-out warehouse that would soon become Kim-berley Square's gymnasium and held it open so Sonya Connelly could enter first.

Judging by her smile, Sonya appreciated the gesture, until she took two steps inside the warehouse, stopped in her tracks, raised her chin, and shrieked, "Christina McIntyre! What on earth do you think you're doing?"

The sudden intensity and sheer volume of Sonya's normally pleasant southern drawl startled Erin so much, her sharp intake of breath sounded to her own ears like a puppy's yelp. She hurried inside. Isaiah Sadler stood on the other side of the room. He held a rope in his hands. Erin's gaze followed that rope up into the rafters of the old warehouse.

Her mouth fell open. High above Isaiah, at the other end of the rope, Christina McIntyre, one of Erin's dearest friends, dangled upside down by her knees from a rafter, clutching what looked like a plastic Safeway bag in her teeth.

Well. No wonder Sonya stopped in her tracks. A smile worked its way across Erin's lips.

"Why are you—?" Sonya's drawl echoed across the warehouse. "Christina! You come down from there!"

Erin's smile faded as a thread of fear laced itself around her heart.

"Right now, young lady! Before you fall!"

Isaiah's soft voice carried to them. "She's fine, now, Sonya. She's almost done." Standing there, holding the rope Chris had obviously used to climb up into the rafters, Isaiah's eyes reflected a hint of sheepishness.

"What is she doing?" Sonya peered heavenward as she and Erin walked closer. "Christina? Are you all right?"

Chris pulled the bag from her teeth. Her voice rained down from above. "Hey, Sonya! Hey, Rinny! What's up?"

Erin couldn't help it. She started to laugh—until Sonya turned and gave her a don't-encourage-her scowl. Her laughter died on a fake cough.

"Yep, Isaiah, I think that'll do it," Chris said. "This bulb is definitely defective. We should take it back."

"Um, okay, Chris." Isaiah didn't look up as he said the words. "I'll take care of that Monday." He looked at Sonya. His face bore a strained smile.

"A lightbulb?" Sonya stopped a few feet from him and put her hands on her hips. "She climbed up there just to change a lightbulb?"

"Little slack," came from above.

Isaiah fed a few feet of rope through his fingers.

Erin glanced up—just as Chris slid down the rope, still upside down, Safeway bag in her teeth, feet flying. She dropped to almost perfect eye level; the rope creaked as she bounced once, then twice. She pulled the bag from her teeth, handed it to Isaiah, then beamed an upside-down red-faced smile at Sonya and said, "Hi there."

For a second, nobody moved. Nobody said a word. But then Chris, hanging like a yo-yo, slowly started to turn as the rope she hung from, the rope she had twisted together around the rafter, started to unwind.

Erin stole a glance at Sonya. Saw a mouth that gaped, cheeks that had flushed into a deep, dark pink.

Chris lowered her feet and lightly touched back down on earth. As the silence lingered, she tugged off her thick leather gloves and rubbed her nose.

Sonya quickly shook her head. Then looked at Isaiah. "Where's Amanda?"

"She's, um . . ." He coughed quietly. "She's in the office pumpin' up volleyballs."

Sonya's voice pierced Erin's eardrums. "AMANDA!"

The little girl's head popped through the office door. "Hi, Grammy!"

"Get your jacket. It's time for lunch."

"Aww, do I have to, Grammy? I'm not finished yet."

"Yes, child. You can come back later." Sonya lowered her voice. "Unless the two of you have more lightbulbs to change."

"Um, no, Sonya. We're done." Chris tossed the rope away, though it came back and slapped against her backside.

The expression on Chris's face eased the fear in Erin's heart. Chris looked like she had just gotten caught with her hand in the cookie jar.

Good. Because she had.

"Hi, Auntie Erin!" Amanda's sweet voice shook as she skipped toward the group. "Guess what! I was blowin' up volleyballs!"

"Very cool!" Erin swept the little girl up into a half hug. "I bet your lips are tired." She let the girl's burst of giggles carry her own.

"Are we havin' pizza for lunch, Grammy?" Amanda pushed her arms into the sleeves of her jacket. "Pep'roni, huh? Or maybe chicken! Yay!" Her sparkly blue eyes peeked out through flyaway blonde curls. "Let's go, Grammy. I'm hungry. Bye, Uncle 'Saiah! Bye, Auntie Chris!" She turned and skipped toward the door.

Happy good-byes and waves came from both Chris and Isaiah, until they glanced at Sonya. Silence descended. Smiles became sheepish grins.

With a quick shake of her head, Sonya turned and started for the door.

Erin stood there another second, then smirked at both Chris and Isaiah before turning to follow Sonya and Amanda outside.

On the other side of the gym's glass doors, outside under the trees, a cold, misty dampness had settled in with the afternoon. The heavy air fell over Erin gently, as it always did. She breathed deeply and enjoyed all the familiar fragrances of her forested inner-city home.

Sonya seemed to be waiting for her, standing there, watching her granddaughter skip and hop, skip and hop across the cracks in the sidewalk.

"You okay?" Erin said, her voice soft as a whisper.

The long silence concerned her. Sonya's face appeared hard and set, until she looked at Erin and said, her voice hushed to protect her little one's tender ears, "She has this thing about . . . being upside down on a rope, doesn't she."

Erin tried to restrain a smile.

"This is what Benjamin told me about."

"He told you about the time she repelled out of the Huey?"

"Yes. But I hardly believed it. Until now."

She couldn't help it. Her outgoing breath carried a hint of laughter.

"How could she do that?" Sonya's voice raised to the next octave. "How could she fall upside down out of a hovering helicopter?"

Erin shook her head. "I really don't know."

"*Why* would she do it?"

She drew in a deep breath. "I don't know that either. For a while, I used to wonder about her."

"Well, I should say so. After what I just saw, I'm beginning to wonder about her."

"Don't, Sonya. She's all right. She just lives life on a different plane than us."

"What is she thinking? Is she trying to prove something?"

"No, she's not trying to prove anything. She can just do these things. She's not like anyone I've ever known before. She's strong. And she's not afraid of anything."

"I didn't even know women like this existed."

Erin only smiled.

"Shows you what I know."

"Look, Grammy! A worm!"

Sonya rolled her eyes. "Don't touch it!"

Erin's smile widened.

"All right, well, I guess . . ." Sonya blew out a deep breath, then turned toward her grandchild.

"Sonya?"

She stopped and looked back at Erin.

"Don't be too hard on Chris," Erin said softly. "She's still trying to find her way here."

"Mercy, child. Listen to you." Sonya's eyebrows lifted. "Do you forget who you're talking to?"

Erin's gaze fell away as she smiled.

"I love that child. Just because I don't particularly understand her at the moment doesn't mean I've stopped loving her."

Erin slowly nodded.

"She's a precious treasure, and we're all so glad she's here. Don't you ever forget that."

"Yeah. I'm sorry."

"Nah. No need to be. Why don't you two come on over for dinner tonight? And bring Scott. There'll be plenty."

"Thanks, Sonya. But Scott's taking me out tonight. To a Blazer game."

"Ahh. Well, that sounds like a plan." Sonya gasped. "Amanda! I told you not to touch that! Come here. Give me your hand." She gathered up her granddaughter and pointed her toward home. "See you tomorrow, then, sweetheart," she said to Erin.

"Bye, Sonya. Love you. Bye, Mandy!"

"Bye, Auntie Erin!"

Erin's smile faded as she watched Amanda's worm scurry back away under a pile of leaves.

"Whatcha doin', Auntie Erin?"

That familiar voice. Erin looked over her shoulder. Chris stood by the gym's doors. "Well, hello there, Auntie Chris." She turned to face her, then lowered her chin and tilted her head. "Are you and Uncle 'Saiah planning any more adventures for today?"

Chris didn't laugh. Didn't even smile. Her gaze traced the outline of the sidewalk for a few seconds. She looked up. "Um . . . Rin? Am I in trouble?"

Erin tried not to laugh but she couldn't help it.

"It was stupid, I know. But that dumb light was driving us nuts, and we took back the lift yesterday. We would've had to wait until Monday to rent it again, plus that would've cost another hundred bucks at least, not to mention all the time it would've taken to get the trailer set up and to go back and get it and—"

"Chris."

"What."

"You were hanging upside down by your knees from a rafter."

"But I had the rope around me. I couldn't have fallen."

"How did you get up there in the first place?"

"Throwing the rope up was the hardest part. You should've seen us. We were cracking up."

Erin imagined it and wanted to smile, yet she kept her face firm. "You should still be taking it easy, and you should still be wearing your collar. You should not be climbing ropes to hang upside down from rafters."

Chris let out a long breath of disgust. "Rinny, I am over wearing that stupid collar. I'm okay."

"Well." Erin let out her own deep breath. "I guess you proved that. If you can crawl up a rope and hang by your knees just to change a lightbulb, then far be it from me to worry about the ruptured muscles in your neck."

"I'm healed, Rinny."

"So I see."

"I'm good as new."

"And crazy as ever."

Chris smiled.

Erin pushed her hands deep into her jacket pockets and kicked a twig off the sidewalk.

"You didn't answer my question."

She met Chris's gaze.

"Am I in trouble? With Sonya?"

"Nah. I think she'll get over it."

"She looked really mad."

"Not mad. Just . . . confused."

Chris's dark brown eyes widened. "Confused?"

Erin nodded. "Yep."

"Confused about what?"

"About you, silly."

Chris looked away as she said, "Great."

They stood in silence for a while. Erin watched two chickadees chase each other through the limbs of a bare oak. She couldn't wait for spring, for the buds to form, for the daffodils, the lilacs, the tulips . . . for her life to settle back down into some form of normalcy, back into her usual happy routine. How had things gotten so out of hand lately? A faint breath of laughter spurted out her lips. She covered it by clearing her throat.

Out of hand. Chris's way of saying insane. The night she smashed two dresser drawers against the wall of her room. Erin rushing to catch a flight to Colorado when she had no idea what waited for her once she arrived. Out of hand. Insane. And yet . . .

Her life would never again be the same. And Chris's life, forever changed. All the insanity. Worth it in every way. *Thank You, Lord,* whispered up from Erin's soul. *Thank You so much for leading us to this place. This moment.*

And yet . . .

She turned to look at Chris. "Are you about done working for today? Have you had lunch yet?"

"Well, um . . . yeah, we're almost done." The response came slowly, as if Chris chose her words carefully, as if she wasn't exactly telling the truth. "We were thinking about putting another coat of paint in the boys' bathroom. But maybe that can wait. I guess."

"Can you stop and take a break for lunch?"

"I'm not sure . . . what Isaiah has planned."

Chris's dark eyes skipped back and forth, up and down, never settling on Erin's face. For spite, Erin moved closer and peered in one of the gym's glass doors. Isaiah sat on a pile of boxes, eating a sandwich. Erin grinned at Chris. "I'd say he has lunch planned."

Chris barely laughed.

"Okay. Look. If you still have work to do, fine. If you're hungry, why don't you come home with me and get some lunch. Then you can come back. I know Isaiah won't mind. Although I'm sure you've found him to be the strictest of taskmasters."

Now Chris laughed aloud. "Strict? Come on, Rinny. Isaiah's a sweetheart. Reminds me so much of Raymond. Makes me miss Raymond."

"Me too. He should come here."

"Who? Raymond?"

"Yeah. We could sure use him. It'd be fun to have him around."

"He wouldn't like living in a city."

Erin's heart clenched. She forced in her next breath. "What's not to like?"

Chris only smiled. A pressed, fake smile that lasted but a second. Maybe two.

Irritation swept through Erin's belly. "So are you coming for lunch or what?" She threw in a goofy grin. "We may have some leftover pep'roni pizza."

Chris's face softened. "No, I want chicken!" And her dark eyes shone. Before turning cloudy. "Um . . . Rin? Is, um . . . is Scott home?"

Erin's heart again clenched. And the way her stomach felt now, she wasn't sure she even wanted to eat. "No. He's out running errands." She knew those were the words Chris hoped to hear. "I don't figure him back until later. Around three."

"Um, okay. But let me go finish up first—put my stuff away. I'll meet you at your place in about a half hour. Is that okay?"

Erin smiled. "Sure. I'll be there."

"Okay. See you in a little bit." Chris turned, pulled open one of the doors, and headed back into the brightly lit gym.

Erin watched for a second, watched the laid-back strides of a woman who had become closer than a sister to her. Of a woman who absolutely, positively drove her crazy.

*Please help her, Lord. Help her find her way here. Help her, dear Lord, to . . .* She hated even thinking about it. Even the slightest possibility of it. *Oh, please help her, dear Lord. Don't let her leave. Please help her . . . to stay.*

She turned and started a slow, solemn trek toward home.

### ✯✯✯

FIRST THE CHUNK OF CHICKEN. Then the chunk of cheese. The fork his wife wielded bore all the signs of a lethal weapon in the hands of a crazed murderer.

"Don't play with your food, Amanda, eat it. Benny, drink your milk."

His wife directed the words toward their two precious grandchildren, yet Benjamin Connelly immediately picked up his glass of milk and swallowed a long drink.

"I'm finished, Grammy," his four-year-old grandson said. "Can I be es-cused?"

"Eat the rest of your apple."

And the boy complied. As did his grandfather.

Another chunk of chicken speared with that fork, with all the vigor of a caveman spearing a mastodon. Ben quietly cleared his throat. And dared speak. "Sonya? Sweetheart?"

"Yes, Benjamin?"

"What's—pardon the pun—eating at you?"

"What?" Her eyes flashed annoyance.

"Pappy, I'm finished now. 'Kay?"

"Take care of your plate please."

"'Kay."

He watched both children carry their plates, silverware, and glasses to the kitchen, then stand on tiptoes to put them on the counter. Amanda returned to plant a sloppy thank-you kiss on her grandmother's cheek that her grandmother happily returned.

The sight about burst Ben's heart.

"Go on over to the church," Sonya told Amanda. "I'll be there rightly so."

"Okay," Amanda said. "Come on, Benny. Bye, Pappy!"

"Bye, Spoofer. Bye, Tiger!"

Little Benny's mighty roar carried back to Big Benny, who only shook his head and laughed. He popped a slice of apple into his mouth and glanced up at his wife. Her face bore a tender smile. Ben saw so much of himself there, in her beautiful pale green eyes.

"You get enough?" she asked.

He swallowed. "Yep."

"You still want to know what's eating at me?"

"Yep."

Sonya took a deep breath. "Well, just a few minutes ago, when I went to the gym to get Amanda, I saw Christina hanging upside down by her knees from one of the ceiling rafters. Now, you know I'm terrible at judging distances, but I'm sure she was at least a good thirty feet up. She said she was changing a lightbulb. A lightbulb, Benjamin! With Isaiah standing right there. He was holding the rope she used to climb up there! What do you think of that?"

Ben didn't know what to think. He knew he didn't want to laugh—knew this was a predicament of a most serious nature—yet, the more he thought about it . . .

"What if she would have fallen, Benjamin? She would have died!"

He wiped his mouth with a napkin to hide his smile. "She wouldn't have fallen."

Sonya jerked back in her chair, her eyes bulging. "How do you know that?"

"I just know."

"She should not have been up there. After all she's been through."

Her words were true. Ben folded the napkin and placed it next to his plate. "I'm sure she must have felt it was necessary to do it. She wouldn't have done it without a good reason. Still . . . I'm sure Isaiah must have tried to talk her out of it."

"Well, obviously, he didn't try hard enough."

"He must have trusted her."

"He doesn't even know her."

"Do any of us?"

That froze Sonya for a second.

"Sweetheart, we have to trust her. To let her be who she is." Ben ran his finger down the droplets of water that had formed on the outside of his glass of milk. "If we try to change who she is, she'll . . . leave."

"I don't want her to leave."

"I know you don't. But you have to realize how hard it is for her to be here. She wants to stay, but is looking for any excuse to leave."

"She mustn't leave, Benjamin. I feel it. She needs us."

"I agree. And, you know what else?"

"What."

Ben looked his wife in the eye. "We need her."

She let out a long, deep breath.

"You can trust her," Ben said softly. "I do. Completely. You're just going to have to take my word for it."

"All right. Well, then, fine." Sonya leaned back in her chair and crossed her arms over her chest. "But I guess, Benjamin, there's one thing we'll just have to make sure we do around here then."

"What's that?"

"Hide all the rope."

✷✷✷

ONLY A BLOCK OR TWO. But at Erin's present pace, the trip would take a full ten minutes, maybe even fifteen. A mosey. At best. And she liked it that way. Especially down her street. Kimberley Street.

Past the Colby's house, with its battered fence and neglected Christmas lights. Past Lenora McClare's house, with her jungle of houseplants choking her front windows, and her cat, Fredericka, curled up against the glass watching, curious, as Erin sauntered by.

She knew every house on her stretch of Kimberley Street. Knew most of her neighbors in the twenty-some blocks of northeast Portland, Oregon, she and her coworkers affectionately called Kimberley Square. Hundreds of people. Children, parents, grandparents, great-grandparents. Dogs, cats, ferrets, and various reptiles. An eclectic conglomeration of the world's cultures neatly packaged in American pride and cohabitating peacefully in the City of Roses.

So, then, yes. What was not to like?

Yes, Chris was born and raised in Denver, Colorado. Yes, as of two weeks ago, she lived in a small log cabin in the middle of the majestic Rocky Mountains. Soaked in her own mineral hot springs. Breathed the freshest air in the world. Viewed the most picturesque of mountain vistas from her own front window.

The more Erin thought about it, the more her stomach ached. She stopped to closely examine a strand of ivy snaking itself around a stalwart Douglas fir.

The apartment above the clinic was certainly no log cabin. The plain bathtub could never take the place of a mineral hot-spring pool. Especially when it was raining.

She carefully rubbed a green-striated ivy leaf between her fingers and drew in a deep breath.

Smelled like car exhaust. Damp leaves. Heavy, moist air.

Nothing like the crisp, pristine air she breathed standing outside Chris's cabin that night. The night the setting sun hit her full in her face, yet only emitted a touch of warmth to her cheeks. Exactly four weeks ago. Almost to the minute.

It didn't seem possible . . . five years had passed since that horrible day at Dhahran's airport. Leaving Dhahran, Saudi Arabia, for home. Desert Shield had become Desert Storm, and the storm had swept through Iraq with a force unrivaled in the modern era. Weeks of bombings and raids. An intense one-hundred-hour ground war. And then it was all over.

The leaf of ivy was perfect—not a blemish, not a misplaced spot of green. Three, no four different shades of green flowing together, yet distinct.

To see Chris again after all those years, to stand on her porch waiting for her to open the door, then when she did, that smile.

To hear Chris's drunken laughter, her anguished sobs, to see such rage in her eyes, then such joy.

Too much. Erin closed her eyes and whispered the Name that soothed her soul. A prayer. Worship. In its purest form.

She let go of the ivy leaf, opened her eyes, then turned and continued her aimless trek down Kimberley Street toward home.

Home. Yes. This place, in only a few short years, had become her home. Yes, Chris had her Rocky Mountains, and Erin had Mount Shasta—the splendor of northern California. Home for her early years, junior high, high school; the place she and her two brothers loved to hunt and fish, rode all-terrain vehicles to hideaways only they knew about, played football and volleyball and ran track for Mountain Lakes High.

Joe Junior, her older brother, still lived there, though Mickey—Mick as he preferred after taking off for army boot camp—avoided the place like a bad dream. Her dad, Joe Senior, still in the army after twenty-seven years, considered nowhere, and everywhere, his home. At the moment, home for him was Hohenfels, Germany.

Home for his only daughter—the daughter he had tearfully cuddled the day she arrived and proudly named Erin Elizabeth, as her mother had so often told her—stood before her now, a two-story duplex with a huge porch swing and a white picket fence.

Kimberley Street. Portland, Oregon. About as far from Hohenfels, Germany, as a person could get. But soon. A few more months. Her sweet dad, big and burly U.S. Army Sergeant Major Joseph Grayson Senior, would cradle and cuddle his newborn granddaughter, or grandson if Scott had his way. Would he cry? Again? This time? Probably.

Erin could hardly wait.

Which reminded her. It was Saturday. She needed to call her mom.

She moved slowly up the stairs of her house and onto the long porch. If she turned left she would end up at her door. If she turned right she could sit on her porch swing and just . . . sit. And swing. She stood for a second, gazing at the door straight ahead. For the hundredth time she read the words etched in elegant calligraphy on the door's smoked glass window. *Kimberley Street Community Clinic. Scott A. Mathis, MD. Erin Mathis, FNP. Kyle Sundevold, MD.*

Her clinic. Her home. Her porch swing. She headed for it. Wearily sat. Heard the chains creak, the wood slats strain beneath her. Maybe she would ask for a new swing this summer. For her birthday, maybe. How she loved to sit here in her favorite spot in the world, surrounded by all she loved, and just swing.

More creaking as she swung. The cold air suddenly bit sharper. She pulled her jacket more closely around her. Then stopped to gently rub her belly. Starting to show now, the unfathomable miracle tucked away in her belly was growing. Stirring. Stunning. Even the faintest flutter froze the breath in Erin's lungs, causing adoration for her Lord to overflow her heart and soul, her entire being. But that first stirring, when the tiny bundle of life inside her stretched and yawned that first time, she had been soaking in a mineral hot-spring pool thousands of feet up in the Rocky Mountains outside Ouray, Colorado. Then, sharing that moment with Chris . . .

Erin closed her eyes, could almost smell the sulfur from that night, almost feel the soothing water reach deep into the marrow of her bones. Yes, a creamy coconut bubble bath in her huge, old-fashioned claw-foot bathtub just upstairs was nice. But that hot-spring pool, those stars, that owl . . . the soft, haunting hoots filtering back to where they sat immersed in steaming water, across the frozen distance.

A scab on Erin's wrist caught on a fiber of her jacket and pulled—she jerked her hand away to look. A tiny drop of blood. So red. So much blood . . . that night.

Her hand curled into a fist.

*Please, precious Lord. Help me. Help me forget.*

The joy in Chris's eyes. The miracle of salvation, of healing. A new life, a soul reborn. Erin rubbed her wrist, focused on the healing, the peace so long elusive, so long taunting, mocking . . . the peace anew, a peace the world cannot give, peace from the Giver of Life. And joy. Erin focused on the joy.

She almost started to cry. Until a UPS truck rumbled down Kimberley, startling her out of her thoughts. She heard footsteps, someone walking up the sidewalk beside her. She quickly wiped her eyes and tucked her hands under her armpits.

Chris. Arriving, finally, for lunch. But, maybe first, a ride on the swing?

Yes. Erin gladly slid over and let Chris sit beside her.

"Cold?" Chris said.

"Not really. Hungry?"

"Not really."

And Erin smiled.

"Are you?"

"No. I can wait."

A thin silence fell over them. Erin wanted to ask all the hard questions, but she waited. And said, "Did you finish up at the gym?"

"Yeah." Chris blew out a deep breath. "Isaiah wanted me to have the afternoon off." She let out a small grunt.

"Good. You've been working like crazy over there. I haven't seen you . . . much at all this past week." One of the hard questions. Asked like a statement. Took some of the edge off.

"Yeah. We really want to get it done. It'll be so nice to have the place full of kids."

"Are you looking forward to coaching?"

Chris let out another grunt. Sounded almost like a laugh. "The kids will probably teach me how to play the game. Alaina, at nine years old, is a better player than I'll ever be."

Erin didn't say anything, but she knew better. She remembered those hot, desert basketball games. Chris had a wicked outside jump shot, though her defensive skills did leave something to be desired.

Chris slouched low on the swing and laid her head back on the top slat. "It'll be fun. Isaiah's granddaughter can really play too. Amazing."

"Jazzy."

"I love that. Jasmine Skye. But, oh no. Don't you dare call her that. It's Jazzy." Chris did laugh this time. Quietly. "What a cute kid."

Erin turned on the swing and pulled her knee up, then rested her left arm on the top slat. She ran her fingers through her hair. Snuck a long look at Chris. Saw those eyes now closed. Allowed her long look to continue. Saw the greenish bruises that lingered on the side of Chris's neck. Pulled her own hand away and studied the ugly ring of healing cuts and abrasions circling her wrist. Knew it was time for a hard question.

"How have you been feeling, Chris?" Her voice barely carried above a whisper. "Really."

Chris's eyes opened and blinked. Her head didn't turn. "Fine."

"Really?"

"Really."

"I haven't had a chance to talk to you . . . almost since we've been back." Erin picked at a splinter on the swing's top slat. "It's almost like . . ." How did she dare say the rest?

"Like what?"

"Like you've been avoiding me."

Chris's head suddenly turned; confusion and fear emanated from her dark eyes. "I haven't been avoiding you."

"I know. It just feels like that."

"I'm sorry, Rinny. I never wanted that."

"I know."

"I've just tried to stay busy. At the gym. You know." Chris looked straight ahead, at the far side wall of the porch. "I want to . . . work. Pull my weight."

"You've been working too hard. And too soon. I'm sorry, Chris. I don't want to be a nag, but you've been doing too much. You should still be taking things slow. No matter what you say, you're not completely healed yet."

A growl. "Thank you, Nurse Mathis."

"Neither am I." Where did that come from? Erin quickly blinked her eyes to fend off tears.

The silence fell heavily, even though cars passed by them on the street and Mildred Conner walked her yapping terrier, Brisco, toward the park a few blocks east.

The silence lingered. Erin glanced at Chris. Those dark eyes looked right back at her. Chris's lips parted, as if she was about to speak, yet nothing was said. She turned her head away.

Erin drew in a deep breath.

"Are you okay, Rin?" The words were soft.

Her breath whooshed out. "Yeah."

"You still think about . . . all that happened?"

"I'm trying to forget. I pray a lot."

Chris pressed her lips. "Yeah. Me too."

Hearing the words, Erin couldn't help smiling.

"He's really been awesome."

"He has a tendency to be that way."

Chris seemed to relax. "I really like going over to Ben's for the home study."

"Good. Me too. It's a special time."

"Andy's a good teacher. He's so patient."

"You can always ask questions. Don't ever feel intimidated."

Chris looked at her. "Oh, I don't. I even ask Isaiah sometimes. Today we talked about the Old Testament a little. He's such a sweetheart."

Erin could only smile.

"It still feels weird, though."

"What does?"

"Praying. I can't get over it. Just talking to God. I mean, I know He hears me, but it feels weird just being able . . . to do it. Without . . . you know. I don't know. A priest, I guess. Or something like that."

*Someone more worthy, Chris?* Sadness tugged at Erin's heart. *Lord, help her know You've forgiven her. That You love her just the way she is.* She waited another second before saying, "When you read the book of Hebrews—that's almost at the end of the Bible—I'd like to hear what you think. It talks about the Lord Jesus being the only priest we will ever need."

"Okay. I'm still in Luke. So far."

A fairly new hunter green Ford Mustang pulled up to the curb in front of the house. For the first time since the day she met him, Erin didn't want to see the man who pulled himself out of it. *Not yet, sweetheart. Couldn't you have given us just a few more minutes?* She hated herself at that moment. Glanced over at Chris.

Chris saw the car pull up. She immediately sat up on the swing.

"He should be bringing groceries," Erin said. "I can fix us something for lunch."

It was as if she could read Chris's mind. She knew exactly what Chris was going to say even before she said the words. "Um, you know? Rin? I'm kinda tired. I think I'm gonna go on upstairs and lay down for a little bit. Maybe take a shower. If Cap's feeling better, we just might go catch a show or something."

*Sure, Chris. Whatever you say.*

Carrying two full plastic bags of groceries in each hand, Scott Mathis stomped up the stairs. His eyes smiled at his wife. Hardened just a bit, but enough for Erin to notice, when they looked at Chris. "Well, hello, ladies," he said. Bright white teeth filled his smile. "Isn't it a little cold to be swinging?"

Erin glanced at Chris, then at her husband. "We were just about to fix some lunch."

"Great," he said. "I'm starved. I got a pound of smoked turkey at the deli. Harvey let me try a slice, and was it ever good. Should make a great hoagie. Got all the fixin's too."

Chris slowly stood. She couldn't mask her weariness.

Erin stood beside her. "Come on, Chris. How can you pass up a smoked-turkey hoagie?" She said to Scott, "Did you get chips?"

"Yes, m'dear. Plain and barbecue."

"Thanks, guys," Chris said, "but none for me. I'm gonna go on upstairs."

"You sure, Chris? There's plenty." Scott still smiled that toothy smile.

Erin tried to give Chris a knowing look. A thought struck her. "You should come to the basketball game with us tonight. Cappy too." She dared not even glance at Scott, to even think about his thoughts at that moment. She kept her eyes on Chris.

Immediate trepidation clouded Chris's face. "Um, no." She shook her head and breathed a polite laugh. "Really, though. Thanks. I mean it. But not tonight. I am so due for a Blazer game. I'd love to see Rod Strickland play. Just not tonight."

"Well, okay. But just say the word, Chris, and we'll go." Scott's voice carried the words just a bit too loudly.

Erin moved a few steps closer to him. Scott shifted the bags of groceries in his left hand to his right, then pulled her into a tight sideways hug. When she could breathe, she gave Chris a warm smile. "If Cap's still sick, let me know, okay? She's too stubborn to tell anyone." Like someone else Erin knew.

"Yeah. Okay." Chris nodded as her gaze fell to the floor. "She was pretty out of it this morning, but I think she went right back to bed. I'll let you know how she's doing."

"Thanks, Chris."

Chris looked up. And she smiled.

"Well, then, see ya later," Scott said, squeezing Erin against him.

"Yeah. See ya, Scott." Chris's smile faded. "Thanks again for the offer."

"Hey. No problem. Anytime."

*Yeah, right. Anytime.* Erin could only watch as Chris moved around between the swing and the front window of the clinic to the corner of the porch where she turned left and disappeared. Erin heard slow steps up the duplex's side stairs leading to Chris and Cappy's apartment.

Her husband's arm still surrounded her, holding her close. Erin turned to look into his light brown eyes. They seemed to long for her, to shimmer with desire and concern even in the gloom of the cloudy day. Lately, his concern, at times, came close to overwhelming her. But with all that had happened in the past month, she couldn't blame him. She lifted her hands and gently pushed back the thick hair from his forehead. "You need a haircut, Dr. Mathis."

"Right now I need a smoked-turkey hoagie."

"Right now?" Erin let her right eyebrow lift a bit.

"Well, right now, at this exact moment, I guess that's not really what I need." Scott lowered his load of groceries to the floor and cupped Erin's cheeks in his hands.

His hands were cold. His touch sent shivers through her, as it always did.

"There isn't any way our good neighbor can see us, is there?" His breath warmed her cheek. Smelled faintly of cinnamon.

"Who, the good Mrs. Taylor?" Erin breathed the words. "She can't see us here."

"I wouldn't put it past her." A feathery kiss tickled her lips. "But I'm willing to take the chance." Another kiss, this one stronger, lasting longer.

"So brave, my fierce warrior." Erin kissed his lips, hungry for his love, tasted sweet cinnamon on his tongue, and sweet joy from his soul.

Yapping barks from the dog named Brisco destroyed the moment. Erin quickly blinked to focus her gaze across Kimberley Street, saw Mildred Conner retracing her earlier steps. She must have decided to forgo the park today.

Erin pushed herself out of her husband's arms, tugged down on the bottom of her jacket, returned Mildred's happy smile and wave, then let out a deep breath as she lifted her hands to run them through her hair.

"We should move out to the country," Scott said as he bent to retrieve the grocery bags. "Out so far where no one can see us." He headed for the front door.

Erin only laughed as she followed him, until she said, "Hey, you. You may have gotten two kinds of chips, but did you get any pickles?"

# TWO

Upstairs in her apartment, Chris closed the door behind her, then leaned back against it and shut her eyes. Her heart pounded, and she couldn't tell if it was from the walk up the stairs or . . . other reasons. Either way, it didn't matter. A pounding heart meant only one thing right now. She was alive.

Alive, yet still irritated. Why couldn't she sit down for two minutes to talk to her best friend without her best friend's husband showing up? Petty, yes. And she knew it. But it was Scott who drew that line in the sand, not Chris. It was bad enough to live so close to the man, but why did he always have to go out of his way to show up every time Erin and Chris sat down to talk?

But then, how could she blame him?

She lowered her head, then thumped it back against the door. *Lord, forgive me. I just miss talking to her.*

Her eyes slowly opened and she blinked. The apartment was quiet. No coughing, no sneezing, no strains of Latin music from Cappy's bedroom. No signs of life at all. She pushed herself away from the door, tossed her keys on the bookshelf, then pulled off her jacket and hung it up on the hook by the door. Turned. Took a long look around.

A comfortable little place. Bouncy couch in the living room. Fully stocked kitchen. Down the hall to the right, Cappy's bedroom. To the left, Chris's bedroom. End of the hall, a fully functional bathroom. At least it had a real bathtub. No tiny shower stall with wood planks for walls. And a real hot-water heater. No water box by the wood cookstove. No need to chop endless cords of wood. No need to light any fires.

She missed her wood cookstove. And her kerosene lamps.

No, here in her new place, though nothing fancy, maybe, just maybe, it was beginning to feel like home. She started for the kitchen for a glass of water, but a note on the kitchen table caught her eye, a note Cappy must have left. It read, *Hey, Chris. Went out for more meds. I'll bring us home a movie. Hasta la vista. Cap.*

Chris smiled. Then laughed. Sergeant Capriella Sanchez was the most notorious female high-mobility-multipurpose-wheeled-vehicle-maintenance assistant in all of the 101st Airborne Division's 4th Brigade. Poker player extraordinaire. Smoked and joked with the best of them. But now . . . Chris still marveled at the clear and unhindered joy radiating all through and out of Cappy's life.

*It's an honest miracle. You saved her, Lord. You saved me too. From all that we were. We needed You. And You didn't let us down. Thank You, Lord. Thank You so much.*

Cappy, Erin, Bettema, Chris. Good friends, fellow soldiers from a desert war in a distant land so long ago . . . and look now. They all happened to find themselves living on Kimberley Street in Portland, Oregon. At their commanding officer's—Colonel Benjamin Connelly's—little inner-city amusement park.

*Home, Lord? Well, I guess if it works for Tee and Cap and Rinny . . .*

Chris let the note drop back to the table. And smiled. A quiet night at home with a fully medicated Cappy Sanchez, some dinner, a movie . . . there were worse places to be.

*Please, Lord. Please make this work . . . for me.*

She walked into the kitchen and poured herself a glass of water. Stood at the kitchen window overlooking the duplex's backyard. Erin's backyard. So much green, evergreen limbs of Douglas fir, lush green grass, the tilled garden spot. Was Erin a gardener? Would she be out there later this summer harvesting ripe tomatoes or cucumbers, wearing a flowery floppy hat and huge white gardening gloves?

No, Erin would be a little busy this summer. Giving birth. Raising a newborn.

Wow. Unbelievable. In just a few months, Erin Mathis would be a mother.

*Oh, dear God, why would I even want to think about leaving here? Please help me to stay.* She swallowed a long drink of water and dumped the rest in the sink. Took one more look at that garden spot. Then headed for her bedroom.

There on the bed, Erin's grandmother's quilt beckoned. Chris flopped down and ran her fingers over the soft, worn stitching. Outside her bedroom window, below her, cars traversed Kimberley Street, the rush of a city on weekend churned all around her. Yet, this was her little spot. Her own tiny corner of the city. Of the world.

The quilt felt so warm, so soft. The fleece blankets she bought in Mesa were still in a box in the closet. Colorful, soft, elegant patterns of sharp contrast, brilliant swatches blended into stunning displays of artistry. Expensive too. She was so glad the men didn't tear them up, like they did everything else in her cabin. But she still didn't want to get them out. Was still a little too afraid. Afraid the sight of them, the scent of them, would make her too homesick.

She closed her eyes and tried to relax. Yet it fell over her. Hard. She missed Raymond. And Sid. And Liz. She missed the station, the work, the mountains. She missed Travis. Oh, how she missed Travis. Heaviness squeezed the breath inside her. She would always miss Travis. Would always treasure the gentle look in his eyes, the way his smile would capture her. The night they first kissed. Awash in the essence of the moment. In love.

The night he died. The anguish of death. Blood.

She held her breath, fighting off burning tears.

But yet, washed by blood. Her new life now. Raymond was so happy when she told him, as she lay in the hospital bed in Ouray with a literal pain in her neck. "I became a Christian, Raymond. Can you believe that? Me!" And the soft, gentle look in his eyes. His tears of joy.

How many tears? How many would wash away the memory of Travis lying on the ground, steam rising up from the blood that had gushed out his chest? How much blood did it take . . . to wash a heart clean?

*Dear Lord Jesus, thank You . . . for forgiving my sins.* Chris wiped her eyes and drew in a deep breath. *Thank You for this place. For my friends here. And for everyone in Colorado. I know now they all prayed for me. Raymond, Sid. Even Liz, I bet. And You answered their prayers. Please. I don't want to let everyone down. Especially Erin. After everything that's happened, I can't let her down. Never again, Lord. Oh, please . . . don't leave me. Help me.*

It would only take about a half hour for her to pack her stuff, load up her truck, and be gone. She'd pick up Interstate 84 and be halfway to Idaho before anyone missed her. But why? She had served her time in the desert, and when her time was up, she left that place without a backward glance. When she first left Denver all those years ago heading for boot camp, she never gave the place another thought. Germany. Alaska. Well, no, not Alaska. She'd love to go back there someday. As soon as possible. But to stay? To live?

Of all the places she had been, no place felt like this place. Never in her wildest dreams did she ever think she would end up in Portland, Oregon. Or in any city. But here she was. The city moved and breathed and hummed around her as she lay on her bed. Cars and buses. Children laughing, yelling. People walking the street, walking their dogs. Police sirens, loud music, car alarms. Airplanes taking off from the airport. The very air itself seemed to absorb every wisp of sound and echo it back to Chris's ears. And yet, the birds at her window sang joyously. Squirrels in the trees chirped at each other, chased each other from branch to branch, playing. Such majestic trees. Such thick, bright green grass.

She could tell by the way Erin looked at her. *She's afraid I'm gonna leave.*

*But, God, dear God, I can't leave. No matter how hard it gets, how weird it feels, how much this city closes in on me . . . Oh, please, God, don't let it overwhelm me. Don't let it beat me. I can't leave here, Lord. I just can't. Of all the places I've been, Lord God, this is where You are.*

*No matter what happens, help me to remember that. I need to stay. Help me, Lord . . . to stay.*

✯✯✯

AFTER ALL THE GOOD FOOD, such intoxicating laughter, cheers for the home team, in the quiet of the moment, in the darkness of the night, his wife's breaths filtered in and out as soft as a baby's whisper. So deeply, so peacefully, she slept. And yet, Scott Mathis could not sleep at all. The nagging pain burned his gut. Simple anger, slowly growing, simmering into intense resentment. Low-grade hatred. And fear.

He knew it was wrong. That made it worse. He was wrong. And he knew it. But watching his wife sleep, knowing how close he came to losing her, he gently pulled back the blanket. Saw her wrist. The healing cuts, burns on her wrist where the lace of a boot had torn her tender skin. The sight infuriated him, beyond anything he had ever known. And the two men who had done this to her, the men who killed their own friend, still had not been found.

Criminals. Murderers. All of them. Even the one that died. Erin had said he was a Marine. That he stopped the other two men from killing Chris. Didn't matter. Any of it. Erin should not have been anywhere near Colorado that night. She should have been home, safe, at her husband's side. She should have been with him.

Lips tightly pressed, teeth clenched, his breath ground in and out of him. He closed his eyes and tried to pray, but prayer was impossible. Yet, it must not be impossible. He needed to pray.

Just across the way, separated only by thin walls, Chris slept in her *new home.* He would see her every day. Would feel the kick in his gut every time he saw her . . . unless he dealt with it. With his anger. He had to pray. Seek forgiveness. Lay everything down at the feet of his Lord. And leave it there. If he only knew how.

For the love of his wife, for her sake, Scott eased himself out of bed, then headed downstairs to sit on the couch. He didn't turn on the light. He sat in darkness. In silence. Slowly breathed. Opened his heart. And desperately tried to pray.

✹ ✹ ✹

BACK TO BED FROM A midnight nature call, Ben Connelly carefully crawled under the covers, loathe to wake his sleeping beauty. He ever-so-gently reached over and guided a stray strand of blonde hair away from her forehead. She barely stirred. But didn't wake up. Ben smiled. Could only stare at her. So beautiful. His feisty southern belle. Spearing chunks of chicken with a murderous fork. Just because she saw Chris . . .

Ben laughed quietly, then held his breath, hoping the little burst didn't wake his wife. No. She slept on. He slowly shook his head.

Murderous forks. Chris had that way about her. It was a good thing Ben's underling lieutenant didn't have a fork in his hand that day as he rushed off to give Chris that authoritative diatribe. Ben never did hear exactly what the man said to her that day. Maybe he should ask Erin sometime. Or Chris.

Lieutenant Gunderson had maneuvered the Humvee across the post, bragging loudly about how the brigade was in impeccable shape, how everything had been falling into line perfectly, how the 4th Brigade of the U.S. Army's 101st Airborne Division Air Assault would be ready, willing, and able to conquer anything and everything Operation Desert Shield required of them. He would personally see to it. Yes, sir. You can trust me, Colonel.

As 4th Brigade's commanding officer, Ben should have been overjoyed at his assistant's assessment. But he only scowled that day. It was too hot and too close to dinner to care too much about the boastings of a second lieutenant fresh out of officer's candidate school. And so far, all Operation Desert Shield required of his brigade was typical continued combat readiness, massive logistical uplinkings, and massive consumption of water.

As Gunderson parked the Humvee on the Tarmac, a UH-1 Huey helicopter hovered. A medevac Huey emblazoned with a bright red cross on its nose and doors. It was the medevac unit Ben had nicknamed his Wild Card. The Huey and its crew of four had arrived a few weeks earlier from a unit outside the 101st, from Fort Wainwright, Alaska, and had gained an experienced trauma nurse from Fort Lewis, Washington, just that previous day.

Sitting in the Humvee, watching the old Vietnam-era helicopter defy gravity, hearing the deafening *whup-whup* of the rotors, Ben's mind wandered. What did they say they called their Huey? Ticket to Paradise?

He blinked. A rope was thrown out the open side door of the helicopter. Gunderson shut down the Humvee and made a point to climb out and stand almost under the intense rotor wash. Whatever was going to happen, the man made sure he had a front row seat.

Ben reclined in his seat in the Humvee, squinted against the harsh sunlight, somewhat refreshed by the brisk wind swirling under the helicopter's rotors, and waited for the show to begin.

For the longest time, nothing happened. He was just about to call Gunderson back so they could get out of the hot sun. But then a figure hopped out the open side door and landed on the helicopter's skid. A soldier. Of the five souls on board, two were piloting the craft. Of the three remaining, two were women. In the shimmering heat radiating off the Tarmac, Ben couldn't tell who stood on the skid, ready to repel.

His heart quickened. The soldier had trained long and hard, in all types of conditions, in all types of weather, for this very moment. Ben couldn't even imagine the winter conditions this soldier trained under in Fairbanks, Alaska. But if he followed his training and relaxed, just followed the rope down—

The soldier fell off the skid. Headfirst. Falling . . . free-falling! To his death! Ben jerked upright in his seat. But—no. In one graceful swoop, the soldier's feet came down, touched the Tarmac, took a few quick steps, and . . . an exaggerated sidestep or two.

Ben stared. What had he just witnessed?

The soldier looked up, tossed the rope away, and waved to his fellow crew members back up in the helicopter, a beaming smile on his face.

Nothing hurt! A wave! Unbelievable!

Had to be Brisbaine, Wild Card's crew chief. Couldn't have been one of the females—

Gunderson. Suddenly in the face of the soldier. Ben's mouth closed as his teeth clenched. Much waving by Gunderson now, over-abundant hoopla. The Huey started to descend. Landed. The engines slowed. The mind-numbing roar of the rotors eased. Wanting to put to a halt the obvious waste of the Huey crew's time, Ben thought about interceding, but didn't move. He only watched Gunderson. Knew he had to dump the kid. ASAP. Send him to Riyadh. Anywhere. Make him someone else's headache.

He scratched his head, then rubbed his forehead and eyes. Then pushed himself up and exited the Humvee. Leaned against it, squinting, knowing soon, yes, he would send Second Lieutenant Roland Gunderson to Riyadh.

No. Couldn't be. Ben had to force his eyes to focus. Through the shimmering dance of the intense heat rippling up from the pavement, was it? The soldier being reamed by his own administrative underling, the soldier standing at strict attention with his flight helmet off and tucked under one arm, the soldier who had just fallen headfirst a hundred feet from a hovering helicopter . . . was a female! Long wisps of blonde hair floated away from her head, out of a French-styled braid. The way Sonya braided her hair sometimes. That pretty braid in Sonya's gorgeous long blonde hair.

The Huey's crew double-timed it out of the helicopter and assembled themselves beside their downed mate. Ben slowly started to smile, but forced it into a smirk. Palmara, Brisbaine, Coffee, and . . . Grayson. Yes. So. McIntyre. His eyes shifted. Specialist Christina Renae McIntyre. His Wild Card medevac medic just performed a free fall out of her helicopter. And survived.

But would she survive Roland Gunderson?

Ben stood still, leaning against the side of the Humvee, simply watching the display, listening. But he made up his mind. Yes. Let Gunderson have this moment. McIntyre would think twice now before taking a dive out of a perfectly good helicopter. As she should. Then Gunderson would take a ride. On the first vehicle heading away. Anywhere. Just away.

Yes. And Ben smiled.

No, he laughed, and again hoped the silliness didn't wake his wife. Ahh, she slept on. Lost in her dreams.

Slowly, so very carefully, he leaned in to kiss her soft cheek. Once. Not enough. He kissed her again. Her breath hummed. *Sleep on, my love. Just sleep.* He closed his eyes. *Sleep in sweet peace for we are safe.* An old sentiment warmed his heart. *Our boys are out there, my love, in all the corners of this world, keeping watch this night. They're out there on the front lines, giving their all.* But he laughed. Again. And amended his old way of thinking.

*Our boys. Yes, my love. And so too . . . our girls.*

★★★

CAPPY'S PHONE WAS RINGING. WHY was Cappy's phone ringing? At—Chris struggled to open her eyes, to focus on the alarm by the bed—six fifteen? In the morning?

"Cappy!"

Still the phone rang. Chris threw off her blankets and barefooted it to the kitchen. With all the cold meds Cappy ingested last night, no wonder she still slept.

"Hello?"

"Chris?"

"Rinny?"

"Yeah. Are you awake?"

"I'm standing in my kitchen."

"Did I wake Cappy?"

Chris looked down the hall. "Her bedroom door's closed."

"Still sleeping then."

"Hopefully."

"But you're up."

"Rinny, I'm up!"

"Good. Get a shower and come on over. You and I are heading to the cape."

Chris blinked. "The what?"

"No time to explain. Low tide's in less than two hours, and it'll take us at least that long to get there."

"What about church?"

"We'll take the Lord with us. Now get moving. There's no time to waste!"

The phone went dead. Chris stared at it for a full ten seconds before replacing it on the hook.

✯✯✯

"AHH, WE SO NEEDED THIS!" Deep in her heart, Erin prayed even as she hoisted her insulated mug of peppermint tea. "Here's to fresh salty air, seagulls, and billions of sand dollars!"

"Here, here!" Chris raised her own mug of tea. Her goofy laughter tickled Erin's funny bone. The still-dirty dark blue Ford Explorer carried them west out of Portland.

"As soon as you see Highway 6, take it," Erin said after a sip of tea. "Left turn. It's not far."

"So where are we going again?"

"Cape Lookout. Land of saaaand—" Erin stretched the word out, trying to milk the last dramatic ounce out of it—"dollars!"

"Whew. I was hoping we weren't heading for the Land of Just Plain Sand."

"Nope. We've already been there."

"Been there and done that."

"And we ain't goin' back."

"Hopefully."

"Nope, no politics on this trip. Only scenery and splendor."

"And donuts. Slide that box over here."

Smiling, Erin obeyed. Raspberry-filled powdered donuts. Between the two of them, over the next sixty miles, they ate the entire box.

Yes. This was just what they needed. No matter what Scott Mathis had to say about it. And he had said just what Erin expected. But the idea struck her as soon as she opened her eyes that morning and nothing would stand in her way. Not threatening rain clouds. Not high gas prices. Not even the confused, hurt-puppy-dog looks her husband repeatedly gave her.

No. There was no mistaking it. Erin positively adored her husband. But lately? Well, lately his adoration for her felt less like love and more like six wool blankets. Smothering under all that wool, Erin needed a break. And so did Chris. And besides, she needed sand dollars.

Her last trip to the cape netted her over a hundred. She could barely lug them all in the five-gallon bucket she carried. Her shoulders ached for a week. It took her almost six months to give them all out. This time, with Chris along for the ride, maybe they'd find two hundred. She could hardly wait.

✸✸✸

STANDING AT THE TOP OF the stairs in the foyer of the Kimberley Street Community Church, Ben Connelly flashed his sweetest smile. "Good morning, Mrs. Crandle," he said to a pretty, white-haired woman. He prepared to hand her a bulletin as soon as she conquered the last stair.

The woman avoided Ben and his smile, making a point to turn away to accept a bulletin from his son instead, saying, as she did, "Good morning, Pastor Andy. My, you look especially handsome this morning."

Ben pulled his smile into a smirk and directed it at his precious son. Even lifted his eyebrow to complete the look.

"Why, thank you, Mrs. Crandle," his son said to the woman. "I hope you enjoy the service." He looked up at his dad. Gave him a wide smile.

"But doesn't that seem odd to you?"

Ben handed a bulletin to Walter Jenks, then looked at Scott Mathis, who stood beside Andy also handing out bulletins. Although not many of the parishioners this morning would say the young doctor had his mind on his work.

"She, um, just left, eh?" Andy made a silly face at the Whitaker's baby.

"Yes! That's what I said! She just up and left. Even when I asked her not to go. It was still dark!"

No one would give Ben a medal for keeping his mind on his work either. Not now, considering the interesting conversation playing out between his son and his friend.

"Hmm." Andy's brow creased as his lips twisted. "Scott, have you given any thought to seeing a marriage counselor? I know a few good ones if you'd like a referral."

"A marriage counselor?"

Ben Connelly could only smile. His son, Andrew, the respected teacher and leader of the Kimberley Street Community Church . . . had a mean streak.

"Yes. You definitely sound like you're having problems." Andy passed a bulletin and a smile and a "Good morning" to the Chavezes.

"Problems?"

"It's obvious to me you've lost control of your wife."

The young man's eyes almost popped out of his head. Ben bit back a burst of laughter. Handed a bulletin to Roy and Lucy Zillnic.

"Scott, from what you've told me, it sounds like she's grown obstinate. Demanding. Spontaneous. First a trip to the coast, next she'll be wanting to paint your entire bathroom some hideous pastel color." Andy flashed pastoral smiles at everyone, saying, "Good morning. Nice to see you this morning. Good morning," to one and all.

Scott Mathis looked like someone had just kicked him in the stomach.

As fun as it was to watch, considering how unfounded the young man's concerns were, still, enough was enough. Ben handed out his last bulletin, then cleared his throat and said, "Son, don't you have a morning service to lead?"

Andy laughed, then turned and socked Scott on the shoulder. "You know I'm just messing with you, buddy. I'm sure nothing's wrong. Just give her a little space. And talk to her. That's the best advice anyone can give you." He grinned at Scott, then turned and made his way through the crowded foyer toward the pulpit.

Yes. Good advice. Ben was proud of his son. Yet, he couldn't help himself. He turned to Scott. Gave him his best scowl. And said, "Lavender. I've seen it many times. It's terrible. Obstinate women love to paint bathrooms lavender."

A green tint settled over the young man's face.

Ben laughed heartily and slapped Scott on the back. "Ahh, now, not to worry. You've come to the right place. Come on. We'll go right on in and request some serious prayer for you."

★★★

COLD, DAMP, CLOUDY. SPURTS OF rain. Perfect sand-dollar-hunting weather. The smooth, relaxing boat ride across the bay . . . perfect. In four hours, Colin would arrive back at the tip of the Netarts Bay spit to pick them up. Four hours. Plenty of time to find two hundred sand dollars.

Erin zipped her jacket all the way up to her chin, tugged her floppy cap lower over her ears, then snuck a glance at Chris.

Chris stood with her chin raised, eyes closed, just breathing in the moment, and the heavy, salty air.

Erin smiled. Closed her eyes. Joy swelled inside her. *Oh, Father . . . Lord God, I love You. Please feel my love for You. May it be a sweet savor to You. Thank You for everything You've done for us. For Chris. Thank You—*

"So. Are we set or what?"

Her eyes flew open. "We are set!"

"Four hours, right?"

"Yep. Did you bring a watch?"

"No. Didn't you?"

Terror gripped her. She spun around and shouted, "Colin! Blast your air horn when you're on your way!"

He blasted it two short toots to say he would.

Erin laughed and waved.

"Okay. We've come prepared."

"Hey." Erin turned and put her hands on her hips. "You can't expect me to think of everything, can you?"

Chris's only response was a burst of silly laughter.

★★★

A TALL GLASS OF MILK, his Bible out and open before him, no pressing engagements, nothing to distract him from the moment. Scott sat down on the couch in his living room and stared at the blues and greens swirling through the fabric of the love seat across from him. He drew in a deep breath. Let it out slowly. "Okay, Lord. This is it. We really need to talk about this." His voice barely carried to his own ears.

"Yes. Again. I know. And I'm sorry to keep bringing this up. I'm trying to leave it all in Your hands, but I can't. I need Your help. Lord, please help me." He covered his face with his hands. "Oh, please, dear God, help me to trust You!"

A quick drink of milk. He waited as the coolness descended through him. Tried to breathe. Hoped the milk and the deep breaths would calm the storm in his gut. If not, Erin had left a pack of Rolaids in the medicine cabinet upstairs.

*Milk's gotta work. This has got to work.*

He pulled his Bible onto his lap. He felt better, just holding it. "Lord," he said softly, "You know I do not want to be overbearing. Or overprotective—she's accused me of that on several occasions." He let out a grunt. "You know I love my wife. And You know I'm still fairly new at this marriage stuff. I really need Your help. I'm not even sure if I know what to ask anymore. Forgive me if I can't say the words. Please, still hear what I'm trying to say."

He ran his finger down the Bible's smooth leather. "There's so much to learn. And now . . ." His next thought almost blew him away. "Lord, I'm going to be a daddy. I can't . . . oh, God, I still can't believe it! Talk about much to learn. Please help me. Please help me get a grip on this marriage stuff, because soon I'll need to get a grip on the daddy stuff. One step at a time, I know. But I can't take any steps until I've taken this one before me, and I can't take this one without Your help."

Another long drink of milk. Another long, deep breath.

"Lord, I'm just going to sit here for a while. And wait. And be still. I know You're going to help me figure this out." His eyes fell closed. "And, Lord? Please? Keep them safe as they're traveling. Please let us hear those men have been caught. Or let them be long gone by now. Please? Protect my wife. Lay Your hand over her. Thank You, Lord. I really mean it. Thank You. And amen."

✷✷✷

"THERE'S ONE!" CHRIS BENT OVER to retrieve another sand dollar, then held it up for Erin to see. "This one's huge. And perfect in every way."

"Except for how it smells." Erin scrunched up her nose.

"I can't believe how many broken ones there are out here."

"That's the joy of finding one that's perfect." She savored the sight of the beaming smile on Chris's face.

"Whole." Chris's smile faded. She closely studied the shell in her hand. "In a sea of broken pieces—" she turned the shell so Erin could see its delicate design—"He finds us. And makes us whole."

Erin stood, staring, overwhelmed by the words.

Chris put the sand dollar in her bucket. Then laughed. "Corny. Huh."

Erin swallowed. Breathed. Said, "Well, we did miss church."

"We're in church, Rinny." Chris glanced sheepishly at Erin.

Erin could only smile. And say, "Yes, we are, Chris. We certainly are."

✯✯✯

NO HARD QUESTIONS TODAY. TIME would work its perfect way among them, between them . . . and Scott. Erin just wished she knew what the major problem was. Yes, her husband was worried. Well, who wasn't? Until Del and Rich were found and put away, everyone at Kimberley felt a little on edge. Everyone prayed for speedy justice. Everyone worried about one thing or another. Did Scott think it was his responsibility to worry more than everyone else?

Yet, Erin wasn't worried. Not really. Her God was too big. And she trusted Him. After all she had seen, how could she—*why* would she—stop trusting Him now?

Okay. So, allow Scott his space to worry. He trusted God too; so it was theirs to figure out. Erin would continue to pray for him, of course. What more could she do? How many more times would she have to tell him not to worry? How many more times would she have to say she was and would be all right?

She was all right. Wasn't she?

She glanced over at Chris. Driving the Explorer, Chris tapped her hand against the steering wheel as a Margaret Becker song filtered through the stereo. Erin looked away and smiled.

Okay, so, the other problems. Scott was a little hotheaded at the hospital in Colorado. No, more than a little hotheaded. Did Chris hear about that? Wasn't she medicated? Sleeping? Could she have overheard their heated discussion out in the hallway? Oh, she hoped not. No. She didn't think so. Chris didn't hear about that.

But then, the next day in the cabin, didn't Scott try to be civil? Didn't he help Chris sort through her ruined stuff, asking what should be saved and what should be "tossed"? He didn't glare at her then. Did he?

The next song on the cassette began to play. Chris reached over to turn up the volume. As Margaret's smooth, sweet voice flowed through the melody, Chris quietly sang along. She knew almost every word.

Erin sat back in her seat and basked in the moment.

Honesty. Healing. If you speak honestly.

Was it time for a hard question?

As the song slowly faded, Erin said, "Chris?"

"Yeah?" Chris turned the stereo's volume back down.

"If I ask you something, will you answer me honestly?"

Her eyebrows shot up.

Erin waited.

"Well, yeah. I guess."

"Tell me the truth, no matter what. 'Kay?"

"Okay."

"Do you like living at Kimberley?"

A slight pause. "Sure."

"Do you like your apartment?"

"Yeah. It's great."

"Great? Remember, we're being honest here."

"Don't worry, Rinny." Chris let out a small laugh. "I'm not planning on running off, if that's what you're afraid of."

"Really?"

"Really."

"Does Scott intimidate you?"

Chris's eyes bulged.

"He is way too protective of me. And I think he's hurt you because of it."

Her head shook. "Nope, Rinny. Not at all."

"So you have no problem with Scott at all?"

"Nope. None."

"Really?"

Another laugh. "Really."

Erin waited.

The silence grew strained.

Chris glanced at Erin and flashed a forced smile.

Erin cringed.

So much for honesty.

★★★

SCOTT HEARD STOMPING ON THE back porch. He hurried through the clinic to open the back door. His wife lugged a five-gallon bucket full of sand dollars. "Wow!" He moved in to help. "How many did you find?"

"Oh, my. Well over a hundred. We'll be cleaning sand dollars for a week." Erin dropped the bucket on the porch.

"Here, let me get that—"

"Leave them out here. They'll stink up the house."

"Beautiful stinky things."

"Thera-peee-uuuu-tic."

"Huh?"

"Oh, nothing." Erin pressed her fists into her lower back as she straightened, then looked Scott in the eye. "How's my main man?"

"Better. Now that you're home." He slowly raised his hands to her face, feeling the cool night on the soft skin of her cheeks. He drew her in for a long kiss. Slowly released her. "You're soaked."

"Turned ugly out there." Erin looked over her shoulder. "Wind really picked up."

"You made it home just in time." Scott turned her face so he could again look into her eyes. And he laughed. "Nice hat."

"Like that?" Her blue eyes shimmered in the faint light. "Velda made it for me."

"She's a wonder with knitting needles."

"I happen to like it very much."

"It's beautiful." Scott lifted it off Erin's head. Then ran his fingers through her hair.

"Are you gonna let me in?"

"Nah. I thought we'd stand out here and neck for a while."

"You know Mrs. Taylor can see us from here. It's a good chance she's watching." Erin laughed as Scott kissed her nose. "You want her to call the cops on us again? She has a cell phone now. She won't even have to leave the window."

"Ahh, what would we do without our dear-sweet-little-old neighbor?" He grinned. Then threw Mrs. Fiona Taylor a wave.

"Behave."

"Hey, I adore the lady. How could I not adore someone named Fiona?"

"She does keep an eye on things around here."

"But she didn't have to call the cops on us. Since when is public display of affection a federal offense?"

"We could take it inside, you know. Make it a 'private display.'"

"Yes, we most certainly could." Still grinning, he moved aside and let Erin go in first as he took one more look out over the backyard. Blustery rain coated everything in glossy black.

"Nasty."

"You got that right." He pulled the door closed behind him. "Are you hungry?"

Erin tossed her wet jacket on the bench, then kicked off her waterproof duck boots. "Nope. We already ate."

Scott pulled her against his chest. "Where at?"

"Colin's."

"In Netarts?" He brushed his lips against her soft cheek.

"Yep."

"That's been hours, then. Let me fix you something."

"Nah. I'm still full." Erin squirmed and giggled as Scott rubbed his whiskery chin under her ear.

"Maybe some ice cream?" he whispered into her ear.

"Well, you know me, sweetie. I'm always up for ice cream."

He kissed the side of her neck, then used his lips to burrow under her sweatshirt to kiss the top of her shoulder.

"I could take that off." She let out another giggle.

"Yes, you could." Just a mumble through his busy lips.

"If you'd let me go for a second."

Kissing and laughing, he lifted her off her feet and carried her out of the clinic through the swinging door leading into their living room.

"Scott! I have to hang up my jacket!"

"Later."

"Put me down."

He carried her to the couch, slowly lowered himself into it, then pulled her on top of him.

"There's one slight problem," Erin said as her lips lightly touched his.

"No. No problem," the words a faint whisper as he kissed her.

Erin laughed through the kiss, then said, "Yes, Scott. I have *got* to go to the bathroom."

"Hmm." Scott gazed into her eyes.

"It's your daughter again."

"Jumping on your bladder?"

"She likes to do that."

"Maybe she'll be a gymnast."

"Or a tap dancer."

He grinned. "You really gotta go?"

"Really."

"Right now?"

"Right now."

"PDA will hafta wait?"

"You know how it is. Hurry up and wait, soldier."

Scott grunted, sighed loudly, then let his arms fall away. Erin pushed herself off him and hurried upstairs.

Not moving an inch, still grinning, a minute or two later, over the howl of the wind, Scott heard footsteps on the front porch. He sat up on the couch. Heard a light knocking on the door. Got up to see who it was. Pulled open the door. Felt his gut twist.

"Erin forgot this."

Scott looked. His wife's wallet.

"In the truck."

"Okay. Thanks." He let Chris drop it in his hand. Slowly glanced up at her. Then back down at the wallet.

"See ya later."

"Yeah. Okay," he said. "Stay dry."

He saw the smirk Chris gave him. He closed the door.

"Who was that?" Erin asked as she moved in behind him.

"Chris. You forgot your wallet in the truck." He turned and handed it to her.

Her eyes bulged for a second. "I am so stupid sometimes."

"Don't say that."

"How could I forget this?" She grabbed her wallet and made a face. "I wonder about myself sometimes. Didn't you invite her in?"

"She looked a little wet."

"I'm sure she was. That didn't answer my question."

Scott didn't answer his wife's question.

"Sweetie?"

"Hmm?"

"Can I ask you something?"

"Sure."

"About Chris."

"What about her?" Scott reached out to pull Erin to him. Her eyes sparkled in the light.

"If I ask you, will you answer me honestly?"

He leaned in to nuzzle her neck, saying, between nuzzles, "I'm not going to lie to you, if that's what you're asking."

Erin gently pushed him back to study his eyes. "You promised me you'd try to get along with Chris. Have you really been trying?"

Scott pressed his lips. Squinted one eye. Said, "Define 'really.'"

Erin's right eyebrow lifted. She waited.

The silence lingered. Scott suddenly couldn't look at his wife, though she stood just a few inches away.

"Baby," she said, "a promise is a promise."

"Yes. Yes it is."

"And you promised me."

He forced his gaze to meet hers. "Yes." He blinked. "Yes I did."

"And are you?"

He didn't know what to say.

"Are you trying to be nice? Hmm? Are you trying to make her feel welcome here?"

"I, um . . ." The truth could not be told. Not now. Maybe later. After the PDA.

"You haven't been trying, have you."

"Well, yeah . . . I have."

"Not very hard then."

"Well . . . now . . . define 'hard.'"

Erin rolled her eyes, pushed the rest of the way out of his arms, then turned for the kitchen.

"Wait a minute, now," Scott said as she walked away. "Give me a second here. I know I've tried."

She stopped at the refrigerator, opened the door, but looked back at Scott.

"I'm trying, aren't I?"

"Scott?"

"Yes, sweetheart?" He once again stood beside her.

"You need to try harder."

Not what he wanted to hear.

### ✦✦✦

PERFECT IN EVERY WAY. ROUND, delicate, yet strong enough to outlast the pounding surf. Once a living critter, now only a skeletal remain. What design, what care and craft, that what was left, what was dead and remained after the life was gone, could be so stunningly beautiful. Perfect. An absolute treasure.

So many broken pieces there on the sand. She picked up and held a broken piece in the palm of her hand, a perfect half of an otherwise perfect sand dollar. Somewhere, out on that beach, the other half still lay in the sand. The surf would soon pound it to sand. Only sand. Until nothing remained.

This shell would never again be whole. To see this shell was to see a broken shell. Just a broken seashell. Leave it in the sand. Look only for the perfect ones. Take them home. Leave the broken ones to be ground away into nothingness.

She wished it wasn't so. Didn't want to think the thoughts, didn't want to look at something so beautiful and feel something so utterly grotesque. Why had she saved this one broken sand dollar? This perfect half. Never again to be whole.

She was that broken shell.

*No. Throw it away, Chris. Don't do this.*

She sat on her bed. Didn't move.

The other half of her. The other half of the perfect heart, the heart that perfectly matched her own, lay lifeless in the frozen ground a thousand miles away.

*No. Don't . . .*

Two people meet. Fall in love. Two souls fuse into one. See themselves in the other's eyes. Ben and Sonya. Isaiah and Emily. Andy and Sarah. Erin . . . and Scott.

She could see what Erin saw in Scott. Handsome. Smart. Fiercely loyal. Love. Beyond love. Adoration. Soul mates. Two perfect halves fused into one. Whole. Perfect. She held his heart in her hands; he held hers.

It was like that. Yes. For those few short months, hadn't she opened her heart, given it to Travis, and hadn't he gently held it in his hands, tenderly caressed it? Touched it? Felt the honor in it? What a wonder to trust the deepest parts of her very soul . . . to her soul's one true mate.

Only to have it all explode in her face. That long knife had cut through his heart. Cut through her own, as well.

A sense of alarm pulled her out of the past, a confusing quick trip back into her present moment. She blinked. Wind whipped huge drops of rain against her bedroom window, battering the glass. A knock on her door broke through the sounds of the storm. Then a voice. Cappy's voice.

"Chris?"

She sniffed deeply and blinked away the remaining darkness. "Yeah?"

"With this storm, I'll bet you two-to-one the power's gonna go off."

She pushed herself off the bed and opened her bedroom door.

"So if we're gonna watch the first part of *A League of Their Own* before church, we'd better do it."

Another gust of wind rattled her window. Chris laughed. "Two-to-one, huh?"

"Maybe three-to-one." Cappy smiled.

Chris tossed the broken sand dollar on her bed. "It's no bet. But I'll make some popcorn."

✯✯✯

WITH THE RUCKUS OUTSIDE HER bedroom window, if she slept a wink this night, she'd be surprised. Maybe she should borrow some of Cappy's Nyquil. Just to help her sleep.

No, as weary as she felt, sleep would come. Sitting on her bed, she looked down at the floor and saw the box in her closet, the box with two thick fleece blankets stuffed into it. They were just what she needed on a night like this. But yet . . .

If she pulled them out they would smell of wood smoke, of a Rocky Mountain miner's cabin tucked away under the trees. The sight of their stunning patchwork of colors, beautifully crafted by the native artisans of Mesa, Arizona, would draw her back to that place. To nights of cool, dry air, the fleece around her shoulders chasing off the chill as she sat and watched the sky slowly fade to black, as a billion stars blinked awake across the expanse of the night.

She felt as far away from the deeply silent desert night as a soul could be. She wanted to go back.

She turned off the light on her nightstand. Her eyes slowly adjusted to the city's gray night.

The blankets would have to stay in the box, in her closet—she'd have to keep that closet door closed. Maybe she should just take the box to Sarah and say, "Give these to someone who needs them." She'd know who would need a blanket. Chris didn't need them anymore. She had Erin's grandmother's quilt. Soft and warm. Why did she need the dumb blankets anymore anyway? Why did she bring them with her when she moved?

She had burned her San Juan Search and Rescue jacket, hadn't she? Tossed it in the fire and watched it burn . . .

Tears again blurred the memory of those flames. The brilliant red jacket splotched with brown dried blood melting away under the bright orange flickers. Glowing orange coals. All of it fading to black. Black and gray ashes, soot, dirt, dust. Nothing but dust.

*That's all we are. All I am. Dust.*

*But . . . that's not true, is it, Jesus. I'm Yours now. That's what I am. I'm Yours.*

Singing the songs from the book, praying with her friends and neighbors in the big church, seeing so many smiles, hearing about the God of Love, about His Son . . . *I'll be Yours, Lord Jesus. Always. If You'll let me.* She almost laughed. *I know You'll let me. Erin showed*

*me where You said it. She said, "A promise is a promise." And You prom-*
*ised never to leave me or forsake me. It's right there in Your Word.*

A long, deep breath. *Lord Jesus, no matter what happens, I can-*
*not leave You. You're all I've got. You, this place . . . and Erin. If I'm ever*
*gonna trust You, I need to do it now. Help me to trust You.*

*Help me, Jesus, Lord, to believe.*

The prayer fell away on the breath of a whisper. Sitting in darkness, listening to the storm's increasing fury, she let the whisper echo
through her. Stillness settled over her soul. Peace. Her prayer had
been heard. It was all too wonderful to comprehend.

She slowly pulled back the covers on her bed and lay down.
Pulled the covers up, tucked them in under her chin. But—wait.
She sat up on the bed and ran her hand over the quilt. Felt the bro-
ken sand dollar, the perfect half she had tossed on her bed earlier.

Feeling its rough edges, holding it carefully, she turned and
placed the shell on the nightstand by the gold chain necklace Travis
had given her. She smiled, then tucked herself back under the covers, and drifted off to sleep.

# THREE

ERIN HELD HER BREATH AND gazed up at the ceiling, feeling a bit silly—if the intense gusts of wind slamming the house ripped off the roof, she could only watch it happen, helpless in any way to stop it.

The roof held. The ceiling remained.

She let out her breath.

Rain pattered the window. Her eyes shifted there, and she waited, wondering if the window would implode.

Beside her, in the gray gloom of the early morning, her husband snored softly, impervious to the storm. Erin was glad, knowing he had slept very little the night before. Knowing the forces he struggled with. Mercy. Forgiveness. Trust. And a wife who demanded no less.

Chris deserved no less.

Erin drew in a deep breath and snuggled closer to her husband, careful not to wake him. Her eyes fell closed.

A sharp cracking sound, deep, distant, then a hideous crash rattled the entire house. Gasping, Erin sat up, eyes wide. Scott grabbed her and pulled her close. "What was that? Erin?"

"I don't—"

"Did you hear that?"

"Yes, baby. It's the storm."

"Storm?"

"Listen to it."

Breathing heavily, Scott turned toward his nightstand, pulling Erin with him, and squinted at the clock. "It's four thirty." He rubbed his face, then ran his hand through his hair.

Erin placed her trembling hand on her husband's chest, felt his heart thumping.

"Wow. It's really blowing." He turned to look in her eyes. "Are you all right? Were you awake?"

"Yes. I'm all right."

Scott's breath rushed through him.

"Shh, baby . . ." Erin reached up to caress his cheek.

"How long have you been awake?"

"About an hour."

"Really? You've been awake? Are you all right?" His eyes darted to the bedroom window. "It's bad out there."

"Yes."

He blinked and drew in a deep breath. "What was that crash?"

"I don't know."

"Sounded bad." In the gray light of the night, he studied her eyes deeply for a moment. Then turned and threw off the blankets, moved to the bedroom window, and pulled open the blinds.

Erin left the bed and stood by his side, allowed him to pull her in close. They stood awash in the faint orange light of storm and streetlights.

"Must have been a tree. Did you hear the cracking?"

"Yeah."

"Close by too." He pushed her back. "Stay away from the window. I'm gonna call Ben and see if he's awake."

Erin grabbed her robe and pulled it on as she followed him to the hall window. She looked over his shoulder out across the street. Torrents of amber rain sparkled under the streetlight. The light pole shook violently in the wind. Light burned through the curtains of Ben and Sonya's bedroom window.

"I'm gonna call him. Stay away from the windows, Erin. Better yet, you should come downstairs." Scott quickly descended the stairs.

Erin stood still another minute, cinching the robe tightly around her, watching the storm batter Kimberley Street. She heard

Scott on the telephone as she carefully made her way down the stairs, squinting against the bright light in the kitchen.

"Thank God. Yeah, tell him I'll come. Yeah. Give me a minute." Scott let out a deep breath as he hung up the phone. "Behind Isaiah's house. One of the firs fell into his shed, but missed his house."

"Thank You, Lord," Erin whispered.

"I'm going over there. Ben and Andy are gonna help Isaiah check it out. They'll call 9-1-1 first. Listen." Scott moved in close to Erin, took her by the arms. "Erin, stay here."

"I want to come. Emily—"

"NO. Listen to me. Stay here. I mean it. You are *not* going down there."

Erin didn't know what to say.

"I'm gonna go check it out. See if there's anything I can do. You stay here. I mean it, Erin. Do you hear me?"

She swallowed.

"I don't want you out in this." He leaned in to kiss her. "*No way* do I want you out in this. So listen to me. Please. Stay here."

She barely smiled. "Okay."

"I gotta go." He pushed away and hurried upstairs. "Maybe? Erin? You could make some coffee. Okay?"

"Yeah, okay." She went to the closet and pulled out Scott's raincoat and boots. "I can make coffee." She muttered the words to herself. "I can't drink it, but I can make it. Sure. Why not." She grabbed the flashlight hanging on the closet wall, clicked it on, then smacked it a couple of times against the palm of her hand.

"Does it work?" Scott quick-stepped down the stairs.

"Yes. And there should be more batteries in the clinic."

"You may want to get them handy." Scott finished buttoning his 501s, then pulled up his socks. "There's a couple more flashlights over there too, aren't there? I know I've got one out in the shed, but don't go out there. I'll get it later." He spun the rain jacket around his shoulders, pushed his arms through the sleeves. "Do not go outside for anything. Erin? Please? Listen to me. And stay away from the windows."

"All right. Heard ya the first time."

He pulled on the rain boots. "There's a couple thermoses in the clinic too. Wouldn't hurt to fill them with coffee. It may just turn out to be a long morning."

"Okay."

Scott stopped. Looked at her. Smiled. Stared at her for another second. "Are you sure you're okay?"

Erin smiled. "I'm fine."

"Don't be afraid."

"What. Of a little ol' storm? Just come back to me, sailor."

Scott laughed and moved in closer. "I'm off to do battle, darlin'." He kissed her full on the lips. Pulled away. Smiled. Then turned and headed for the door.

"Hey, wait, soldier." Erin handed him the flashlight. "Don't forget your weapon."

"I shall return."

"Coffee'll be waitin'."

✳ ✳ ✳

IT BREWED. DRIPPED. ERIN FINISHED washing the thermos she found in the kitchen cupboard, then headed for the clinic for the other two she knew were there. And the flashlights. And the batteries. In a storm like this, it wouldn't be long before everything went black.

Wiping her hands on a dishtowel, she pushed through the swinging door into the clinic's back room. Heard a strange, frightening sound. Over the wind, the rain, the howl, and the patter, she heard stomps on the front porch. She tossed the towel on the counter, then headed for the clinic's front room. Moved carefully to the clinic's front window. Her blood froze in her veins.

Someone stood outside on the porch by the swing. Reaching up, they were trying to unhook it. The wind tossed the swing into whoever it was, almost as if in defiance. The person doubled over for a second. Erin rushed to the clinic's front door, unlocked it, pulled it open, and gasped. "Chris! What are you doing?" Rain blew in her eyes as the wind almost tore the door from her hand.

"Rinny! We gotta take this down! It'll go through the window!"

*Lord!* Erin ran back inside for a chair.

Chris met her at the door. "Yeah, this'll work. Stay in there. Don't get wet." She pushed Erin back and pulled the door closed.

Erin stood there. Her mouth hung open. She watched out the window as Chris climbed up on the chair, unhooked each swing cable, and let the swing drop to the porch floor. Breath gushed out of her. Chris gathered up the chair and headed for the door. Erin quickly let her in.

"Whew! That was exciting!"

Still stunned, Erin could only laugh at the bright smile on Chris's face. She pushed the door closed and locked it.

"Man, Rinny, I came down the stairs and saw the swing—it hit the window. We are so lucky it didn't shatter."

Her eyes widened. "Wow. Thank You, Lord."

"Yeah. No kidding."

"Are you okay?"

Chris pushed off the hood of her jacket and swiped her hand down over her face. "Yeah."

"I saw it hit you."

"Yeah. Took one for the team there." Another brilliant smile.

Erin absorbed every bit of it. "I bet you could use some coffee. Help me grab some stuff in here first. Okay?"

"Sure."

She tossed the hand towel she had been using to Chris, then led the way to the clinic's back room where she gathered up the thermoses, handed them to Chris, then grabbed the flashlights and batteries. Everywhere Chris stepped, her jacket left drops of rain in her wake.

"Where's Scott?"

Erin pushed through the swinging door back into her living room, then held it open for Chris. "He went down to Isaiah's. Did you hear the crash?"

"'Bout gave me a coronary. Isaiah?" Chris lowered the thermoses to the kitchen counter.

"It was a tree near Isaiah's. Took out his shed, I guess, but didn't hit his house."

"Is he all right?"

Erin moved in beside Chris. "Yeah, he's fine. His shed, however …"

"Scott went down there?"

"Yeah." One of the flashlights slipped out of Erin's grasp and crashed to the floor. "Well, that was good. Probably broke it."

"I'm going down there."

Erin quickly looked up. "What?"

"Right now. I'm going."

She put the flashlight on the counter. "It's all right, Chris. I'm sure Isaiah's all right."

Chris swung the hood of her jacket back up over her head. "I'm gonna go find out." She started for the door.

"Wait!"

Chris turned around.

Erin didn't know what to say.

"You should stay here, Rinny."

For the briefest of seconds, the words infuriated her. "No. I'm coming too."

"Rinny …"

She hurried to the closet for her long rain jacket and boots.

"It's too wet out there, Erin."

"Too wet for me, but not for you?"

"I'm the crazy one. Remember? You're the smart one."

"That's why I'm coming with you." Erin gave Chris one of her best smirks. "Someone has to keep you out of trouble."

★★★

SPLINTERS OF DOUGLAS FIR LAY mixed in with splinters of the two-by-fours Isaiah had used to build his backyard shed. Scott could only stand and gape. The shed had literally exploded under the weight of the tree. White and yellow paint had squirted a good twenty feet out of crushed cans. The handle of Isaiah's lawn mower looked untouched, though it was now connected to the side of the tree, the mower itself crushed beneath it.

"Well, now, that's a disappointment."

Scott turned at the sound of Isaiah's voice, which barely carried over the roar of the wind and a fire truck's rumbling diesel. "Looks like you won't have to mow grass for a while."

"I just tuned up the motor too."

Scott laughed. Then slowly shook his head. "I'm really sorry about this, Isaiah. Though, of course, I'm glad it wasn't worse."

"Could've been a lot worse."

"Yes, sir, it could have been."

"Lord's pretty amazing, isn't He?"

The old man's smile spoke wisdom Scott only wished he could fathom. "Yes, sir, He truly is."

"You should get on home now. We can deal with this come sunup."

"You sure? You need anything, Isaiah?"

"Need for you to go home, son. Thanks, though. I mean it."

Scott nodded. "All right, then." He gave Isaiah's shoulder a gentle slap. "I'll see you come sunup." He grinned.

Isaiah smiled, then laughed, then slowly turned and headed for Ben and Andy and the small congregation of firefighters and police officers around them. Scott watched for another second, until a gust of wind blew his hood off. He quickly grabbed it, pulled it back on, tugged on the strings, wiped the rain out of his eyes—saw two figures approaching Isaiah. One stopped to shake Isaiah's hand. Isaiah seemed happy to see whomever it was, gave him a bright smile. The other person . . .

Scott squinted against the rain, focused his gaze.

The other person carried what looked like a thermos. And the jacket he wore . . . looked vaguely familiar.

The first person turned his head toward Scott. Through the darkness, the rain, the wind, the water in his eyes, Scott saw familiar dark eyes. And that familiar look. His stomach roiled.

Chris.

Scott quickly lowered his head and stared at the ground. The wind drove the rain under his hood, against his soaked jeans, against—

His heart clenched. Breath in his lungs burst out.

He lifted his head and strained to see the other person standing beside Chris, talking to Isaiah.

He knew that person. It was his wife. It was *Erin!*

✵✵✵

NOT FAST ENOUGH TO CAUSE her to trip, yet his steps as firm as the set of his jaw, his hand resting between her shoulder blades, Scott led Erin back down Kimberley Street, up the steps of their house, through the door, and into their living room. The entire trip, neither one of them said a word.

Erin stood staring at him, her cheeks enflamed as embarrassment coursed through her. Rain dripped off both their jackets onto the hardwood floor, into little pools at their feet.

Still his eyes blazed. The muscles in his jaw rippled as his teeth ground.

"Scott—"

"Don't say a word, Erin."

*"What?"*

"Just let me look at you. Let me try to figure this out."

"Figure what out?"

"Just be quiet! Please!"

His words weren't yelled, but were sharper than any she had ever heard him speak. Her own teeth started to grind.

"I told you to stay here. Didn't I?"

"Do you want me to answer that?"

"No."

Her teeth begged to grind. She forced her jaw to relax.

"I asked you nicely. Didn't I? Was I being demanding? Overprotective?"

She waited. Didn't move.

He looked into her eyes. "You can answer that."

"No."

"No?"

"No, Scott, you were not being overprotective."

"Demanding then?"

"No."

"Then, Erin, why didn't you listen to me?"

She couldn't look at him. "I don't know."

"You should not have been out there! Look at you! You're soaked!"

"Just my jacket." She eased it off, grateful that she was truly dry underneath.

She started as Scott's hand came quickly toward her face—he gently cupped her cheek in the palm of his hand. "You're cold."

She smiled. "Scott, I'm fine."

"You're wet and you're cold. You should go upstairs and take a hot shower."

She drew in a deep breath. "That sounds like a wonderful idea."

"Yes." But there was something more in his eyes.

"Are we . . . done here?"

As he blinked and his gaze drifted away, Erin saw such hurt in her husband's eyes, hurt that cut to her soul.

She took a step closer. "Sweetheart, I'm fine. And I'm sorry. You told me to stay, and I just didn't."

His eyes found hers again. "Why?"

"I don't know. I'm sorry."

"Erin, I know why. You know why. I wish you'd admit it."

His words didn't make sense. "Admit what?"

"It was Chris. She made you go."

Erin took a step back. "What?"

"No, I'm sure she didn't say the words. I'm sure she didn't 'make' you go. But you went because of her."

Her mouth fell open.

"You defied me . . . because of her."

"Scott—"

"It's the truth, isn't it, Erin?"

"What's the truth, Scott? You think that I purposely defied you . . . because of Chris?"

"She came here."

"Yes. She heard the crash, came down the stairs, saw the swing about go through the clinic's window. She's the one who took it down, Scott. She said it hit the window, almost shattered it."

"She came here, you told her about Isaiah, she wanted to see for herself, and you decided to join her."

Erin sighed. "Yes. Play-by-play? That's what happened."

"I knew it."

"You knew what?"

"Erin, if she would not have come here, would you have gone out?"

*Careful . . .*

"Answer the question. Would you have gone out?"

She couldn't speak the truth.

"No. You wouldn't have. You would have stayed right here. Made coffee. Been warm and safe and dry."

"Scott, stop this."

"Again, Erin, you have put your friendship with Chris before your own safety."

She glanced away.

"Say it. It's true. Before your own—"

"Enough, Scott!"

"And . . . the safety of our child. The child you carry."

"Stop this." But her words barely left her lips.

"Stepping out of this house in this storm, you were putting your life, and our baby's life, at risk."

She met his gaze. "Our lives, Scott? How? From attack of the 'killer raindrops'?"

"You think this is funny?"

She blinked and looked away. "No."

"Can you even hear what I'm saying to you?"

"Yes. I can."

"You can?"

"Yes."

"What am I saying, Erin. Say it back to me."

"Why, because you want to hear that you're right?"

His voice rose. "Because I want you to finally admit that Chris is dangerous. She doesn't think about you, about your safety, she just does whatever she wants, and you just love tagging along."

She glared at her husband. "Don't make this ugly, Scott."

"This *is* ugly, Erin! For me, it's as ugly as it gets."

"You're wrong. I know how you feel about Chris, but she's not—"

"You know how I feel? Do you?" He grabbed her right arm, lifted it, then pulled back her sweatshirt's sleeve. "When I see this . . . Do you think you have even a clue as to what I'm feeling? Even a clue?"

Tears filled her eyes. She tried to blink them away, looked down, saw the sickening marks on her wrist.

"Oh, God, help me." Scott pulled Erin into a gentle, yet intense embrace. "Baby, I love you so much. You are everything to me." His voice softened, shook. "I love the Lord. You know that. I am so grateful to trust my life to Him. I am so grateful He gave me such a gift. You, Erin. You are a gift. I mean it. And I'm trying to trust God on this. I am trying to get along with Chris. I'm really trying! But when she . . . when *you* do stupid things because of her . . . or maybe not because of her, I don't know what I mean. I'm sorry. I'm tired. I'm angry. But, Erin?" He pushed out of the embrace to gaze into her eyes. "Babe, please. Help me here. All I want is for you to be safe."

Tears stung her cheeks as they fell. Sudden weariness engulfed her. She couldn't think of anything to say.

"You know that, don't you?"

"Yes." Just a whisper.

"Not even a month ago, Erin, *three weeks* ago, I almost lost you. And the guys responsible for that are still out there. In that cursed war that you *volunteered* for, you almost died! You don't realize your own fragility. You think you're invincible. But you have to stop thinking that way. You have to take care of yourself. And our baby."

She nodded slowly.

He lifted her chin, waited for her eyes to look into his. "Erin, please hear me. I don't hate Chris. You should know that. But you've been through so much. You need to rest. In a few months, our baby's gonna come. Think about it. You need to be strong then, your body well." His eyes studied her entire face for a moment, then focused on her eyes once again. "I'm concerned about the stress you've been under. I'm concerned about the seriousness of your past injuries. And you hit your head again, just the other week. I know you told me it was nothing, but if you sustain any more concussions, even the slightest one . . ." His eyes reflected anguish as he tenderly caressed her face. "My love, the stress of giving birth will be extremely hard on you. The pressure on your entire body, but especially on your brain. I'm . . . afraid." Tears flooded his eyes. "Erin . . . my sweet love . . . I'm afraid."

Her bottom lip shook. She could only whisper through her aching throat. "Scott, it'll be all right."

"I'm sorry."

She tried to smile. "Don't be."

"I'm trying to trust . . ."

"We need to pray."

"Yes." His lips pressed as he swallowed. "After."

"After what?"

"Your long, hot shower." In a quick, gentle swoop, he lifted her into his arms, then carried her up the stairs to the bathroom.

Erin nestled against his chest and let her tears fall into the drops of rain on his jacket.

***

*STUPID! HOW CAN YOU BE SO STUPID! She should not have been out there. How can you blame him for the way he reacted? How can you blame him one bit?*

Chris threw her wet jacket into the corner of the dining room.

"Whoa! You all right?"

She glanced down the hall toward Cappy's bedroom door. Then away. "Hey, Cap."

"Chris?"

"I'm fine." She drew in a quick breath. "You?"

"Ugh."

"Go back to bed."

"What was that crash?"

"Tree blew down on Isaiah's shed."

"His shed?"

"Yeah. But he's all right. Didn't hit his house."

"Wow. That's amazing. Thank You, Lord."

Chris nodded.

"And you? You're not all right."

"I'm fine, Cappy."

"Okay. I'll take your word for it. But I'd hate to see you when you're not fine."

She lifted her head and put a smile on her face. "Go back to bed, Cap."

Cappy slowly grinned.

"Go."

"I'm going."

"Anything I can get you?"

"A new nose? Mine's just plain drivin' me nuts." A sniff.

"I'll see what I can do."

"Okay. Later, lady."

"Later, Cap." She let a deep breath calm her.

"Chris?" came from inside Cappy's bedroom.

"Yeah?"

"You know I'm prayin' for you, don't you?"

Her breath caught in her throat. "Um . . . yeah, Cappy."

"Okay. 'Night." And Cappy's bedroom door closed.

Chris slowly walked over to where her jacket lay, picked it up, and hung it on the hook by the door.

★★★

"Sweetie? Are you awake?"

Erin blinked open her eyes. "Yeah?"

"Ben's called an 'all hands.' Things are getting a little . . . well, crazy around here."

She pushed herself up in the bed. "The storm?"

"It's bad. All over the state. Up into Washington." Scott shook his head.

Erin looked at the clock by the bed. No numbers.

"Power's out. It's a little after nine."

She threw off the blankets and spun her feet to the floor. "We're meeting at Ben's?"

"Yeah. In ten."

"Just let me change my clothes." She stopped. Looked at Scott. Gazed deeply into his eyes.

He shook his head slowly. "Don't, Erin. It's over with."

She wanted to cry. "Is it?"

Scott let out a weak laugh. "Well, I hope so. I hope we never have to discuss it again."

"No. I'll be more careful. I promise."

He nodded. "Okay."

"And a promise . . ." Erin stood and wrapped her arms around him.

" . . . is a promise." Scott barely finished the words before his lips captured hers in a warm, passionate kiss.

✷✷✷

"YOU SHOULDN'T BE HERE, CAPRIELLA. You look terrible, sweetheart."

Ben agreed with his wife, then almost laughed as Chris gave Cappy an *I-told-you-so* look.

"All hands is all hands, Sonya." Cappy's nose sounded completely plugged.

"Nonsense. You get on back up to bed. Immediately, child. I'll make sure someone brings you some hot soup later."

"Go," Ben said, with a hint of purposeful command in his voice. He was pleased to see the stubborn young woman finally go.

"I tried to tell her," Chris said, watching Cappy's exit. "She can't even breathe."

Cappy stopped just long enough at the door to say hello to Erin and Scott as they walked in. Ben glanced at Chris. Saw immediate regret in Chris's eyes. Chris turned to study the family pictures on Ben's fireplace mantel. Ben glanced at Erin. Saw an odd seriousness there, in her eyes. Glanced at Scott. Didn't like what he saw there either.

*Lord, I think You're right. But . . . You've got to help this work. You're the only One who can make this work.*

Clearing his throat, Ben drew in a deep breath and blew it out quickly. The time had come. Peering out over the crowd of people in his living room, his heart swelled. His family, his friends, his brothers and sisters. A call for help, another overwhelming response. *Thank You, my Lord, for this place. For these people.* He lifted his hand and rubbed his wife's back. Smiled as she looked up at him. "Dear? Shall we?"

Sonya grinned, then drew in a breath, raised her fingers to her lips, and let out the most blood-curdling whistle Ben had ever heard. He could only smile.

It was amazing how quickly silence fell. He cleared his throat again. "Okay, folks. Listen up." He waited for all eyes to find him. Felt the honor of command, as he always did. Such a privilege to command such incredible people. "The city's put out an 'all hands.' We've faced this before. It's time to face it again. This storm has taken everyone by surprise. And now forecasters are saying it's only going to get worse. They're expecting wind speeds to increase, the intensity of the rains to increase, and they expect it to last at least through tomorrow. Maybe longer. They're expecting warming temperatures, so very little ice or snow, but there may be hail. Thunder and lightning. They just don't know. If it stays warm, they're worried about the snowpack melting too soon. And flooding. Well, one thing's for sure, it should certainly be exciting."

Everyone reacted, most with shaking heads and subdued smiles.

"As you all know by now, the tree behind Kenny's place fell this morning, taking out Isaiah's shed and Olivia's garage. And her car, unfortunately. But, the way the tree fell, it missed all their houses, and now simply lies in state in all their backyards, rather than, well, towering over them like it once did. Once again, we have the Lord to thank for His protection." Ben lifted his eyes. "And we thank You, Lord!"

A chorus of "Amen!" and "Thank You, Jesus!" swept across the room.

Ben let the moment linger just another second. Then continued. "However, there will probably be more blowdowns. Douglas fir are notorious for shallow root wads. With this wind, this will be a great concern. As you're out there, if you see anything that would indicate an unstable tree or a downed power line, call it in. If there's blowdown that we can clear ourselves, blowdown that's clear of power lines, of course, go ahead and clear it. We're in the process of gathering up chain saws, but remember, only those qualified to work them should. Kenny, Ryan, Isaiah, myself, Andy, and . . . Chris, I do believe you've worked a chain saw in Colorado."

Her eyes found his quickly. She couldn't hide her surprise. "Um, yes, sir."

"Good. But remember, all of you. Do not do more than you can handle. If the job is too big, call it in. The city has crews all over the place, and they're obviously able to handle anything. Our job is to just make their job a little easier, to get out and help wherever we can. We hope to be part of the solution, right? Not . . ." He waited.

" . . . part of the problem," came from every corner of the room.

Ben laughed. "Yes." He looked at his wife. Saw her silly grin.

"Okay. So. The city has closed all schools and government offices. They've put out the word for people to stay home. The roads are flooding since drains are blocked with debris. If you're going to be out, be careful. While you're out there, if you see kids or transients on the streets, send them home or to the mission. Get them there, if need be. We need to get people off the streets. And keep on the lookout for looters. If you see anyone looting, do not do anything." Ben waited for the words to sink in. "I'll say it again. Do not do anything. Call 9-1-1, or call John here at the house and report it. Even if the looters get away, at least the police can contact the building's owners and get them out there. Everyone got that? Do not approach looters."

A few mumbles. More nods.

"Okay. Here's how we're going to split up. I can tell right now there are going to be some changes, so listen up." He waited for his wife to bring up a blank page on the notebook she held in her hands. Then again looked out over the crowd. "Okay. Isaiah? I'd appreciate it if you could take one more look at the generator at the church, make sure it's up and running correctly, then you and Kenny go on home to stay close to your own 'disaster scene.'" He said the last few words with dramatic flair. "At least for the rest of the morning anyway. Make sure everything's okay. The city has already cleared the alley and some of the debris on the street, but you guys go ahead and stay close to home. If you want to come by here later, we'll find something for you to do."

He waited for the two men to give him a nod.

"All right. Then, Kay? You and Sonya head up to the women's shelter and see if they need help securing that. Take their emergency boxes. Andy? Can you help get stuff loaded into Kay's van? You two, then, stay as long as you're needed. They should be fine, though, I would imagine. All their systems are in place."

Kay gave Ben a nod. "After the last ice storm, they got their act together quite nicely."

"Good. If you're not really needed up there, come on back. We can use you here, that's for sure."

Kay gave Ben a thumbs-up.

"Okay. So, Sarah?" Ben enjoyed the surprised look on his daughter-in-law's face. "You and Maria and . . . Mildred? Are you here?"

He saw a hand pop up in the far corner of his living room. The woman's face peeked out from behind Isaiah.

"Hey. There you are." He allowed his smile to linger a second longer. "Would you like to join them? If the three of you could head over to the church and start up the kitchen, that'd be great. If there are any problems with the generator or anything like that, let me know. Let's open up the entire basement for walk-ins." Ben shifted his eyes toward the door. "Erin?" He gave her a warm smile. "Let's not have you go out this time. And I think we should keep the clinic closed. Let's have you set up a table or something like that in the corner of the basement for any first-aid necessities that may arise. Is there any reason why the clinic will have to be open today?"

"No." Scott coughed quietly to clear his throat. "I called and cancelled all appointments for today and tomorrow."

"Will you be needed at Good Sam?" Ben asked him.

"No. Not really. I've been on light duty over there all last week anyway so I could be closer to home. It runs through this week too."

Ben glanced at Erin. She stared at the floor. The scene from earlier that morning—Scott's reaction to seeing his wife out in the rain—flickered through Ben's mind. He pressed his lips and forced the image away. "All right. That will work out well, then. Let's keep the clinic closed for a few days. Keep things centralized in the church basement. And the basement, folks. Let's not track up the sanctuary, if possible."

He saw nods of approval around the room.

"Okay. So. Well, then, Bettema and Mason are needed at home— Mason's mother's house lost part of its roof. And Cappy's still sick, so we sent her home. Erin? Could you check on her after we dismiss? She didn't look very well at all."

"Sure, Ben," came Erin's soft reply.

"Thanks. And tell her to stay home. I don't want to see her around here."

Erin smiled and nodded.

"So. With that, I think we've got everything covered. Andy and I will go out, but we'll stay in the Square, as usual. We'll take my Explorer and make the rounds. If any of you need one of us, just call in. John and Elaine will stay here at the house monitoring the phone and radio. They'll be our liaison with the city. If you have any questions, call here. They'll get you an answer."

More nods.

Good. Ben knew this group would rise in strength to face this calling.

Except for . . .

He looked down at the floor and swallowed deeply. *Okay, Lord. Here goes.* He lifted his head and focused his gaze toward the back of the room. "Scott?" He flashed the young man a quick smile. "Andy and I will cover the Square, could you and . . . Chris . . . cover the outer areas? Take the Blazer. Make the rounds out there. Please?"

Ben held his breath, waiting for Scott's reply.

It came silently, in the undeniable expression of pure shock, then outrage in Scott's eyes. His mouth fell open.

Ben gritted his teeth, then smiled and said, "Thank you." He glanced at Chris. Saw the same reaction there, less the outrage, in Chris's eyes. "Thank you both. Be sure and take the radio. John will let you know about any specific needs that come in. And he has the list of folk that will probably need a visit. We'll try to get by to see them all."

Ben glanced down at his wife. Shock widened her eyes. He tried to give her a look that said, *I know, sweetheart. It'll be all right.*

Oh, if only he believed it.

# FOUR

"BEN, I NEED TO SPEAK WITH YOU."

"All right, Scott. Give me a minute."

"Now."

Ben looked up and met Scott's gaze. "Is there a problem?"

Scott's teeth clenched.

Ben waited.

"Why—?" Scott glanced around the room. "Can Andy go with me? Chris is new to this neighborhood, new to this work. Andy would be of more help to me."

Ludicrous. But Ben kept a stony face. "I need Andy with me." Not the complete truth, but not a lie either.

"But Chris could go with you. You and she could cover the Square. You could show her around to everyone. Introduce her."

"Hmm." Ben pretended to consider that. "No."

Scott's eyes bulged. "No?"

"I need Andy with me. We need to stay close to home. Besides, the two of you, being medical professionals, should be able to work well together. You'll be a big help to those who live outside the Square." Ben tried to keep his expression firm, though he wanted to cringe. His ability to verbally improvise through tight situations was waning in his old age.

"You really need Andy with you?"

"Yes, I do. And this will give you a good chance to introduce Chris to our friends outside the Square." He smiled.

Scott could see through the thin facade.

"I've got to go. I'm sorry. If you need anything, give John a call. He'll know where I am."

"Right. Thanks, Ben." Scott turned and marched out the front door, ignoring Erin, ignoring everyone else in the room. Especially Chris.

Ben glanced at Chris. Apprehension clouded her face. His heart ached. *Oh, Lord. What have I done?*

✳ ✳ ✳

THE SLOW WALK ACROSS BEN and Sonya's living room seemed to drain Erin's energy. She looked at Chris. Tried to smile. "Hey."

"Hey."

"Looks like you're gonna get a little wet today."

"Yeah. Looks that way."

Chris was already soaked. "Do you have a warmer jacket?" Erin asked.

"It's warm enough, Rin. I'll be fine."

"Yeah, that's right. You like it cold. But don't get too wet, okay? With this wind, it'll be cold."

Chris didn't say anything.

"Come in if you get too wet, or too cold. Promise me. Okay?" She nodded. "Yeah. I will."

Erin let out a deep breath. Tried again to smile.

"Do you want to go see Cappy now? I'll go with you. I want to grab some stuff before we leave."

"Yeah. All right." Erin turned and led the way past the few remaining people in the room, then across the street to Chris's apartment. Wind drove drops of rain under her jacket hood, and both women lowered their heads and quickened their pace. Up the stairs, through the door, they didn't talk. Against the storm, they would have to yell to be heard. At the moment, nothing was worth saying that desperately.

Erin tiptoed down the hallway. Stopped to knock lightly on Cappy's door. Glanced up to see Chris watching. Heard Cappy's voice.

"I'm awake."

"Cappy? It's Erin."

"Hey, lady, come on in." And a cough.

Erin glanced at Chris. Barely smiled.

"I'd, um, better get going." Chris moved past her, heading for the bathroom.

"Chris? Wait for me. Okay?"

Chris turned. Looked surprised.

"Wait." Erin only breathed the word. She turned to smile at Cappy.

Low-grade fever, congestion, sinus pressure, headache . . . in her misery, Cappy endured the cold. But she'd be fine, if she stayed put and slept. She promised to keep taking her meds. Erin promised to bring her some oranges and hot soup later.

Easing herself through Cappy's bedroom door, she looked for Chris. Saw her waiting by the front door. Erin smiled. Though it trembled on her lips.

"Will she live?"

"I think so."

"You ready to go?"

Erin nodded. Chris started to pull the door open, but Erin rushed to her and pushed it closed. Chris quickly turned, eyes wide. Erin looked into those dark eyes. She couldn't stop tears from blurring her vision.

"Rinny?"

Too much to say. Too much to explain. No time. No words.

"What is it?" Barely a whisper.

"Chris . . ." Erin tried to blink away her tears. Then quickly leaned forward and pulled Chris into an embrace. "Please, be careful." She whispered the words into Chris's ear. "Don't be afraid. It's all gonna work out." A sob stole her breath. She fought to get it back. "Just don't be afraid."

She pushed Chris out of the way, tore open the door, and raced down the stairs, across the street, blindly out into the storm, running anywhere . . . away.

★★★

UNDER THE DRIVE-THROUGH BACK PORCH of the Kimberley Street Community Church, Scott Mathis tossed another plastic bag full of blankets into the back of the Blazer. "So, here's the deal," he said as he worked. "We'll start about eight blocks north of here, and work our way west. I've got a list of about fifty people we need to check on." Another bag. He pushed on them, forcing them into the small cargo space of the Blazer. "Obviously we won't be able to check on everyone today. We'll just take things as they come. About ten or so of those people we must see today. Make sure they're all right. We'll knock on their door and ask if they need anything. Nothing to it. If they need something, we'll try to get it for them. If they've got stuff blowing around their property, we'll get it and secure it. If they're in any danger that we can tell, we'll either fix it or call it in. Got all that?"

Chris McIntyre. A five-foot-six-inch two-year-old. Her stomach burned the way it always did after she'd ingested a crock of Raymond's five-alarm chili.

"We'll just try to cover as many names on the list as we can today. No big deal."

Chris nodded. Standing by the side of the Blazer, she only watched as Scott continued to load equipment into the back.

"Several folk will need us to check their home-care equipment. With the power out, they all should be on battery power; so there should be very few problems. But as this storm drags out, the need will increase."

He really did think she was a complete idiot.

Isaiah approached—Chris's heart swelled with joy.

"Howdy there, Chris. Scott." Isaiah's smile fell over Chris like a healing flood. He carried a small chain saw in a black case in one hand and a small can of gas in the other. "You guys want to take these? May come in handy."

Scott reached out to take the saw from Isaiah before Chris had the chance to move.

"Thanks, Isaiah." Scott squeezed it in beside the bags of blankets. Then grabbed the can of gas.

Chris smiled. "Yeah. Thanks."

"You two be careful out there. Remember, nothing heroic."

"Just get the job done. Yep, Isaiah, we'll remember that." Scott turned to look at Chris, bore down on her with his eyes. "Won't we, Chris."

She swallowed. "Of course."

"We don't need any heroes around here. We only need the job done."

Chris tried not to smile as a gust of wind blew Scott's jacket hood off.

★★★

SO. YES. JUST A JOB. And Chris certainly didn't want to be a hero. She'd just do her job, try to endure, adjust, and overcome. This too shall pass. Hoo-uhh. Semper Fi, dudes. Yeah, yeah, yeah.

So far, so good. Scott drove like a half-blind centenarian, easing the Blazer over debris-covered streets, wipers going but not keeping pace with the rain. Already the windows were fogging up. Chris wiped her window again with the palm of her hand. Between the roar of the storm outside and the roar of the defroster inside, no words could be spoken even if either person wanted to speak. She liked it that way. She sat still and quiet. And, deep in her heart, she prayed.

Deep breaths. Adjust. Overcome. Stay focused. Do the job at hand. *I mean, Lord Jesus, this job isn't as bad as a field exercise in the interior of Alaska, is it? There aren't any mosquitoes, and the wind is warm. I handled all that. I can handle this, can't I? And besides, putting up with Scott Mathis isn't near as bad as putting up with Teddy Brisbaine. Is it?* Chris stared out the window.

Putting up was still putting up. And she didn't need it. Didn't have to sit there and take it.

Did she?

She let her head fall back against the top of the seat. Closed her eyes.

No. She didn't have to take it. Erin knew that. That's why . . . earlier . . . Erin broke down into tears.

Chris could up and leave in a heartbeat, and no one would stop her. If she set her mind to it, no one could stop her. Making up her mind was easy. But convincing her heart was another story.

*Pray. Try to pray.* She drew in a huge, deep breath, knowing, as she let it out, it would fog up the windows even worse. She drew in another. Slowly let it out. Kept her eyes closed. And deep in her heart, she prayed.

★★★

"It's pretty ironic," Scott yelled over the roar of the defroster, "that the first person we're gonna check on doesn't even go to our church. He's a codger, that's for sure, but he's harmless. He's kind of a pet project. We figure if we pester him enough, maybe someday he'll come to church."

Chris glanced at Scott but said nothing. She didn't think he was expecting her to say anything anyway.

"He's got emphysema, and a plethora of other ills. He should be all right as long as his home nurse can make it out in this weather. I know her. She'll try, that's for sure."

The Blazer splashed into the river of runoff flowing down both sides of the street, then thumped over a submerged branch as Scott pulled up to the curb. He cut the engine and pushed open his door to get out.

Chris drew in another deep breath. Time to make herself useful.

Up the walkway to a small thirties-style bungalow, Scott led the way as Chris lowered her head against the driving rain. Up the stairs onto the front porch, Scott peered in the window, waved, then knocked on the front door. Testing the doorknob, finding it unlocked, he pushed the door open and quickly herded himself and Chris inside.

"You should lock your door, Chester." He pushed the door closed. "You never know who's gonna burst in."

Inside the man's cozy home, cigarette smoke hung in the air like thick fog, assaulting Chris so severely she coughed.

"Well, if it ain't the doc. What are you doin' here?" The old man didn't get up. Strapped to an oxygen tank and planted firmly in his recliner, Chris didn't think he could get up even if he wanted to. She pushed off her jacket hood and tried not to breathe.

"Just checking up on you." Smiling brightly, Scott moved in close to shake the man's beefy hand. "How do you like this storm? Are you doing okay?" He added a degree of volume to his voice. Chris wondered if deafness was part of Chester's plethora of ills.

"You're drippin' all over my floor, Doc," Chester hollered through an almost toothless grin.

"Well, it is a little wet out there."

"Who's yer friend? This ain't yer wife, is it?"

Chris coughed again, then tried not to laugh at the look Scott gave her.

"This is Chris, Chester. She's a medic. She's new to Kimberley. She'll be helping Isaiah run the gym when they get it finished."

The man listened intently to what Scott said, studying Chris with every word.

"Hello, sir." Chris gave him a small wave and a smile.

"Well. Chris." The burly man flashed another toothless grin. "How you likin' Kimberley? They got you singin' in the choir yet?" He roared with laughter, then broke into a fit of coughing.

Chris didn't think any response beyond her smile was appropriate.

Scott slapped the man on the back. "Come on, Chester, breathe." The man stopped coughing, but still laughed.

"We've come to see how you're doing. Will you be all right if this storm lasts a few days?"

Chester cussed under his breath. "I've seen worse, Scotty. You don't gotta worry about me."

"Is Linda coming today?"

"No."

"Why not?"

"Ain't her day to come. She'll be here tomorrow."

"And you're good until tomorrow?" Scott quickly checked the collection of medical equipment by the man's recliner. "Is there anything you're gonna need?" He adjusted a knob or two.

The old man looked at Chris, for a second his eyes seemed to twinkle. "You could bring me a couple cartons of Luckys."

Chris smiled as Chester barked in laughter.

"Chester, the air's already so thick in here, I'm catching my death just breathing it."

"Can't have that, Scotty. You'd better leave." Chester winked at Chris. "You can stay, though, purdy lady."

Chris laughed.

"Sorry, old man, but she's got work to do." Scott gave Chester a friendly pat on the shoulder and took a few steps toward Chris and the door.

"Hey, I know something you can bring me."

Scott stopped and looked back.

"You can bring me a case of JD."

Chris's heart quickened. She lowered her head and closed her eyes for just a second.

"We are not bringing you any whiskey, Chester." Scott laughed as he finished his trek to the door.

"Then why in tarnation did you come here for, if you ain't gonna bring me what I need? Smokes and sauce. Them's two of the four food groups."

"Come on, Chris." Scott carefully pulled open the door. He turned back to Chester, who was again laughing hoarsely. "We'll come by tomorrow. If you need anything, give the church a call. You've got the number, right?"

Chester threw Scott a dismissing wave. "Yeah, it's around here somewhere."

"Well, use it. We'll come by again if you need us."

"Didn't need ya this time."

With the sounds of Chester's laughter filling the room, Chris studied the bright smile on Scott Mathis's face. She liked what she saw.

His eyes suddenly found hers. His smile lingered. "I think we're done here."

She hoped the smile she gave him said more than she knew how to say. She quickly turned to Chester and hollered, "Nice to meet you, sir!"

"You come on by anytime, young lady," Chester said. "And bring the doc's missus with you. She's a peach, that one. Like you."

Chris's eyes widened. She snuck a glance at Scott, who only rolled his eyes.

Laughing to herself, Chris pulled her hood up and walked through Chester's front door back out into the blustery gale.

Halfway down the walk to the Blazer, Scott touched her shoulder. Chris turned.

"Let's walk his property, make sure everything's tied down," Scott hollered over the roar of the wind. "You take that side, I'll go over this way. Let me know if you need a hand."

"All right," Chris shouted. Moving around to the west side of Chester's house, she found a bucket blowing in the wind and a window screen that must have blown off an upstairs window. She grabbed both and met Scott in the backyard. He carried a stack of shingles in his hand.

"Let's put this in his shed," he shouted.

Chris followed, then helped Scott gather up Chester's garbage can. All went into the shed. Scott made sure the shed door closed securely, then gave Chris a nod and pointed toward the Blazer. Chris nodded and followed.

As they opened the truck's doors, wind blew rain inside, coating the dashboard and seats. Chris sat and slammed her door shut, then let out a deep breath. Hot. Too hot. Under her jacket, she was sweating.

Scott let out a big, "Whew!" as he settled in the driver's seat, then reached down to fire up the Blazer. Water dripped off his nose and splashed onto the steering wheel.

Reaching behind her, Chris felt inside the bag she had brought. She found a towel, quickly wiped her face with it, then slowly, cautiously, offered it to Scott.

He looked at her. Then down at the towel. Couldn't hide his indecision. Chris's heart fell. But Scott accepted the towel, wiped his face, and handed it back. Without giving her as much as another glance, he pulled the Blazer away from the curb and drove on down the tree-lined street.

Chris tossed the towel over her shoulder into the back, then settled into her seat, feeling drops of sweat already forming on her face, dripping down her chest. She laid her head back.

Chester's cigarette smoke lingered on her jacket. Nauseating smell. She had never smoked a cigarette in her life. But a triple shot of Jack Daniel's Tennessee whiskey would definitely work for her about now.

Her eyes fell closed. *Forgive me, Lord.* She drew in a deep breath and let it out slowly. *We can do this. Help those we'll visit today. Help me.* She blinked open her eyes as the Blazer again slowed in front of a house. Alta Fitzsimons's house, Scott announced. Nice lady. Chris listened. Yet, in her trembling heart, she prayed.

\*\*\*

DOWN THE STAIRS LEADING TO the basement of the Kimberley Street Community Church, Ben Connelly lingered on the bottom step and leaned forward, looking inside the huge open room, yet not going in. A flurry of activity greeted him, people he loved as his own family working to set up a type of . . . well, central command. He laughed to himself, then allowed his gaze to continue its aimless trip across the room. Sarah and Mildred stood in the kitchen making sandwiches as Maria spread a colorful tablecloth over one of the many folding tables. Ryan and Andy carried boxes filled with all kinds of collected emergency supplies out the back door to put into Ryan's truck. Ben's grandson, Benny, and Benny's best friend, Jeffrey, on their knees pushing Tonka trucks across the floor, appeared and disappeared through the open door of one of the classrooms. Squeals of laughter came from that direction, and Ben smiled. Bertha Myers had braved the storm to come and sit with her friend, Julia Mullins. They sipped coffee, or maybe tea, and worked on their knitting as the stereo beside them played soft praise and worship music.

In the far corner of the room, Ben watched as Erin guided his granddaughter's hand as she drew on something, a piece of poster board maybe. Curiosity captured him. Ben finally entered the room.

Sarah, his lovely daughter-in-law, immediately looked up and gave him a smile. He returned it, then detoured to her location to grab up a half of one of her egg-salad sandwiches piled on a platter on the kitchen counter. He hummed in delight as he chewed, then gave her a silly grin as he swallowed.

Finishing his last bite, he quietly moved closer to where Erin and Amanda diligently worked on their project. Ben craned his neck to see. It was a sign. First Aid Here. With a bit of her tongue sticking out, Amanda colored the last part of the word *Here*, then stepped back to admire her handiwork. Ben's heart swelled when he saw the joy on her young face.

"It's perfect, Auntie Erin!"

"Yes, Miss Connelly, I do believe it is." Erin held the sign up for a better look, but caught Ben's eye and smiled sheepishly.

Amanda suddenly turned. "Pappy!"

Ben swept her up in his arms, then plastered her cheek with whiskery smooches, causing the youngster to squeal and giggle. He glanced at Erin. Saw a joyous smile on her face.

Ahh, after all that had happened that morning, how he needed to see a joyous smile on Erin Mathis's face.

"We're makin' signs, Pappy!" Amanda wriggled out of his arms. "Come see!"

Her tug on his shirtsleeve pulled him closer to the table. "Well, yes, I see. And they're beautiful!" He patted her shoulder. "And what's this one say?"

"It's for outside, Pappy. So people walking by can see it."

Ben read aloud the words on the second sign Amanda had drawn. "Find Shelter from the Storm Here." Bright red letters with bright yellow borders, finished with bold purple and blue flowers, all carefully colored with crayons and magic markers. "Yes. A magnificent job, Spoofer."

"It may not hold up in the wind." Erin's voice carried little strength. "We're trying to figure out a way to put it up outside. Out front, so people can see it from the street."

"We need more yellow, Auntie Erin. People need to see it in this awful dark storm."

"Yes. Mandy, I think you're right. Go ahead. Make sure everyone can see it." Erin smiled at Ben as Amanda immediately went back to work.

Ben's heart clenched inside him. "Um, Amanda," he said, leaning over to puff a breath into the child's ear, knowing she loved, yet hated, to be tickled like that. "We'll go get you some clear contact paper to help protect your sign from the rain."

Amanda did not look up from her work. "Okay, Pappy!"

Did she even know what clear contact paper was? Ben wanted to laugh. He used his eyes to motion Erin away from his granddaughter.

"There's some in the closet, I think," Erin said.

"We can line it on both sides, then use zip ties to fasten it to the sign out front."

Erin brightened. "Yeah. Okay. That's a good idea."

They stopped at the Sunday school supply cabinet where Erin quickly found the roll of plastic paper and a pair of blunt-tipped scissors. She looked up at Ben.

"I'll go get the ties from the maintenance shed," Ben said.

"Okay." Erin waited, still looking at Ben, waiting for him to move.

He didn't move. He pressed his lips.

A flash of confusion swept Erin's face.

"I hope I did the right thing." Ben barely breathed.

"What do you mean?"

"Sending Chris and Scott out together."

Confusion immediately gave way to apprehension. Erin glanced down at the floor, then at the roll of contact paper in her hand.

"I just thought that maybe, if they could work together, they would get to know each other. Maybe . . . they would even become friends."

A long pause. "I guess we can only hope it will work." She lifted her head. "It'll either work, Ben, or it'll blow up in our faces."

He hated what he saw in her eyes.

"We'll just have to wait and see." She tried to smile. "Excuse me." She moved past him and headed for the table where Amanda worked.

Ben stood still and simply watched her go.

✫✫✫

A GUST OF WIND BATTERED his already battered car. He had pushed the jalopy hard from Colorado, was impressed his quick fix of the radiator hose held. In front of him, an immaculate dark green metallic Ford Mustang was parked. Rain fell on it, then instantly beaded and rolled off in rivers, making the car sparkle in the dreary gray light of the day. Well waxed. Someone loved that car.

He drew in a deep breath, let it out with a huff, then wiped his arm over his side window. He'd been staring at the Mustang, and the huge church across the street, for maybe an hour now, though his watch was broken and he had no idea of the time. The entire neighborhood and the upper level of the church remained gloomy and dark, yet brilliant light shone out the windows of the basement, illuminating the wilted flowers someone had planted, probably last summer. Through the windows, he could see the tops of people's heads. Women. Smiles. Quite a little gathering. Nice place to hide away from the storm.

He slouched in the seat. He'd been hiding for weeks now. On the run. He didn't like it. Not one bit. He never felt so alone in his life.

Kimberley Street Community Church. A Bible-based House of Worship. Come and Worship the Lord with Us. He had read the sign on the front of the church at least a hundred times. Worship? He didn't even know the meaning of the word.

Though he knew about God. Yes. Just over two weeks ago, he had whispered the name of God. And not even as a curse. He had searched out this place, this Kimberley Square. Knew the two women he needed to find would be here. But he didn't know if he wanted to stay . . . or run away as fast as he could.

Del would laugh at him if he didn't finish the job. Deep in his heart, he hoped he would never have to see Del again. Ever.

Movement. The front door of the church opened. A person stood there, carrying a large floppy sign, gripping it as gusts of wind tried to rip it away. Just a figure, hood up, pulled tight, face hidden in the mist.

He reached up and swiped the sleeve of his shirt over the fogged-up window again.

Trying to hang the sign, to attach it to the sign already hanging there . . . Come and Worship the Lord with Us.

Wind blasted the person, yet whoever it was persevered. The sign remained fixed to the front of the church. The person stood back for a second to admire his work.

Large red letters over bright yellow. Find Shelter from the Storm Here.

He blinked. The sight shimmered. He blinked again, blinked away a tear.

The person moved slowly, so slowly, as he turned around. He lifted his arms and pulled away his hood.

No. It was a woman. Lifting her face into the rain, letting the wind slam her from all sides, she smiled. Then stuck out her tongue. The woman stood there, face lifted into the storm, eyes closed, tongue out, tasting the rain. Laughing at the storm. She slowly started to lift her arms.

His heart slammed to a stop. His breath caught in his throat.

He knew that woman.

Yes. It was *her*.

His hand found the car's steering column, the key hanging there. He quickly turned it, the engine rumbled to life, and he floored the gas pedal, spinning the old car's tires on the wet street in his rush to escape.

✸✸✸

*OH, FATHER, IF SCOTT WERE HERE, if he saw me now, out here, in the rain, he'd seriously pitch a fit. A bona fide, old-fashioned fit.* Erin almost laughed. Raindrops pelted her cheek, her eyelids, dripped down her chin, down her neck, her chest. Chills raced up and down her entire body.

*Please don't let him be watching. It's okay if Mrs. Taylor's watching. She already thinks I'm a little ... strange. But the last thing I need right now is for my loving husband to see me and pitch a ... another ... fit.* She reached up and pushed her hood off. Lifted her head and smiled. Stuck out her tongue. And laughed.

*Lord God, he's out in this. Chris too. They're soaked, like this. Cold. Tired. Hopefully they're not hungry, are they? They took sandwiches, didn't they? Someone out there has to feed them!* Her eyes popped open, yet quickly closed as rain splashed her face. *Corissa would have fed them. Oh, Lord, what am I worried about? Everything that's going on ... yet You're still in control. Let the wind blow! Let the rain fall! You are Lord of all!*

She shook out her hair in the wind. Slowly raised her hands to heaven.

*Bless the Lord, O my soul. And all that is within me, bless His Holy Name!*

*But, Lord! I shouldn't be doing this! This is crazy!*

Rain flowed down her hair, under her sweatshirt collar, then down her back. She hopped a few times as chills bolted through her. Her hair hung matted to her head.

*No, let the river flow. Fall all over me.*

She laughed again, then heard something . . . a car start up, just across the street. The tires spun in the driver's haste to leave the area.

*Oh, no. I did have an audience.* She watched the car as it raced down Kimberley Street.

Saw the Colorado license plate.

Her laughter died on a breath. Something deep inside her shrunk a bit at the sight. She wiped her face and blinked, focusing on the car as it turned the corner and disappeared. Concern, then confusion filled her. She shook her head quickly, then headed for the front door of the church. A gust of wind almost toppled her. She ran up the last few steps and slammed the door shut behind her.

# FIVE

ALTA FITZSIMONS. RAUL AND REYNA Melindez. The Corwins, all
seven of them. Jack and Corissa Foley. Wind and rain and flooded
streets. Branches down. Trees split, blown down. Power lines down.
Candles flickering in dark windows. Wood smoke filling the air.
People at home hunkered down around their fireplaces and wood-
stoves while their garbage cans blew trash all over the neighborhood.

Inching the Blazer around storm debris littering the street, Scott
seemed to be genuinely enjoying himself. Seemed to genuinely care
about his neighbors. Even the ones who didn't attend the Kimberley Street Community Church.

So. He didn't hate everyone in Kimberley Square. *Just me.*

Chris sucked in her bottom lip and bit into it.

*No, Lord.* Hate *is too strong of a word. Scott doesn't hate me. Does
he? I know he may not like me, with good enough reason, but he certainly doesn't hate me.*

But then ... what was that look in his eye earlier that morning
when he pulled Erin away from Isaiah and Ben and marched her
home like a disobedient child? If looks could kill, Chris would have
been as obliterated as Isaiah's shed.

But he smiled at her at Chester's. Even smiled again at the Corwins'. Yes, he was eating a big slice of cherry pie smothered in melted
vanilla ice cream at the time, but he looked right at Chris and
smiled. And didn't let the smile fade like he usually did.

But then, he had growled. Literally growled, through a snarl,
when Mrs. Foley asked Chris about being in the army. She had heard
about Chris from Sonya. Met Chris once at church. Chris didn't
remember Corissa Foley. Corissa Foley remembered Chris. Wanted
to know all about Operation Desert Storm.

And Scott had literally growled.

Shivering with cold, yet too warm, she had abandoned her rain jacket. Under her sweatshirt, sweat drenched her. Without her jacket, rain had soaked her to the skin. The ponytail of her French braid felt weighted with lead, had actually whipped in her face a few times, stinging her cheek, when caught by a gust of wind. Water slogged in her boots. Socks soaked, her feet were shriveling, hot, sweating as though drowning in floodwater.

All in a day's work. And what a good day it was.

Adjust. And overcome.

Six years in the army—how many times had she been this miserable? More times than she could count. All in the day's work. Frozen solid into an Alaskan block of ice, melted away on her cot in that horrible Land of Sand. Feet festered with classic jungle rot after weeks of war games and exercises in the field. Brain numbed by week after week of unbearable boredom in the desert. Funny, how the military dictated her life in two distinct ways. Hurry up. And wait. Her less-than-distinguished U.S. Army career fell into four distinct categories: hurrying, waiting, melting, and freezing. In any and all random combinations. On any given day.

She'd take freezing to melting any day. And being dry.

Either way, any way, she was slowly beginning to realize she'd take any other place in the world . . . but here.

*Lord, I'm sorry, but I just want to go home.*

✼✼✼

"YOU THINK SHE MIGHT LEAVE."

Erin tore off another peel of orange, maybe a bit too aggressively. A tiny squirt of juice shot up and sprayed her cheek. "I don't know, Cappy." She sighed deeply as she wiped her face with the back of her sweatshirt sleeve. "No. I do know. Yes. I think she's going to leave."

"You're afraid."

Her hands stopped their work. Erin looked at her friend. "Admitting my fear would be admitting my lack of trust in the Lord."

Cappy's face revealed nothing. Her poker face.

"Yes. I'm trying to trust, but you're right. I'm afraid."

"Why in the world would Chris want to leave here?" A section of orange disappeared into Cappy's mouth. For a second, Erin was glad. Cappy would at least stop asking hard questions when her mouth was full.

Erin tore off another chunk of peel.

"She wouldn't leave because of you."

A grunt. "I should hope not."

"She certainly wouldn't leave because of me. I'm the greatest."

Erin glanced up. Noticed the goofy grin on Cappy's face.

"And she certainly wouldn't leave because of Isaiah, or the gym. I think she's really excited about that."

"Okay, Cap. Say it."

All of a sudden, an innocent look widened Cappy's eyes. "Say what, Erin?"

"Why would Chris want to leave? Because of Scott. Say it. Because of Scott."

"Has he given her reason to leave?"

Erin slowly shook her head, then tore off a section of orange and let it rest on her tongue for a second, savoring the tangy sweetness, before squishing it against the roof of her mouth.

"He has been a bit of a jerk at times."

She almost spit the orange across the room.

"But he hasn't given Chris reason enough to leave."

She swallowed and looked at Cappy.

"You know he hasn't, Erin. If Chris left, she could use Scott as an excuse, but it'd be her own choice. Her own . . ."

She waited.

Cappy met Erin's gaze. " . . . failure."

Erin lowered her head and picked at a bit of orange peel caught under her fingernail.

"And, Erin . . ."

"What, Cap."

"Have you ever known Chris to fail? At anything?"

She glanced up.

"She's not gonna leave. She'll fight this. She has a home here, and she wants to stay."

"I hope you're right, Cap. I really hope you're right."

"If I was the betting type . . ."

Erin started to smile.

" . . . I'd like the odds."

"Thanks, Cappy."

"Not so fast, Erin. There's something else. I've got this nagging feeling in my gut. And it's not my cold, that's in my nose."

Erin laughed.

"I just think . . . it's gonna get a lot worse before it gets better."

They sat in silence, listening to the storm beat against the house, eating the rest of their oranges, for a long while.

✯✯✯

CHRIS COULD ONLY WATCH. IF she moved just an inch closer to Scott and that chain saw, he would turn and slice her in half with it.

She heard him grumble as the wind blew rain into his ears. His hood had blown off ages ago. His lips moved. He was grumbling, though no words carried over the whine of the saw.

No wonder he struggled so. He was pinching the blade. Cutting at the wrong angle. Doing it all wrong. But would he let her show him how to do it right? No. Would he just let her do it so they could get out of the wind? No.

She sighed.

Men.

No, not all men.

*No. Absolutely not.* If she thought about Travis now, in her present state, she would start crying right on the spot.

Teddy. *Yeah. Think about Teddy. The jerk.*

Her heart squeezed the breath from her lungs. Tears stung her eyes. *No. Don't think about Teddy either. Poor guy.*

*God? I'm sorry. I'm so sorry.* She turned and trudged back to the Blazer, not caring anymore if Scott A. Mathis, MD, cut off a critical body part with that saw. *Forgive me, Lord.* She pushed herself into the passenger seat of the Blazer, slammed the door shut, grabbed her towel, covered her face with it, and let her tears fall.

★★★

HE CURSED THE STORM. MISERABLE weather, miserable place.

Oh, he had been to Portland before. Spent time in Washington, working in a mill. Hours on end, running slabs of Douglas fir through the saw. Day after day. But, at week's end, he and a group of his buddies would hit Portland. Drink up whatever wages remained after the week's debts had been paid.

He usually didn't drink that much. He usually didn't have that much money left after all his deductions.

His ex had found him. Made a big deal out of it, going to the judge to have his wages garnished to pay back child support. Miserable woman. Miserable, spoiled son. Worthless as his daddy.

The gin burned his mouth, yet he savored it, let it roll around his teeth for a few seconds before swallowing it. He sat in his car, drinking. Not smart for a wanted man. But he had no place else to go.

He was done running. Tonight, he would put that one special bullet back in his .38, put the barrel back in his mouth, and this time pull the trigger.

Last night, the sharp metallic taste of the gun barrel had surprised him as it touched his lips. He licked them now, tasting only the gin that lingered there. The awful taste had shocked him so much he jerked the gun out of his mouth, then didn't have the guts to put it back in. If he had just pulled the trigger instead . . .

Find Shelter from the Storm Here. As brilliant as a picture, the homemade sign appeared in his mind's eye. The crazy woman standing out in the gale-force wind, raising her head, laughing . . .

She was crazy that night in the cabin too. Not hysterical-crazy. She wasn't scared. Not at all. Didn't act like it anyway. Didn't fall apart. Didn't panic like most women do when they're terrified.

He never should have listened to Del. Never should have gone with them to that cabin. He never should have fought with Matt.

He never should have come to Portland, Oregon. To this place. Kimberley Square.

He reached across the seat for the .38 revolver he had stashed in the glove compartment. Pulled it out, held it gently in the palm of his hand.

No. They had gone to that cabin for a reason. For a good reason. Del was right. Wayne was their friend. With two quick shots from this gun, he could finish what they started that night. For Wayne. A little payback. Wasn't that why he came all this way? In this wretched storm? To this place?

Yes. Everything Del said was true. With two quick shots it would be done. And then, with one more shot, he would finish what he started last night. He would put the gun barrel back in his mouth and, this time, pull the trigger.

Three quick shots would finish the entire job. Yes. For Wayne. For Del. For Matt. He grabbed the bottle from the seat beside him and drank it dry. Threw it into the corner of the car.

Yes. He would finish the job. After he bought some more gin.

✵✵✵

"ARE YOU ABOUT READY TO HEAD HOME?"

Chris forced her eyes to look at Scott. "Is it about that time?"

"Almost. I think it's about five. Are you hungry?"

She wanted to ask why he even cared, but didn't. "Yeah. A little."

"Me too. We'll make one more stop, then call it a night."

Chris nodded. *Anything you say, sir. Just lead the way. I'll be at your six, just doing my job.* She wanted to laugh, but in her present state, laughing seemed impossible.

*Oh, suck it up, Chris. You've seen worse. No matter what, this man is a teddy bear compared to . . . Teddy.* She did laugh. Just a quiet, silly grunt. *And besides, this man has just cause. Now doesn't he?*

She let her mind wander a bit. *Wonder what Erin's up to? And Cappy. Is she feeling better yet? If she spent all day in bed while I've been out here busting my behind . . . Maybe I should have faked a cold. Probably won't have to fake it in a few days. If I don't catch something after all this . . .*

Scott turned down a familiar street. Chris blinked. They were only few blocks from home. This was Velda's street. And that . . . was Velda's house. Her mood brightened. She actually smiled when Scott pulled the Blazer up to the curb and cut the engine.

"Velda's?" Hope flooded her heart.

Scott looked surprised. "Yeah. You've been here before?"

"Yeah. Erin brought me here last month. When Velda was sick."

"Oh. Well, I'm sure she's fine, but I just want to make sure. Andy and Ben may have come by here already. But I don't think she'd mind the company."

Was that a smile?

*You know? Lord?* Chris let the words continue in her heart as she pushed herself one more time out of the Blazer. *Sometimes this man can be charming. How can one man be so charming one minute and so absolutely infuriating the next?*

Wind and rain slapped and tugged at her as she walked up the steps to Velda Jackson's porch. By now Chris barely noticed.

"For heaven's sake, you two, what are you doing out in weather like this?"

A wide smile stretched across Chris's entire face. She couldn't hold it back even if she wanted to.

Velda Jackson, sweet, large, dark, old, yet teeming with energy, stood at her door waving Chris and Scott into the house. "Come on now, children. Get in here."

"We just wanted to make sure everything's all right with you," Scott said while being ushered into Velda's front room.

"Ahh, Scott." The woman pulled him in and planted a smacking kiss on his cheek. "Everything's fine, now that you're here." She turned to Chris. "And you! Precious Christina. Look at you, sweetheart, you're soaked!"

Chris held her breath to keep from crying. The fact she was soaked didn't stop Velda from wrapping her up in a huge hug.

"And you're freezing! Oh, child." Velda pushed away. "You come in here and warm yourself by the fire. You too, Scott. I'll go get us some coffee. Russell's done brought me a thermos full each of coffee and sweet black tea. I'm set for at least another week!"

Chris let the woman's laughter and rich southern sway fall over her like a blanket. But she needed no warmth and avoided the fire. She may have been cold on the outside, but inside she was still burning up.

"No, Velda, we don't need coffee." Scott turned to look at Chris. "Do you?"

She quickly shook her head and said softly, "I'm fine."

"You save that. You may just need it next week if this storm doesn't break."

Velda's laughter carried to them from the kitchen. "You sure? There's plenty, Scott."

"No, Velda, please. We're fine. We're just about ready to call it a night and go get some dinner anyway. They've got everything set up at the church."

"So you two have been out all day in this?" Velda returned to the living room carrying a plate of cookies.

Chocolate chip. Chris's mouth watered at the sight.

"Take a handful, both of you. They were in my freezer for a rainy day, and the day couldn't get any rainier!"

Chris took three cookies—they were small—then glanced sheepishly at Scott.

He gave her a grin, then took four.

"Come. Sit. You two. Look at you. My, how I love my family. Thank You, Jesus. Y'all are the sweetest you can be to me. Why, Pastor Andy and his daddy were here earlier this morning. They unpacked the rest of my freezer into that there cooler. Full of ice. Wasn't that nice?"

Chris couldn't respond. The cookie in her mouth was too incredibly delicious to hastily swallow.

"You know we love you, now don't you?" Scott's eyes shone in the faint light of Velda's assortment of candles. "We have to look out for you."

"You two come on in, now. Sit."

"No, Velda, thanks. We're too wet. We just wanted to say hello. Make sure everything's all right."

"Well, I'm good, Scott. Really. I sure appreciate you two stopping by."

Chris swallowed, then chomped into her second cookie.

"How have you been takin' to your new home, Chris? Do you like living here with us?"

She struggled to clear her mouth. Then grinned. "I'd like it better if it wasn't a typhoon out there."

Velda laughed. "We tend to get these crazy storms from time to time. Ahh, the Friday the Thirteenth Storm of '81 about blew us off the map. But the Columbus Day Storm of '62, well, now, that made the Storm of '81 look like a summer shower!"

"The Big Blow, they called that one," Scott said to Chris as he chewed his third cookie. "It only lasted for two hours. Is that weird or what?"

"That's right," Velda said. "Two hours of pure terror. Almost clean wiped us out." She slowly shook her head. Then smiled at Chris. "When this storm calms down a bit, you and Erin must come see me again. I did so enjoy our last visit. And now . . . now that you're my sister in the Lord . . ." She tilted her head back and lifted her hand. "Praise You, Jesus! Thank You for saving this precious child. Thank You, Lord!" She held her hand up for another second, then let it fall to her lap as her eyes found Chris again. "I can't tell you how happy I am for you. Ahh, you did so look like a lost soul the last time you were here."

Chris didn't know what to say. She only chewed her cookie. And smiled.

"How is Erin, Scott?" Velda looked at him, then gave him a wink. "She's starting to show a little. Ahh, you two must be so happy."

"We are, Velda. Very much. She's the love of my life."

"Ooh, look at me!" Velda rubbed her arms. "I've got goose bumps!" Her laughter filled the room. "Love is such a precious, precious gift, now isn't it? Thank You, Jesus."

"Yes, ma'am, it certainly is." Scott glanced at Chris as he pushed another cookie into his mouth.

Chris looked down and finished the last one of hers. She pressed her lips as her tongue ran across her teeth, gathering up what remained of the sweetness. *Yes. Thank You, Lord, for love . . . and for chocolate chip cookies.* She smiled, but hid the smile as she worked her tongue through her mouth. *Thank You for Your love for me.* She swallowed one last time. Looked up.

Velda was pulling a jug of milk from the cooler Ben and Andy had brought. "Don't know where my head is," she said as she carried the milk to the counter. She poured two juice glasses full. "Cain't have chocolate chip cookies without milk."

Chris accepted the milk with a smile and a polite, "Thank you," then drank deeply. Gratitude suddenly overwhelmed her. *Thank You, Lord . . . for chocolate chip cookies . . . and ice-cold milk. Two of my four food groups.*

For the first time that day, joy tickled her heart. She let it surface in the smile that stayed all through the rest of their visit with Velda. She hoped it would flow out of her and warm the woman's heart, would tell her, *I love you too, sweet Velda, my sister, my friend.*

★★★

FUNNY, HOW THE LINGERING REFRAINS of chocolate chip cookies echoed on the taste buds long after the last morsel had been swallowed. In the stomach, what remained of the golden delicacies mixed with powerful acids, horrible-tasting acids, acids that would burn the throat . . . if it weren't for the milk. Cold, thick, fresh milk, coating the throat, washing down all the sweetness . . . except for what so joyously remained to linger on the tongue.

Ice cream did that too. Or cherry pie. Especially cherry pie with ice cream. Even if it was melted. What was melted ice cream anyway, but extra-thick, extra-sweet . . . milk?

Was she losing her mind?

It wasn't raining anymore. And it was very dark. She blinked. It wasn't raining and it was very dark because Scott had pulled the Blazer under the overhang behind the church. Ahh. They were home.

Well, close enough, anyway.

She turned to look at Scott. He sat there looking right back at her. A tiny smile pulled his lips. "So. I didn't lose you."

"Huh?"

His smile widened. "I just thought I'd lost you there for a second. You were sort of . . . gazing off into space."

"Oh."

"I was afraid I'd have to carry you inside." Scott turned to push himself out of the Blazer. "I've already carried you once, and didn't much care for the prospect of having to carry you again."

Slam.

Chris sat still for another minute. Wanted to dig a hole in the ground and completely disappear into it.

Scott had carried her that night. The night she passed out in Erin's arms.

Her eyes fell closed as her head thudded back against the seat. Why did he have to bring that up now? And she was in such a good mood.

She pushed herself out of the Blazer and trudged, more like sloshed, to the door of the church basement.

Erin stood there, holding the door open. The smile on her face quickly disintegrated. "Oh . . . Chris. Why aren't you wearing your jacket? You're soaked! Come in and get dried off."

At that second, all Chris wanted to do was . . . "No, I think I'm just gonna go home."

"You've got to come in, Chris. Come and get some dinner. There's sandwiches, hot soup, coffee . . . Please come in."

The last thing she wanted to do was stand there and argue with her best friend. No, the absolute last thing she wanted to do was go through that door. "I'm all right, Rinny. I'm going on home. Thanks, anyway."

Erin looked as if she was about to cry. "Can I fix you a box to go? Maybe one for Cappy too?"

Chris smiled. It hurt her heart to see Erin so sad. "Sure."

"Please come in. Get out of the cold for at least a minute. While I get them together."

She barely nodded, then walked through the door Erin still held open for her.

Erin quickly headed for the kitchen, but Chris stood just inside the door. Almost everyone she saw wore happy smiles as they sat at the long folding tables eating sandwiches and soup. Though wet and disheveled, they seemed to be basking in the joy of being together, sheltered in the time of storm. Wasn't that how that song went?

She cared about these people. Had grown to love a few of them. Like Isaiah. And Mildred. Mildred Conner had the cutest little terrier dog. What was his name? He barked all the time, her little protector, her little vicious dog. Ankle biter. But no one would mess with Mildred when . . . Ahh, what was that dog's name?

"Hey, Chris. You look a little wet."

She turned to seek out the source of that soft voice, the voice she recognized as Bettema Kinsley's, yet was amazed at how much effort just turning her head required.

Her neck was still stiff. Sore in more ways than she would ever let on.

"Hey you," she said to her lanky friend. "Come on in and have some soup."

"Yikes, girl, you aren't wet, you're soaked."

"Heard you had some adventure of your own in this storm."

Bettema let out a laugh. "Adventure. That's a good word. It's amazing how little you appreciate the roof on your house until it blows off."

"I hear that. Is Mason's mom all right?"

"He's been wanting her to move out of that house. Now he finally got his wish. She's moved in with him."

Chris laughed. "That'll learn 'im."

"Certainly will."

She enjoyed how Bettema's smile played out on her face.

"What are you doing, standing here?"

"Rin's bringing me a 'to go' order. One for Cappy too."

"I just came from seeing Cappy. She's one sick puppy." Bettema gave Chris a hairy eyeball. "You'll be one too, girl, if you don't get out of those clothes."

"Nag, nag." But Chris knew her smile refuted the words.

"Hey, Tema." Erin handed the box she carried to Chris before standing on tiptoe to give Bettema a quick hug. "How's Mason's mom?"

"Missing her roof, but other than that, just fine."

The box was heavy. Chris lifted a corner to see what all Erin had packed away inside it.

"Don't now," Erin said. "Go on home and dry off. And eat. Before it gets cold."

Chris playfully glared at Erin for a few seconds, then at Bettema. "Nags. Both of you."

"It's only 'cause we care," Bettema said through a goofy grin.

"Aww. Well, right back at ya both." Chris headed for the door, then stopped and looked back at her friends. "Tell Mason I said howdy," she said to Bettema.

"I will," came with a warm smile.

"See ya, Rinny. Thanks. For this." Chris lifted the box a little.

Erin only nodded.

Chris allowed her eyes to stay on Erin's just a second longer, wanted them to say what she could not . . .

The small, teary smile Erin gave her said that she heard just fine.

★★★

"LUUUCY, I'M HOME!"

"Oh, goodie, goodie! What'd you bring me?"

Chris pushed the door of her apartment closed against a gust of wind determined to force its way inside. Then spun the deadbolt. Blew out a breath. And said, "Soup."

"More soup?"

"Whaddaya mean, 'more soup'?" She squished into the living room and saw Cappy sitting on the recliner all wrapped up in blankets surrounded by tissues and candles, listening to the Christian station through a transistor radio.

"Erin brought me soup for lunch. I was hoping you would've taken into account my poor beleaguered condition and brought me . . . pizza."

Chris dropped the box onto Cappy's lap. "Well, lady, the only place open in Kimberley Square at this hour is the Church Basement Restaurant, and all they're serving is soup. And sandwiches, I guess. See what all Rin put in there. It weighs a ton."

"Girl, you are soaked."

"Really, Cap? Ya think so?"

"Aren't you freezing?"

Chris headed for the bathroom. "Nope. Not at all. Just pruned."

"What?" came from the living room, but Chris didn't feel it necessary to reply.

It took her twenty minutes to get cleaned up, dried off, and wrapped in her soft cotton sweatpants and her favorite extra-soft Mesa State T-shirt. Her hair was still damp, and probably would be for quite some time, but it felt nice to free it from the French braid and to run her brush through its shoulder-length strands.

She finally padded back out to the living room where Cappy held what looked like a bag of chips. Sounded like chips crunching in her mouth. Chris flopped down on the couch and stretched out, laying her head on the pile of pillows in the corner.

"You gonna eat?" came from Cappy's full mouth.

"Later." Her eyes fell closed as she let out a long, exhausted breath.

"There's a ham and Swiss sandwich, a roast beef and Swiss, and another bag of chips. Plus chocolate cake. And a jug of milk, and what I think is peppermint tea. Smells like it, anyway."

Erin's face appeared in Chris's mind. She smiled as warmth flooded her heart. Erin knew Chris loved Swiss cheese. And peppermint tea. She ventured ahead. "What kind of soup?"

"Well, I already ate the chicken noodle. But there's some kind of creamy, cheesy soup in the other jug."

Chris's eyes popped open. "Cream of broccoli, maybe?"

"Maybe. I didn't taste it."

She pushed herself out of the couch and reached for what was left of Erin's box.

"Wait, I want one of the oranges."

Chris pulled it out and tossed it to her. Then settled back into the couch with the box on her lap. Yep, roast beef and Swiss. Oh, to only have a grill to toast it up so the Swiss would melt. Dijonaise. Perfect. And ham and Swiss. With Dijonaise. And, yes, cream of broccoli soup.

Her eyes closed. *Oh, Lord, thank You. Thank You so much . . . for Erin. I can't tell You how much she . . . but I think You already know. Thank You. Lord Jesus, I really mean it. Thank You so much.* She opened her eyes. *And thanks for this food!*

★★★

"YOU'RE REALLY QUIET."

Erin smiled, then slowly reached up to caress her husband's face. On the couch in their living room, he had pulled her onto his lap, drawing her in as close as he could against him. They sat like that for a long while. Just silently listening to the storm.

"Are you tired?" he asked.

"No. Not really." She leaned in to kiss his cheek. "Are you?"

"A little."

She wanted to ask about his day, but didn't know how.

"Are you hungry?"

"No. I'm okay."

"Comfortable?"

She hummed. "Completely."

He squeezed her gently. "Me too."

Minutes passed. Erin had no idea how many, or even what time it was. It was dark, that she knew. The few candles they had lit burned brightly, but threw only shimmering shadows across the room.

"You wanna go upstairs?" she whispered.

He didn't answer her question. Didn't seem to have heard it. "Erin," he said softly, "can I ask you something?"

"Sure."

"About Chris."

She tried to look into his eyes, but saw little in the darkness. "Um . . . I guess."

"When she was here last month, when you two got back from Dandy's . . ."

Erin waited, suddenly a tiny bit afraid.

"Chris came down the stairs and said she was leaving. Do you remember that?"

Scott's voice was soft and quiet, and there didn't seem to be anything hidden in the words. Erin said, "Yes."

"But you went up and talked to her. But she still blew up."

Where was this going? Erin waited.

"She blew up, but then you guys talked again. And that's when she fell asleep in your arms. I had to carry her back to her room."

"I remember, Scott." She almost wanted to smile. Chris wasn't the only one Scott carried that night.

"If she would have stayed mad and left that night, do you think she would have gone out and . . . ?"

She waited for what seemed like forever for him to continue.

"Erin, do you think if Chris would have left this house that night, she would have gone out . . . and killed herself?"

Her breath stuck in her throat.

"She was so . . . desperate. And hard. And there was such urgency in you about her. There still is." He looked at her. Candlelight flickered in his eyes. "That's it, isn't it. You were afraid Chris would leave . . . and take her own life."

She didn't know what to say.

"That's why you had to make her stay. To save her very life. And . . . you did. You helped her come to know the Lord."

Her eyes closed for a second as her heart swelled with unsettled joy.

"She was that close to . . ."

Erin again met his gaze.

"Why, Erin? I mean, obviously because her friend was killed."

"Travis was more than her friend."

"Do you think she was in love with him?"

"Yes. I'm sure of it."

"Hmm." He glanced away.

"Why, Scott? What are you asking?"

"Erin, if Chris was to leave here and go back to Colorado, would that be such a bad thing? I mean . . ."

Her mouth fell open. Just what did he mean?

"That sounded horrible. I'm sorry, sweetheart." He gently squeezed her.

"Don't be. Just say what you mean."

"She really does need you."

Erin pushed herself up in her husband's arms to see more clearly into his eyes.

"I mean, if she goes back to Colorado, you're afraid she'll fall away from the Lord. She needs you, and all of us here, to help her gain her footing with Christ."

She wanted to cry. "Yes, love, but I don't understand—"

"I guess I knew that. I just didn't want to admit it."

"Admit what?"

Scott gazed deeply into her eyes. "She can't leave here."

Erin waited, feeling a thread of fear weave itself around her heart.

"She won't leave here. Not if you have anything to say about it."

"I really want her to stay, Scott. But it's completely her decision."

"And not mine."

"Oh, Scott . . ."

"No, Erin, that's not what I mean. I can see it now. Chris needs to stay. She needs all of us here at Kimberley." He rubbed his forehead, then reached up to run his fingers through Erin's hair. His hand cupped her cheek. "You should have seen her today at Velda's. The look on her face . . . it made me wonder if she's ever been loved like that. By someone like Velda. Just . . . loved. Pure and outright."

Tears filled Erin's eyes.

"Chris needs to stay here. So I've gotta get with the program."

"Honey, don't—"

"No, really, Erin, this is a good thing. I've been stupid. It's all so obvious to me now." His thumb gently swiped the tear that fell from her eye. "Hey, don't cry. This is a good thing. Really."

"I'm so sorry about all of this. How it's hurt you."

"No. I haven't been hurt, Erin. I'm just a little slow on the uptake." He grinned.

"You heard that from Ben."

"And hey, speaking of that, you don't, like, have any plans to paint the bathroom, do you?"

Erin could only stare, mouth gaping, until Scott playfully pulled her back down against him and planted a laughing kiss on her lips. Their laughter quickly faded as the kiss lingered. And lingered.

★★★

"HE CAN BE A PAIN, CAN'T HE."

Chris's eyes flew open. Lying on the couch, full of soup, sandwich, and peppermint tea, she turned to look at Cappy who still sat in the recliner.

"He's cute and all, but he can be a bit pigheaded at times."

"And whom, Miss Sanchez, are we talking about?"

Through the sleepy darkness, Cappy grinned. "Erin's husband."

"Scott?"

"Yes. I think that's his name."

Chris settled back into the couch's soft corner pillow.

"You haven't told me about your day."

"What's to tell?"

"Well, how did it go?"

"Fine."

"And how will it go tomorrow?"

She turned to look at her friend again. "How do I know?"

"You don't have to go out with him tomorrow. If you tell Ben you'd rather not, he won't make you."

"I'm fine with it, Cap. If I can help, I want to help."

"You don't have to."

"I know."

"Do you? Really?"

Chris sat up in the couch and spun her feet to the floor. "Yes, Cappy. I know. Quit being a nag. I got enough of that today from both Erin and Tema."

"To nag you is to love you."

She stood and stretched her arms above her head. "Right. Thanks. Right back atcha."

"Anytime."

"I'm going to bed."

"Sleep tight."

A sudden gust of wind shook the house. Chris heard creaks from several different corners of the room. Her breath stuck in her throat.

"Man. That wasn't good."

Chris stood still, listening.

"You remember how it howled in the desert . . . on G-Day?"

"Like being in a sandblaster."

A moment of silence fell between them while the wind howled. Until Cappy said, "Someday . . ." That was it for a second. She pulled her blanket up to her chin. "Someday I'd really like to hear what it was like for you."

"What *what* was like?"

"Being in the desert. All of it. Flyin'. Working with Teddy. And with Erin. And what happened . . . that day."

Chris sighed deeply.

"No, not now. Right now you've got enough on your mind. But someday. Okay? I'd like to hear about everything. We've never talked about it. But someday. Okay?"

"Okay."

"Until then, if you need to talk about Scott, I'm here. You hear me, Chris?"

She smiled. "I hear you, Cap."

"You're gonna be all right."

She didn't know what to say.

"This is all gonna be . . . all right."

Another violent gust of wind battered the house. More creaks from every direction.

"Go to bed, woman."

Chris smiled. "Yeah. I'll see you in the morning."

"Not if I see you first. Throw me a pillow."

A laugh. A toss. The pillow landed on Cappy's lap.

"Nightie night."

"'Night, Cap."

"Oh, hah hah. That's very funny. Original too. Like I've never heard that one before."

Chris only laughed. Turned and walked down the hall toward her bedroom. Outside, out in the late-night storm, something caught in the wind clanked and crashed. Slowly padding down the hall, Chris felt just as caught in the storm. Tossed around by winds unseen. Not too sure where she would land.

*Will we, Lord?* She stopped at her door and raised her head, listening. *Will we really be all right?*

# SIX

SHE DIDN'T NEED AN ALARM clock to tell her it was time to get up. Out her bedroom window, the heavy, cold dark of night had given way to a lighter shade of black, a deep gray, a hint of morning light squeezing its way through thick swirling clouds, clouds that hurled billions of fat raindrops into everything foolish enough to be standing in their way.

*You don't have to go out with him tomorrow. If you tell Ben you'd rather not, he won't make you.*

She let the words float through her grogginess. Cappy's words. What a nag.

Of course, Chris didn't have to go out with Scott again today. She could stay right where she was, tucked under Erin's grandmother's quilt all day if she wanted to, and not lift a finger to do anything. No one would blame her. Ben wouldn't even cut her pay.

So tempting. The morning had simply come too soon. Too dark, too dreary. The wind roared against her bedroom window. Rain smacked the glass, the way it had smacked the windshield of the Blazer all day yesterday, and splashed off her cheeks, stung her eyes, bore into her ears. She felt bruised, sore, weary of being weary, and cold.

She pushed up to sit on the edge of the bed. Slowly rubbed the sore spots on the back and sides of her neck, then rubbed her forehead, then her eyes.

Ugh. Was she catching Cappy's cold? Her entire body ached. Deep, icy dampness had settled into her bones.

*Oh, God. This new day . . . I'm not ready for it.*

She reached to her nightstand for the matches to light the candle. Squinted against the brilliant flash of flame. Lit the candle, blew out the match, then sat and watched the flame rise to its full height on the candle's wick. Brilliant and beautiful, the sharp edges of the flame danced on invisible currents, sending soft orange light flickering through the shadows across the room.

The flame warmed her heart. She barely smiled. *I may not be ready for this day, Lord Jesus, but it's ready and waiting for me. I'll go out with Scott again today, if You want me to. If he wants me to.* She rubbed her nose. *And if he doesn't want me to? Well, I won't be sad.*

She laughed. *Sorry, Lord. You can disregard that last part.*

She pushed herself out of the bed and, carrying her candle, headed for the bathroom.

✴ ✴ ✴

PRAYER. IT WAS STILL TOO amazing. Her head should have been bowed, her eyes closed, yet she peeked around the room, watching the people who had joined her in the basement of the Kimberley Street Community Church. Together they sat, praying for strength and guidance, for help in this time of storm. Ben's deep, soothing voice carried each word of his prayer like a line of pure poetry. Each word filtered into her soul, filled her heart, eased the night's weariness from her bones.

She peeked to her left, saw Erin looking at her. She looked away, but not before giving her best friend a small, sheepish grin. She closed her eyes. Held on to the sight for a few seconds longer. Felt gratitude well up inside her, flooding her entire being. She let herself fall into the poetry of Ben's prayer.

" . . . and we thank You, heavenly Father, for Your Son, our Lord and Savior, Jesus Christ. We love Him, and thank You for giving Him to us. Thank You, Lord Jesus, for giving to us life, truth, and peace. You are our peace, even as we go out into the chaos of this storm. Thank You, Lord. We pray these things in Your precious name, amen."

The word was repeated by several in the room. "Amen." Chris slowly opened her eyes and blinked. And smiled. *Yes, Lord. Thank*

*You for . . . everything.* She lifted her head and saw Sonya. Felt touched by her gentle smile. She tried to return it, tried to tell Sonya how much she loved her through the simple smile. She looked away and saw Isaiah, then his wife, Emily, then a few people she didn't yet know. She glanced at Ben. He stood by the kitchen counter talking with Scott. Scott's eyes turned directly to her.

She froze. Couldn't look away. Couldn't figure out what she saw in his eyes. Scott looked back at Ben. Nodded his head. Turned away. His shoulders seemed to sag as he filled a cup with coffee from the urn on the counter.

So. It would be another day.

Chris lowered her head and stared at the floor. *Lord, You've got to help me with this. Don't let me blow this. Unless You help me, I know I'm gonna blow this. I'm sorry. I'm really sorry.*

"Are you okay?" Just a whisper. Erin's whisper.

Startled by it, Chris turned her head quickly. "Hey, you."

Erin barely smiled.

Chris saw nervous tension in her eyes. "I'm good." She smiled warmly. "Really."

"Did you get enough to eat?"

"Yeah. Plenty. Thanks."

"Are you, um . . . are you sure you want to go out again today?"

"Yeah. If Ben wants me to."

"But it's not up to Ben. If you don't want to go . . ."

"I know, Rinny. But I want to. I enjoyed yesterday."

"You enjoyed it?"

"Well, you know what I mean."

Erin grinned. "Heard you met Chester."

And Chris laughed. "Yeah. He's a character."

Erin's grin faded too quickly. "Be sure and take a thermos of coffee with you. And wear your jacket this time."

"Yes, mum."

"I mean it, Chris. Don't get so wet. Or cold. Like yesterday."

"I hear you. Don't worry, Rinny."

"I always worry about you, Chris." Erin's voice barely spoke the words. "I'll see you later." She smiled and turned for the kitchen.

The words fell heavily over Chris. Didn't sit well. She sighed deeply. Then stood as Ben approached.

"Hello, Chris."

"Hi, Ben." She restrained a grin. When would she lose the persistent urge to salute every time she saw the man?

"Would you like to go out again today? With Scott? We've had several calls from people who'd like a home visit."

All the fuss and concern was starting to wear on her nerves. She tried to keep it out of her tone. "Yes, Ben. I'd like that very much."

"You're sure, now?"

She swallowed down a surge of temper. "Yes, sir. Very much. I want to help out wherever you need me."

"We appreciate that, Chris. We love having you here with us."

"Thank you, sir. I love being here." She almost cringed. Too much sentiment.

Ben's hesitation matched what she saw in his eyes. "Good. I, um, gave the list to Scott. Let us know if you need anything, all right? Just call it in."

"All right. I will."

"Good." Ben's smile seemed genuine, yet strained. He slowly turned and walked away.

Chris drew in another long, deep breath. Held it a second. Let it out. *Well, that could have gone better.* She grabbed her rain jacket, then her small bag of towels and dry socks. Looked up just in time to see Scott heading out the back door of the basement, keys to the Blazer dangling in his teeth as he swung his rain jacket around his shoulders.

Another deep breath. She started toward the door after him, then stopped and looked back toward the kitchen. Sarah, Erin, and Mildred stood inside it, laughing and talking. A huge plate of cranberry-orange muffins sat on the counter. Chris quickly detoured to that plate. Snatched up one of the muffins. Gave Erin a warm smile. Then followed after Scott once again to begin her new day.

### ★★★

*COME ON, YOU DUMB THING. START!*

Scott ripped on the chain saw's cord again. And again. Only hums. Not a spark, not a chance of starting. Again. His arms were tiring. Again. Again.

No. This was not how this day was supposed to go. First the flood of drainage filling both his boots. Then the transient cursing his offer of help. Then Mr. Potts's rantings about the failures of the city, the failures of the power company, the failures of the president, the UN, the global economy . . .

Another rip on the cord. Nothing.

Chris was watching. Of course, she was watching. Was she laughing at him? Probably not. Yet, he wouldn't look at her, no sir. Another rip on the cord. Nothing.

No, he wouldn't look, wouldn't show even a hint of the aggravation he felt. Another rip. Another. Nothing.

What was he doing wrong? He had worked this stupid machine yesterday. There was nothing to it. So why, today, wouldn't it start?

Out of gas. Of course! That must be it. He sucked in a deep breath and blew it out. Then headed for the back of the Blazer, for the gas can he knew was there. Lifted the Blazer's tailgate.

"What are you doing?" came from Chris in the front seat.

Scott simply chose not to answer that question.

"It doesn't need gas."

How would she know? Did she check the tank? Scott glared at the back of her head for a second. Then checked the tank.

Full.

Well, sure. What did he expect? This entire day, no, this entire week had turned out to be a complete pain in his backside. He tossed the chain saw into its carrier. Snapped the lid shut. Slapped the Blazer's tailgate shut. *We'll just call this one in to the city. They can clear it. Dumb, stupid thing.*

Gritting his teeth, he climbed in the driver's side of the Blazer. Reached for the key to start it.

"We're leaving?"

"Yes." He pumped the gas pedal to rev the engine.

"We're not going to clear this."

"No. I'll call it in to the city." He picked up the radio to contact John.

"For this little twig. Don't you think they have enough to do?" Chris gazed at him.

Their eyes met. One second. Two. Five. Scott keyed the radio's mike and drew in a breath to speak. Chris suddenly turned and pushed herself out of the truck.

Scott unkeyed the mike.

Chris opened the back door of the Blazer. Scott heard the chain saw's case being opened. Then slapped shut. The Blazer's door came down. Through the howling wind and driving rain, Chris appeared at the passenger's side window, gave Scott a disgusted look, flipped a switch on the chain saw, and with one quick tug, brought the dumb thing roaring to life. She stood there another second, then headed off for the downed branch blocking half the street. Immediately went to work.

*The kill switch! Of course! You forgot to turn the dumb thing on!* Scott curled his right hand into a fist and pounded the steering wheel with it. Wanted to curse. But didn't.

He was such an idiot. He glanced up. Watched her. Through the streams of rain pouring down the Blazer's windshield, he couldn't see much. Just that Chris was wielding the chain saw like the experienced sawer she was. The broken branch fell away from the old elm tree. She kicked at it, then set to work slicing it up into firewood.

Scott shut down the Blazer, eased back into the driver's seat, then allowed himself to relax. He blew out another deep breath. Laid his head back. Closed his eyes.

He saw his wife's face. Her gentle smile. Her gorgeous blue eyes. Heard her laughter. Saw the dimples on her cheeks as she laughed. Felt washed in her love.

*Oh . . . Erin. My sweet one. Dear God, how I thank You for my wife, my love. She came to me, a gift from You. You saw me in my lonely state, and gave me . . . such a gift. A gift I'll never be able to repay. You've been so good to me. Given me so much.*

He wiped his hand down over his face. *Lord, I'm sick of being wet. Cold, wet, and cranky.* His eyes blinked open. *But Chris has been out here this whole time with me. She's cold, wet . . . and she's cranky too. But she's been a big help, Lord. I need to tell her that. But how?* He ran his fingers through his wet hair.

*She's been a big help out here. People like her. She has a terrific laugh. Until she looks at me. Then all I see is fear.*

*And I put that fear there. It's my fault she's so afraid of me. But it's her fault I'm so afraid for Erin! Lord, what's the truth, huh? The truth is . . . in the last month, because of Chris, Erin has almost been killed— not once, but twice! Crazy murderers wanted to kill her because of Chris. Then she's in a bar. A bar! Of all places! And she falls and hits her head. Oh, Lord God! With her past injuries . . . just one more concussion, and she may die! She may fall into a coma. A permanent coma! Is that something I can just shrug off? Don't I have the right to be worried about her?*

His teeth ground. The chain saw's whine stopped. He stared through the foggy windshield, watching Chris stack the chunks of wood on the edge of the sidewalk. Cleaning up the mess.

*Should go out and help her.*

Scott grunted. *She can handle it. She repels out of helicopters, doesn't she? Kills all kinds of bad guys, saves the day for everybody. She can certainly handle stacking a few pieces of firewood.*

He growled. *Lord, You've got to help me with this. Forgive me. Please. Help me to see Chris . . . as You see her. As Ben sees her. As . . . Erin sees her. Please help me see what everyone else sees in Chris. 'Cause when I look at her, all I can see, Lord, is the danger she brings to all I hold dear.*

*Forgive me, Lord. Please. Help me understand.*

★★★

"ANYTHING INTERESTING?"

Erin glanced up from the Tuesday *Oregonian* in her hand and smiled as Sarah Connelly lowered a steaming mug to the table beside her. Peppermint tea.

"One sugar, right?"

"Perfect. Thanks, Sarah." She held her smile as Sarah sat down across the table.

"You're very welcome." Sarah sipped her own tea.

"I can't believe the mess this storm is causing." Erin turned the paper so Sarah could see a large picture of the Willamette River overflowing its banks.

"Is it true they think downtown may be flooded?"

"Right now they're not sure. Mayor Katz is calling for volunteers to fill sandbags to shore up the waterfront."

"I'll be so glad when this is over."

"Me too." Erin folded the paper and left it on the edge of the table.

"How are you doing, Erin? Are you feeling all right?"

She met Sarah's gaze. "I'm fine."

"You look a little pale."

She smiled. "I feel a little pale. But it's nothing."

"Why don't you go on home? We can certainly hold the fort around here."

"Nah. I'd rather be here."

"I'm worried about you."

The words stunned her. "Don't be. I'm fine." She could feel Sarah's gaze as both women quietly sipped their tea.

"Wanna hear a secret?" Sarah said a minute later.

Erin leaned closer. "Sure."

"If you tell anyone I told you, I'll deny it."

"Cross my heart."

"I heard Isaiah and Scott talking about building a cradle."

Her eyes bulged. Her loving husband was a healer, not a builder.

"They seemed really excited about it."

"A cradle?"

"It won't be long, you know."

She grinned. Then sipped her tea.

"Has she been kicking?"

"Some." Erin's grin gave way to a full-blown smile.

"Kayley didn't kick hardly at all. Not like Benny. I still think Benny is going to play professional soccer."

Erin slowly shook her head as she laughed.

"All right, woman. If you tell me you're okay, I'll believe it. I've got to go round up my little soccer player. It's time for his lunch." Sarah gave Erin's hand a gentle pat, then pushed herself up from the table. "See ya later."

"See ya, lady. Thanks for the tea." Erin watched her go, then fell lost to her thoughts.

Isaiah and Scott. Building a cradle? When did this come about? She laughed quietly, then let her eyes close. *Oh, my love. You're going to be a daddy. You're going to be the best daddy in the whole world.*

Sudden tears stung her eyes. She blinked them away.

*Thank You, Father, for my precious love. You have given me everything I could ever hope for. Thank You for Your love. For all You've done. For all that lies ahead.*

She winced as her stomach suddenly burned.

*Lord? For right now? Wherever they are. Whatever they're doing. Please help them. Please keep them safe. Please . . . keep them from killing each other.*

She wanted to laugh, but couldn't. The prospect was too close to the truth to be funny.

✷✷✷

"So, what are you saying? You're going to stay out here?"

Ben Connelly did not look at his son. He stared at the rain coursing down the windshield. "I am not going in, and that's all I'll say about it."

"Dad, when are you going to get over this? Mrs. Crandle is a harmless old woman."

"Who passionately hates me."

"No, she doesn't. She just hates the uniform you once wore."

"And that's not enough?"

"Dad, look. The more you show her who you are, the less she'll hate you."

He turned to meet his son's gaze. "Son, my dear firstborn son, listen to me. I am not going into that woman's house."

Andy looked away, laughed, then slowly shook his head.

"Now, go and see what she needs. I'll just wait right here. And take a little nap." Ben slouched into the seat of his Explorer, then laid his head back on the headrest.

"Fine. I'll be back."

"I'll be here."

Andy laughed as he exited the truck.

Ben crossed his arms over his belly.

*Naggity old bitty, anyway. What's she got against those who have served her country? Ultraliberal extremist. Doesn't she realize even soldiers hate war?*

It only took a second. He spoke the words aloud. "Sorry, Lord." Was he?

"Really, Lord. I'm sorry. Forgive me for feeling this way about my sister in You."

He shuddered. The thought of Mrs. Verlene Crandle being his sister ruffled his feathers.

He sighed. Closed his eyes. Peace fell over him, flooding him with tender compassion. *Thank You, Lord, for Verlene Crandle. I know why she's so bitter. From what I've heard, John was a fine husband, and a fine soldier. He was too young to die, in a war that had simply gone awry. Forgive me. But, Lord, thank You. Thank You for every young man and every young woman who has ever worn a military uniform. This country—the very freedom that courses through the heart of this country—owes its very existence to those who have served. And are serving. We owe our freedom, our very lives, to them all. And, of course, to You, precious Lord.*

In his mind's eye, one particular soldier stood across from him again, as she often did. Dressed in dusty desert camouflaged Battle Dress Uniform, hair pulled back in that French braid, dirt on her nose, booney hat tucked into the pocket of her trousers.

Specialist Christina Renae McIntyre. One of the most remarkable soldiers he had ever had the privilege to command.

She stood there that day, waiting to hear that her most unusual request had been granted. Even to this day, Ben could not understand it. He kept his eyes closed and let himself drift into the memory.

She had respectfully made her request. Ben didn't understand it, but he pursued it for her anyway. He contacted General Myron Spenser, Chris's commanding officer at Fort Wainwright, Alaska, to ask permission for Chris to stay in Saudi Arabia to serve out the remaining weeks of her enlistment by assisting in the massive debarkation effort about to be carried out. Operation Desert Shield in reverse. A complete 180—getting all hands and equipment back to where it came from. Home. Specialist McIntyre could navigate a forklift, could assist at the aid station, could present herself willing and able to assist in any capacity to anyone who required her services. She would help upload supplies and equipment for Operation Provide Comfort. Would help disassemble and pack combat aid stations and hospitals.

It was her decision to stay. Ben had tried to talk her out of it. Had said he'd have to clear her request with her CO at Wainwright. The okay had arrived within the hour. Her request had been granted. While thousands of her fellow Desert Storm veterans lined up to march in lavish welcome-home victory parades, Specialist Christina McIntyre, sitting in a rumbling forklift, would line up to carry another load of materiel out of the desert.

By her own choice.

It didn't make any sense.

"You do understand what this means, McIntyre," Ben had said to her that day.

"Yes, sir, I do. Completely."

"You don't have to spell out to me your reasoning behind this decision. Truth is, I don't want to hear it. But you must convince me that this is your decision, and that you fully comprehend what you are asking."

She raised her head just a bit, squinted her eyes, as if focusing them more clearly. Her eyes betrayed the facade of strength she tried so diligently to portray. The facade of invincibility. "Sir, I have no reason to return to Wainwright at this time. My unit has moved on without me, and the unit I came here with . . . well, sir, I never really did belong to that unit in the first place."

"No. That's not enough, McIntyre. You do have a reason to return. One very good reason."

Her eyes reflected sudden confusion. "I do, sir?"

"Yes, you do. To get the hey-day out of Saudi Arabia."

She seemed to restrain her smile. "Yes, sir. Sorry about that, sir. You are right about that."

"You do want to leave this place then?"

"Oh, yes, sir. Very much, sir."

"Okay. That makes me feel better. It's not like you're going to end up running with a band of Bedouins. It's not like you actually enjoy living in the desert."

A laugh. "No, sir. I am still tried-and-true blue-blooded American, sir, and I can't wait to see home again."

"Good. All right. Fine. You've got your stay. I'll make a few calls and assign you to a unit this afternoon. I'll need someone to keep an eye on you."

Another smile.

Good. It did Ben's heart good to see this soldier smile.

"Thank you, sir. Will that be all?"

"McIntyre?"

"Sir?"

"Are you in that big of a hurry to escape my presence?"

Her eyes widened. "No, sir. Not at all, sir."

"Good. Then relax. Stand at ease. And I mean it this time."

She reached up to rub her nose, conveniently hiding another smile in the process.

"There's something I need to say to you." Ben waited to see her reaction.

She tensed in the silence. Her eyes narrowed. "Sir?"

Ben stood and walked around the front of the heavy folding table serving as his command desk to sit on its corner edge. "You're from Denver. Is that right?"

She blinked. "Yes, sir."

"Do you consider that area your home? Will you return there someday?"

Her eyes hardened. "No, sir." The words carried that hardness.

Ben barely nodded. "Where will you settle down when you get home?"

She continued her hard gaze. Ben could almost read her mind. *What business is that of yours?* She looked down at the floor. "I'm not really sure, sir."

"Will you stay in Alaska? Are you a 'mountain person,' McIntyre?"

Finally. A hint of a smile. "I tend to think so, sir."

"They've got a few in Alaska."

"Yes, sir. One of the biggest." Definitely a smile now. "I, um, sir, I have thought about settling down in south central Alaska. Around Seward, maybe. Or Homer."

"Beautiful country."

"You've been, sir?"

"Once. But I'd love to go back."

Her smile faded. She said nothing.

"You're positive you want to end your enlistment? It's not too late to change your mind and stay in the army."

"Yes, sir. I'm sure."

DONNA FLEISHER

"Did you enjoy your six years in this army, McIntyre? Now, I know 'enjoy' is a relative term, but ... will you carry fond memories of your army career with you to Seward?"

"Yes, sir. Mostly."

Ben nodded. "Good. Mostly is good. Remember the good, Chris. Let the bad go."

Her eyes shifted.

"Will you try to do that?"

Almost a whisper. "Yes, sir."

"Good." Ben stood and moved back behind the table. "There's one more thing." He pulled out a manila file folder from under a stack of papers.

"Sir?"

"I've compiled all the reports from Dustoff Five."

He looked up at her. Saw such trepidation in her eyes he hated himself for saying the words.

He slid on his reading glasses and perused the list he had scrawled on the first sheet of paper in the file in his hand. "Palmara's, Coffee's, Franklin's, Corday's, Everson's, and Verdov's." He glanced up over the rim of his glasses. "I've finished my report. I'm ready to send it up to CentCom. They've been asking for it. But I wanted to talk to you first."

The tension he saw in her eyes had filtered through her entire body. She stood rigidly, her hands behind her back. She said nothing.

He pulled his glasses off and tossed them onto the table. "I'm adding a recommendation to my report, Chris. I'm nominating you for a Star."

Her mouth fell open. Her eyes bulged.

"The United States Army is pleased to give the Bronze Star to individuals who have distinguished themselves through combat heroism, outstanding achievement, or meritorious service. The Star was conceived for those who show great courage in combat, for those who act out on that courage to perform uncommon feats that reveal their true integrity in the face of immediate harm."

Her teeth clenched. Her eyes blazed.

"I'd like to see you receive the Bronze Star, Chris, for your valor, and for your acts of courage and combat heroism on 25 February 1991 during the medevac mission designated Dustoff Five."

Her upper lip trembled.

"I just wanted you to know, since I may not see you again. Cent-Com will have it ready to give to you by the end of next week, at least. But by then I'll probably be in Riyadh. I'll try to make it to the ceremony, but there's a chance I won't be able to."

"No. Sir."

Ben heard her words clearly, yet still asked, "What did you just say?"

Chris strained to swallow what appeared to be a grape stuck in the back of her throat. Her lips pressed together. Her eyes would not look at her commanding officer.

"McIntyre?"

She met his gaze. Just for a second. Let it slip away. "Sir, I—"

Ben didn't move. Didn't lessen his stare. Or the confused expression he knew contorted his face. He waited.

"Sir, with respect—and that's a lot of respect, sir. It has been an incredible honor for me to serve with 4th Brigade, with the 101st, and with you. Sir."

His chin dropped a bit, yet his eyes stayed on the soldier standing before him, the soldier struggling with emotion, with control, with ways to express both. Ben gave her no slack. "What are you trying to say, McIntyre?"

Chris pulled in a sharp breath. "Sir, with respect, I will not allow you to nominate me for a Bronze Star." Glancing up, seeing her commanding officer's immediate reaction, she quickly added, "That didn't come out right, sir. I apologize."

*You got that right.* "Take a moment, soldier. Make it come out right."

She nodded. "Yes, sir. Thank you, sir."

She took her moment.

"Sir, I appreciate what you are attempting to do. I really do. I appreciate your desire . . . to recognize me for my actions at the Dustoff. But, sir . . . I respectfully request that you do not turn in that nomination. For reasons I'd rather not divulge."

*Not divulge?* No, that wouldn't do. "I need to hear your reasons, Specialist McIntyre."

She struggled for words. "Yes, sir. I know you do." She would not raise her eyes to look at him. "But . . . I'm really sorry, sir, it's just that my reasons . . . You're not going to think my reasons are good enough to validate what I'm asking."

"They would have to be doozies."

"Yes, sir, they would. They . . . are."

"Try me."

"Sir?"

"Give me one reason why you should not receive the Bronze Star. I could give you at least a hundred reasons why I think you should."

Staring at the stack of papers, the file of reports in Ben's hand, Chris said, "Because I don't want it, sir."

Ben swallowed. Let the words echo in his mind. Felt the full impact of each word. Felt like throwing something through the canvas wall of his command tent. "And that's the best you could come up with."

Tears glimmered in Chris's eyes.

"You just 'don't want it,'" Ben said, his voice firm as his heart ached.

"Sir . . ." Chris sniffed and straightened, regaining her composure. "Please, sir, understand how grateful I am. To wear a Star . . . is to feel the army's full force of gratitude toward you for the job you've done. For your service. For your sacrifice."

Ben only nodded.

"Colonel, if you were standing here presenting me with the Star, right now, I would not refuse it. I'd be dishonoring you, sir, dishonoring the entire army, dishonoring the very institution of the medal itself. I am proud to have served in my country's army. I am proud to have served you, sir. And I am so grateful for what you are trying to do. Really, I am. But please, sir. Please throw the nomination letter away. Just file your report with CentCom, sir, and . . . let the rest go. Please, sir. Just let it go."

Ben stared at the collage of various shades of brown on Chris's desert-camouflaged BDU shirt.

"Please, sir."

He looked up. Sighed deeply. "Are you sure?"

She gave him a trembling smile. "Yes, sir. I am."

Ben slowly shook his head. He didn't understand. But he didn't have to. "All right, McIntyre. I'll tear this up." He let the file in his hand fall open, pushed past all the papers, and pulled out the last sheet. He gave Chris a stern look, tossed the file on his desk, then tore the nomination letter in two. Turned it. Tore it again. Turned it. Tore it again. He continued to tear the sheet of paper until it was only a stack of tiny neat squares in his hand. He slowly leaned over and, watching Chris the entire time, tossed the pieces into the trash can beside his desk.

He straightened. Continued to watch. The woman appeared to be breathing easier. Appeared to be more relaxed. "Thank you, sir," she said softly.

"McIntyre?"

She tensed. Looked up at him. Finally looked him in the eye. "Sir?"

Ben again made his way around the side of the table, stopped only a few feet from Chris. He lifted his head and said, gently, "Stand at attention, soldier, and face me."

Chris snapped to attention and performed a brisk left-face.

Ben stood about a foot away from her now, so close he could see the fine particles of sand affixed to her nose. He studied her eyes, such dark brown eyes, reflecting fierceness, a surety, strength. Hidden strength. A kindling fire.

In that second, standing there, he remembered the day he saw her free-fall out of the Huey. The day she stitched up the cut on his arm. Such tender administrations, such genuine concern. His mind replayed the contents of the file on his desk—the reports, written summarizations of the few witnesses of the events of 25 February, on that medevac mission dubbed Dustoff Five. Specialist McIntyre was not asked to file a report about what happened during Dustoff Five. What would she have written if she had been asked?

Didn't matter. Any of it. All of it. Every single bit of it. At that present moment, Colonel Benjamin Connelly knew the American soldier standing before him deserved to wear a Bronze Star. And she would. She would, at least, in her heart. He hoped this moment would be a moment she would remember, would cherish, all the rest of her life.

"McIntyre?"

"Sir." Quiet response. No impatience. No questioning.

"I wasn't present to witness the events of 25 February, on New-market, during Dustoff Five." He waited.

"No, sir." Barely a whisper.

"But there's one thing I do know. Do you want to know what I know, Specialist?"

"Of course, sir."

"All right, I'll tell you. If you would not have been there in that spot on the Main Supply Route Newmarket on 25 February, during Dustoff Five . . . if you would not have done what you did that day, we still would have won this war."

A tiny breath. A tiny smile.

"Granted?"

The smile widened. "Granted. Yes, sir."

"We still would have liberated Kuwait, we still would have dec-imated the enemy, and we still would have done so in record time. Do you concur, Specialist McIntyre?"

"Yes, sir. I do concur."

"And this is what else I know. Do you want to know what else I know, Specialist McIntyre?"

The smile lingered. "Of course, sir."

"All right. I'll tell you." He paused. "Chris, if you would not have been there at that moment to take out that Iraqi—if that grenade in that Iraqi's hand would have exploded anywhere near that tanker, the resultant fireball would have ignited the Humvee, which would have ignited the crate of M-60 ammo in the back compartment—you didn't even know there was a crate of M-60 ammo in the back compartment, did you? But there was, and the fireball from the grenade igniting all that diesel would have ignited that Humvee, and that ammo, and that would have caused an explosion that would have taken out you, Grayson, your Huey, all souls aboard your Huey, the MSR—" he paused again to take a breath—"and at least three of the trucks in that convoy."

Her features hardened with every word.

"We needed that MSR, McIntyre. Newmarket was the essential main supply route for the flow of fuel and materiel to arrive on location at the forward operating base so designated Cobra. Sure, teams would have cleared a path around the explosion, would have detoured the convoy, all that. But what we needed most that morning was to keep that convoy moving. Your actions not only accomplished that but also saved the lives of at least eight other people, saved millions of dollars of equipment, and who knows what else. Will we ever know how a two- or three-hour interruption of the flow of supplies to Cobra would have affected the more forward operation areas? Hmm. I guess that's something I don't know, Specialist McIntyre. Something we'll never know."

She only swallowed. Her lip trembled a bit.

"So. Here's what I'm telling you. Listen up, soldier."

"Sir." The word broke on her lips. She cleared her throat.

"You may not want a Bronze Star; you may not think you deserve a Bronze Star. But you're wrong. For your actions that day, and for just because of who you are, you deserve it. I'm telling you. You deserve it."

A sudden, heavy silence fell. Chris barely touched it, with the words, "Thank you, sir."

"Don't thank *me*, McIntyre. I'm thanking you. If you won't let me secure a Star for you, then at least shut up and let me thank you in this way."

She blinked.

Ben took a step backward. Centered himself directly in front of her. "Look at me, Specialist McIntyre."

She shifted her eyes to meet his gaze.

"Please accept my gratitude for a job well done. For exhibiting to me, and to all the 18th Corps, the heart and soul of a true American soldier. Thank you, Chris." Ben extended his right hand.

Chris looked down, then back up into Ben's eyes. A second later, she reached out with her right hand to shake her commanding officer's hand. She seemed to absorb the sight of their hands together, didn't look up until she pulled her hand away to lift it slowly, then sharply to the corner of her eyebrow in a perfect salute.

Ben's heels clicked together as he snapped to attention, then he lifted his right hand and returned the soldier's salute. He held his hand in position a full five seconds longer than usual. Then slowly lowered it to his side.

Chris's hand lowered as well. Her eyes shone with tears. "Thank you, sir," was just a whisper.

"You're very welcome, Chris." Ben's heart swelled. "God be with you. Wherever your new journeys may take you."

A trembling smile. "Thank you."

Ben's smile trembled a bit too. He pulled in a deep breath, broadened his smile, and said, softly, "Dismissed."

Specialist Christina McIntyre gave him one more long look, another trembling smile, then turned sharply and hurried across the tent, let herself out the flap, and disappeared into the bright sunlight.

Ben Connelly did not see her again. Until the day she walked into his living room almost five years later.

Out of sight all those years, but never out of his heart. Never out of his prayers. Never out of the tender care of the One who created her. And loved her.

# SEVEN

WEARINESS REACHED DEEP INSIDE HIM, deeper than he had ever known. He wanted to sleep. Needed to sleep. Yet sleep would not come. He wouldn't allow it. He honestly believed that if he closed his eyes, he'd wake up to discover his life to this point had all been a dream. A cruel dream. He didn't deserve the life he lived. He didn't deserve the love of the beautiful woman who lay sleeping beside him.

Tears stung his eyes as he lay facing her, listening to the soft hush of breaths filtering in and out of her, as soft as baby's breaths. In the faint orange hint of flickering light reaching her from the single lit candle on the nightstand, she was so beautiful, her face perfect in every way, her lips full and soft. Her hair . . . he gently lifted away a stray strand from her forehead. His breath caught as the backs of his fingers brushed her forehead. Her skin felt warm, soft, so very soft. He wanted to scream for the entire world to hear, *Oh, Erin! How I love you! Oh, you are my sweet and priceless treasure!*

And the babe she carried, the wonder of life growing with each new heartbeat inside her, cell upon cell forming exponentially. He didn't deserve such perfection. Such priceless gifts. His eyes pinched shut. A tear fell to his pillow. *Lord, I cannot begin to thank You. My God. You have given me so much, so much that I do not deserve.*

Grace.

*So much grace. So much love. Thank You, Father. Lord Jesus, thank You.*

Sleep.

*No!* His eyes flew open.

No. Not now. Later. Maybe. Right now he needed to see her. Hear her soft breaths. Watch her as she slept. The way he watched her that one night a few weeks ago. It had been almost morning by the time she returned to bed. She had slowly, carefully, lowered herself into bed beside him while he pretended to sleep. She lay quietly, yet he could tell she did not sleep. Until much later. As distant sunlight lit the morning sky. He had turned then to face her, to watch her as she slept.

*Lord, just when I think I'm starting to understand . . . I can't let it go.*

The memory of that night hung vividly in Scott's mind. Well after midnight, Chris had come home drunk. Unable to sleep, Scott tossed in the bed until he heard the car pull away. Heard the front door downstairs quietly close. He remained in bed, yet strained to hear his wife and Chris talking in the living room below.

It wasn't right to listen in on their conversation. But none of it was right. Nothing he felt for Chris McIntyre was right. If he had his way, he would erase even the memory of the woman from everywhere, from everything. He rued the day she was born. The day she met Erin.

"I can't take it, Rinny," Chris had said, her voice quiet, yet clear, though Scott knew she was drunk. "Being here. I don't belong here."

And she was so right.

"Where *do* you belong?" Erin asked. Scott heard nothing more, until Erin said, "You belong here. With me."

Oh, no, she didn't! She didn't then, and she doesn't now. Scott's eyes clenched. *Forgive me, Lord!*

Erin's voice. "Where do you belong, Chris? Tell me."

Chris's response. "Nowhere."

"That's a very lonely place."

"It's safe there," Chris said. "Safe . . . for you."

What did that mean? What did any of it mean?

"Maybe I don't want to be safe," Erin said. Scott almost leaped out of bed that night, hearing those words. And on this night, as Erin slept peacefully beside him, he wanted to rant and scream and kick. Oh, to turn back time, to erase certain moments, to rewrite the past, to clean up such a mess.

But then Erin had said, "I'm perfectly safe around you. You saved my life."

He had quietly crept to the stairwell to sit on the upper step, barely breathing, listening. He heard Chris say, "I did not. I'm why you got shot."

His heart slammed to a stop, freezing all breath and thought inside him.

"I shoulda listened to Teddy," Chris went on to say, "and left that dumb ring."

None of it made sense. Erin never wanted to talk about that day during Operation Desert Storm. Second day of the ground war. That was all Scott knew. No, that wasn't all together true. Scott never wanted to listen to any more. He never wanted to know, to fully realize how close he came to never holding Erin Grayson Mathis in his arms.

But . . . leaving a ring. What ring?

"What would that have done?" Erin had asked.

"Saved Teddy's life."

Was Chris responsible for this man's death?

"It shoulda been me, Rin."

Yes. It should have been.

*God, please* . . . Tears burned his eyes. *Please forgive me.*

"Don't say that." Erin snapped the words.

"It was stupid."

He stopped listening then, sitting there on the top step. None of it made sense. All of it infuriated him. But then Chris started to cry. Such desperate crying. He couldn't hear or understand any of her words, yet her crying, such anguished crying, then her shout of, "NO!"

He gripped the stairwell handle then, keeping himself from running down the stairs and throwing Chris out the front door.

"It's okay, Chris . . ."

How many times had Erin said those words that night? It's okay. It's okay, Chris. It's okay, Scott.

*No, Erin. It's not okay.* He reached again to lift a strand of hair away from her forehead. *Lord, I'm sorry. But none of this is okay. I'm going to find out what happened. Chris almost got Erin killed. She admitted it. I've got to know how. And why. I've got to know everything. Don't I have that right?*

His hand trembled. He pulled it away and rubbed his eyes.

*Lord, I'm gonna find out. I mean it. And if I don't like what I hear, then I'm gonna throw Chris out. That's all there is to it. She'll leave. I'll make her leave. I don't care what anyone says. I don't care if everyone thinks she has to stay. If she in any way endangers my wife or my child, ever again, I'll drive her back to Colorado myself.* His stomach burned. He pinched the bridge of his nose.

A soft hum, soft as the faintest whisper, carried on his wife's gentle breath.

*Oh, Erin. God. I'm sorry. Please help me do what's right. Please help me understand.*

✯✯✯

ON HIS FIFTH TRIP THAT morning past the Kimberley Street Community Church, instead of trying to see through the brightly lit basement windows, he looked the other direction, across the street, and allowed his watery gaze to follow each house, each bush and tree, each pathetic white picket fence. Why did people insist on pretty little white picket fences? Did they actually think a fence like that would stop someone from walking across their precious yard? Would a white picket fence stop him if he wanted to bust out a window and break into that house?

A grunt of amusement bubbled out of his throat. His throat burned, yet he still reached for the bottle on the seat beside him. Lifted it to his lips. Poured a huge slug into his mouth. Struggled to swallow. Continued to cruise. And gaze. At pathetic little people with their pathetic little white picket fences.

He slowed the car to a crawl. Grinned. There, parked in front of a white picket fence, sat that shiny dark green Mustang. Even in the dreariness of the blustery steel gray morning, the metallic flakes in the paint sparkled. The rain still beaded up and rolled off. Perfect wax job.

Who would own such a car? Who could afford it? A lawyer, maybe? Or a politician? Or, maybe, a doctor.

He glanced up at the house so fiercely, so loyally protected by that white picket fence. Saw two doors to the house. Must be a duplex. Saw writing on one of the doors, yet he couldn't focus his eyes to read the writing. No matter. He didn't care what was written there anyway.

What he cared about was behind him. Back in that big, beautiful church. Probably down in that basement. Two women. Soon, very soon, he would walk right in, seeking shelter from the storm. He'd walk right up to them. Say hello. Then finish it. He'd finish everything. Bang, bang, bang.

Soon. Very soon. He was running out of gas. And money. And time.

He stomped the car's accelerator and sped off down the street.

★★★

THREE DAYS IN A ROW. Heavy, dark clouds. Torrential rain. Sustained winds, violent gusts.

*This stinking storm will never end. None of this will end.*

His stomach churned. He wished he had thought to pack Erin's Rolaids in the glove compartment. Especially when he thought of what he was about to do.

*Don't be stupid. The day's almost done. Let it go.*

*You can't do this.*

Scott suddenly pulled the Blazer over to the curb. *I'm doing this. If I don't do this now, I'll never be able to let it go. Right here, right now.* He shoved the gearshift into Park, reached for the key, and shut down the Blazer's engine. He stared at the dash. Didn't look at his passenger.

A long moment of silence passed between them. His voice sounded gruff to his own ears. He didn't care. "Chris, I'm sorry about this. But we've got to talk."

He didn't look at her, and wasn't surprised when she said nothing.

"I am really sorry. I mean it. I don't want for any of this to come out wrong. I don't want you to think I'm angry or that I don't like you. I'm not angry. And I'm trying to like you. But we've got to talk." He quietly cleared his throat. "These past three days were fine. But if this storm lasts, if we have to go out again tomorrow . . . I'm sorry, but I can't work with you anymore until I find out exactly what happened . . . that day . . . when Erin was shot."

Silence fell quickly and heavily. Thick and black. He almost welcomed the roar of the wind, the smattering of rain beating the truck.

Still, he didn't look at her. "I'm trying to deal with all this. About you being here. About all that's happened. I'm trying to understand. But it's too hard. There are too many unanswered questions. Questions Erin can't—or won't—answer. I know she loves you—that the two of you are friends, and that's okay. That's not what this is about. I want you two to be friends. But I also want you to understand that I am her husband and I have a right to know exactly what happened . . . so that I can prevent anything else from happening."

*Oh, that didn't come out right. Please help me, Lord.*

He forced himself to relax. "Chris, I have been praying about all this, and I am trying to trust the Lord, but I need to know the truth. I need to know what happened. And I need to hear it from you."

His hands were trembling. He tightened them into fists and pulled them under his jacket. Then slowly, inch by inch, he turned his head and studied the woman sitting beside him.

Her face had paled to a deathly white. Her eyes stared at the glove box door. Her teeth were clenched.

Scott pushed himself back into his seat and laid his head back. "I'm sorry, Chris. Please believe me. I know this is hard for you. And I know . . . you know . . . this is hard for me." He waited. And was pleased to hear her voice.

The words were soft. Broken. "I know. Don't be sorry."

Erin's words. For a second, Scott wanted to cry. *Help me, Lord. Please. Forgive me. I'm so sorry.*

They sat in silence for another long moment.

He pulled in a deep breath. "So, will you to tell me what happened that day? During the war? I do know . . . you saved Erin's life."

He could barely hear her voice over the pelting rain. "I didn't exactly save her life."

*Didn't exactly?* "All right, well, would she or wouldn't she be here today if it wasn't for what you did that day?"

Another long moment of silence fell. Until, "I guess she wouldn't be here."

"So you did save her life."

"Sort of."

Just what did that mean? Scott cleared his throat to conceal his growl. "Was it . . . Chris, was it because of something you did . . . that put Erin's life in danger to begin with?"

Another long pause. He didn't think Chris would respond. He turned his head to look at her.

"Yeah." Her expression did not change. "Sort of."

He jerked his eyes back to the Blazer's dash. *I knew it. I knew it, Lord!* "What. Did you disobey an order or something? What did you do?" He waited.

"I guess you could say that."

"You disobeyed a direct order, and Ben wanted to give you a medal?"

"It wasn't like that. There was no direct order."

"Who told you not to do what you did?" Scott glared at Chris.

She swallowed deeply. Seemed to be struggling with her reply. Finally, she said one word. "Erin."

Scott's eyes bulged. "Erin?"

"Yeah. She told me not to . . . do what I did."

"And she was your immediate supervisor, right? She was an officer, and you were just an enlisted person. Right?"

Chris's upper lip pulled into a sneer. "Right."

"She gave you an order, and you disobeyed it."

"Yeah. That's exactly what happened."

"What did you do? It involved a ring, didn't it?"

Her eyes slowly found his. Reflected pure misery. "Yes. I went after the ring when I should have just left it."

"What ring?"

"Archie's wedding ring. It was sewn into his boot. They had to cut off his boot to get his foot out of the Humvee."

"And Archie was . . . ?"

"The reason for the Dustoff."

"Dustoff. Erin said that's what you called a medevac."

"That's right."

"And this man, Teddy. He was killed."

A whisper. "Yes."

"Who was he?"

"Our crew chief."

"Why did he die?"

Chris looked out her side window. "Because I didn't obey an order."

No. Scott drew in a sharp breath. "Don't lie to me, Chris. I need you to tell me the truth."

Chris turned her head, glared at him. "I'm not lying to you. I wouldn't do that. You're asking what happened that day, and I'm telling you."

"No. There's more to it. Ben wanted to give you a—"

"So what, Scott! Ben wanted to give me a medal. Ben wasn't there, okay? Only Erin was there. Erin and Teddy and Angelo . . . and Teddy died because I didn't listen. Erin was shot and almost died. Okay? That's the truth. I'm sorry, but that's the truth."

He wanted to punch something. Anything. Chris. *Lord! Help me!* "All right, look." He forced his anger down, forced himself to regain control. "I know Erin loves you. She wouldn't love you if you were careless and caused that man's death. That I know."

"Depends on how you define 'careless.'"

His stomach burned. "No. I'm not going there. Forget that." He pulled in a breath. "I know Erin wouldn't love you if you were the reason she almost died."

He glanced at her. Saw her bottom lip tremble.

"If it was your fault that Teddy died, Ben would not have wanted to give you a medal. He would have thrown you in the brig. So stop wasting my time and tell me the truth."

Chris reached for the Blazer's door handle.

"Don't you dare run out on this. I know that's what you do. You run. Well, you can't run from this, not if you want to stay here. If you run . . . I'm gonna chase after you. You are not leaving Kimberley. Do you understand me, Chris? You can't. I know that. And besides." Scott softened his voice. "If you leave, Erin will kill me. And we can't have that, now can we?" He tried to smile.

Chris didn't turn to see his smile.

"Ahh, Chris. God knows I'm trying to understand. And He knows how sorry I am to be doing this."

"Stop being sorry, Scott. Like you said. You have every right to know the truth."

A long, stormy silence fell over them.

"Why did Ben want to give you a medal?"

Chris's voice barely carried. "Because I killed an Iraqi soldier."

"The one who shot Erin?"

"And Teddy."

"How did you kill him?" Scott immediately regretted his stupid question.

"I shot him. Five times."

"Five times?"

"Yeah. Five times. At least."

"Wanted to make sure he was dead?" Another stupid question.

Chris suddenly turned. Her eyes burned with anger. "Yes. Dead. I had to kill him before he threw the grenade."

"Grenade?"

Chris turned to look out the window again.

"The soldier had a grenade?"

"Woulda gone boom. Woulda blown up the precious supply route. And all of us. That's why Ben was so determined to give me a Star."

"Why wouldn't you take it?"

Another harsh glare. "That's my business, Scott. And none of yours."

He wanted to slap her hard across the mouth. His stomach heaved at the thought. *Oh, Lord, I'm out of control.*

The silence worked to calm him. He only worried about breathing. In and out. Slowly. *Help me, Lord Jesus.*

All that time, Chris said nothing. She stared out her side window.

So many questions bombarded his mind. So many angry, cruel questions. Sorting through them, he was startled to hear Chris's voice.

"What are you afraid of, Scott? Just say it."

He couldn't believe he heard the words.

Chris turned to look at him. She was waiting for an answer.

What was he afraid of? Could he be honest?

"You're afraid I'm going to hurt Erin. You know I could never . . . that I would never allow myself to come between you two. That's not what has you so terrified. You're afraid I'm going to hurt her. Or physically, somehow, get her hurt. Aren't you?"

Scott swallowed. He couldn't think of one thing to say.

"Will you believe me if I tell you that's what has me terrified too? I've hurt her so many times before. I don't know why. It just seems like . . . things always happen to those . . . I love."

"You love Erin."

Chris glanced away. "She's the best friend I've ever had. Yes, Scott. I love her with all my heart."

"And yet . . ."

"You've just got to know, Scott . . ." Chris turned to look him in the eye. "I would never do anything to hurt Erin. Or your baby.

Or . . . you. I'd rather die. I mean it. I would leave . . . before I let anything hurt either of you."

Scott sat in silence, gazing into the darkest, saddest eyes he had ever seen.

"I should just leave here. I am so sorry about all the hurt I've caused you."

"No. No." He couldn't say anything more. His head shook. "No."

"I will leave, Scott. If you want me to leave, I will. In a heartbeat."

"No. Chris, that's not what I want. You can't leave."

"Erin and I will still be friends. We'll always be friends. I'll just go back to Colorado. Get my old job back. I like it there. I have friends there."

Her eyes told a different story.

"I'll leave today. Take me home. I'll be gone in an hour."

"Stop it."

"It's what you want, isn't it? You want me to leave, don't you?"

"No. I don't. You can't leave, Chris."

"Stop saying that. I can leave. And I will."

"No! Stop it!" Scott's fists thumped the steering wheel. "Listen to me, Chris. You've got to understand what I'm saying here! There is no way I want you to leave. You must stay here. And I'm serious. If you leave, I'll track you down myself and haul you right back. Do you hear me?"

Chris looked away.

"This isn't about me wanting you to leave. I don't want you to leave. It's just . . . if you're going to stay, there are a few things I need to understand. There are a few things . . . I need you to understand." He stared at the steering wheel and drew in a deep breath, hesitant to press on. But he had to press on. He had come too far. He needed to finish saying what needed to be said.

"Chris, I love my wife. I'll do anything I have to do to protect her. Anything. You need to understand that. She's accused me several times of being overprotective. Well, I'm sorry about that, but, then again, I'm not. I'd rather be overprotective if it means saving her from harm."

Chris didn't make a sound.

"She's carrying our child. My child. The last thing in the world Erin needs right now is stress. And this past month . . . there has been nothing but stress in her life. That must stop." Scott paused to let those three words sink in. "For her own health, and for the safety of our child, at least until she delivers, she must rest and keep up her strength. That means there must not be any more stress."

He glanced at Chris. The pink on her cheeks was deepening into a dark red. Her head slowly nodded.

"No more trips to Dandy's. No more trips to Colorado. No more sleepless nights or careless, stupid decisions. The other morning when I saw her at Isaiah's, Chris, that almost made me insane. I know she only went there because of you. If you hadn't gone, she wouldn't have gone either."

Chris's face turned hard. Her eyes cold.

"I'm sorry about all this. But I need you to understand what I'm saying."

Silence.

"Do you understand what I'm saying?"

More nodding. Then her lips parted. "Yes."

"You're not still drinking, are you?"

His heart cracked at her reaction to his words.

"I'm sorry, Chris." He let out an exasperated growl, then briskly rubbed his face, ran his fingers through his hair. "That was uncalled for."

"No, it wasn't."

"Yes." He sighed deeply as his hands came down. "Yes, it was. I had no right to say that." He stared at the rain coursing down the windshield. Watched the rivers of rain . . . and had no idea what to say next. Maybe there was nothing left to say. "I'm sorry about all of this, Chris."

She rubbed her eyes and nose. Her voice still barely carried. "If you say that one more time, I'm gonna punch you."

He laughed quietly. Then slowly reached for the Blazer's door handle. "Listen. I've got to get some air. Will you give me a few minutes to sort all this out?"

Chris only nodded.

"Wait here for me. Don't get wet. I won't be long." Scott looked at her. "Okay? Just give me a few minutes."

She only nodded.

Scott sighed deeply, then pushed himself out of the Blazer into the gusty rain. *Lord God . . .* swept through his heart as he walked aimlessly across the street and down the flooded sidewalk. *Lord, I'm so sorry.*

✷✷✷

ANOTHER SWALLOW. AND ANOTHER. NAUSEA coursed through her belly, but if she stayed calm, maybe she could swallow it down.

*Breathe. Just breathe. Oh, Jesus.*

Scott had every right. She couldn't blame him at all. She knew this moment would come. And yet, hearing his words, his concern . . .

Breathe. And swallow. She laid her head back. Closed her eyes. Her entire body trembled.

It was all true. Everything he said. He loved his wife. It was that simple. Erin was so fortunate to have such a loving husband. And he was not being overprotective. *No, Lord, not at all. Erin thinks he is, but it's only because she's making excuses . . . for me. Blaming Scott for my mistakes. My carelessness.*

Breathe.

*How could I have been so stupid? Oh, Lord, everything he said was true. I disobeyed a direct order. Got Teddy killed. If I just would have left that stupid ring, Erin would not have been shot.*

Quiet and still, Erin suddenly lay on that bed again, on board the *Mercy*, her forehead cut, her eyes almost swollen shut, her entire face bruised, unconscious . . .

Chris violently rubbed her eyes as they filled with tears. *No, God, please! Lord, I can't . . . I can't take any more of this.*

Tears smeared across her face as she rubbed—she jumped when Scott opened the driver's side door of the Blazer and climbed in. She wiped her face with her wet sleeve and quickly sat up, embarrassment flaming her already burning cheeks.

"Whew! I am so ready for this storm to be done with!" Scott pulled the door closed against the gusts of wind forcing its way inside. "Enough is enough!" He turned to look at her.

Chris glanced at him and felt her lips tremble as she tried to press them into a smile.

His face softened. He looked away. It took a few seconds for him to speak. "I don't know about you, but I don't think I can be of any help to anyone right now. We've been out here long enough anyway. Let's call it a day."

They still had at least three more people on their list to visit. Yet . . . yes. She wouldn't be very helpful either.

Scott started the Blazer and pulled a U-turn back toward Kimberley Street.

Chris sat quietly, not wanting to speak, not wanting to cry anymore.

She only breathed. And swallowed down the bile in her throat.

✯✯✯

HE HAD PAID GOOD MONEY for it. It fit in the palm of his hand, a perfect fit, as if it had been made just for him. Small, black, smooth barrel. A classic .38 caliber revolver. Six bullets fit into the cylinder. But today he had only put in three. Three bullets were all he needed.

He had come to Portland for this one reason. He told Del he would finish what they started that night in McIntyre's cabin. But he wasn't a cold-blooded murderer. Sometimes he saw that look in Del's eyes. Del had it in him to aim his piece at a guy's head and pull the trigger. Del could kill a man. Outright.

*"Are you with us, Rich? Don't just stand there."*

If he didn't do it, Del would. He would kill both women. Then track Rich down and kill him too.

*"Make up your mind, man. Quit being so pathetic."*

He spit out a laugh. He was pathetic. Even now, here to finish the job, he knew he couldn't go through with it. Not outright. He would leave it to chance. Test the fates. If there was a God, he'd leave it in His hands.

He would play a little Russian roulette. Three bullets in his .38. He would spin the cylinder and pull the trigger. Three times. And see who died.

Yes. He had played this game before. One bullet in the cylinder. A one-in-six chance. Not bad odds, actually.

Of course, the gun didn't fire.

He was still alive.

Three bullets this time. Much better odds. It was a very good chance that today, someone was going to die. Maybe all three of them. That would suit him just fine.

But what if he killed one of the women and not the other? No, that wouldn't do. Yet, maybe, if he only killed the one he knew best, Erin, beautiful Erin, then maybe McIntyre would really suffer for killing Wayne. And Matt. She'd know how it felt to have a friend die—

No. Wait. McIntyre did not kill Matt.

*I did. I killed Matt.*

*Should've killed Del when I had the chance.*

He drew a bottle of gin to his lips and sloshed a huge gulp into his mouth. Let it burn . . .

*Yeah. Face it. Del's right. About everything. This is for you, Wayne. All for you. I'm so sorry about killing Matty. I didn't mean it.*

Another deep, burning swallow of gin.

*Three bullets. That's all I need. Let's get it on. Spin the cylinder, pull the trigger . . . and let's see who gets dead.*

★★★

IN THE CORNER OF THE church basement, at her improvised first-aid station, Erin ever-so-gently dabbed a spot of Neosporin onto the small carpet burn on Jimmy Thurman's elbow. "Easy now," she said softly as the little boy squirmed. "Nothing to it. You'll be good as new in just another . . . second."

Chasing Benny and Jason, Jimmy had tripped on his oversize high-tops and crashed to the floor. Except for the nice raspberry, he'd conquered the fall without a trace. But the abrasion had to burn.

Erin unwrapped a Bugs Bunny Band-Aid and carefully stuck it on the boy's elbow. "Leave this on until it stops stinging, all right?"

His big dark eyes glimmered with unshed tears. "Yes, Miss Erin."

She pulled off her rubber gloves, tossed them on the table, then pulled the little boy into a monstrous bear hug. "And why don't you tighten those shoelaces, you goofy dude? Before you fall again."

Jimmy pulled away, his new front teeth shining against his dark skin. "Can't tie 'em, Miss Erin. That's not how yer 'posed to wear 'em!" He pulled away and ran across the room to find Benny and Jason, high-tops clomping.

Erin laughed, watching him go. Until the basement's back door was pulled open with such force . . . wind and rain blew a man inside. Her husband. Erin stood and moved toward him.

He pushed off the hood of his jacket and gazed into her eyes. His face bore a strange shadow. Until he smiled at her.

"Hey, stranger. How was your day?" She saw that strange look again. "Are you all right?"

"Hi, love." He moved in to kiss her lips.

His face was so wet, after the kiss Erin wiped her nose and cheek with her sleeve.

"I need to talk to you, sweetheart." His voice carried a hint of tension. "I . . . I need to ask you some things."

"What are you talking about? What's wrong?"

"Nothing's wrong." He pulled off his jacket and ran his hand down his face. "I need to finally get some answers from you."

Erin backed up a step. "Scott, where's Chris? Where is she?"

His face hardened. "I don't know where she is. She looked tired, and I'm too worked up to do anyone any good out there today, so we just decided to call it a day and come back in."

"What? Why are you . . . ?"

"I had to talk to her. I said some things—"

"Scott, where is she?"

"I told you, I don't know. Last I saw her, she was heading home."

Erin's teeth clenched. "Stay right here. I'll be back."

"What? Where are you going?"

She didn't turn around as she ran across the basement to the stairs leading to the church's front doors. She ran up the stairs, pushed the heavy door open, ran down the front stairs—Chris was halfway across Kimberley Street, heading for home.

"Chris!"

She stopped and turned around.

Wind whipped fat raindrops into Erin's ears. She had run out without a jacket, without thinking. She didn't really care. "Wait!"

Chris's eyes hardened. Anger saturated her voice. "What are you doing? Are you crazy?"

Already the rain had soaked Erin's sweatshirt, had flattened her hair against her head. It ran down her face, into her eyes. She had to shout above the wind. "Where are you going?"

Chris shouted too. "Where do you think I'm going? Home!"

"Why? What happened?"

"Nothing happened." She almost spat the words. "Go back inside!"

"No! Chris, tell me what happened! What did he say to you?"

"Who? Scott?"

"Yes! What did he say?"

"He didn't say anything to me! Erin, stop this and go back inside!"

She couldn't move. Couldn't speak. She could only stare, blinking as the rain stung her eyes.

★★★

WHO WAS THAT WALKING ACROSS the street right in front of his car? Walked like a woman. A woman in a hurry. Where did she come from?

He tried to blink away his drunkenness.

Another woman suddenly burst through the front doors of the church. Ran down the stairs. Yelled at the first woman. The first woman turned around.

He blinked.

McIntyre. It was Chris McIntyre! He couldn't believe his eyes! And then, could it be? Could the second woman be . . . ?

Yes.

A breath of glee slipped out his lips as he tossed the bottle of gin to the floor and grabbed the pistol from the passenger seat. Holding it, he caressed the cool metal, the smoothness of the barrel, the firmness of the black rubber grip. He used his thumb to flick off the safety. Pulled it up to look at it. Popped open the cylinder. Counted his three bullets.

What better time. He couldn't believe his luck! There they stood. Right there in the street. Right there in front of him.

They were going to make this easy for him! Laughter rumbled from deep in his chest. He cranked down his window, then cursed as the storm blew into his car. Cursed the storm. He was so ready to see an end to it all.

Today. Right now. What better time.

# EIGHT

"Erin! What is wrong with you?"

Her mouth hung open, yet she couldn't find the words to say.

Chris grabbed her by the upper arms and pushed her back toward the church. "Get back inside! Now!"

"No!" She slapped Chris's hands away.

"You can't be out in this!"

"Chris, tell me if you're all right."

"Me? Erin, I'm fine!"

"Scott said you two talked."

"So what! We've been working together for three days!"

"Please tell me what he said to you!"

"No! I won't!"

Erin pushed her hair out of her eyes. "Chris, please. He said you're tired. Come back to the church with me and—"

"You know what, Erin? I am tired." Chris's eyes flashed with anger. "And so what! I'll get over it. Listen to me. I'm fine. So stop worrying about me!" She again pushed Erin toward the church. "Go back inside! You're gonna get sick!" She turned to walk away.

Erin grabbed Chris's arm. Pulled her back. Was crushed to see such rage in Chris's eyes.

A curse. "Let me go!"

"Chris . . ."

"What, Erin? What? What do you want?" Chris ripped her arm out of Erin's grip.

Erin couldn't move. Couldn't speak.

Chris glared at her.

Standing there, no words to say, not knowing what to do, Erin couldn't have hurt more if Chris had swung out and punched her in the stomach.

✯✯✯

OH, MY, MY, THEY'RE HAVIN' *a little tiff! Isn't that special.*

Yet he couldn't just sit there, gaping, wasting time. Who would be first? Didn't matter. As the wind blew rain into his eyes, his ears, into his car, he grinned, spun the cylinder of the pistol, snapped it back into place, pulled back the hammer, then steadied his aim against the half-lowered window.

McIntyre. Of course. She would have to be first. First to die for killing Wayne.

He blinked deeply, trying to focus through his haze, through the rage of the storm. Gritted his teeth. Carefully steadied the gun, aimed at McIntyre's head, held his breath . . . gently pulled the trigger.

A click.

Blood froze in his veins. He blinked. Blew out his breath.

Hmm. Well. So. It wasn't McIntyre's time . . . to die.

He pulled the gun inside and wiped his face with his shirtsleeve. Cursed the storm. Lifted the gun, popped open the cylinder, spun it, then snapped it back in place. His heart raced inside him. Fun little game, this game of fate. He cranked the hammer back, steadied the pistol once again against the top of the window. Aimed at Erin's head this time. Steadied it against the gusts of wind . . . held his breath . . . pulled the trigger.

A click.

No.

No! This couldn't be right! They stood right there! Three bullets in the cylinder. One should have fired by now! McIntyre should be dead. If not McIntyre, then Erin!

He moved the gun a half inch to the left. Steadied it. Held his breath.

Chris would die. She had to die. He came all this way to kill her. And he was not going home.

Should he spin the cylinder? He blinked. Blew out his breath. Stupid, stupid game. No. Just pull the trigger. Get it over with.

He steadied the gun . . . held his breath . . . aimed . . . pulled hard on the trigger.

A click.

No. Curses ripped through his mind. He stared over the top of the gun barrel, focused on the woman standing right there in front of him.

★★★

"Erin, please!"

Water dripped down Erin's back, tickling her. The sensation stunned her. Felt so out of place in her sudden nightmare.

"Go back inside."

She could only nod. Slowly.

Chris turned and leaned into the wind as she trudged the rest of the way across the street.

Erin watched her for a moment longer, then turned and headed back toward the church.

★★★

He watched Chris turn and start walking. Then Erin slowly turned, walked back to the church, up the stairs, through the doors, and disappeared inside.

He had blown his best chance. They stood right there, almost asking for him to shoot—no, begging—and he had blown it.

He pulled the gun inside and quickly rolled up the window. Stared at the dash for a second. Then wiped his hand across the rain-spattered windshield. They hadn't seen him. They had no idea he was even there. Good. He watched Chris walk down the porch of that house, the one with the green Mustang and the putrid white picket fence. Just down a bit, and across from the church. She continued on around the corner of the porch. Then she was gone.

All right. Fine. Maybe not today, but there was still plenty of time. Wasn't there? Why was he in such a big hurry? He gazed down at the pistol in his hand. He knew where McIntyre lived now. Maybe later that night he would pay her a private visit. No more playing around. He would fill the pistol's cylinder with bullets. Use all six if he needed to, to make sure she was dead.

Yes. A private little midnight visit.

And there was no need to kill Erin anyway. That night at McIntyre's cabin, she was just in the wrong place at the wrong time. Yes. Erin didn't deserve to die. It was Chris McIntyre who deserved to die.

She deserved it almost as much as he did.

Maybe later tonight. Maybe tomorrow.

*Tomorrow?*

The word floated through his mind. Then suddenly sickened him. He swallowed down a rush of nausea.

Maybe it was the gin.

No. It wasn't the gin. It was that word.

There would be no tomorrow. There would be no tonight, no private midnight visit. His moment had passed. The moment he had waited for. Right there in front of him. And he had blown it. His perfect opportunity, and he had let it slip away. He insisted on playing his stupid little game. And because of it, he had blown his one and only chance to finish what needed to be done. For Wayne. For Del. For Matt.

He looked down, then slowly lifted the gun in his hand. He would play his stupid game of fate just one more time. Staring straight ahead, he popped open the cylinder, spun it, snapped it back in place, cranked back on the hammer, then quickly pressed the pistol's barrel against his temple.

Three bullets in the cylinder. Fifty-fifty chance. If one chambered ...

Right now. This moment. It was time to find out.

★★★

SHE SHIVERED, THOUGH HER CHEEKS burned. She wanted to scream, cry, throw something, kick something. She slammed the church's front door and turned—and almost ran into her husband who stood just inside the foyer. She stared at him. Watched his eyes transform from concern to pure fury.

"Why did you do that?" His voice was restrained, yet still sharp.

Erin pushed her hair out of her eyes, then stood still, glaring at him, keeping her lips pressed, quiet.

"You're soaked! Look at you!"

Scott took a step toward her. Erin took a step back, hitting the door. She only glared.

Sudden confusion narrowed his eyes. "Please tell me why you felt it was necessary to run outside! Without a jacket—why didn't you at least grab a jacket?"

She refused to answer his question. Refused to say a word, though several came to mind.

"Erin? Answer me!"

"I will not."

"What's wrong with you?"

"I might ask you the same thing."

His eyes closed for a moment. He backed up a step and turned away. "I told you. I'm just a little worked up right now."

"And what has you so worked up? What happened?"

"I told you! I had to talk to Chris."

"Well, so did I."

Scott glanced at her. Slowly shook his head. "I didn't mean to upset her."

"Well, you did."

"And I'm real sorry about that, Erin. But I needed answers." He looked around. Lowered his voice. "We can't discuss this here. Come home with me."

"No."

His eyes bulged. "What?"

"I'm staying here. I still have work to do."

"What. At your first-aid table?"

Erin's teeth started to grind.

Scott tossed his head back, gazed at the ceiling. Then closed his eyes. "Erin . . . love, I'm sorry. I didn't mean that."

"I had to clean and dress three very serious wounds this morning, I'll have you know."

Scott's eyes opened.

"I used up the rest of the Bugs Bunny Band-Aids."

His head lowered as he slowly started to smile. "We'll have to make sure we order more."

"Yes. As soon as possible." Erin allowed herself to relax, yet her words remained firm. "Until then we'll have to use the Winnie the Poohs."

"Yes. And the Tiggers too." Scott's voice fell into a whisper. His eyes softened. "I'm sorry, Erin."

She pushed her right eyebrow up.

"I know, I know. But I am."

"I think this time I'll allow it. You should be sorry. Tell me what happened."

"Please come home with me. We can talk about this at home."

"Just say it, Scott. What do you feel you need to talk about? What is left to talk about?"

He scowled. "Everything, Erin. You haven't told me anything."

"What? What's that supposed to mean?"

"You haven't told me about Chris. Or about the day you were shot. Do you want to discuss this here?"

"What's to discuss? Is that what you were asking Chris about? Stuff that's long been forgotten?"

"All right, Erin. I understand what you're saying. So I'll only ask you one question. Just one. Okay? If you give me an honest answer, I'll forget everything else and be happy as a clam, like everyone else, that Chris is here with us, making herself at home in Kimberley Square."

The words struck Erin hard, shooting bolts of rage through her entire being. "Scott, you need to go home and calm down. I'll be home later."

"Will you discuss this with me later? Or will you put it off, like you always do?"

"What have I been putting off? You want to talk about Chris? What's to talk about? You know her, Scott. She's not hiding anything. And I've told you everything you need to know. Yes, there are some hard things in Chris's past—in my past too. But I have repeatedly asked you to trust me, and to trust Chris. Some things you just don't need to know! Some things are just none of your business."

"How can you say that? I'm your husband! I love you!"

"You know what, Scott? Sometimes, when you say that, I don't want to hear it. You use it as an excuse so you can act like a fool. Your love for me should not hurt someone else."

For a moment, Scott fell silent. Then he shook his head quickly. "Erin, if I'm going to be able to deal with Chris living around here, I need to know exactly what happened and how she was responsible for you getting shot."

The words felt like a slap. "She was not responsible in any way!"

"Well, I needed to find that out. You obviously were not going to tell me. You obviously don't want to tell me anything. So I asked Chris, and she told me that maybe she *was* responsible."

"That's ridiculous."

"Did you give her a direct order that day? You were an officer. She was just an enlisted person. Right? Did you tell her not to go after that ring?"

Erin's mouth fell open. "Who told you about a ring?"

"Come on, Erin." Scott lowered his voice and quickly looked around. "Did you or did you not give Chris a direct order that day?"

She allowed her confusion and then her fury to show on her face. "I don't remember, Scott. That was five years ago!"

"Well, think, Erin! This is important to me!"

She could only stare.

"If you gave her a direct order, and she disobeyed it, then she *is* responsible for you getting shot. And for that man's death."

"Who. Teddy?"

"Yes. Teddy. She said he was your crew chief."

Erin allowed some of her fury to surface. "Chris did not disobey a direct order that day. I did not give her a direct order that day. Do you want to know how I know that, Scott?"

"Yes, Erin, I do."

"Because in the entire time we served together, I never gave Chris a direct order. I never felt like she was 'just an enlisted person.'"

"She told me you did. She told me you ordered her not to go after the ring."

Breath burst through her throat. "If I did, it certainly wasn't a direct order. It wasn't an order at all."

"Maybe it should have been."

She pushed herself away from the door and walked a few steps into the foyer. Ran her fingers through her wet hair. Slowly turned to look at her husband. "I can't believe we're having this conversation."

"It's about time we had it."

"You still think Chris is dangerous."

"I don't know what I think, Erin."

"But you're not letting that stop you, are you?"

"I have to know what happened."

"Why, Scott? Why can't you just let it go?"

"Do you hear yourself? For how long have I been telling *you* to let it go? And now you're telling me?"

Erin let the words flow through her, then slowly moved in close to him. "I can never let it go. That's what you must understand. It's too much a part of me. For so long, you haven't wanted to hear about any of it. You've never wanted to talk about it. I never really worried about that because some things I really didn't want you to know anyway. I figured if you weren't going to ask, then I wasn't going to volunteer the information. But now, are you telling me you do want to know? Are you telling me you're ready to hear about the war? About all of it? Even the day I was shot?"

Scott's eyes filled with confusion. Regret. Then surrender. "Yes. I guess I am."

Erin gazed deeply into his eyes. Then drew in a long breath. Let it out slowly. "Are you sure?"

He blinked and looked down. "Right now, I'm not sure about anything."

She barely smiled. Then moved in closer to him, laid her head on his shoulder. Tears flooded her eyes as he pulled her into a tight embrace.

"Okay, I take that back."

"Take what back?" A whisper as her lips brushed his cheek.

"Here's one thing I'm sure about."

"Okay. Let's hear it."

"You . . . are wet."

She blew a small breath of laughter into his ear.

"And . . ."

Lightly kissed his earlobe. "And?"

"I cannot tell you how much I love you. There are no words."

She pulled back to look into his eyes. "None at all?"

"Not right now."

"You're just too tired."

"Yes. That I am."

"We need to go home." Erin caressed his cheek.

"Yes. Yes we do."

"We'll talk later, okay? When you're ready, I'll answer any question you have."

"Later."

"Yes. Later."

"Right now I need coffee."

Erin grinned. "I'm sure there's some downstairs."

"And food."

"Plenty of that too."

"Thank you, Erin."

"For what?"

"I don't know. I'll think about it and tell you later."

She broke into laughter, then gasped as Scott pulled her to him and swept her away with a deep, intoxicating kiss.

✯✯✯

THE STORM RAGED AROUND HIM. Gusts pounded his beat-up car. His breath hung in his throat. His eyes slowly closed.

Blood coursed through him. He felt each pump of his heart. Didn't matter. He was ready. He'd been ready for a long, long time.

Still, the pistol shook in his hand. Trembled against his temple.

He cursed. Maybe Del was right. Maybe he didn't have the guts for any of this.

He cursed again. Drew in a deep breath. Held it. Pinched his eyes shut. Clenched his teeth. Pulled the trigger.

A click. Nothing more.

His eyes blinked open. His mouth gaped. Breath and life, time, hope, fate. All of it, everything at that moment ceased to exist. Suspended in disbelief, he sat, staring straight ahead.

The gun barrel trembled against his temple as his hand continued to shake. His eyes blinked, yet through the rivers of water snaking down the car's windshield, the wet smears that had coated the inside, the sudden flood of tears into his eyes . . . he couldn't see a thing.

Nothing . . . but light. He turned his eyes toward it. Saw bright yellow light pouring through the bushes from the basement windows of the big church. He blinked. Felt the pistol still in his hand, his hand still raised, pushing the barrel into the side of his head. He lowered his hand to his lap, blinked tears from his eyes, stared at the heavy black object in his hand.

He was wet, drunk, miserable. Breathing. Deep in his chest, his heart thumped. He was alive. He had played his silly game. And won.

Three bullets in the cylinder. Three people should have died.

He blinked. Blinked again. Tears dripped down his cheeks. Flowed like the rain. Still he stared at the gun in his hand.

What just happened? Why did he still breathe? Why did his heart still beat?

*I'm alive.*

*Oh . . . God . . .*

He lost all control as his head fell forward against the top of the steering wheel, the gun falling from his hand to the floor of the car, as great, violent sobs overwhelmed him.

★★★

THANK YOU, LORD.

It was still there, where it was an hour ago, in the church's back lot where Chris had parked it after their trip to the beach on Sunday. Seemed like ages ago.

Erin allowed herself to relax. As long as that dirty dark blue Ford Explorer still remained in that spot, Chris still remained in Kimberley Square. And that was all Erin needed to know.

She pushed the basement door closed against the wind and turned to lean back against it. Peered out across the room. Ben had decided to hold the Wednesday night Bible study down here instead of upstairs in the sanctuary. People were gathering, moving chairs and tables together, making room for the service. She looked at her husband, who sat sipping coffee, talking to Andy and Ryan, not far away. She jumped away from the door when it thudded against her back. Turned and saw Cappy. She smiled and said, "Hey, you. It's good to see you out and about."

"Yeah," Cappy said sheepishly. "I was getting a little cooped up." She forced the door closed against the wind. "Needed to get out and get some air. Or some wind, I guess I should say. When's this storm gonna end?"

Erin shook her head. "I have no idea. Shouldn't last much longer, I would hope."

"No kidding. I'm about over it."

"Me too. How are you feeling?"

"Better. I'm good. Thanks for all the soup and oranges."

"No problem." Erin waited another second. "Chris didn't come with you?"

Cappy pressed her lips into a grim line. "No. She came home a couple of hours ago and went straight to her bedroom. Didn't say a word. I didn't get the impression she wanted to talk about it."

Erin frowned.

"Is she sick?"

"No. Just sick and tired, I would imagine."

Cappy nodded. "It's been a rough couple of days." She gave Erin a knowing smile, then gently squeezed Erin's shoulder before heading for the coffeepot on the counter of the kitchen.

Erin watched her for another second, glanced at her husband, then down at her watch. Should she? What would be the harm in having her own prayer meeting, just in another location? The Lord would understand. He'd come with her. But would her husband understand? She walked over to where he sat. Said hello to the guys.

Scott immediately brightened. "Hi, love." He lifted his arm and Erin sat beside him, allowed him to pull her into a sideways hug.

She kept her voice low. "Um, Scott, I'd, um ..." She waited for him to look at her, then smiled warmly to soften the blow. "I'd like to go over and see Chris. Is that all right?"

He hesitated only for a second. "But the meeting's about to start."

"I know. I just want to check on her. I'll try to be back before the service ends."

Scott lowered his gaze to his empty coffee mug, but slowly nodded.

"We'll talk tonight. Like I promised. Okay?"

He looked up and smiled. "I know. We will. It's okay, Erin. Go ahead."

"I'll see you later."

His smile wavered, yet Erin saw nothing heated in it. She leaned in to kiss his lips, then turned and left the basement, grabbing her jacket on the way, pulling the hood up and over her head as she walked. Out the church's front door, down the concrete steps, across the street, into her own house, she left her wet jacket on the kitchen counter, then found a large candle and lit it. She carried it carefully through her living room, through the swinging door into the clinic, and up the back stairs leading to the apartment above. She opened the hallway door and stopped, listening, then peeked inside Chris and Cappy's apartment. She waited. Heard nothing but the wind. She slowly moved inside.

"Chris?"

Not very loud. Maybe Chris was sleeping.

She tapped softly on Chris's bedroom door. No response from inside. Except for the wind and rain lashing the house, all was quiet. And very dark. Her candle threw shadows everywhere. She slowly turned the door knob. Eased the door open. Leaned around the door frame. Squinted into the darkness.

She pulled her candle inside the room, saw Chris lying on the bed, saw the dark-dampened colors of one of Chris's Navajo fleece blankets wrapped around her as she lay, wrapped so tightly that she appeared as if she had been wrapped in a cocoon. A brilliant colorful cocoon.

Erin slowly moved into the room. Smelled a faint hint of wood smoke. Closer to Chris's bed, the smell grew stronger. Erin smiled. The fleece blanket had come from Chris's Rocky Mountain cabin. No wonder it still smelled of wood smoke.

She headed for Chris's nightstand to place the candle on the square of tinfoil there, thought about lighting Chris's candle too. Her foot kicked an empty box on its side at Chris's closet door. Big empty box. She waited a second to see if the clunk had awakened Chris. No change in her soft breathing. No movement. Erin pushed the box out of her way with her foot and lowered her candle to the nightstand. Waited a second, made sure it wouldn't fall. Then turned her head. Looked at Chris.

She heard long, soft pulls of air, faint breaths, in and out. Chris slept quietly, bundled in the blanket—no, two blankets. Chris had pulled both of her fleece blankets out of the box and wrapped herself up in them.

Erin's heart ached.

It wasn't all that cold in the room. Chris had wrapped herself so tightly in the blankets, even up over her head. She must have been freezing. She hadn't even pulled the quilt on her bed back. She lay wrapped only in her blankets.

Erin lowered herself to her knees at the edge of Chris's bed. Chris breathed through her mouth. In the faint light, her eyes and nose were splotchy and swollen. Erin's eyes closed as sadness swept through her. Chris had been crying.

Erin reached out blindly, though ever so gently, and touched the blanket, felt its soft fibers, felt the warmth of the person laying under it. *Lord God . . . Precious Father.* She held her breath as tears stung her eyes. *Lord, we need You so much. Please hear my prayer. Please allow her sleep to be sweet. Give her Your rest. Heal her, dear Lord. Heal us all. Lead us through this storm.*

She listened to the hushed breaths, to the relentless gusts beating the house, whirling through the dead power lines. Her eyes slowly opened. Candlelight danced across Chris's face. *Oh, Father. Your strength, Your wisdom . . . we need all of You. We need You so much. We need You to heal us.*

So much healing so far. So much more yet to be done. Mess upon mess these past few weeks, yet healing would come, Erin was sure of it. This storm would not last.

Gritting her teeth, she lowered herself the rest of the way to the floor, then just sat there, watching the candle throw faint orange flickers around the room, listening to the blustery wind outside. She prayed without words. Simply implored her Lord to do. And to be. Only as He willed. Only in His perfect time.

She leaned back against Chris's closet door and stretched her legs out. Laid her head back. Closed her eyes. In her heart she prayed on, yet as weariness settled over her, words and thoughts languished in her mind, and she desperately wanted to sleep.

"Be our sweet rest," she whispered to her Lord. "So gracious and kind. In Your love we do hide. In Your mercy we abide. When on clouds we will ride." Her voice shook. "To our home in the sky." She struggled to finish the prayer. "Forever . . . by Your side."

Her eyes blinked open. The prayer, one of her mother's favorite bedtime prayers, always soothed as sleep crouched near Erin's bed waiting for her heavy eyelids to fall. Her mother's soft voice, the melody of the rhyme . . . until that word. *Mercy.* Erin ran her fingers through her hair. Let out a long, deep, quivering breath.

Even in the simple rhyme, the word struck her, took her back to that place. To the war, to the Persian Gulf, to the USS *Mercy*, that floating naval hospital where she had awakened into her continuing nightmare. Running down that path in the desert, dust obscuring the one she ran for, only to awaken days later and see that one, to gaze upon those tear-filled eyes. To hear such relieved laughter, the sweetest sound she had ever heard, even to this day, as it echoed through her heart.

Over time, the memory was fading, and for that she was grateful, yet still it seeped through the recesses of her mind rousing deep terror. Such deep pain. So long ago. Yet still so sharp it cut to her soul.

On board the *Mercy*, lying in the hard bed, she had forced her eyes to open, heard words, a voice, that familiar voice. She wanted so desperately to see the person speaking the words, but she couldn't make her eyes focus through the fog and numbing pain.

"Come on, Rinny. That's it. Open your eyes and look at me."

She did not want to remember the pain. Never before had her head throbbed the way it did that day, as she forced her eyes open, forced them to focus.

"Please? Rinny? Stay with me this time. You can do it."

She had blinked and blinked against the harsh light, squinted, searched for the one softly calling her name.

"That's it, Rinny. That's it."

She so wanted to speak. Her lips wouldn't work. Her tongue lay in her mouth like a lump of damp clay. With great effort, she forced her lips to part. Forced her tongue to move. Forced one word out through her dry, aching throat. A croak. "Chris?"

And the smile that appeared across that face . . . even now, Erin's eyes welled with tears as she remembered it.

"Yes, Rinny. Yes. Oh, thank You, God. Rinny?"

Easier to focus, the light not so bright, Erin gazed at Chris McIntyre, saw that smile, saw those dark brown eyes shimmer with tears.

"Ahh, girl. Rin. Welcome back. You really had me worried."

Another croak. "Really?" And a pitiful attempt at a smile.

Chris held a chunk of ice against Erin's lips. Let the ice melt, held it carefully so Erin could draw in the water, could wet her lump of a tongue, her lips, her throat. Said, as she did, "Nah. Not really. I knew you'd be all right."

Erin sipped the melting ice water. It felt as sweet and as cold as anything she could remember.

"I told Angelo you'd be all right. I just knew it. And here you are. I told 'em, Rinny. I knew it. You're gonna be all right, girl. Listen to me. You're gonna be as good as new in no time."

She had wanted to say so many things, yet she could only sip the water and swallow it as she listened to Chris's voice and believed what she said. She would be all right. If she could just get rid of the headache.

A doctor had come in then, hadn't he? Too much time, too long ago, the memory was fading. But it was later that night, after her headache had eased a little, her throat felt better, her eyes could focus, that Chris returned. Sadness seemed to pull at her. And tension. Anger.

"Are you all right?" Erin asked her.

"I need to tell you something. It's . . . hard."

"All right."

"I don't know how to say it, so I'm just gonna."

Erin had waited for Chris to find the words. It took another minute.

"Rinny, Doc Cornum's Blackhawk went down a few hours ago. They were on a medevac. It's confirmed. She's MIA. One of the Pathfinders too. The rest are . . . gone. They didn't make it."

Hard words. The look in Chris's eyes. The pain in Erin's stomach, all breath being crushed out of her lungs . . . that's what she still remembered, would never forget. They had talked on about it, about the search, and about Doc.

Major Rhonda Cornum was more than one of the 101st Airborne Division's flight surgeons. She was a friend.

Missing in action. Cruel, hard words. Later, prisoner of war. Erin had watched many days later, tears streaming down her face, as Major Rhonda Cornum slowly eased herself down the steps of the big jet that carried the American Operation Desert Storm POWs home. Both of her arms broken, hanging in slings out in front of her, still she smiled, laughed even, when being greeted by the brass on the Tarmac.

Erin had cried hard that day, sitting alone in the second-floor nurses' lounge at Fort Lewis's hospital, watching the television coverage of the POWs' return.

She had cried hard that day when Chris left. When Chris said, "I've gotta go, Rin."

Just like that. Without warning.

"Where are you going?" Erin asked her. "Are you coming back tomorrow?"

"No. I've got orders. I've got to report."

"Orders?" It was still hard for Erin to think straight. Her headache had eased, yet still raged.

"I'm sorry. I've gotta go."

That was it. No explanation. No reconsideration. Chris walked out the door of Erin's room, walked off the hospital ship, and just disappeared.

It wasn't fair. Wasn't right. Orders? The war was almost over, wasn't it? Wasn't Chris going home like the rest of them? Couldn't she wait to report, at least for a few more minutes so Erin could say good-bye?

There was no good-bye. Chris had simply walked out. Erin heard later that night from Doctor Cayman that Chris sat by Erin's bed the entire time Erin was unconscious. Two days. Just sitting there, reading some, sleeping, waiting. Erin had awakened, saw Chris, saw the doctor, then later that same day Chris had returned with the news about Doc. Less than an hour later, she walked out that door and disappeared. With just a, "Gotta go, Rin." No good-bye. No nothing.

Erin pinched her eyes shut as she prayed. Sitting on the hard floor by Chris's bed, her body started to ache. Too weary to care, she let a tear fall, then slowly wiped it away when it tickled her cheek.

So many tears. Each one had burned a swath through her soul.

First at Fort Lewis, then home in Shasta Lake, in the days, then weeks, then months after the war, Erin had looked through every magazine, watched every news broadcast, studied every documentary and every highlight film, read every newspaper, looked through everything that had anything to do with Operation Provide Comfort or the cleanup of Kuwait, Saudi Arabia, the Persian Gulf, or Iraq. She watched TV with the volume down, searched every soldier's face, trying to catch even a glimpse of Chris. But she never did. She didn't expect to. She knew if there was a camera anywhere near Chris, Chris would be turning away from it, if not running away.

Almost two years after the war, Erin started hearing reports of Gulf War veterans becoming sick from exposure to chemical weapons. Sick from the remnants of exploded ordnance, of waste accumulated during cleanup. Sick from abandoned ammunition dumps, or dumps exploded by her country's own military. Sick from exposure to the oil well fires. To disease. Sick . . .

Constant worrying, wondering about a ghost. Praying for her safety. For her salvation. For her very soul. Praying to remember every moment they shared. Praying to forget the horror. The pain. Erin prayed and prayed for the friend she used to know. The friend she knew she would never see again. Unless her prayers were answered.

First arriving at Kimberley, she found kindred spirits, those who remembered Chris, those who would share her burden of prayer. Not long after, when she met the man of her dreams, he had helped heal all the war wounds so deep inside her, still open and raw. His love had filled her so completely, had taken her to new and higher places, to heights she had only ever dreamed of reaching. Their faith in each other, their ever-increasing faith in their Lord, all of it helped ease the misery she carried. Slowly, bit by bit, she learned how to lay it down. To give it up. Chris McIntyre became a fond memory. Just another memory of a very exciting chapter in Erin's life. Little of the pain remained. Little of the agony of losing one so dear.

She almost laughed aloud at the irony of it all. She had been trucking along quite nicely in her new little world, loving her husband, longing for the babe in her belly to leap into her arms. Her career, her home, had all taken shape quite happily. Until that one afternoon last month. Almost five weeks ago. Ben Connelly had walked through the door of the clinic. Carrying a newspaper. Portland's *Oregonian*. Back pages. But the look on his face . . .

He had waited patiently, standing by the front window, as Erin scheduled Mrs. Vargas for an appointment on Wednesday, the following week. Mrs. Vargas had said, "Thank you, missus," in her broken, yet courteous attempt at English. Still struggling with her own Spanish, Erin said, "*Vaya con Dios*, Mrs. Vargas. *Hasta la* . . . next week."

It was then Ben approached the counter where Erin stood, still carrying the paper, saying a friendly good-bye to the kind Mexican grandmother. He looked at Erin, who still grinned at her pathetic Spanish, grinned when she said hello to Ben, grinned when she said it was about time he moseyed over for a visit. His eyes seemed to ache as he lifted the *Oregonian* and placed it on the counter, as he pointed out to Erin the small story near the end of one page.

She read the story, but it made no sense to her at all. An escaped convict, Wayne LaTrance, somebody from a jail in Arizona, had killed a search and rescue worker in Colorado, only to be killed by another search and rescue worker from the same station. Sad, but why did Ben want her to read it?

"Erin, I read this yesterday morning. This is yesterday's paper." Ben's voice broke. "It bothered me all day. All through the night. So this morning I made a few calls." He swallowed deeply. "The man in charge of the search and rescue unit is someone I served with in Vietnam. We've kept in touch somewhat over the years. His name is Sid Thompson."

"Wow. You know him? That's really terrible what happened, Ben. I'm sorry."

Her words, though heartfelt, seemed to frustrate him. His face hardened. "I called him, Erin, to offer my sympathy for his loss. The man who was killed worked for him. His name was Travis Novak."

Erin slowly shook her head. "I'm sorry, Ben, but I'm not sure why you're telling me this."

"The woman who killed the convict also works for Sid. He told me who she is. I couldn't—" Ben's voice broke again. His face darkened as he tried to regain his composure. "I couldn't believe it when he told me who she is. Erin . . ." He looked at her, eyes brimming with anguish. "It's Chris. The woman who killed the convict . . . is Chris McIntyre."

The words suddenly meant nothing to her. Her brain could not make sense of any of it. Yet, she knew that name, and as Ben explained it all to her again, as her knees gave out and she fell into the closest chair, as her blood turned cold inside her, she heard everything. Put it all together into something she could process. It spelled out loud and clear in her heart.

Chris McIntyre lived in Colorado. Worked at a search and rescue station. Just lost a coworker. Just killed a man.

That one single moment changed every single tiniest fragment of Erin's life as she knew it. The way she looked into her past. The way she looked into her future. What she heard from her husband. What she heard from her heart.

Seventeen hours later she sat on a plane on her way to Ouray, Colorado.

Not how she expected all of her prayers would be answered.

Yet, here she sat just a few feet away from Chris McIntyre. Just weeks from that first encounter in five years. Just days from seeing Chris reborn. Just hours from being pushed away by the woman as she cursed in rage.

Here Erin sat. Praying. Still.

Her eyes fell closed as a smile barely pulled her lips. *Lord God,* she whispered from deep in her soul, too weary to even try to whisper the words aloud. *Somehow, I know Your hand is in all of this. In every raindrop falling, in every tear we've shed. Here we are. Me and Chris. We are Yours. And that's a good thing, Lord. Because . . . You are here too. And . . . we really need You.*

# NINE

SOMETHING FELT WRONG. SHE BLINKED open her eyes and rubbed them. There was nothing wrong with her eyes. Through the gray light of morning she saw the poster of the Heceta Head Lighthouse on the far wall of her room. Remembered the hike up to the base of it, overlooking the pounding surf of the Pacific. What a day that had been. The memory made her smile.

She saw one of her closet doors was still open, saw the empty overturned box that held her blankets. She saw the splash of brilliant color wrapped around her.

Her eyes were fine. It was her ears. They didn't work. She couldn't hear anything. Positive silence. What did it mean? She yawned. Heard her eardrums pop. Heard, yes, something . . . the soft melodic patter of rain, gentle rain falling on the roof. Soft, spring rain. With no wind.

And no storm.

*Oh, thank You, Lord.*

A bit of good news, yet, the old day's heaviness still shrouded her soul. Echoes of words, all spoken with fear, in anger. Her eyes pinched shut at the thought of the new day. She hated to move, wanted to keep hidden under the sweet-smelling blankets surrounding her, a refuge from the old day's mistakes. She had to move. Her shoulder ached and the bathroom called.

Another new day. Get up and live life, or bury yourself away . . . and die.

*My goodness. So morbid this morning.* She started to pull away the blankets, but they were still wrapped so tightly around her she had to sit up and push them down first. She leaned to her nightstand and lifted her watch to read it. 8:14. Time to get up and start her new day.

A half hour later, back from the bathroom, shaking off the chills of her icy bath, she stood at her bedroom window wrapped in her robe, looking out across Kimberley Street. To Ben and Sonya's house. To the big church on the corner, its basement windows filled with light. To the empty space where a huge tree once stood, the tree now lying across Isaiah's backyard, on top of his shed. She gazed at the sky out across the tops of the trees, over the collection of roofs and chimneys, and saw thick clouds, yet lighter clouds, gentle spring rain sort of clouds. Not the stormy monstrous clouds of the past four days. Today was a new day. The storm had passed.

She hoped.

Pulling on her clothes, she wondered what the new day would bring. Coffee would be hot at the church. Erin would be there. And that's how Chris's day would start. She needed to apologize, to say the words Erin wouldn't want to hear.

*I'm so sorry, Rinny.* She sat on her bed and rubbed her face and eyes. *Lord, I'm so sorry about what I said to Rinny. And how I said it.*

She needed to talk to Cappy too. Right away. Tell her the same thing. *I'm sorry for ignoring you last night, Cap. I wish I could go back and change this entire week. Make everything right. Oh, Lord, forgive me for everything I said. Or didn't say.*

She ran her fingers through her wet hair, then separated strands to work into a French braid. Closed her eyes as she worked. Felt that persistent ache spread through her neck, up the back of her head, like thin creepy fingers reaching deep into her brain, as she worked. At the end of the braid, she spun the elastic into place like she'd done a hundred times before. Yet, this was the first time tears fell from her eyes . . . as she did.

*Lord Jesus, please help me. I'm losing this battle. I'm so sorry.*

✷✷✷

MORE THAN USUAL, THE COFFEE left a bad taste in his mouth. But that didn't stop him from refilling his mug at the giant urn on the kitchen counter. He refilled Ben's too, then carefully carried both mugs back to the table where Ben sat.

"Thanks, Scott." Ben's tone masked the weariness playing out on his face.

"Are you all right?" Scott asked as he sat at the table.

Ben swallowed a drink of coffee. "Yeah. I just can't tell you how glad I am that this storm has ebbed."

"I hear you." Scott slurped his coffee, then wished he had grabbed another muffin.

"Did you see the paper this morning?" Ben slowly shook his head. "There's extensive damage all over the state. Floods, landslides, contaminated water supplies, bridges wiped out, beach erosion . . . If it wasn't for all the folks who showed up to sandbag, downtown would have been completely flooded. And we were fortunate here too. The damage in the Square is minimal compared to other parts of the city. Of the entire Northwest."

"I can't believe how widespread this storm was."

"One of the biggest of all time." Ben let out a deep sigh. "We'll have to get Isaiah and Ryan up on the roofs today as soon as possible. Let's hope everything's still intact."

Scott drew his mug up for another drink of coffee.

"Now I'm going to ask you what you just asked me. Are you all right?"

He pressed his lips into a smirk. "I'm the doctor, Ben. I'm allowed to ask that question."

"But not answer it?"

Scott let out a small laugh. "I'm fine." He hesitated a second, then met Ben's intent gaze. "Can I ask you something?"

"Certainly."

"How did you . . . survive all those years in the army? I don't mean, how did you dodge the bullets, but . . . how did you stay sane? Through all the danger. The chaos." As soon as the words stopped,

Scott regretted every one. It took determined effort to restrain a grimace, and the words, *Forget I said that.*

Ben's eyes hardened as he seemed to consider his response. "Do you mind if I ask why you want to know?"

Cut to the chase. Good military strategy. "Erin and I had a long talk last night."

The way Ben leaned back in his chair, Scott could almost hear him say, *"Ahh."*

"She told me things. Things that will haunt me the rest of my life."

"Your wife was a soldier."

Sometimes the simple truth spoken simply could simply . . . irritate. "Yes. Thank you for reminding me of that, Ben."

"Your wife was a good soldier. A true warrior. She still is."

*Please.* Scott stared at the coffee in his mug.

"What's the problem?"

He looked up. "My wife followed her dad, who followed his dad, who followed his dad into the army."

Ben didn't reply. But by the way his jaw clenched . . .

"I'm sorry, Ben. It's just that . . . when our baby grows up, he's not following in his mother's footsteps."

"You remind me of someone."

Scott waited. "Who?"

"Verlene Crandle."

He almost choked. "What? Ben, please."

"But she has every right to feel the way she does. She lost her closest friend in a war. She lost her husband."

"In Vietnam. I know, Ben."

"She has every reason to hate the military."

"I don't hate the military."

"You just hate that your wife was a part of it."

"No, Ben. I hate that she can't forget about it. Or she won't." Scott swallowed a gulp of coffee. Why did he even bring this up?

"You hate the fact that now you know what she went through. You're not ignorant anymore."

A growl. "No. I'm certainly not."

"I liked you better ignorant."

The words stunned him. Yet didn't anger him. As he sat there, and they echoed through him, they slowly calmed him, slowly opened his eyes to the truth. "Me too," he said after a long while. He looked up at Ben and tried to smile. "I'm a fool."

Restraining a smile, Ben leaned forward and pulled his coffee mug to his lips to take a long drink.

"What did she look like? As a soldier."

Ben swallowed and wiped his mouth with the back of his hand. "You've never seen a picture of her?"

"That's not what I mean. Of course, I've seen pictures of her."

Ben gazed at something over Scott's shoulder. "She was relaxed. Confident. She enjoyed being a soldier. An officer. She enjoyed helping people. And she was good at it."

"She told me she carried a gun."

His gaze returned to meet Scott's. "Every day. A nine-millimeter pistol."

"But she would never use it."

"Oh . . ." Ben's eyebrows lifted. "I bet if she had to, she would have."

"To shoot someone?"

"To defend. Yes. If the enemy threatened one of her fellow soldiers or one of her patients, she would have, without hesitation, used that weapon."

"She would have killed another human being."

"If the situation called for it. She would have followed her training and performed her duties as an officer of the United States Army."

"I can't believe she would ever kill anyone."

"Well, she didn't. So don't even think about it."

"Will she revert back to her . . . *training* if, say, an . . . *enemy* around here threatens one of her coworkers or one of her patients?"

"Why. Did she go out and buy a gun?"

He couldn't help it. The absurdity of it pushed a laugh through Scott's lips.

"I appreciate you talking to me about this, Scott, but—" Ben waited until he looked at him—"you're up to your neck in cow excrement."

More laughter escaped his lips. "Think so, huh?"

"I can smell it. And it ain't pretty." A smile crossed Ben's face.

"Yeah." Scott pushed his mug away and leaned back in his chair. "Maybe you're right."

Across the basement, the back door opened. Chris McIntyre stepped inside, then pushed the door closed behind her. She looked across the room . . . met Scott's gaze. She held her eyes on him just a second longer, then looked away. Slowly walked toward the kitchen. Saw Erin and Sarah there. Talked to Erin.

Scott saw his wife smile.

His heart surged. That smile always made his heart surge. Yet, his joy quickly soured. He turned to look at Ben. Drew in a deep breath. Let it out, then said, "What kind of a soldier was Chris? Ben? Please, tell me the honest truth."

Ben glanced at Chris. "The best."

Scott's teeth clenched. He forced himself to relax. "Why? What made her so special?"

Ben's eyes shifted back to his mug. "She did what she had to do. Didn't hesitate. Didn't panic. Didn't give up."

"That day at the Dustoff?"

He met Scott's gaze. "Every single day I knew her."

Scott hoped his growl wasn't audible. "What does that mean, Ben? She was gung ho?"

"Not at all."

"Then what? She displayed leadership qualities? Had a knack for military strategies?"

Ben's gaze became a glare. "She is who she is. Nothing more, nothing less."

Scott waited for more, but there was no more. "What does that mean?"

Ben slowly pushed his chair back from the table and stood. Then let out a deep sigh. "Are you available today to run some errands? Squire's going to open his shop so we can pick up some shingles. There's enough laying around in the yards around here to make me think we may need a couple of packs. So, of course we'll need nails." He reached into his back pocket and pulled out a small piece of paper. "Here's a list of what else Isaiah says we need." He held the list out to Scott. "You can take my Explorer. I'm going to stay put today. Andy's helping Ryan at Olivia's. They want to try to unbury her car sometime this morning."

Scott peered up at Ben, allowed his eyes to harden into a glare, then reached up and accepted the list.

"And then, if you could make one last trip through the outer areas, that'd be great. Chester called this morning. Sonya talked to him; so I didn't hear exactly what he needed, but he said he'd like a visit later. And we should really check up on Alta again. And Velda. They should have the power back on in a matter of hours. If you could pick up the cooler at Velda's, that'd be great."

Scott laced his words with attitude. "All right, Ben. Anything else?"

"And take Chris. One last day. You'll need her help lugging stuff. And running the chain saw. The Foley's had a tree go down last night against their house. Just a small one, but if we can clear it, we should. Oh, and be sure and take Chris with you to Velda's. She's just what Chris needs."

Scott hung his head in defeat. His words this time flowed through an impish grin. "All right, Ben. Anything else?"

Ben leaned his head back, looked up at the ceiling, and reached up just as impishly to rub his chin. "Nope. I think that'll do it." His grin gave way to a bright smile as he laughed.

Scott slowly stood, then rolled his eyes and shook his head. He tried to keep a straight face, but failed.

★★★

As he walked toward Chris, Ben's words replayed in his mind. Nifty sidestepping. Purposely vague answers to Scott's simple questions. Fair questions, he still thought. Questions demanding answers. And if Erin and Ben couldn't answer them—or wouldn't—whom else could he ask? If they refused to tell him the truth about Chris, then who would?

She sat at the kitchen counter eating a blueberry muffin. She didn't look up at him as he approached, only reached for her coffee.

Scott looked at his wife. The smile he saw on her face, in her eyes, made his foolish heart go pitter-pat. He couldn't help himself. He moved in and kissed her. Gently caressed her face as he gazed deeply into her eyes. Then turned and said, "These are excellent, baby. Did Sarah make them?" as he reached for another muffin.

"No. Mildred did."

"Mmm." Scott chewed a mouthful. "Excellent."

"I'll tell her you said so." And another gorgeous smile.

Scott wanted to kiss those lips again. And again. Right there in front of everybody. He chewed his muffin and tried to resist the urge.

"What are your plans for the day?" Erin asked him.

Beside them, eating her breakfast, Chris had yet to make a sound.

Scott swallowed, then pined for a tall glass of milk. He swallowed again. "I'm going out. Imagine that. Of all things, Chester called this morning. Can you believe that? So I figured I'd go on over and see what he wants." He popped the rest of the muffin into his mouth and turned to Chris. Still chewing, he said, "So, um, do you want to go with me? Once more for old time's sake?" He chewed and grinned.

As she looked at him, her face said no. Yet her lips pressed open to let one word escape. "Sure." She barely smiled.

Scott nodded and swallowed. "Ben's asked us to go to Squire's too, to pick up some supplies. And there's a tree down at Foley's." He looked at Erin. "I don't think it'll take us all day, baby. They should have the power back on soon. And I want to go over to Isaiah's later tonight. See what he's been up to."

Erin's right eyebrow lifted for just a second. Until she smiled and said, "All right. Be careful, you two."

Scott gave in to his urge, leaned over and kissed her, then pulled away and gave her his warmest smile. Then he turned to look at Chris. "So. Shall we?"

Chris quickly swallowed the last of her coffee, then stood, zipped up her jacket, pushed her hands deep into her pockets, looked at Scott, and said, "Yes, I guess we shall."

And the smile she added to her words almost looked heartfelt. Almost.

### ✦✦✦

JUST ONCE MORE. FUNNY, HOW Scott repeated those words as he commandeered Ben's Explorer. Just one more time out in the rain. He was grateful for the help. Yada, yada, yada.

All in a day's work.

Chris watched as he pulled Ben's seat up a few notches so he could reach the gas pedal. She turned to look out her side window. And tried not to laugh.

So, okay, fine. One more day. And the rain falling today was completely vertical. No wind to speak of to blow it off course. She could handle one more day. And another visit to Chester's. Maybe tomorrow the sun would shine. Maybe tomorrow they would give her the day off.

Maybe today was looking better already.

### ✦✦✦

HIS CIGARETTE TASTED FOUL.

Why did he ever think he could switch to one of the cheaper brands? Lousy waste of money. First place open and selling cigarettes, he would stop in and buy an entire carton of his usual brand. That would burn up the rest of the cash in his wallet, but, then again, with the 9mm Beretta tucked inside his waistband, maybe he could persuade the clerk to give him a discount.

His upper lip curled slightly at the thought.

But with the power out, where would he find an open store?

At least he found the right church. There were three churches on the long stretch of Kimberley Street he had followed through northeast Portland. One looked more like an abandoned pawn shop; so he knew that wasn't it. No, the church he was looking for would be a grand church. Grand enough to support all kinds of happy little programs for the needy little community.

And there it stood. Grand. Yes. The Kimberley Street Community Church. A Bible-based House of Worship.

Quite grand.

He spit out a laugh, almost losing his cigarette in the process. Dumb thing anyway. He lowered his truck's window a few inches and tossed the burning half-smoked waste of money out onto the street.

Happy little street. Trees and porch swings and happy little cars in front of grand little homes with white picket fences. Without electricity, the place looked deserted. Closed up for the winter. Maybe he should nose around some. Find out who bugged out for the storm. Find out if they remembered to lock that upstairs window. Find out what they left in their useless refrigerator. Even a warm beer would hit the spot about now.

He needed another cigarette already. A growl rumbled up through his chest. He pulled out the pack from his shirt pocket and tapped one of the worthless things out. Even foul, it would have to work. At this point, maybe foul suited him. Matched his mood.

He let his truck idle and coasted down the street as he lit the cigarette with a match, then glanced left and right, hoping to see a familiar brown Plymouth, a piece of junk, really. He would be surprised if he saw it, surprised if it survived the trip all this way from Denver. But, then again, Rich was a half-decent mechanic even if he did have lousy taste in cars. He had kept that clunker on the road for almost two years now. Quite an accomplishment, considering the dumb car should have been crushed a decade ago.

Not seeing the car would actually be a good thing. That would mean maybe Rich was smart enough to switch cars on the way. He'd have to know the police would be looking for them, that there were APBs out on them. So which car would he grab? Another clunker? Was it here? Was his old buddy Rich sitting here in one of the slick-looking parked cars lining both sides of the street?

Another foul cigarette. Enough was enough. He tossed this one out the window too, then stepped on the gas and continued on down Kimberley Street, hoping he would spot his old friend sitting in anything but an ugly brown Plymouth, praying he would find an open store soon, any store, maybe even a not-open store, any place that carried his brand of cigarettes. And beer. Yes. Even if it was warm, he needed a beer.

★★★

"So, TELL ME AGAIN WHY Chester *needed* for us to go see him today?" Chris rummaged through the bag of goodies Alta Fitzsimons had given her and found the seedless grapes. She pulled them out. "I mean, he looked fine to me. Didn't he look fine to you?" She rubbed a grape on the leg of her jeans, then popped it into her mouth.

"As good as he gets," Scott replied. "I think he just wanted to see you again."

*Please!* Chris almost spit her grape out. She swallowed it, trying not to laugh. Then held the bag of grapes out to Scott. "Wanna grape?"

He glanced at her, almost smiled—no, he did smile. And pulled about five grapes off the bunch.

They just sat and ate grapes as Scott drove the Blazer down one street, then another, on their way to the Foley's to clear their downed tree. Chris wondered if Scott would let her run the chain saw this time. She wondered, but didn't dare ask. She would just wait and see when they arrived.

The day had been full, quiet. Blessedly quiet without the raging wind. She was wet, though not drenched, and warm, but not sweating like before. Even her feet were dry. Deep down in her soul, she knew she had no reason to complain. She drew in a long breath and let it fill her with peace. It felt almost tangible, something she could reach out and grab. Something she could spread on a piece of toast. Filling her heart and soul, tingling her toes, and stirring up laughter from deep in that usually dark, silent place. That place she had always feared. That deepest, most terrifying place. That place, now flooded with light. Open and flooded with . . . peace.

For now, anyway.

Her eyes closed as she laid her head back. She heard her own voice, just a whisper, carry up from her soul. *This is real. You in my heart. You taking my life, then becoming my life. This is Your way. This is truth. Oh, Lord Jesus . . .*

Another soft whisper. Yet, different from her own. *Yes, My beloved, My precious child . . .* Just a breath. Maybe just the wind.

She blinked her eyes open. It couldn't have been the wind. Today, there was no wind. Only the quietly falling rain.

No. Deep in her heart, a gentle wind blew. Still too amazing to even begin to comprehend. Too wonderful to know. Yet, she knew. And believed.

*This is what is, Lord. You in my heart.* Her eyes again fell closed. *It's too much. Too much for me to know. But please help me to learn. Please, keep teaching me Your ways. I want to know You. I want to learn to love You more. And trust You. Please help me to trust You, Lord . . . more.*

She opened her eyes as the Explorer slowed to a stop in front of the Foley's house. The wipers slushed rain off the windshield. The defroster hummed, clearing the glass. Outside, up and down the street, lights again burned in the windows, beamed down from the lamps above.

"Well. Look at that," Scott said as he shut the Explorer down. "It's about time."

Chris drew in a deep breath and pushed herself up. "Yes, it certainly is," she said softly. She turned and gave Scott a warm smile.

***

DEL SAT IN HIS TRUCK and watched the streetlights over Kimberley Street flicker on one by one. A porch light here and there. Lights in several upstairs windows.

Too bad. It was too late for the can of beer he held in his hand. Beer needed to be cold. That was all there was to it. The fact that it was free didn't help. But finally, the cigarette he smoked tasted like a cigarette should. And since it was free, it tasted all that much better.

Someone had hit the store earlier. Made it easy for him. The locks were already broken. Half the store's cigarettes were gone. Yet, there they were on the floor, an entire carton of his favorite smokes just calling out to him. The beer had called out to him too. He shouldn't have wasted the time it took to grab it.

And maybe, just maybe, he shouldn't have wasted his time tracking Rich to this place. What if the fool hadn't even made it? What if he was broke down in some two-bit town in Idaho? What if the fool wimped out and couldn't go through with it?

No. Rich was here. If anything, he was methodical. Patient. He would have cased the place out for at least a day. Figured out his plan. Unless he drunk himself into oblivion, which would have pushed back even his best-laid plans.

He was here. Or he would be. It wouldn't be a waste of time. It would be worth it to finally see his friend show some guts and take some initiative. Maybe the man wasn't pathetic. Maybe he had a few redeeming qualities after all.

***

ON THEIR WAY TO VELDA'S, Chris couldn't look at Scott. She rested her right elbow against the window ledge, then rested her chin in her hand. Used her fist to hide her smile. Looked out the steamed-up window as Scott maneuvered the Explorer through the soggy city streets.

For the past hour and a half, Chris sat at Corissa Foley's dining room table, sipping peppermint tea and talking with her about all sorts of things, from the weather to the war, as Corissa Foley's husband and Erin Mathis's husband stood outside in the rain clearing the tree that had fallen against the side of the Foley's house. Not really a tree, just a branch from their neighbor's tree, yet big enough to look like one. Big enough to take two burly men an hour and a half to clear.

After pulling up to the Foley's house and watching Scott retrieve the chain saw from the back of the Explorer, Chris had turned around to see the Foleys standing in their front window. She returned their friendly wave, then followed Scott to the side of the house, staying close to him, wondering with childish expectancy, waiting to see if he would let her run the chain saw. After their last chain saw debacle, she honestly had no idea what the man had in mind that moment.

But at that moment, just as Scott lowered the saw to the ground and turned around with his mouth open to say something to Chris, Mr. and Mrs. Foley slogged out to them, wrapped up in rain jackets and wearing bright smiles. Mr. Foley quickly began orchestrating the downed branch's demise, while Mrs. Foley grabbed Chris by the arm and said, "Now, you just come on inside with me, Christina, out of this rain. Let's have some tea! How does that sound?"

Being pulled toward the Foley's front door by the firm grip of Corissa Foley's left hand, Chris looked over her shoulder to see Scott looking back at her, great anxiety pouring out his eyes.

Well, okay. Maybe she had imagined the great anxiety. Maybe Scott just looked at her with trepidation. Or was it a hint of jealousy? The more she thought about it, maybe his look carried the warm, fuzzy sentiment flowing through his heart as he looked at her and thought, *Go, Chris, stay warm and dry. Have a nice cup of tea and relax. I'll stay out here and take care of this. You've worked so hard every day this week, it's the least I can do.*

Yeah, right.

The peppermint tea tasted sweeter and mintier than any Chris had ever tasted. And the strawberry-drop sugar cookies literally melted in her mouth. Mrs. Foley had warned that they were only "store-bought," what with the weather and all. Store-bought or not, with the sweet tea and the delicate cloth napkins, the pleasant chatter and the warm, loving smiles, Chris had a wonderful time at the Foley's. While Scott just got wet. And maybe . . . a blister.

*Oh, Lord, I really need Your forgiveness for that one. There is no need for that kind of . . .*

Smiling, she let the prayer fade as Scott turned the Explorer onto Velda Jackson's street. Down the block, looking very near to Velda's house, a thick black column of smoke billowed.

"What is *that?*" came from Scott, almost in a whisper.

Black smoke meant only one thing. Where there was smoke, there was—

The Explorer lunged forward as Scott stomped on the gas. Another second later, Chris could see . . . it was true. Fire and smoke poured out through broken windows. A few people stood in the street watching Velda Jackson's house burn.

Velda's house was on fire.

"Stop the car!" Chris jumped out of the Explorer and ran across the street. Staring at the flames, gaping, her mind paralyzed, she started up the front walk almost to the stairs when a wall of heat slammed into her. She raised her arms over her face.

It wasn't possible! So much heat, so much smoke!

Behind her, Scott screamed her name. She turned. He ran toward her as four, maybe five people stood on the sidewalk gawking up at the house.

"Chris! Don't—!" Scott raised his arm to shield his face from the heat. "They said they called! Fire's on their way!" He grabbed Chris's arm, pulled her toward him.

"NO!" She shoved him away. "Have they seen Velda? Do they know if she's in there?"

Scott's expression told Chris he hadn't even asked.

She turned and ran up the stairs onto the front porch.

✫✫✫

THE HAM SANDWICH IN HIS hand tasted bland. But it wasn't his daughter-in-law's fault. Or Mildred's, if she made it. It had everything a great ham sandwich required. Swiss cheese. Mayo. Just enough mustard. Fresh rye bread. Not too rye. Light rye. Just right.

No. It wasn't the sandwich's fault. He was just too tired to eat. Strange. Maybe it was true. Maybe he was getting old.

Ben Connelly grunted at the thought. But then took heart. One more day, and this storm may have beaten him. But, here he was still standing, so to speak, and the storm had surrendered.

Whew.

He chewed and swallowed, then drew in a gulp of ice-cold milk. Maybe next week he would call the fitness center and sign up for a membership. Maybe if he strength-trained again, lifted a few weights like the good old days, he'd be able to keep up with the young dogs again.

Nah. Maybe it was time for him to face the sad truth. He couldn't play with the kids anymore. Maybe it was time for the old dog to live out the rest of his days letting the young pups fight the battles. Wasn't that why he retired from the army? After all the great years?

Scott had asked him how he had survived all those years. Ben laughed again, then gnashed a fierce bite out of his sandwich. He didn't know if he would ever stoop to give Scott an answer to that question. Ahh, maybe someday. When Ben's pride recovered.

No, that wasn't it. It wasn't bruised pride smarting from Scott's words. The army had given Ben purpose back when nothing else seemed to make sense. It had given him a home, good friends, and a calling. Even in the ugly years, he held that calling dear. Even when his calling changed, when God Almighty spoke his name and set his feet on a different, narrower way. The army gave his life purpose. God gave his life meaning. Between the two, Ben had no regrets.

Maybe Sonya carried a regret or two. But she never complained. She couldn't have stood by her husband any closer than she did. All those years. It would have been impossible. Every minute they were together. Every minute they were apart. Sonya trusted and cherished her husband. And her husband trusted and cherished his wife.

Ben pulled his glass to his lips and let the cold milk pour into his mouth. He swished the mouthful through his teeth. Swallowed it down.

It was good then, that Scott married Erin after her term of enlistment was up. Scott would have made a terrible military spouse. He would have made life unbearable for Erin. No. Didn't do any good even thinking that way. Scott Mathis never would have looked Erin Grayson's way if she still wore an army uniform. Even if only part-time, say, in the guard or the reserve.

Some people just weren't able to accept what they didn't understand.

Maybe, soon, Ben prayed, Scott would understand and would accept what he couldn't change, then would move on and enjoy life as it played out around him. Because at that moment, the man was missing a good, no, a precious life. Ben glanced up at Erin, saw her standing in the kitchen leaning back against the refrigerator talking with Sarah.

*Soon, Lord. Help him understand and move on. For Erin's sake.*

He started to look away, then hesitated as Erin lifted her hand to her belly. Ben watched her. No, nothing to be concerned about. She still laughed and talked with Sarah. Even as she slowly rubbed her belly.

Erin's face glowed as she laughed heartily at what Sarah said. She laughed and talked on as her hand made small circles around her belly.

The sight so touched Ben's heart, it was hard for him to breathe. He looked away, down at the table, at the crumbs of bread on his paper plate.

Scott Mathis was a good man. A good friend. A good husband. And he would be a terrific father. Of that, Ben had no doubt. Yet it hurt him, infuriated him, that Scott held so lightly what Erin held so dear.

She had heard that same call. As a healer and a soldier, she lived to serve others, to serve her country and her God. And she did all things well. Almost gave her life heeding that call.

It seemed like last week, maybe only last year, that Ben stood in Erin's room on board the USS *Mercy* pinning a Purple Heart to the fabric of her shirt. He could not believe it had been five years. The memory still painted a vivid picture in his mind. All the colors. And the laughter of that day.

He had joked that the purple in the medal matched her eyes, still swollen and bruised from the blow to the head she had received. It was a good-natured little remark, nothing personal or even remotely true. Erin had slapped his arm and laughed, which helped Ben relax in the awkward moment, considering Erin was a first lieutenant and still felt comfortable enough around him to slap him even though he was her commanding officer and a full-bird colonel. As she laughed, of course. Joyous laughter, even after all she had been through.

Ben let his eyes close. Let a prayer whisper up from his soul. *Lord God, Father, please bless the little one growing so big and strong inside Erin right now. Please help Erin, strengthen her as the baby grows. Lord, You've got to deal with her husband. Because if it gets left up to me, I won't be gentle with him. I'll tell it like it is. And he won't like it. But I don't much care. He needs to learn that sometimes, some things are just out of our control. Help him to trust You, Lord. And his wife. And . . . Chris.* Ben blew out a deep breath as his eyes opened. *Please help him to trust Chris, dear Father. And help her . . . to trust You.*

He lifted his glass of milk for one last long drink. Stared at the cup in his hand. Tried to shake the memory of Erin's swollen, bruised eyes. The sight of that Purple Heart pinned to her chest. *Lord, thank You for seeing Erin through to this place. For bringing her here. And Chris too. And Cappy and Bettema. What a wonder it is for me. The four beautiful soldiers You've placed here with us at Kimberley.*

*The beautiful changes You've brought about in each of their lives.* He let his next breath carry a faint laugh. *And I'll say it again, Lord. I really wish I had the chance to pin that Bronze Star on Chris. It would have been an honor. One of the finest moments in this old dog's life. But, of course, it wasn't to be. And so be it. She's here. And she's Yours. What more could I ever hope for?*

✯ ✯ ✯

SCOTT TOOK A FEW STEPS closer to Velda's house, the heat and smoke burning his eyes. Already on the porch, Chris tried the door. Pushed against it with her shoulder. It didn't open. She ran to the front picture window.

"Stop it!" he yelled at her. "Chris, you can't—!" He quickly climbed the stairs and stood beside her.

She glanced at him, hesitated only another second, then raised her foot and kicked through the window.

The glass shattering, the ear-splitting shock of it giving way to a shower of falling shards scattered what little breath remained in Scott's lungs, what little thought still flowed coherently in his brain. Chris kicking through it, the look in her eyes . . .

They both cowered for a second, turned their backs and covered their eyes as the glass fell. Yet as soon as the last crash faded, Scott turned to look—Chris stood, facing the hole, looking into the flames.

"Are you crazy?" The words wrenched Scott's throat. "Stop this!"

She didn't say a word, didn't even look at him—only lifted her foot and continued to kick, breaking out the rest of the glass that stood in her way.

"Stop it, Chris! You can't go in there!"

Did she even hear what he said? She took three steps back, then ran toward the hole and jumped through headfirst, almost a dive— no, it *was* a dive. Headfirst into Velda's burning house.

Scott couldn't move. His mouth hanging open, he only stood and stared.

# TEN

AT THAT MOMENT, REALITY SHORT-CIRCUITED; every tiniest thread of anything in his world even remotely rational or true or sensible vaporized. Dumbfounded, he stared, unable to comprehend what he just saw.

Gray smoke flowed through the top of the broken window, long eerie fingers escaping into the fresh outside air. The movement caught his attention, then abruptly brought him back to his present reality.

Velda Jackson's house. Smoke. Fire. And Chris just dove through the window to get inside.

He blinked. What if Velda was still in there? What if—? *What if!*

He ran to the window. Inside, swirling black smoke and brilliant orange flames engulfed the entire front room. His heart cried out for help as he saw the jagged shards of glass that lined the window. Chris's way was the only way.

Backing up five steps, he gritted his teeth, sucked in a sharp breath, then ran forward and dove through the window . . . crashed on the floor by Velda's couch, knocked the breath from his lungs. Screams poured from his heart. *Help me, Father! This is insane!* He lay on the floor, eyes pinched shut.

Breaths came quickly. So did his coughing. Smoke circled above him, lowered the ceiling to about three feet. He stared at it a second, mesmerized by the flowing rivers of a multitude of grays, swirling . . .

Coughs came again, deep and violent. His throat ached as he breathed, sucking the poison into his lungs.

He rolled onto his stomach, drew in a deep breath, then tried not to cough it all back out as he opened his mouth and shouted, "Chriiiissss!"

He blinked. Tears flooded his burning eyes. His nose ran as he coughed.

He had to move. Find Chris. Find Velda! He pushed up to hands and knees and searched left, right, saw only smoke, flames leaping out of Velda's kitchen. The entire back half of the house burned—a solid wall of brilliant orange flame.

The heat!

He pulled his T-shirt over his face, the hood of his wet jacket up over his head. Looked right. Thought he saw . . . it was! Chris! Again, he shouted her name. Again, she ignored him.

He quickly crawled toward her. She had pulled open the door of the stairs. Thick gray smoke poured out the open door. Scott reached out and grabbed her ankle. Then quickly ducked as she kicked her foot out—almost caught him in the face. She turned to glare at him.

"You can't go up there!" Scott shouted, then he coughed. "Too much—!"

"She's got to be up there! She's got to be!" Chris coughed, kicked away, then started crawling up the stairs.

A curse ripped through Scott's mind. He clenched his teeth. Heat seared his back. But he followed, crawling on hands and knees. His eyes burned as tears dripped down his cheeks. He held his T-shirt between his teeth. Tried to breathe through his mouth.

Inside the stairwell, the heat's intensity eased. But the smoke thickened. Blinded him. He bumped his head against the door frame at the top of the stairs.

Chris shouted, almost screamed Velda's name. Over and over. The word, the screams, pulled all of Scott's conscious thought to the prayers crying out from his soul.

*Please! Lord God! Don't let her die! Velda! Please don't let us die!*

At the top of the stairs, he pushed himself onto the floor of the hallway. Looked behind him. Then ahead. He tried to see through the smoke, blinking, coughing, eyes burning. Chris was just ahead, kneeling to push through one of Velda's bedroom doors. Scott dropped to his stomach, snaked across the floor behind her.

"Velda! VELDA!"

Her wild screams terrified him. She stopped only to cough, violently, and to spit. Again she screamed, "Velda!"

Behind him, flames climbed the far wall of the hall. The second floor was now completely engulfed. A wall of flames spread toward them. Scott blinked through his tears as Chris crawled out of the room. By the time he reached her, she was on her stomach, pushing herself forward toward the last room at this end of the hall.

"Velda! Velda!"

"Chris! We gotta—!" Scott's voice gave out. Still he shouted, "CHRIIISSS!"

She continued crawling away from him, coughing, frantic, but not panicked.

Panic ripped through Scott. He wanted to run back down those stairs, jump back out that broken window, get in Ben's Explorer, and drive away from this place. Go and find Erin and drive away with her until—

"VELLLDAAAA!"

The scream shot adrenalin through his veins. He squinted through the smoke and saw Chris slithering through the last bedroom door. He tried to catch her, but could only watch her feet disappear into the room.

They were going to die. The smoke, soon the flames . . . They had to go back down those stairs. There was no other way out. Carrying Velda. And Chris too, if Scott didn't get to her soon and get her out.

Burning smoke in his throat and eyes crazed him. Coursing insanity slowed his brain. He couldn't catch up with Chris. She was gone. Inside that room, maybe she found Velda. But they wouldn't get her out in time. None of them would get out of this in time. Alive.

Chris was ready to die, risking everything to save Velda. Dying in the attempt.

Scott loved Velda, yes. But this? To die in this place? Like this?

No. He didn't share Chris's willingness to die. Even for a friend. Sweet Velda. If he turned around right now and ran back down those stairs, he might save his own life.

No, he didn't have any of what Chris had. Proved he didn't know her at all.

Proved how much he knew about himself.

★★★

"How was your sandwich, Ben? Did you get enough?"

He tossed his jacket over his arm, his plate and cup into the trash, then looked up at Erin and grinned. "Yes, I most certainly did. But I could use one of those pickles you got there to wash it all down. You're not hoarding them, now are you?"

Her outburst of giggles must have embarrassed her. Her face instantly tinted pink. "It's not like I carry them with me wherever I go." She held out a jar of dill spears. "Please, sir, have a pickle."

"Nah. I was just teasing you." For a second, Ben enjoyed the stunned look on her face. "But you know, what I really want is a couple of those cookies that just came out of the oven. Are they what I think they are?"

Sarah held the plate out to him. "Only if you're thinking they're chocolate peanut butter chip. There's about six here with your name on them."

Erin leaned closer to the plate for a look. "Oh, really? Well, I see this one right here has my name on it." She picked one up from the plate, stuck it into her mouth, then glanced up and gave Ben a mischievous grin.

He turned to Sarah. "Someone should teach this lady how to read." He grabbed up four of the cookies and gave both Sarah and Erin a warm smile. "Thank you both, by the way, for all your help this week. You too, Mildred. Thanks so much for everything. All the great food, all the hours you put in . . . we couldn't have done it without you."

All three glanced down at the floor and grinned sheepishly. Mildred actually blushed and tossed Ben a dismissing wave.

Just the reaction he expected. He laughed. "And since we've pretty much conquered this storm, now, ladies, without further ado, I think I'm going home to reclaim my recliner."

"You are looking a little tired, Pap," Sarah said, her voice soft with concern. "Are you feeling all right?"

Ben let out another laugh. "Nothing a good nap won't cure." He gave the three women a wave. "I'll see you all later. And thanks again. I really mean it." He absorbed their good-byes, then turned to force himself up the stairs on his way out the front door of the church. Stopped, just for a second at the top of the stairs to glance around the foyer, to listen for anything amiss. Only silence. Friendly silence. And that familiar smell. How he loved this old church. And the One they honored here. Such joyful fellowship. Wondrous praise. He let a few echoes of *A Mighty Fortress* waft through his heart as he turned and pushed through the main doors. As he chomped into another cookie.

At the top of the stairs, he stopped and looked out across Kimberley Street. A gentle rain still fell.

His eyes narrowed. A huge black cloud rose into the sky only a few blocks away. In the distance, sirens wailed, growing more severe, more intense—police and fire working their way toward it.

Pulling on his jacket, Ben quickly descended the stairs, then walked up the street toward that black cloud, praying the Lord's protection upon all those involved, finishing his last cookie on the way.

✮ ✮ ✮

THANK GOODNESS FOR THAT FIRE. The old man at the top of the stairs almost looked right at him. But as soon as he spotted the smoke, away he went. Didn't want to miss any of the excitement.

Del breathed a deep sigh and tried to relax. It was hard. Just sitting there in his truck, waiting, watching out for his fool friend was dangerous. Especially with the open containers littering the passenger's floor of his truck. But hey. If anyone gave him grief about his open containers of warm beer, he'd lay out a little grief of his own. And why not. He'd done it before.

And he was due to lay out a little grief. As soon as he spotted that ugly brown Plymouth. He still couldn't figure out why Rich had taken off like he did to come here. He was so drunk that night, shouting stuff like, "You don't understand, Del," and "Matty's dead! We never should have gone there!"

It only took one good pop upside the head to make him shut up and listen. He needed to understand how things were. With Matt dead and those two rat-women spelling out to the cops exactly who killed him, it would only be a matter of time before they'd be busting down the door.

Though they would never find Matt's body. And they would never be able to prove what those two rats said they saw. Unless they got to Rich. If they twisted him, even a little, Rich would sing like Patty LaBelle. He would rat Del out in a heartbeat.

No, the man needed to understand how things stood. From aggravated assault to B and E, he was going down for all of it. Maybe even for murder too. They wouldn't care about his claims of self-defense. Performed in an act of armed, aggravated assault mixed in with a little breaking and entering and a little destruction of private property, well, yeah, it made sense they would list Matt's death as murder. Even without a body. Even though it really was self-defense.

Or a dumb—no, an unimaginably stupid—accident. Rich standing there, saying the gun just went off. "We were fighting, Del, and the gun just went off!"

Idiot.

Oh, Rich would pay. He would burn for all of it. Just like Del would.

There was no other way out. Before the two of them pulled out of Denver and hit I-25 for Mexico, they needed to finish what they started in that rat-woman's cabin outside Ouray, Colorado.

With all that said in the way Del said it, Rich understood. Or, at least, he was starting to.

Idiot.

He pulled one last long drag from his finished cigarette, then flicked the burning butt into the corner of his truck. Blowing the smoke out through his nose, he reached to his shirt pocket to immediately tap out and light another.

He held the burning match in front of his eyes, watched it burn down to his fingers, then slowly flame out. A long wisp of smoke snaked away. Cursing, he tossed the spent match into the corner of his truck with all the other garbage. Reached up and pulled the burning cigarette away from his lips. Blew out a deep breath. Watched the smoke twist and curl as it rose from the cigarette's glowing tip.

The truth of it had been gnawing at him for weeks. Burned at him, like the first deep swallow of sour-mash whiskey or the flame of a match dying out on his skin. If he could go back and do it all again, if he could turn back time and make things right . . .

Of course, Wayne wouldn't be dead. If Del had left Matt and Rich at the hunting cabin and gone after Wayne himself like he wanted to, he would have been there with Wayne when that—when *Christina McIntyre* showed up. Yeah, he wouldn't have killed her either. Wayne had it right. Just shut her down without her even knowing what hit her. And clear out before she woke back up.

Yeah, Wayne wasn't stupid. But Del was. Stupid for waiting on Rich and Matt. Waiting while they unloaded the supplies. Waiting while they unloaded their snow machines. Waiting while they picked their nose, wasting precious time.

Oh, what he wouldn't give to go back to that moment. To make it all right. For Wayne. Hadn't Wayne trusted him? Wasn't the plan rock solid? Meet up at Timmons, maybe spend the night if the weather turned bad, then take the back way to their hunting cabin to hide out until Wayne's trail went cold. Del had looked forward to spending two weeks at the cabin with Wayne and Rich and Matt. They would live large off the land, just sitting life out for a while. Before heading south to disappear forever.

That was the plan. And that part did not include Rich. Or Matt.

Both had their lives to go back to. Matt was toying with the idea of asking his girl to marry him. No, Rich and Matt had no reason to run off to Mexico. It was Wayne's behind in the sling. And Del would gladly give up his own miserable life to join his best friend on the trip. South of the border. On the run, maybe. But running was living. Staying where they were only meant dying. Slowly. A slow, painful death. Rotting away in a lousy job. Or a cell in an Arizona prison.

And after all of it, all the planning, the dreaming, then executing the plan, Wayne had to go and get killed. By a woman no less. Shot with his own gun.

After all this time, the thought of it still turned his stomach so hard he groaned.

Rich and Matt were fully behind him. They knew what had to be done. It didn't take much to convince them. Matt was in line. Rich didn't hesitate. They planned their next job from their cabin tucked deep inside nowhere. Knew they had a little less than two weeks to wait. But that didn't matter. They would wait. And then pay little miss hero Christina McIntyre a visit.

He pulled the cigarette up to his lips and drew in a deep drag. Forget the beer. He needed a stiff belt of tequila. Something that would burn hotter than the burn already consuming his soul.

What a joke. Their perfect plan. Considering how everything turned out at Miss McIntyre's cabin.

They never should have left without finishing the job.

Stupid. He had been so stupid. Even driving away, he knew he should have turned back. When they passed that old man heading up McIntyre's road, he should have turned around right then and gone back to that cabin. Gone right back and killed every single one of them. Even that old man. Didn't he give Del a good long look as he pulled over to let them pass? Wasn't he heading up that way to see McIntyre? Wasn't he the reason the cops got there so quickly? They barley made it down the mountain before the cops headed up.

No. None of it sat right in his gut. He should have finished the job. Even after he tossed Matt's body into his truck. He should have turned on Rich and blown him away. Then gone back to that cabin and finished what they started. Then stopped right there in the road and killed that stupid old man.

All of them. Dead.

Then he would have been free. Maybe Mexico, though actually, Canada suited him more. Up in the far northern Rockies. Maybe up there he could lose himself in his beloved Rocky Mountains. Just a few miles north of Uncompahgre. Like two thousand. But just as spectacular. Just as removed from the world.

It wasn't far from where he sat to the Canadian border. Maybe he could recalculate his plan. Maybe, just maybe, he could disappear after all.

One thing now was perfectly clear. His old buddy Rich would not be making the trip. This was one trip Del would make alone. After he finished the job. If . . . Rich hadn't finished it for him already.

Del wanted to laugh. Surely, if there had been a double homicide on Kimberley Street in the past few days, he would have heard about it.

No. Rich hadn't yet finished the job. He had better show up quick and get it done.

✳✳✳

"VELDA! NOOO!"

The scream ripped through his panic, cutting jagged edges across his soul. Chris screaming like that—did she find Velda? Was she—?

Scott forced himself forward, pushing, pulling his way down the floor, his face rubbing against the carpet, his lungs desperate for just a gasp of clean air. He squirmed to the door and looked inside the room, saw only light gray smoke hovering, felt a hint of cooler air brush his burning face.

Chris had reached up to open this door. Yes. This door was closed. At the far end of the hall, away from the fire, this would be the last room to fill—Scott quickly looked behind him. Flames filled the hall. Smoke and flames reached the door of the stairs. Their only way out. He turned back to Chris. Rubbed his eyes to clear away the sooty tears.

Chris had pulled the comforter off the bed and now sat on top of it, her face buried into it, coughing. Was she weeping?

Scott crawled into the room, then turned and slammed the door closed behind him. Chris immediately jumped up and tried to push him away, screaming, "No, Scott! She's still out there! I need to check down the hall!"

He grabbed her arms and shook her. "There's nothing left, Chris! It's all on fire!"

"NO! Let me go!"

He wanted to shake her again, to slap her, but the expression on her face, the intensity in her eyes, such focused determination . . . Scott almost ducked, afraid she would reach out and slap him.

She only cried. Huge tears dropped out her bloodshot eyes forming pink lines through the soot on her cheeks. Until she coughed. She doubled over in his arms and coughed so hard Scott held her gently, aching for her, desperate now to find a way out. To get her out.

The window. Their only hope.

He started to pull her up, to pull her toward the window.

She suddenly jerked out of his arms, screaming, "NO! NO! We can't—!" She pushed him away, then stumbled for the door. "Scott! We can't leave without Velda!"

"NO!" He grabbed the back of her sweatshirt and pulled her back to him with such force she fell backward to the floor beside him. She tried to get back up but Scott held her down. "Stop it, Chris! We have to get out of here!"

"No!" She tried to push him away, then broke into a fit of ragged coughs.

Should he hit her? A good hard slap across the side of her face would get her attention. One solid punch would knock her out cold.

She tried to push out of his grip. Still he held her down. She cursed at him, called him some very interesting names. Still he held her. Coughing, almost retching from the smoke, Chris struggled to break free from him, to get back up, to go back out that door, to find Velda.

Scott blinked tears from his eyes while he held her down, desperate to make sense of what he saw in her eyes, on her face, the intensity of her struggle, the tenacity, the absolute inability . . . to accept defeat. At that moment, Chris would rather run into the flames than give up on her friend. She would rather die . . . than quit.

He had heard about it, but never seen it. Could only imagine what would drive a firefighter into a burning building or a Marine to storm an enemy-infested beach. But at that moment, he stared into the face of it. Into the eyes of one who lived it.

Mouth gaping, he could only stare.

✵✵✵

POOR OLD RICH. THE MAN had a way about him. Had a way of always ruining everything. His three marriages. His what, fifteen jobs?

Smoke blew out Del's nose and mouth as he laughed.

And the funniest thing of all, that night? At Miss McIntyre's cabin? If Rich hadn't left to walk up to Del's truck for more smokes, then that other rat-woman, Erin, would have run right out the door when she started to. She would have made it back to their truck—

what was it, an Explorer? If she would have made it out of the cabin, she would have called for help on the radio in their truck.

No. If she had run out of the cabin, Matt would have chased her down and killed her. Right then and there. No fooling around. Then they would've had their fun with Chris, like they planned, before killing her too and leaving her to rot.

If only Del hadn't run out of smokes. If only Rich hadn't walked up to the truck to get more. If only Matty hadn't gotten cold feet. If only Rich hadn't lost it and killed him.

That night, just last week, when Del and Rich stood face-to-face discussing things—when both could barely stand from drinking too much—when Del had said that, about Rich losing it and killing Matt, Rich swung out and popped him on the mouth. Just remembering the punch pulled his lips into a grin. He sucked in a deep drag of his cigarette and pulled it away from his lips.

When his head cleared that night, Rich was gone, but not before Del was sure he heard him say he would finish the job. At least that was what he hoped Rich said. Because if it wasn't, and Rich came all this way just to jerk Del's chain, Del would finish it, that was for sure.

Afterward, he would disappear. Canada. Yes. Sounded better and better all the time.

He finished his cigarette and tossed the butt into the corner of his truck. Then wondered if he shouldn't be a little more careful. He didn't want to start a fire down there in all the trash and warm beer. He laughed. Reached to his shirt pocket for another cigarette. Slowly lit it.

And what was the funniest thing of all? To think that maybe the reason Rich lost it that night at McIntyre's cabin was because Matt lost it first and actually shot Del. Even to this day, he couldn't believe Matt shot him. The kid actually chose the little hero—uh, *heroine*—over his brother's closest friend. Fine. But why did he have to shoot him? His shoulder still felt like it was packed with white phosphorus.

No, nothing made sense anymore. Nothing fell into line the way it was supposed to. When Wayne had called that night and said he had cleared the state and was free, Del couldn't wait to meet up with him, to hit Mexico with him to live free and wild until the day they died. But then little Miss McIntyre had to show up and ruin the whole thing.

And then Rich had to go and kill Matt. Matt was a good kid. He didn't deserve to die.

Neither did Wayne.

No, neither did Wayne.

✯✯✯

THE EXPLOSION GOT HER ATTENTION.

Scott was almost glad for it. Being knocked back against the bed tore him from his own daze as well.

Chris pushed herself up from the floor and turned to look at him. Her wide eyes finally revealed what Scott had been shouting at her all along. *We have to get out of here!*

"Come on." He grabbed her by the arm and pulled her to the window. "We have to jump." He peered out and saw the roof of the back porch below them. "Just step out, then we'll jump."

Chris's eyes burned with sadness as she looked at him. "She's . . ."

"She probably wasn't even here."

"How can you say that? Her car is—!" Chris broke down, coughing.

Scott tore the curtains off the wall and tossed them aside, then unlocked the window and jerked it up. Popped the screen out with one push. "Come on!" He grabbed Chris's arm again but she instantly pulled it away.

"Don't touch me!" She turned her head and gazed back at the door.

Scott grabbed her again, this time with enough strength she couldn't pull away. "Come on. We have to go now!" He pulled her to the window, then, when she hesitated, pushed her out onto the roof of the porch.

Oh, she did not like that, not one bit. Yet she stood and waited for him pressed against the side of the house.

And, no wonder she waited. The cold damp air tasted sweeter than anything he had ever known. The rain pelting his face felt truly heaven sent. He wanted to stand there and just breathe—

Chris coughed, then slipped on the wet roof. Scott threw out his arm to grab her. Too late. As Chris fell backward, Scott also slipped and fell, and the weight of both of them sliding to the edge brought the entire roof down underneath them.

As Scott hit the ground, mud slapped up around him. He heard the splat. Felt the cold mud soak into his jeans. Cool the heat across his back. He could barely breathe. Felt like someone had punched him in the gut. Then kicked him in the head.

He turned his head. Through the sparks and stars, the rain splashing on his face, the sooty tears in his eyes, he heard a groan. A horrible cough. Chris was in trouble.

A breath found its way into his lungs. He coughed, then used what air remained to say, "Chris?"

She pushed herself up to her elbow, coughed and coughed, then fell back into the mud.

Scott slowly rolled over, taking stock of his appendages, his vital internal organs. Everything seemed intact. Functional. Everything seemed to be happening in a parallel universe to some other Scott Mathis, to some other crazy fool who only looked like him. None of this could be really happening. Not in his—the real Scott Mathis's—world.

He coughed, then drew in a refreshing breath of that sweet Portland, Oregon, wintertime air. Heavy with rain, so fresh, so much smelling like the soggy earth he lay in. This was his world. His reality. His, and . . . he repeated his earlier word. "Chris?"

"Don't—!" She still struggled to breathe.

"Are you all right?"

"Don't talk to me! Don't!" She rolled away from him, then worked her way back up to her elbow. Coughed again.

"Just breathe. Lay still a minute. Try to relax."

"Don't tell me—! Don't, Scott." Up on her knees now. Holding her shoulder, she gritted her teeth and pushed up to stand. Swayed. Took a step backward. Stood. Muddy water dripped down her face and back.

Scott started to lift up, until a wave of dizziness hit him. He laid back down to let it pass, then winced as his head touched the ground. He reached back to feel a cut. A deep one. Pulled his hand to his eyes. Saw blood.

Chris stumbled toward the gate in the back of Velda's yard.

Scott again tried to stand. Kept his eyes closed against the dizziness as he said, "Where are you going?"

She kept walking.

"Chris, wait!" He caught her just before she reached the gate. "Wait a minute!" He grabbed her arm.

When would he learn? Chris quickly threw out her arm as if trying to knock Scott's head off. But she grabbed her shoulder instead, didn't follow through with the backhand.

"Sit here a second. Let me take a look at it."

"Don't touch me."

"Okay. I'm sorry. I won't—"

"Don't tell me you're sorry. Don't you dare."

"Chris, I—!"

"We let her die, Scott!" She turned to push him away, both hands connected with his chest, yet she put no strength into it. The push didn't even cause Scott to have to step backward. "We let her die." Chris lifted her hands to her face.

His heart ached. After everything, he couldn't bear to see her cry. "Chris, we did everything we could."

"No!" Her eyes blazed. "I didn't check the other end of the hall! What if she was there? If she was, she's dead!"

"She may not have been in the house! Have you considered that?"

"Her car is right there, Scott! Don't you see it? Where would she go without her car?"

It was true. Velda rarely went anywhere without her car. She even drove the few blocks to church three times a week. In the rain, today, with her car still in the carport, Velda was probably at home. Not downstairs on her couch or in her recliner, she was probably upstairs tucked in her bed in that room at the other end of the hall, taking an afternoon nap. The smoke would have overwhelmed her. Hopefully she didn't suffer.

"We let her die . . ."

The whimpered words sliced Scott's heart. He slowly lifted his arms, not knowing how to show Chris how sorry he was, how much he wanted to comfort her even as his heart bore his own agony.

"No!" She backed away from his hands, then looked up to glare at him. "You shouldn't have followed me inside. Why did you even follow me?" She took another step back.

Scott could only shake his head.

"We had time. We could have checked that other bedroom. If you hadn't stopped me!"

Enough was enough. "Chris, the place was on fire. You made a choice. You checked two of the three bedrooms. That was all you could do!"

"You could've checked the other one."

His teeth ground. "You know what? Maybe I could have. I'm sorry I didn't. I'm sorry I didn't live up to your expectations."

"She's dead, Scott. We had time to get her out and we didn't."

He watched her eyes, could tell she was winding down. Saying things . . .

"You shouldn't have followed me." She turned and kicked open the gate so hard it swung and crashed into the fence. "Don't follow me now." She took off down the alley, then suddenly stopped and doubled over to cough.

For the first time in his life, at the same moment, love and pure hate burned like a roman candle inside him. He did not like how it felt.

✭✭✭

QUICKENING HIS PACE, BEN TURNED the corner of the street, then stopped so suddenly he almost slipped on the wet leaves. Before him black, billowing clouds of smoke poured out of a house about halfway down the block. A part of him refused to believe what he saw, what his brain was trying to tell him. That house was . . . Velda Jackson's house. Her home, all her things, even her car, all of it—was being swallowed up in flames. His bold prayers disintegrated into whimpers. *Oh, dear God, please, dear God . . . don't let Velda . . . don't let her be in there. Please, God.*

He forced his feet to carry him closer, couldn't pull his eyes away from the brilliant flames and the smoke. So much smoke. Such evil flames, roaring, devouring the poor woman's house. The roar of the fire trucks' diesels, the putrid smells, the cries of those who had gathered to watch, to weep, and to pray. For Velda. *Father God, oh, Lord God, please let her be all right.*

A young boy ran up to him. Jimmy Thurman. Benny's little friend. Yes. Ben blinked, trying to focus on the lad, on the words he was saying.

"Mr. Con'ley, Mr. Con'ley! Velda's with Unca Russell. Velda's with Unca Russell!"

It didn't make any sense. Didn't register. Until he finally heard the words through the boy's frantic delivery. *Velda's with Russell!* He grabbed the boy by the arm. "Are you sure, Jimmy? Are you sure? How do you know?"

"My momma's got her on the phone right now, Mr. Con'ley! Come on!" Jimmy grabbed Ben's hand and pulled him closer to his mother. Ben had no choice but to follow.

With one hand holding a cell phone to her ear, Darnice Thurman held up her other hand as they approached. "Oh yes, you sweet thing. Yes, we will. No, we'll be careful. You're coming then? Yes. Yes, they'll want to talk to you." She glanced up at Ben and smiled. "Yes, Velda. Hey, just a minute, honey. Talk to someone." She handed the phone to Ben.

His mouth fell open. He could only thank her with a quick smile as he raised the cell phone to his ear. "Velda? Is that you?"

Her voice sounded sweet as sugar in his ear, saying words that made him laugh—and yet, it was hard to hear with all the noise, the firefighters shouting. Hard to stay focused on her words, especially when he saw his Explorer parked askew in the middle of the street.

"You're sure you're all right?" he asked, then he felt a little stupid. Obviously Velda was fine, miles away from the fire ravaging her house. "I, um, have to go. I'll see you soon, okay? I'll be here when you get here. You better hurry, Velda. But be careful."

He heard Velda's response, but wasn't really listening. He handed the phone back to Darnice and said thanks. All the while, he slowly moved toward his Explorer, wondering why it would be here, parked the way it was. Where were Scott and Chris?

Scott and Chris.

Ben grabbed his chest as his heart seized, as his blood froze in his veins. His mouth fell open, yet he couldn't breathe as he slowly turned to gaze at Velda's burning house.

✳✳✳

DEL CLOSED HIS EYES AND rested his head against the truck's back window. It pained him that he would have to ditch this truck. He had grown quite fond of it. It was one of the few pickups that fit him. Most cramped him and wouldn't let him stretch out behind the wheel the way he liked. Maybe he should move up to an extended cab. Expand his options a little.

Another long drag on his cigarette. Then he reached up and pulled it away. Blew out the smoke and peered through the steamed-up windshield of his truck, and saw an ugly brown Plymouth sedan slowly turning the corner onto Kimberley Street. He blinked his eyes deeply a few times. Was tempted to wipe off the inside of his wind-shield. Maybe turn on the truck's windshield wipers. But he didn't want the movement to attract Rich's attention.

Yep. It was his old buddy Rich. And the stupid fool didn't even have the brains to switch cars. Not even to switch license plates. Del let a smile stretch his lips. He even let a laugh burst up. Sure enough. Good old Rich. As stupid and predictable as a hangover.

So. What were the man's intentions?

Rich pulled the sedan into a vacant spot halfway up the block. Turned off its headlights. Then nothing more.

Del frowned. Smoked his cigarette. Crushed the butt into the seat of the truck. Tossed it into the corner. Lit another, hiding the flame of his match with his hand. Blew out the match. Sucked in on his cigarette. Growled.

Obviously, Rich intended to wait.

This could be a long night. Del cursed under his breath.

The car's door opened. A few seconds later, Rich pulled himself out and stood in the street. A few seconds after that, he pushed the door closed. Then he stood for a while longer, in the rain, just gawk-ing up at that big church across the street from him. Just standing there, getting wet.

Del wanted to laugh.

His hands deep in his jacket pocket, Rich lowered his head and walked across the street, up the sidewalk to the steps of the church, then turned and headed up the stairs. He pulled open the door at the top of the stairs. And walked inside. The door closed behind him.

Hmm. Very interesting. Rich didn't hesitate one bit as he walked through that door. Maybe he was a man on a mission.

The time had come. Yes. And Del loved a good mystery. He quickly jumped out of his truck, tossed his cigarette into the gutter, then reached behind him, under his shirt, to make sure the big pistol back there wouldn't fall out. When it felt right, he pulled his shirt back down, spit a flake of tobacco off his tongue, then headed down the sidewalk to the stairs of the Kimberley Street Community Church.

★★★

SHE WANTED TO RUN, BEGGED her legs to carry her faster down the alley, yet all she could do was cough. And every cough tore at her throat, her chest, caused her to bear down over her knees just to get herself through it.

*Breathe. Just breathe.*

The cool moist air. The fat drops of rain falling out of the peaceful puffy clouds. She tilted her head back, let the rain fall over her burning, filthy face. She slowly lifted her hands to pull back the stray strands of hair that had worked their way out of her French braid. Lifting her hands hurt. Across the top and back of her shoulder, through her chest, across her entire lower back. She almost groaned, but the outgoing air caught in her throat and made her cough. Again.

She wanted to fall to the ground right on the spot. Break down into a million tiny pieces and just float away on the storm's runoff. Yet she forced her feet to move, forced her legs to carry her away from that place, away from the moment she had just endured.

Velda was dead. Precious Velda. *Oh, God . . .*

She fell to her knees and whimpered as gravel cut through her jeans, yet she didn't cry. Not until she started to pray. Or tried to.

*God, I don't understand! Why? Why would you take someone like Velda? Why . . . dear God.*

She wanted to lie down right there in the alley and fall asleep dead. Wanted to stand up and run and run and run.

Her head fell forward into her hands. For just a second. She pulled them away and cupped them in front of her, letting the rain pool in her palms, a small puddle of cool rain that she carefully lifted to her lips, carefully poured into her mouth. At first it burned her raw throat, then soothed, slowly working its way through her chest. She held her hands out again, let the rain pool . . .

Her eyes filled with tears. Her bottom lip started to shake. Instantly infuriated, she let the water fall through her fingers and abruptly stood, then walked, then ran down the alley and across the street, down the sidewalk to the next street, then turned away from Velda Jackson's house and ran away as fast as she could.

Which wasn't very fast. She slowed to a stop and leaned over the hood of a car to cough. And to breathe. She turned and continued down the street. One step, then another. *Just keep walking. Don't stop. Don't turn around. Don't look back.*

Her eyelids fell closed as she walked. She didn't care. She continued to walk. One step, then another. Farther down the street.

*God . . . Oh, dear God, I can't—I can't believe she's gone. It's not fair! It's not—!* She opened her eyes and wanted to kick the first thing she saw. She stopped. Her breath stuck in her throat as her heart slammed to a stop.

She stood exactly between two long-ago-abandoned stores, looking into the small vacant lot between them. A rusted Safeway shopping cart lay wedged in the far corner. A broken concrete slab no bigger than a truck lay in the middle of the lot surrounded by weeds and garbage, the walls of the stores decorated with tags, artistic graffiti, and faded Customer Parking Only signs.

She had seen this vacant lot before. Though maybe not from this angle. She had stood behind Erin, right over there, peeking over Erin's shoulder to watch a blonde-haired little girl dribble a basketball around and around her tightly laced high-top sneakers.

This was Alaina's playground.

The sight of it, the thought of the precious child playing in this hole, Chris let her tears fall as she walked into the lot and fell against the wall, then landed in a heap on the ground. She leaned back and pulled her knees up to her chest. Lowered her head to the top of her knees. And cried.

It wouldn't take long. With the power back on, she could take a hot shower, then pack only what she needed and leave Kimberley within the hour, before anyone even knew she was gone. No one would stop her. No one would blame her.

She couldn't stay for one more minute in this town. Yet, she couldn't summon even an ounce of strength into her legs to make them move. Her head lifted, then fell back against the wall behind her. Her legs fell away from her chest. She struggled to straighten them, to ease some of the pressure on her wrenched lower back.

Still, the rain fell. Against her face, it splashed away some of the soot. Cooled her burned skin. Washed away her tears. She opened her mouth and slowly stuck out her tongue. Let the rain ever so slowly spill into her mouth.

*Please help me get up, God. I can't stay here. Not anymore. I'm sorry.*

Not one part of her moved. Not even her tongue. Rain continued to collect in her mouth.

*I won't blame Rinny if she hates me for leaving. She'll get over it. We'll still be friends. She'll come back to Colorado. After her baby's born. Someday.*

She pulled in her tongue and swallowed just as a sob burst out. She pulled up her left leg and rested her elbow on her knee. Let her head fall into her hand. She sat, crying, for a long, long time.

# ELEVEN

HE WATCHED HER STUMBLE DOWN the alley for another moment, then glanced away as she fell to her knees. His eyes closed as the fire in his gut flickered out. He didn't hate this woman. Even though he wanted to.

A rumble startled him. He turned and saw a fire truck splashing through the alley's puddles. Even before it roared and hissed to a stop beside him, two firefighters jumped down and started pulling hose from the back of it. Another approached him. Scott gave him a weary smile.

"Are you all right?" the firefighter hollered over the noise of the truck.

Scott nodded. "Yeah. We were hoping to find Velda, but we ran out of time."

"Her too?" The man pointed down the alley at Chris. "Is she all right?"

"She will be."

"We were told the owner of this house is at her son's. In Canby."

Scott blinked.

"She's on her way here, I guess."

"Who told you this?"

"Several of the neighbors standing out front. One of them had a cell phone. I guess she called her."

Scott's head fell back as he gazed up at the sky. His eyes closed as the gentle rain pattered his face. *Thank You, Lord.*

"You sure you're all right?"

"Yeah." He looked at the firefighter. "I am now."

"I hear that. But if you need care, don't be shy. There's a bus out front."

"Thanks." Scott slapped the man's shoulder. "You guys be careful."

"Always." The man grinned, then helped his buddies pull the hose close to the back of the house.

Scott peered down the alley hoping to see Chris, but she was gone. He lowered his head and walked across Velda's side yard to the front of her house, then around the line of fire trucks with their flashing red and blue lights, past the scores of people watching, to Ben's Explorer. He quickly turned when he heard a familiar voice call his name, almost laughed when he saw the expression on Ben Connelly's face.

"I knew it!" Ben jogged up to Scott and grabbed him by the upper arms. His face bore a huge smile. "I knew you two went in there!"

"It was Chris's idea," Scott said, then instantly regretted his defensiveness.

Ben's eyes flashed a look of something Scott couldn't quite read. "Yes, I bet it was."

He laughed in spite of himself.

Ben released Scott's arms and took a step back. "Are you all right?"

"Yeah. I'm fine. Is Velda really all right?"

"She's at Russell's. I talked to her on Darnice's cell phone."

"Really? How'd she sound?"

"Grateful to be in Canby, that's for sure. But she's on her way here."

Scott nodded. "Good." He gazed down the street, hoping to see—

"Where's Chris?"

"She took off. Have you seen her?"

"No. She hasn't come this way. Is she all right?"

Scott squinted his burning eyes. "I think so." In the distance, someone was walking away, almost stumbling down the sidewalk. It looked like Chris.

"Are you sure you're all right?" Ben asked. "You look terrible."

"A little singed." Scott glanced at Ben. "I need to go talk to Chris. She still thinks Velda was in the house."

"Dear Lord . . ."

"We'll be all right, Ben." He took a few steps, then turned around and said, "But could you do me a favor, Ben? Please?" He walked backward for a few steps.

"Name it, Scott."

"Could you, um, pray for me?" He grinned, then turned and hurried after Chris.

$$\ast\ast\ast$$

GLANCING LEFT AND RIGHT, DEL quickly climbed the stairs of the big church, then stopped at the front door and turned around. He gazed up and down the street in each direction.

Police sirens. Fire trucks. Smoke. No one stood in the rain watching him. No one peered out of their front windows to see what he was up to. He laughed. Throw in one little well-timed diversion and the entire Kimberley Street Neighborhood Watch program goes to pot.

He turned back to the thick door and put his ear against the cold damp wood. As thick as it was, he would have been surprised if he had heard anything, anyway. But, it was always prudent to err on the side of caution.

He slowly pulled the door toward him, using his body to block some of the light from filtering inside. Tried to see into the dark room behind the door, but couldn't. He turned his head and put his ear into the crack. Heard nothing but heavy silence. So heavy, he pushed open his jaw to pop his eardrums.

Another quick look over his shoulder. Still no one standing in the rain. Or at a window. He pulled the door open a little more. Stuck his head inside. Saw a wide-open room, an empty coat rack, a door with a small sign that read Pastor's Study. He looked hard left, down the stairs where light poured up. And women's voices. Faint.

Quiet. Nothing hinting to murder and mayhem running amuck. Rich must have taken a different route.

Straight ahead, Del saw two swinging doors, and through their small windows, a faint golden light. Still hearing only the women's voices, he pushed himself inside the church and let the door quietly close behind him.

He swallowed. He never did much like being inside a church.

Laughter filtered up with the light from below. Straight ahead, through the swinging doors' small windows, beams of wood reached out, illuminated golden in the otherwise pitch black. He moved a step closer, straining his ears to hear more than just the pleasant conversations from below. He stepped lightly, hoping the floor wouldn't creak as he walked. He eased his way to the two swinging doors, peered through one of the windows, saw the golden beams of a cross hanging high above where a preacher would stand, where good Christian folk wearing hideous white robes would sing praises to their God.

*Careful, boy.* It was as if he could still hear his grandmother's voice. *Don't be showin' no disrespect to the Good Lord, now, ya hear? He's a'watchin' ya, boy. And if'n He don't a'getcha, then the ol' Devil a'certainly will.*

He wanted to laugh. Easy to see how that turned out.

He blinked. Rich stood at the front of the church. What was he doing? Just standing there, looking up at that cross.

The man must have completely lost it.

Great.

If Del wanted to kill Rich now, he would have to wait until Rich came out of the church. Even the Devil himself wouldn't kill a man in a church. Especially if that man was staring up at a cross.

Fine. He would wait.

He hated to wait. Especially when he needed a cigarette.

★★★

HE HEARD HER BEFORE HE saw her. Soft cries, sniffs, a cough. Then, when he saw her, his heart fell. She had been crying hard.

She lifted her head and looked at him. A snarl captured her entire face.

Trying to ignore it, Scott moved into the vacant lot and asked, "Is this seat taken?"

Chris only rolled her eyes, then stared out toward the street.

With a grunt, then a deep sigh, Scott sat across the lot from her, about twenty feet away, then leaned back against the dirty wall. A green weed poked at his elbow.

Dirt and gravel muddied his already filthy jeans. He looked around the small lot, noticed a Safeway cart, the colorful graffiti here and there, a terribly faded Customer Parking Only sign on the wall above Chris. A clever retort fluttered through his mind. He didn't have the strength to put it into words.

He looked at Chris. Saw her eyes. Her frown. Her misery.

"Velda's okay." The words croaked out his throat, yet he knew Chris heard him just fine by the way her eyes quickly found his. "She wasn't in the house."

"Are you sure?"

Her voice croaked as well. Scott wished he would have asked the firefighters for a couple of bottles of water. He nodded. "Yeah. I'm sure."

"Who told you? How do they know for sure?"

"Ben told me. He talked to her. She's at Russell's. Velda's with Russell."

The name meant nothing to Chris, Scott could tell.

"Russell is Velda's son. He lives in Canby. About a half hour from here. Darnice Thurman, you know, Jimmy's mother? She had a cell phone. Ben talked to Velda. He said she sounded grateful to be in Canby, though she's on her way here."

"Ben told you this?"

"Yep. Just now."

"He talked to her? He was sure it was her?"

Scott breathed out a laugh, but tried to squelch it. "Yes. Ben talked to her. She's fine, Chris. She's okay."

"She was at her son's."

He gentled his voice. "Yes. He must have come and picked her up when the storm dragged on. He picked her up and took her to his house."

When Chris blinked her eyes, Scott wasn't sure if she could push them open again. "So, she wasn't there."

"No. She wasn't." He waited in silence for the words to sink into Chris's brain.

It took a few seconds. She finally met his gaze again. "And we were running around in her burning house like a couple of fools."

He barely smiled. "Well, I wouldn't exactly say that."

"Her car was there."

"It's all right, Chris. You thought she was there."

"If I would've known she . . ."

Scott smiled. Waited.

"What was she doing at her son's? Watching Oprah?"

A laugh ripped out of him. "Probably."

"She was at her son's watching Oprah, when we were crawling through her burning house looking for her."

"Yep."

Chris shook her head. Then let out a long breath. Her eyes fell closed as she leaned her head back against the wall.

Scott let the silence play out between them. Heard the gentle hush of the rain falling around them. Heard a car splashing through the rain as it sped up the street. He waited for the silence to return. Looked at Chris. Spoke the truth. "You really look terrible."

She didn't open her eyes. "So do you. You've got black stuff all over your face."

He waited a second. Rubbed his cheek with his hand, then wiped his face with his sleeve. Ran his fingers through his dripping hair. Let his hand fall with a thud to his lap as he sighed. Then said, "Are you all right?"

"Never better. You?"

He let out a small laugh. "Well, I think I still have all my eyebrows."

A breath of laughter pushed out of her, which immediately brought on violent coughing.

Scott listened to her struggle, his heart aching as he waited for her to recover. He let a whispered prayer for her lift up from his soul.

Wincing, she slowly leaned over to spit into the weeds beside her, then pulled her sweatshirt neck up to wipe her eyes and nose with the inside of it. Black stains showed through the fabric as she pushed it back down. She settled back against the wall, then slowly looked up at him. "Not very ladylike, huh."

Scott only smiled. A faint press of his lips.

Chris shifted her eyes out to the street, slowly blinked, slowly breathed, watching a car or two pass by, letting the rain fall over her.

Scott watched her. And, deep in his heart, he prayed.

✯✯✯

UNBELIEVABLE. DIDN'T PASTORS KEEP ANYTHING in their offices except Bibles and books about Bibles?

Standing in the middle of Pastor Andrew Connelly's study, Del frowned and shook his head. He looked again at the picture of the man, the good young pastor and his beautiful young family. Three darling children. A beautiful wife. He wanted to laugh.

If the good young pastor had a vice, and he probably almost certainly did, he didn't bring it to work with him. Too bad. After picking the lock and searching the man's entire office, Del found no cigarettes, no girly magazines, no beer, no stale potato chips, no nothing. Just Bibles. And books about Bibles. And the picture in his hand.

And Rich still stood at the front of the church, looking up at that cross.

Del tossed the picture back onto the pastor's desk, then breathed a deep sigh. Not only did he need a cigarette, he needed to use the men's room. But, considering Rich hadn't moved in fifteen minutes, maybe there was time to snoop around the church and find one. And maybe to slip outside for a smoke.

Even the Devil himself wouldn't smoke in a church.

✳✳✳

HER EYES WERE OPEN. YET she barely breathed. Didn't move at all. Only blinked.

Sitting across from her, Scott watched her. He couldn't help it. She looked so dirty, soaked to the bone, her sweatshirt sooty and stained, her jeans just plain filthy. Her hair was still confined for the most part in a French braid, though much of it had worked its way free. Rain dripped down her face, yet she made no move to swipe at it. Dripped from her chin. She didn't even seem to notice.

He closed his burning eyes for a second. Wiped his hand down his face. They both needed to go to the clinic and breathe pure oxygen for a while. To use the eye wash. They needed to take showers. And they needed about a week's worth of deep, uninterrupted sleep.

Chris moved her hand, then reached up to rub her nose. She slowly turned her eyes to look at Scott, then waited, probably to see what he would do, to hear what he would say next.

If only he knew.

Nothing needed to be said. Yet, with both of them too tired to stand, what better time to clear the air. The gentle rain falling over them seemed to caress them. Chris actually lifted her chin and closed her eyes, letting the rain fall on her face.

Scott quietly cleared his throat. Then said what was on his mind. "If I hadn't stopped you, you would have died."

Her head fell as her eyes leveled on his. He could almost read her mind. *Oh, please.*

"No, I'm serious. If I hadn't stopped you, literally sat on you, you would have run out that door and back out into the flames to try to find Velda." He didn't know why he even spoke the words. Yet, he needed to understand. Now more than ever. "I don't understand, Chris. I'm sorry, but I don't ... understand."

"What's to understand?" The words growled out of a nasty snarl.

"I'm sorry. I just—" Scott gasped as Chris quickly stood, so quickly she almost reached the edge of the sidewalk before he could say, "Wait! Chris!"

Breathing heavily, Chris leaned against the wall. Slowly lowered her head and closed her eyes.

If she continued to walk away, Scott didn't think he had the strength to follow her. He couldn't even imagine trying to push himself to his feet right now. He let his head fall back to the wall behind him. Breathed out a deep sigh. Said, "Come back and sit down."

"Don't tell me what to do." She didn't open her eyes to say the words.

"You're just gonna stand there?"

"Maybe."

"For how long?"

She didn't say anything. Still didn't move.

"Come back and sit down."

She quickly turned. "Scott!" Her face burned with anger.

"What? You want to leave? Where would you go?"

"I don't know."

Scott spaced the words out, yet spoke them as softly as he could. "Come on back here and sit down."

"No."

Her stubbornness was caving in. Scott wanted to smile almost as much as Chris wanted to sit down.

"I don't even know what I'm doing here." She barely spoke the words as she pushed away from the wall and turned again to look out at the street.

"Chris, please come and sit down."

She slowly met his gaze.

He gave her a lopsided grin.

She let herself slide down the wall to sit right where she stood. Her breath stuck in her throat as she sat. She held it another long second before letting it out. Blinked. Then looked up at him and glared.

"Erin and I talked about the war."

He knew the words would hit Chris hard, but not that hard. "You're kidding, right?" Her eyes blazed. "You're going to bring this up now."

Scott stuck out his bottom lip. Shrugged. "Why not? I'm here. You're there. We're both not going anywhere for a little while."

Her teeth clenched as she glanced away.

"You want to go? Go. I won't stop you."

She didn't say anything.

"If you sit there and answer my questions, help me . . . understand you, I may be able to help you . . . stay."

Again, her eyes blazed.

"You don't want to leave Kimberley, right? You like it here. Don't you?"

Nothing.

"Erin wants you to stay. She really does."

"It's not Erin's decision to make."

Scott slowly nodded. "Yes, you're right about that."

"What do you want, Scott?"

He quickly tried to prioritize his long list. "I want to be able to trust you."

Her eyes flickered.

"I think I'm learning that I can."

She looked away.

"I mean, before, I couldn't figure out how you could kill a man. How any person could kill another person. But you, a friend of my wife's, how you could stand there and look at another human being, and then shoot them and kill them. I'm sorry, Chris, but that's the truth."

"Stop being sorry."

"I'll admit it. In all my life I've never even tried to imagine what it would take to kill another person. Yet, since I've known you . . ."

Her lips parted. She stared at him, but didn't speak.

"I used to think you were dangerous. That you purposefully did things that put other people at risk. Especially Erin."

Her teeth clenched.

"You have to admit, Chris, that Erin's been through a lot since she met you."

She didn't admit anything, though her eyes betrayed her silence. Scott could tell his words didn't sit well.

"But still, with all that said, what I saw in your eyes back at the fire . . . when you screamed at me to let you up so you could go back out to look for Velda—"

"I didn't scream at you."

He tried to restrain his grin. "You know, I think I'm finally starting to understand. At least a little bit. It makes sense to me now, what Ben said. He told me during the war you did what you had to do."

"When were you talking to Ben about me?"

"Earlier this morning."

A cold sneer. "You've had a busy day."

Scott quickly blew off the comment. And the sneer. "He didn't tell me much, so you don't have to worry. I mean, that was all he told me. He said you did what you had to do. And that you were a good soldier. No." He almost laughed. "The *best* soldier. I asked him what he meant by that, if he just meant that day at the Dustoff, and he said no, every day he knew you. I thought he was feeding me a line. A couple of lines, actually. But now I see he wasn't. He was right."

Chris made a show of rolling her eyes. "So, this is a special moment for you, huh? You're finally starting to figure me out?" She let out a grunt of a laugh. "You know what, Scott? Once you completely figure me out, let me know, okay? I'd love to hear what you've discovered."

"That's what he said. You do what you have to do. You don't think about yourself, or the consequences. You just do what needs to be done."

"Please, Scott. I was just kidding—"

"Like in the fire." He hoped she would look at him. She didn't. "Chris, it's true. If Velda would have been anywhere in that house, you would have gotten her out."

"What's your point, Scott? Make it so we can get out of here."

"You can leave any time. I'm not keeping you here."

She grunted again and let her gaze follow a passing car.

"Tell me what happened the day Erin was shot."

She shook her head in disgust. "I already told you."

"Tell me again. Erin told me she did not give you a direct order that day."

"You know what, Scott? I don't even remember. And I don't care anymore."

"No, that's not true. I can tell you still care very much. And I know what you were telling me the other day was only what you thought I wanted to hear. You were basically lying to me."

Anger flared in her eyes. "What? I have never lied to you."

"You cannot make me believe you have stopped caring about that day at the Dustoff, about what happened to Erin, and to Teddy as well. Deep down in your heart, you know what happened that day was not your fault."

She spit out a laugh. "You know what? Deep down in my heart? I don't know that. Not for sure."

"It's easier for you to blame yourself than to believe the truth."

"Yeah, okay, whatever. Whatever you say."

"Well, I'm not going to know enough to say anything for sure unless you tell me the truth."

She leaned forward and lifted her hands out to her sides. "What truth? Huh? What are you talking about?"

"Just answer one question for me about that day."

Her hands tightened into fists as she brought them back to her lap. "Why? Why are you doing this?"

Scott clenched his teeth for a second. "If you think I'm doing this for me, you're wrong. I'm not doing this for me. If it were up to me . . ." He swallowed deeply. "I am doing this for my wife. She loves you, Chris, and she wants me to try to get along with you. But, you know what? A part of me thinks she doesn't even know you anymore. That she never really did. So, here I am. Again. I want to find out if you're that person Erin is sure you are, or if you're that person she only hopes you are or wants you to be."

Chris's mouth fell open.

Scott suddenly hesitated. "Did that come out right?"

"Crystal."

"Good. I think."

"Thanks for sharing, Scott."

"Well, you asked."

Chris looked away. Her head slowly shook. "You're still steamed that Erin came to see me in Colorado."

A grunt pushed through his lips. "Of course I am! You think I can just forget about that?" But he couldn't fake his vehemence any longer. He looked down and put a hint of a whine into his voice. "I wanted to come with her. I've heard about Ouray and that area. I've heard it's really beautiful. Why did she get to go off traipsing around the glorious Rockies when I had to stay home and work?"

Chris stared at him for a full ten seconds, until the faintest of smiles barely twitched her lips. She looked away and lifted her hand to push the rain off her face.

Scott sighed deeply. Turned his hands palm up to catch the rain. Watched the drops splash into the tiny puddles forming there.

"Erin always did try to see the best in me. She always hoped for the best."

He smiled. "Yeah, she has that way about her."

"I'm not the same person I used to be."

He spoke the words as tenderly as he knew how. "I know, Chris."

"Just meeting Erin changed me. Having her as my friend . . ."

The falling rain softened the silence of the moment.

"What do you want to know, Scott." The words, Chris's voice barely broke the silence.

"Do you want to talk about this now?"

She met his gaze. "If I say yes, will we ever have to talk about it again?"

He pulled his lower lip up into a pout. "Probably not."

"This will be it? 'Cause I want to forget it, Scott. I have to. The more I think about it, the more . . ."

*It haunts you. I know, Chris.* Scott waited another second for a prayer to slip through his heart. "This will be it. I'm hoping from now on we'll have better things to talk about."

Her smile touched her weary eyes.

And it touched Scott's heart. He tried to return it, tried to put as much warmth in his smile as he could. He slowly let it fade. Then said, "Can you tell me why you went after the ring?"

Her face fell with sudden hardness.

*Lord God, please help me here.* Scott let out a deep sigh. "Erin told me what she remembered from that day, how things happened up to that point. And that it was you that got her out of there. You sat by her bed all that time. I guess the only thing I can't figure out . . . is why you ran down to the wreck to get that ring."

She glared at him for a second, then blinked the glare away. "I don't know why."

"Can you think about it? Try to remember?"

The muscles in her jaw rippled as her teeth clenched. Until she blew out a deep breath and let her head fall back against the wall. "This is insane, Scott. I wish you'd just let it go."

"Tell me first. Then I will."

"I don't know what to tell you, Scott! I don't know why I did it!" Her voice thundered through the lot. Her frown seemed to radiate all through her. "I wanted to get it for Archie, all right?"

"Archie, the newlywed."

"Yes. Well, I didn't know he was a newlywed at the time. All I knew was that he wanted that ring. But I was so stupid for going for it. Anyone else could have dug it out for him later, after they cleared away the wreck. They could have seen that he got it later when he was on the *Mercy*."

"Maybe."

"It wouldn't have been that difficult."

"If someone cared enough about him to take the time to do it."

"Somebody would have."

"Unless that Iraqi soldier standing by that tank would have thrown that grenade at the tanker and blown up the entire place."

She swallowed. "Well, yes. I guess if that would have happened, it would have set things back just a tiny bit."

"Blown you up too, in the process. And your helicopter."

"Yes, that would have been a real shame. That helicopter had been through a lot."

"And Erin."

She glanced at him only for a second. Didn't say a word.

Scott wiped his face with his hand. "Okay. That's all I need to know about the Dustoff."

A huge sigh. "Thank goodness."

"Can you tell me what happened to Travis?"

When he dared look at her, he saw a mouth that hung open, eyes that bulged with disbelief, then with pure rage. She glared at him another second, then quickly started to push herself up to stand. She struggled to get her feet under her.

"Come on, Chris."

She cursed when her legs wouldn't cooperate. Plopped back down on the ground. Then winced sharply and held her breath as she waited for the moment to pass.

Scott waited as well. It took almost a full minute. "Where do you feel it?" He barely said the words aloud.

Her breath was forced through her teeth. "Where don't I feel it?"

He hesitated. Then said, "There's a bus back at the fire."

"Oh, give me a break, Scott."

"If you're hurt, Chris, then you need to tell me."

She used a shaking hand to push the hair out of her face. "That's right. You're a medical doctor. You know? For a minute there, I thought you were a shrink."

He let out a weak laugh. "Nope. Never felt called in that direction."

"Until now, obviously."

"Well, I guess you just bring that out in me."

"And how does that make you feel?"

Chris held her straight face as long as she could, then burst into soft giggles. Scott hoped they wouldn't break her down into a coughing fit.

She stopped laughing. Slowly looked at him. "You really want to talk about this stuff?"

He made her wait for his response. Made sure she was really listening. Was really ready for what he was about to say. "I hate the way I've been feeling about you." He let the words echo in his heart. And knew it was true. "I don't want to hurt you, Chris. I really want to understand what makes you tick."

"You want to be able to trust me. You want to make sure I won't hurt Erin. That's why you're so concerned."

"If that was the only reason, Chris, wouldn't that be reason enough?"

She lowered her eyes.

"Yes, I'm concerned about Erin. I love my wife. But her safety is not the only reason why I'm concerned about you, and you know it."

"Right now, Scott, I don't know anything."

"Nah. You're just tired. It's okay." He looked at her a long while before saying, "Tell me the one and only thing you know for sure. Listen to me. Look into your soul and tell me what's there. Even after everything that's happened today. After everything that's happened this past month. What's there, Chris? What's in your soul? In all of this craziness, what's real? Can you tell me?"

Her eyes closed as her head slowly fell back against the wall. She sat like that for so long Scott thought she might have fallen asleep. But then she slowly let a smile stretch her lips. She said one word. "Truth." She said nothing more.

But for Scott, that word was enough. "Yes. Truth."

Her faint smile lingered as the rain gently fell on her face.

Scott laid his head back and let the rain fall.

A few cars splashed by them on the street. They sat in otherwise silence for a long, long time.

Chris's voice finally broke through the silence. "Did Erin tell you that Travis believed in God?"

Scott had to clear his throat. "Yes. She did."

Another moment of silence fell. Until Chris whispered, "I really loved him, Scott."

He lowered his head to look at her.

"You have every reason to believe I'm incapable of love. But I'm not. I really loved him."

"I know you did. Erin told me you did."

"He was . . . the man I wanted to share my life with."

There were no other words for Scott to say. "I'm so sorry, Chris."

She let out a weak laugh.

The moment stretched into silence once more. Until Scott said, "What was your first reaction when Erin showed up at your door?"

Heartier laughter bubbled out of her. "Oh, you wouldn't want to hear my exact thoughts at that moment."

"You were mad?"

"Shocked out of my tree was more like it." She smiled. "I thought it was a dream. A miracle."

"Did she tell you I didn't want her to go?"

"She didn't have to tell me. I knew."

"What did she tell you about me? Not that I'm all that curious, of course."

Another faint smile. "Not that much at first. We talked about you later. She really loves you, Doctor Mathis."

He basked in the sudden rush of heat to his heart. "Did she tell you how mad I was when I got to Colorado that night? After I heard about all that happened at your cabin?"

Chris looked at him. Her eyes flickered with a hint of disgust.

"She didn't tell you, huh."

"She doesn't tell me everything."

"I know."

"But you just verified what I already knew." She pushed herself up against the wall to sit straighter. Seemed to push her back into the wall.

Her back was bothering her. Scott could tell. He watched her. And lifted up another quick prayer.

"Sometimes I just know things without being told. I knew you were upset the minute Erin told me you existed. She didn't need to explain why. She still doesn't. And neither do you."

The words hit him hard.

"I saw it in you the moment we met. You were standing by Ben's fireplace. We shook hands, and I saw it in your eyes. You were not thrilled to meet me."

He couldn't look at her. "I'm sorry, Chris."

"No. Don't be. I mean it, Scott. You have every right to feel the way you do about me."

He quickly looked up. "No, I don't."

"Hating me for what happened to Erin in my cabin . . . Scott, you have every right."

"Stop it, Chris. Just because you think I have the right doesn't mean . . ."

Chris waited. Barely smiled. "I know." She let out a deep sigh. Coughed once, then swallowed. "Well, maybe now that you're getting 'to know me' a little better, you'll feel a little better. Maybe you'll even learn to relax. Maybe I'll learn to relax. Maybe, together, we can just . . . relax."

Laughter worked its way up through him.

"But if I relax any more right now, I'll be asleep. I mean it. And then you'll have to carry me again. And I know you're not up for that."

More laughter. "No, I'm afraid I'm not." Scott glanced around. "Maybe we should get out of here."

Chris lifted her hand to point, though with her eyes closed, Scott had no idea what she pointed at. "Maybe . . . that sounds like a plan." Her hand fell to her lap.

Sounded like a great plan. If he could move.

Chris didn't make any immediate or even detectable attempt to move either.

The two of them just sat there.

As the rain fell.

# TWELVE

"YOU KNOW? I THINK PAP had it right. Going home. Doesn't that sound like a good idea?" All of a sudden, Sarah Connelly looked straight at Erin and said, "Why don't you go home? We can finish cleaning up around here, can't we, Mildred?"

Sarah and Erin both turned to gaze at Mildred Conner, who put her hands on her hips and said, "Well, heavens, yes, Sarah. You go on home, Erin. We can take care of this."

What was Erin supposed to say to that?

They stood there staring at her, waiting for her to speak, to toss in her towel, to do something.

"Why do I have to go home?" Erin said with a shrug of her shoulders. "Why not one of you?"

"Okay." Sarah glanced at Mildred. "Let's take a vote. Who all wants Erin to go home?"

Erin laughed as both women raised their hands.

"It would appear you've been outvoted. See ya later, lady."

"Sarah . . ."

"Go. Put your feet up."

"Take a nice hot bath," Mildred said, adding exaggerated dramatic flair to her words.

The image fell over Erin suddenly, yet so very softly, reached deep into her soul, flooded her entire being with . . . yes. Creamy coconut bubbles.

"Good-bye, woman."

Erin looked at Sarah. "You sure?"

"Mildred, are we sure?"

"If she's not out of here in ten seconds . . ."

"Okay, okay." Erin tossed in her towel. "But I won't forget this, you two."

"Happy soaking," Sarah said as she laughed.

✶ ✶ ✶

HE HAD BEEN WATCHING FOR them, hoping they would be all right. Hoping they would make their way back his direction. Soon. He watched the firefighters maneuver long beams of water into the flames engulfing Velda's house. Heard the trucks' rumbles, the quiet concern of Velda's neighbors, the excited yammers of Jimmy and his little friends as they danced and played in the rain. He hoped to see his wife soon. She had said she was quickly on her way. He hoped to see Velda soon. Another prayer of thanksgiving flew heavenward from his heart. Then his prayers turned more urgent. He prayed for Scott and Chris. Hoped they would arrive . . . soon.

Shattering glass, radio static, shouts of direction, squeals from the children. So many red trucks of all shapes and sizes, two ambulances, the battalion chief's sedan. So many umbrellas. So many people. So much commotion.

He peered down the street. Pushed back his jacket's hood and squinted his eyes. Was it? Yes. Finally. He saw two living, breathing answers to prayer walking toward him.

*Oh, thank You, Lord. Please let them be all right. Please, Lord, help them to be all right.*

They didn't exactly hurry back to where Ben stood waiting for them. They didn't seem to be in any hurry at all. No, that wasn't it. They didn't seem capable of hurry right at that moment. And that was all right. They were up, walking, side by side, slowly making their way closer . . .

Ben stepped off the sidewalk and into the street. Tried to restrain a giddy smile. Forgot all about the fire and its commotion. He stared at those two friends walking toward him. And in his heart, gratitude swelled.

As soon as they were close enough, he stepped up to meet them, saying, "Hey, you two! There you are!" But his heart almost broke. Chris McIntyre looked worse than he had ever seen her, and during the war, he had seen her at her worst. She walked toward him completely soaked, from the top of her head to the shoes on her feet. She wore waterproof boots. Ben hoped, at least, her feet were dry.

And she was filthy. No, filthy didn't even begin to describe her. Dirt and soot smudged and stained every inch of her face and her clothes. She looked singed, her face flushed and sullen, yet, as she looked up at him, she almost smiled. No. Wait. She did smile. Wasn't that a smile?

"Hi, Ben," she said, though her scratchy voice barely carried the words. She reached up to rub her nose. Her dark eyes looked swollen and sore.

Ben glanced over at Scott, saw a small, reassuring smile on his face. He looked back at Chris, hesitated for another second, then slowly lifted his arm and held it out to her.

She moved in and let him wrap her up in a hug.

Ben closed his eyes. He held Chris tightly against him, close to his heart, so close he was sure she could hear his heart pounding. "Are you all right?" he said to her softly.

"Yeah," was just a breath, yet her head pressed a bit tighter against him when she said it.

Ben didn't know what to say. His heart flooded with prayers, overwhelmed with the moment. He held Chris a few seconds longer, then slowly released her.

She pulled away wiping her eyes. She wouldn't look up at him.

Didn't matter. He smiled, then gazed at Scott.

Scott barely nodded. And he smiled.

"You two need a long hot shower and a good hot dinner." Ben laughed. "And the sooner the better."

"Is Velda here?" Chris asked, finally lifting her eyes to meet his.

"Not yet," Ben replied. "Russell's bringing her. But they wanted to stop and pick up her daughter first."

"I think we're going to go get cleaned up quick," Scott said as his hand lifted to rest on Chris's shoulder. "It's not like we need it or anything."

"Oh, no." Ben laughed.

"We'll be back." Scott peered out over the chaos around them, at the flames devouring the house. "I think we both need to see Velda. Just to know."

Ben nodded. "I'll stick around here. When I see her, I'll tell her what you tried to do."

Chris slowly shook her head. "No, don't upset her. Just tell her how glad we are that she's safe." She looked up at Ben and tried to smile. "That's all she needs to know anyway."

As Chris turned her head to look at the fire, her dark eyes, bloodshot and swollen, still glimmered in the light. Ben closed his eyes for a second as another grateful prayer lifted from his soul. He let out a deep sigh. "All right," he said as he turned to look at the flames. Even as the devastation before him broke his heart, a faint smile pressed his lips.

*★★★*

ALL RIGHT, ENOUGH WAS ENOUGH. Patience was a Christian virtue.

Standing at the swinging doors, looking through the small window into the dark empty hall of the church, Del growled, then reached back to his waistband and pulled out his 9mm pistol. He loved to look at it. Loved how it felt in his hand. He dropped the magazine into his palm just to make sure it was full. Pushed it back with a satisfied grunt. He always loved that sound, when a full nine-mil magazine clicked perfectly back into place. He resisted the urge to pull back on the slide to chamber a round. No. Not in church. Though he loved that sound too. The smart clicks of a bullet chambering.

Patience. Compassion. Forgiveness. All good Christian virtues. So no one would blame a helpless lost sinner like him for losing his patience and dragging an unforgivable man out of a beautiful church so he could kill that man on the street. That would be okay, wouldn't it? They would give him credit for not committing murder in a church. Wouldn't they?

He blew out a laugh, then stuffed the pistol back inside his waistband. He could wait for a few more minutes, at least. Thank goodness he had found the john. And had taken the time for a smoke. Really hit the spot. And it brought back a few fond memories. Smokin' in the boys' room. Even if it was in a church.

He let out a deep sigh, then growled as he glared through the window into the hall of the church. No, the sanctuary. At least that's what the sign above the door said. Four-dollar word.

Well, at least Rich had taken a load off and made himself comfortable. He sat now, almost in the front-row seat, still looking up at that cross.

Del cursed. What was Rich waiting for? A sign from God?

*No, the question is, What am I waiting for?*

His teeth clenched. He needed another cigarette. He reached to his shirt pocket. This time, he would smoke it right where he stood.

✯✯✯

IT DIDN'T TAKE LONG FOR Erin to gather up her first-aid bag and her jacket. Stopping at the foot of the stairs, she turned and said to Sarah and Mildred, "Ladies? Any last regrets? This could be you standing here." She added her own dramatic flair to the words, "On the verge of a long, hot, bubbly baaahh-th." She held her pose without flinching.

Until Sarah hollered, "Get outta here!" and Mildred said, "Yeah, go on!"

Erin laughed and threw them both a kiss and a wave. "Well, all right, then. I'm off. *Vaya con Dios*, ladies!" She turned and started up the stairs, still laughing as Sarah and Mildred hollered their spirited good-byes. A few more steps up, Erin let a thought play out in her mind. A short detour. Just a quiet moment of peace and solitude after all the chaos of the storm. Of the week. Of the past month. Of . . .

She laughed to herself as she climbed the stairs.

Just a few minutes sitting, maybe even praying, but mainly basking in the splendor of that big, sacred place.

She topped the stairs and stood for a second, looking at the doors leading into the sanctuary. Yes. It seemed to call to her, the quiet, the sacred peace of that place. She couldn't wait for it to revive the peace in that sacred place of her heart.

She walked toward the doors and pushed herself through into the sweet-smelling soul of the church, lifted her eyes to the cross on the wall above her . . .

✯ ✯ ✯

HIS CIGARETTE MADE IT TO his lips, but the match never got lit. He heard a voice, almost a familiar voice, a woman's soft voice radiate up from the stairs. He listened, then bit back a laugh. Maybe he should forget about his old buddy Rich and follow the lady home just to make sure she enjoyed her long, hot, bubbly bath.

He pulled the cigarette out of his mouth and tucked it back in his shirt pocket. Glanced at Rich. Turned his head to look behind him. Listened.

Except for her faint laughter, the happy woman barely made a sound as she climbed the stairs. Del ducked back into the pastor's study and closed the door to a crack. Looked through. Saw the woman step up the last stair, then stop to look at the sanctuary doors. She stood there for another second, then turned and slowly walked through the doors into the sanctuary.

He blinked. Couldn't breathe. Couldn't believe his eyes.

It was Erin. Erin from the cabin. The rat-wench from McIntyre's cabin. The very same one.

He slowly grinned. Too bad she didn't go straight home. He definitely would have followed her.

He pulled the door open and quietly stepped out of the pastor's study. Slowly, painfully slow, he eased back to the double doors to peer through the window. Saw line after line of benches—pews, he thought they were called. Saw his old buddy Rich sitting down at the front of the hall, saw Erin standing just a few feet away from the doors, down the aisle facing Rich, standing there looking at Rich . . .

Del tried to quiet his thoughts, the rush of blood in his veins.

He wanted to laugh. If ever there was a sure bet, this was it. Little Miss Erin-from-the-cabin never in a million years expected to walk through those doors and see her dear old friend Rich standing there in front of her. Del had to hold his breath to keep the laughter from bursting up from his gut.

Well, well. And finally. Some excitement. Maybe now something would happen. Standing at the window, Del settled in to watch the show.

Maybe now, someone would finally die.

✳ ✳ ✳

SHE STOPPED AS SOON AS her eyes laid hold of it. The wonder of that cross, the symbol of all of Christ's suffering, all of His pain. Yet, in the wonder of that cross, in the obedience shown by the One who hung there, all of her pain, all of her suffering, all of her sin was gone, forgiven, and forgotten. Her heart had been washed clean by the blood that fell from the One who hung on that cross.

Her eyes closed as her breath rushed out. *Oh, Lord Jesus . . . dearest Lord . . .*

Her blood seemed to quicken in her veins. Her heart pumped against her chest, filling every last bit of her body with literal lifeblood as her lungs filled with the scent of the place, with the peace . . . with the very breath of God.

Laughter rang up from her soul as her eyes pinched shut. She hugged her jacket close to her chest, felt the weight of her first-aid bag in her hand, wanted to dump it, to throw her jacket away, to run down that aisle and straight into the arms of her Lord.

She opened her eyes and—froze. Completely. Quickly looked down at her feet, felt her cheeks flush with heat. She laughed at herself.

Someone sat in the first-row pew also looking up at the cross.

Biting her lip, Erin wanted to quietly back up, back out through those doors, wanted to turn and run home and pretend she didn't just barge into the middle of someone else's quiet time. She gazed at the person sitting so far away. Squinted her eyes to see through the gray light.

It was a man. Someone she had never seen at church before. He turned his head and stared right at her.

Cheeks burning, Erin wanted to lift her hand to wave at him, to back right up and out those doors, saying, as she did, *"Sorry! Didn't mean to disturb you!"* She didn't move. Didn't say a word. She only looked at him, trying to see him clearly through the dim light.

The man slowly stood. He continued to stare at her. Didn't say anything. Just kept staring.

She blinked. Who was this man?

He slowly took a step toward her.

An icy chill slipped into her blood. But she almost laughed. The man was just being nice. Oh, she hoped he wouldn't want to leave on her account. He had seemed so intent as he looked up at the cross.

He slowly lifted his hand, not to wave, but just to hold it out to her, as if he wanted to say, *"Wait,"* yet, no words were spoken. He took one more step forward, then stopped. His hand reached out to her.

The chill in her blood intensified. She pulled her jacket back up to her chest and hugged it. Her mouth hung open as she gazed at the man, at his hand, into his eyes. Across the distance, through the dim light, Erin saw emotion in the man's eyes. Such imploring. Concern. Almost . . . fear.

She blinked. Blinked again. She knew it was crazy to be standing there staring, mouth gaping. She should quit being rude and say hello. Tell him he could stay. She didn't mean to disturb him.

She knew those eyes. She knew that man.

"Erin."

The word barely reached her. Then stunned her.

This man knew her.

Her heart slammed to a stop. The heavy bag in her hand fell to the floor. This man knew her. And she . . . knew him.

*Oh, God. Oh, Lord God!*

"Don't be afraid."

Flooded with terror, she almost laughed. *Don't be afraid?*

"I'm not going to hurt you."

Her hand covered her mouth as her lips trembled, as panic swept nausea through her belly.

"I'm not going to hurt you, Erin." The man took another step forward.

Laughter. Sarah's laughter. Filtering up from the basement. Erin quickly turned her head to look at the doors behind her.

"Don't—run. It's all right."

Erin turned back around. The man had taken another step toward her. She threw up her hand and shouted, "Don't!"

Rich stopped and straightened. "All right. I'll stay right here." Both of his hands reached out toward her, palms out, as if to say, *"Okay. It's okay."*

Sarah's laughter again rang up from below. The laughter, the panic—Erin bit down on her cheek. The sudden pain helped keep her focused.

"I'd like to talk to you, Erin. Just talk. To you . . . and to Chris too."

Words burst out of her. "She doesn't want to talk to you."

Rich lowered his gaze and nodded. "I know. And . . . I know you're afraid." He stared at her again. "But please, Erin, don't be afraid. I will not hurt you. I'm not here for that. Not this time."

Her teeth clenched.

"I just want to talk. I swear to God."

"Don't speak to me of God." Her words again burst out. Deep in her soul, she struggled for control.

"I was hoping, Erin, that you would speak to me . . . about God."

The words slammed into her. "What?"

Rich stepped closer. He stood now about fifty feet away.

Erin backed up a step.

Rich stopped. Again held out his hands. "I'm changed, Erin. I don't know how, or why. But I'm changed."

"You have a lot of nerve to come here."

"I knew I'd find you here. You . . . and Chris."

"Leave her out of this. She's . . . not here anyway. She's away."

"What she said to Matt that night. Erin, that's what changed me."

She desperately tried to control the myriad of bitter thoughts racing through her mind.

"She forgave him, Erin. I heard her. She helped him get right with God. Matty died . . ." Rich looked down at the floor. His shoulders seemed to sag. "Matty was a good kid. And I killed him. If it wasn't for Chris, Matty would have died . . . and not been right with God." He lifted his head and met her gaze. "I'm usually not a God-fearing man, Erin. But that night, when I saw Matty die, and heard his last words . . . Erin, that's the only thing, the only thing that's kept me going, that's kept me sane since that night." He let out a weak laugh. "But it hasn't been enough. I've tried to kill myself several times. But—" The words ended.

Erin pulled her mouth closed and swallowed, then barely turned her head and strained to hear . . . Sarah's voice, then what sounded like Andy's voice, then Ryan's. Their voices, then their laughter filtered up from the basement. Erin glanced at Rich. With Andy and Ryan so close, maybe she could . . .

Rich pushed his hand across his forehead, then ran his fingers through his thin hair.

His words, what he just said, repeated in Erin's mind. Faint echoes of his voice, his . . . honesty. She slowly allowed her terror to give way. She saw the man before her, heard his last words echo, and said, "You tried to kill yourself?"

He looked at her. "Several times." A sad smile stretched his lips. "I can tell you firsthand, the barrel of a .38 Special tastes terrible."

Fear and panic fell away so quickly inside her, Erin let out a breath and let herself relax.

"I tried to kill you. And Chris too. You stood right there in front of me."

Her mouth fell open.

"I tried, Erin, but it wasn't to be. I played a game of fate. Left it in God's hands. And He didn't let a bullet into the chamber. Not once. Erin, of all the times I pulled the trigger, no bullet ever chambered. No one died. Not even me."

Erin slowly lowered her hands and let her jacket fall to the floor beside her. She stepped over her first-aid bag and walked slowly toward Rich. A thousand thoughts tangled her mind. She couldn't say a word.

Rich's face softened with a smile.

Erin walked, until she stood only a few feet from him. She saw his face clearly in the faint light. Saw the pure misery in his eyes.

"Please don't be afraid of me, Erin."

She shook her head slowly, telling him, *"No, I'm not,"* even as the words refused to leave her lips.

"I promise you, I will not hurt you. Or Chris. Ever again. I'm so sorry I hurt you before."

Her wrists. She slowly lifted her hands and rubbed them, amazed that his words, his very presence, made them start to ache.

"Can we sit? And just talk?"

She tried to pull in a deep breath. Succeeded. Then nodded. "Yes."

Rich's smile almost burned away the last of her terror.

Almost.

★★★

FROM BEHIND THE DOOR, DEL peered through the window, so close his breaths left small clouds of steam on the glass. His gut burned. He needed to hear what Rich and Erin were saying. And with the party that had suddenly sprung up downstairs, he had no hope of hearing anything through the door. He glanced around behind him, then watched as Erin finally walked farther inside the big hall, down the aisle closer to Rich.

*Finally.*

With the lull in the party noise, the darkness in the long hall, and Rich preoccupied with the little miss making her way toward him, maybe, just maybe, Del could pull it off. On hands and knees, he eased himself ever so slowly through the swinging doors heading for the first pew to his right, his movements slow, stealthy as a cat stalking his prey. Holding his breath, he hid behind the back of the pew, then waited for Rich's voice to shout his name, for footsteps to march up the aisle toward him. He waited. Heard nothing. Let his breath out slowly, then leaned out around the edge of the pew for a cautious look.

Rich still stood up front, watching Erin's slow progress toward him. Neither of them had even noticed Del had just slipped into the room. They were oblivious.

He let his laughter surface, yet made sure it was silent laughter, the kind only he could hear.

And oh, it was hilarious. Del heard everything play out, could barely contain himself as Rich pleaded his case to the rat-woman. Del wanted, no needed, to jump up and join their conversation. With just a few choice words, he would quickly set them straight on how things were going to go. Yet, as hard as it was, he waited, hiding, trying not to laugh, straining to hear what they said.

It was difficult to hear. They sat close to each other, keeping their voices low. He cursed under his breath. He had to get closer. Somehow. Or, he had to listen harder. Somehow, he had to shut out all the thoughts of what he couldn't wait to see happen.

And all thoughts of what he couldn't wait to do.

✷✷✷

WHAT WAS SHE DOING? HAD she completely lost it? Sitting so close to the man, her heart thumped, forced ice-cold blood through every inch of her veins with every violent beat. *Lord God . . . Oh, I hope You know what You're doing here. Help me to know what I'm doing here!*

Rich's eyes suddenly widened as he looked toward the doors.

Erin swallowed hard, then barely turned her head to listen. No laughter this time, just Sarah's voice, then Sonya's, then what sounded like a herd of elephants racing up the stairs. Andy's voice. Sonya's again. But Erin couldn't hear what any of them were saying. She glanced at Rich, who turned to look at her. They waited, watching each other's reactions, as the herd left the church out the front doors.

Silence fell throughout the sanctuary. Throughout the entire church. Deep, hard silence.

Rich licked his lips.

Erin tried to control her breathing. Prayed desperately that she wouldn't hyperventilate.

"I mean it, Erin."

She only gazed at him.

"I'm not going to hurt you."

She let the words register in her mind, then said, "Ok—" Her throat clogged. She coughed to clear it. Gave him a quick nervous grin. Tried again. "Okay."

"You believe me?"

Did she? Could she? "Yeah." She barely nodded. "But please . . ."

Rich waited.

"Please don't make me regret it."

✮✮✮

FINALLY WARM, CLEAN, AND DRY after his first hot shower in days, standing in the examining room of his clinic, Scott tried not to smile as he gently palpated Chris's shoulder, as she squirmed and whined, acting just like a small child having her teeth pulled.

She suddenly hollered, "Oww!"

"Oh, did that hurt?"

"Well, I certainly didn't say 'oww' for no reason!"

He clenched his teeth to keep from laughing, pressed his lips to keep from grinning. Continued palpating. "There's swelling. I think you may have dislocated it. Are you sure you didn't dislocate it?"

"No. I told you. It's not that bad. I just jammed it. It's all right."

"Hold still." He sat on the rolling stool and reached for a tube of Neosporin. He squirted a glob onto his gloved index finger and rubbed it over an abrasion on the back of Chris's arm. "You know, if you're brave, I'm sure Kyle's got a bag of lollipops around here somewhere." He couldn't help it. He smiled at his poor choice of words.

Chris let out a laugh and relaxed. "I'll take a sucker, but I'm through being brave. I'm too played out to be brave anymore."

"Good. Leave all that braveness for the people who get paid for it." He gently covered the abrasion with a Tigger Band-Aid.

"Oh. You mean, like firefighters?"

"Yes. Like firefighters."

Chris turned her arm to look. "Is that really necessary?"

"What. You want Neosporin all over your sweatshirt?"

"Hmm."

Scott let out a deep sigh. "Any other boo-boos you haven't told me about? Not that you have told me about any so far. I'm only going on what I think needs attention here."

"No, Doctor Mathis. No more boo-boos."

"What about your back."

Something flickered in Chris's eyes.

"Did you hurt your back or not?"

She swallowed. Whispered, "Just wrenched it."

"Wrenched and jammed. These are not very insightful medical terms, Chris. I expected more from you. Wrenched, as in, muscular or skeletal?"

"Muscular. Nothing to worry about. Nothing a few Tylenols won't fix."

"Any pain in your legs? Shooting pain or otherwise?"

"Nope. None."

"Good." At that moment, as hard as she was pulling it, Scott's own leg was starting to hurt. He pulled off his gloves and tossed them into the garbage pail. "If you're not lying to me, I think you may live to see another day." He gave her a grin. "If you are, then I'll make no guarantees."

"I'm not lying to you."

"Good."

"So. Your turn."

His eyes widened. Then he grimaced. "I told you I'm fine."

"That's what I told you and see how far that got me."

"But I am."

"Whiner." Chris grabbed a pair of gloves, then moved behind Scott to look at the cut on the back of his head. He knew his head had connected with the edge of Velda's porch as he went over, but didn't think the bump drew enough blood to need stitches.

She prodded and poked. "You're gonna need stitches."

"No, I'm not. Oww! Take it easy!"

Chris laughed. "Would you like a lollipop, Doctor Mathis? You have to be real brave to get a lollipop."

He felt her fingers dabbing the antibiotic cream on his head. "Did you give out lollipops to the troops?"

"Sometimes. If they were really, really brave." He heard Chris's gloves come off. "I could shave some of the hair away from it and put on a butterfly."

"I think not."

"Okay, fine. It'll leave a scar, but, otherwise, I think you're gonna live too. You've got a concrete brainpan."

"Good. I've always wondered about my brainpan." He spun around on the stool and gazed into Chris's eyes. And smiled. "You look a lot better without all that soot on your face."

She tilted her head, clicked her tongue against the roof of her mouth, and said, "Right back atcha, Doc."

She laughed softly, but Scott could hear weariness in it, could see deep exhaustion in her eyes.

"Hey, um, Scott? I, um . . . I said some things to you back at the fire."

"Forget it."

"I didn't mean it."

"I know. Neither did I. Remember? I said some things too."

Her eyes softened with a smile.

He hesitated for a second. "Are you, um . . . I know you are, so can you tell me how bad it is? I know you're still feeling stiffness in your neck from . . ." He let the words fade.

She couldn't hide her surprise. Her lips parted, but she quickly pressed them into a firm line. "Nah. Well, maybe. Just . . . a little."

Scott spun again and scooted himself on the stool across the floor to the glass med case. He quickly unlocked it, grabbed two packs of Extra Strength Tylenol, one pack of Tylenol PM, locked the case, pocketed the keys, then scooted back to Chris. "Here," he said as he handed them to her, saving one pack for himself. "This one's for now, the other's for tonight. That's why it's got a PM on it. Get it?"

She smirked.

"And pack some ice on your shoulder and back. Tonight, stop by before you go home and I'll give you some packs if you need them. Try to rest for a while tonight with your knees up as you ice them both. No heat, no really hot showers, at least for a few days. Let the swelling ease."

Chris gazed at the floor. "Okay, okay."

A moment of silence fell over them.

Until the words, "Thanks, Scott." Chris closed her fist around the pills and met his gaze. "For . . . everything."

The words made him smile. He gave her a nod. "Don't mention it, Doctor McIntyre."

✯✯✯

HIS KNEES ACHED FROM KNEELING so long. Yet he was almost afraid to move. The room was so quiet, their voices so low, he was afraid any noise would give away his presence. That any movement would keep him from hearing what they were saying to each other, sitting there, halfway down the aisle.

He didn't need to move closer to hear them. He could hear them just fine. Talking about everything that happened that night at the cabin. What happened afterward, when Rich and Del fought about finishing the job. What happened then, when the moron rushed off to Portland to try to finish the job.

Del's jaw ached from clenching his teeth. Violent curses rang through his mind, and it was all he could do to keep from opening his mouth and letting them spew. It was all he could do to stay still, listening, without jumping up, pulling his nine-mil out, and emptying the magazine into both of them.

Still, he listened. Waited. Cursed.

His knees ached.

He heard a sound. The church doors opened. Footsteps tromped down the stairs.

He quickly flattened himself against the floor and slid under the pew, holding his breath, praying his knees wouldn't pop or his gun wouldn't rap against the wood just above him. He lay still, listening, barely breathing. Hearing his heart pound against his chest. Hearing the man he hated most, talking to the woman he hated most.

No. That wasn't true.

He didn't hate Erin. Not really. It was Chris he hated. He hated Chris McIntyre more than anyone else in the entire world. And he hated a lot of people.

Right there, in that moment, lying on his stomach on the floor of a church, everything in his muddled mind suddenly became clear. A plan materialized with such vivid detail, he could only stare at the carpeted floor in awe. And anticipation.

It was so true. None of this was about Rich. Who cared about Rich anyway? He was a louse. And it wasn't about Erin, either. She was just there that night, a sad victim of circumstance. No, he didn't hate Erin. She was actually a good-looking woman. It would have been so much fun watching her relax in her bath, even if he would have stayed hidden and never even let her know he was there.

And . . . yes. None of this was about Matt, either. The poor kid. Another miserable victim of circumstance. Even if it was Del that brought him in and made him part of the plan.

No. Everything, right now, all of it . . . was about Wayne. Only Wayne. The best and only true friend Del ever had, from those early days of riding motorcycles in the mud pits and throwing cherry bombs into that jerk's chemistry class, to that last day when they slammed the doors shut on him in Arizona.

All of it, every last bit of it, was about Wayne LaTrance. And the woman who killed him. The woman who killed him with his own gun.

Right now, with Wayne dead, it was all about Christina McIntyre.

From that very moment until the moment it was done, nothing else mattered in the world but killing Christina McIntyre. Very, very slowly.

Sticking with the plan. And finishing the job.

✵✵✵

WALKING ACROSS KIMBERLEY STREET, CHRIS tagging along at his side, Scott glanced up toward heaven—and stopped right in the middle of the street. "Wow."

"What."

"When did it clear up?"

Chris slowly looked up. "Wow! I don't know."

Patches of fading blue lay behind faint swirls of orange and pink. The sun was setting.

"Thank You, Lord." Just a whisper. Chris's whisper.

"Amen to that." Scott turned and smiled at her. No wind, no rain. Streetlights flickered above them. The storm had completely moved on.

They continued across the street, up the stairs of the church, and through the heavy double doors. Scott turned left and headed down the stairs leading to the basement and the kitchen just beyond, Chris right on his heels.

The place looked deserted. Scott glanced around, was almost tempted to yell out his wife's name. He went to the refrigerator and pulled out a platter of sandwiches, then plopped it down on the counter, and grabbed up what looked like a ham and cheese.

"Think they heard about the fire?" Chris grabbed what looked like a roast beef and Swiss.

"I guess so. They all must have headed up to Velda's." Scott chewed his sandwich and took a long look around.

"Erin too, you think?"

"Probably. Let's go find out." Scott tossed the platter of sandwiches back into the refrigerator and headed for the stairs. He lugged his weary self up, finishing his snack on the way.

Across from him, Chris said, "I don't know about you, but I'm gonna sleep like the dead tonight." She ate her sandwich with one hand and pulled herself up the stairs by the handrail with the other.

Scott laughed. "Nice choice of words, but you know, I was thinking just about the exact same thing."

At the top of the stairs, instead of turning and walking back out the front door, he walked into the foyer, then looked inside the soundproof room for mothers with crying infants. Erin sometimes liked to hide out in the room, just rocking and enjoying the silence. The room was so dark he had to open the door to look inside. It was empty. He looked at Chris and shrugged. "Thought maybe . . ."

"Think she may be in there?" She glanced toward the sanctuary doors.

No light could be seen through the windows. But maybe . . .

He walked up, pushed through one of the doors, then held it open for Chris as she followed him in. Standing inside the broad open hall, he allowed himself to absorb the wonder, the peace of this favorite place. He blinked a few times to adjust his eyes to the darkness. His eyes found the only light burning in the room, the one illuminating the cross above the back of the stage. He savored the sight for a second, then heard Chris beside him say, "There she is. Hey, Rinny." She started walking down the center aisle.

Scott quickly followed as his heart swelled.

# THIRTEEN

THERE SHE WAS, INDEED, SITTING on the end of a pew about three-quarters of the way down the aisle. His love, his sweet and precious . . . *two*. Not just one anymore. Scott wanted to smile and say something syrupy sweet to his wife, but only grunted as he kicked something, almost tripped. Her first-aid bag. He kicked it aside, started again toward his wife, started to tell her it wasn't smart to leave—

He saw a man. Sitting in a pew across the aisle from her.

Erin quickly stood. Scott wanted to give her a smile, but the look on her face . . .

The man across the aisle from her stood. He appeared nervous, almost frightened.

Who was this man?

Right in front of Scott, Chris stopped so abruptly he sidestepped to avoid running into her.

"What are you—?" Chris gaped, then rushed past Scott to stand in front of Erin. She faced the man, glaring.

Scott blinked deeply, trying to comprehend her actions. The way she stood, the way she pushed back against Erin, as if to protect Erin, as if the man across the aisle—

"It's all right, Chris. Really, it's all right."

The words flowed softly from Erin's lips through a gentle smile, yet Scott's heart started to race. "What's going on here?" He moved closer. "Erin?"

She turned to look at him. "It's all right, Scott. Really, it is." She continued to smile. "Come on, Chris. It's all right. Why don't we all just sit down."

The concern, the fear, the pure hate Scott saw on Chris's face terrified him. He shook his head. "No, I'm not sitting down. Tell me what's going on!" He moved to stand beside her, suddenly angry that a pew stood between them.

Chris hadn't moved. She stood directly between the man and Erin, blocking her view of him. Blocking the man's path to Erin.

"Please, sweetheart, it's all right." Erin's voice barely reached a whisper. And still a small, gentle smile played in her eyes. No fear at all.

Scott looked at Chris. Deep concern hardened her face. Her eyes blazed at the man.

Scott glanced across the aisle. He had never seen this man before. Hefty, but not tall, the man stood with his hands raised in front of him, palms out. He seemed to cower under Chris's glare. He seemed genuinely afraid of her.

Erin lifted her hands to Chris's shoulders. "Chris, it's—"

"What are you doing here?" The words were a growl, especially with Chris's voice still wrecked from the smoke and violent coughing.

The man's lips moved, but he said nothing. His palms remained up, out, almost as if he implored Chris to stay calm. To hear him out, though he had yet to say a word.

Who was this man? A sudden thought turned Scott's blood to ice. *Is he . . . one of the men . . . from Colorado?* His hands tightened into fists as his eyes flicked from the man to Erin. She had lowered her head, closed her eyes. It didn't seem possible. She was praying. Her hands on Chris's shoulders, gently squeezing, she prayed. Scott sensed no fear in her. None.

*Lord? What is happening here?*

He swallowed. And breathed. And slowly, painfully, waited.

"I just . . . I had to talk to you guys." The man licked his lips. Slowly moved his hands to punctuate his words. "I . . . had to find you. To talk to you about . . . what happened." He glanced at Scott.

"Who are you?" Scott's voice boomed through the empty hall. "Talk to them about what?"

"Scott . . ." Erin turned to look at him. Her eyes seemed to cry out to him, begging him to understand. To trust her. "This is Rich. He was . . . one of the guys . . . who was at Chris's cabin that night."

Scott's breath stuck in his throat.

"He was a friend of the young Marine who was killed," Erin said.

"No, no, no." The man shook his head as his hands finally lowered. "I was the one who killed him." He grabbed the top of the pew to steady himself.

"It wasn't like that." Erin leaned around Chris to see him. "You didn't mean to hurt him. You fought for the gun."

Standing there, mouth gaping, Scott could not comprehend what he was hearing. He watched Chris. Could tell she couldn't comprehend any of it either.

"No, no, no. I killed one of my best friends." The man stared at the floor. "Ahh, Matty. He was just a boy." His voice shook. "I got so crazy. Got too caught up in the moment. Del wouldn't let it go. He got so messed up when Wayne died." He looked up at Chris. "He's the one who wanted you dead. It wasn't Matt. Not at first. Del put him up to it. Matt and Wayne weren't even all that close."

Chris's jaw muscles tensed. She was grinding her teeth. Scott forced his own teeth to part, his jaw to relax. It was difficult.

"Chris." Rich's entire expression reflected deep sadness. "You forgave Matt. That night. I heard you." He lowered his gaze back to the floor. "Could you ever forgive . . . me?"

Scott stared at Chris, waiting. For what, he didn't know.

Chris turned her head to look at Erin. Confusion filled her eyes. Anguished confusion. Anger. And a hint of fear. Chris slowly looked down at the hand on her shoulder, at Erin's hand, at the healing cuts on her wrist, where the bootlace had torn.

*Lord God.* Scott's upper lip twitched, his teeth ground as he glared at Rich, wanting to rip out the man's throat with his bare hands.

Chris glanced at Rich. Then down at the floor. "I don't think . . ." Her voice cracked, and she seemed to struggle to swallow. "I don't think I can ever forgive you for what you did that night."

"Hey." Erin pressed closer to Chris, so close the sides of their heads touched. "Chris, it's okay."

Chris didn't look up. "No. No, it's not, Rinny. This man didn't hurt me. He didn't even touch me. But he hurt you." She quieted her voice. "He tried to kill you, Rinny. I saw him. His hand over your mouth and nose . . . I saw you struggle. For what he did to you, I will *never* forgive him."

The words burned white hot through Scott's soul, so hot he started to tremble. He stared at the man across the aisle. Let his heart scream, *Dear Lord God! I want to kill him! Please let me kill him!* Erin's arm suddenly stretched across his chest. Her touch restrained him.

Her voice broke through the chaos in his mind. "I know what you saw, Chris. I know what this man did to me. But . . . Chris . . . I've already forgiven him."

Scott's mouth fell open.

Erin pulled her hand back to Chris's shoulder and leaned in to whisper into Chris's ear. "And now . . . you need to as well."

Scott heard what she said. He couldn't breathe.

Chris glared viciously at the man before her, her face burning with anger.

Scott couldn't move. He couldn't think. Silence fell. Heavy, awkward silence. He waited. Glanced at Erin. Heard his heart whisper, *Please, Lord God, what is happening here? What should I do?*

Chris's mouth hung open as she drew in long breaths. The anger on her face slowly dissipated. After a long while, she closed her mouth and swallowed. Pressed her lips open. "Rinny?"

"It's okay, Chris." Erin's words were barely whispers in Chris's ear. "Really, it is."

"I can't." Chris stared at Rich, as if she was afraid he would bolt if she took her eyes off him for even one second.

"You forgave Matt."

"He had every reason to hate me."

"No, he didn't, Chris. Neither did Del."

"I haven't forgiven Del."

"Someday you will. That day will come. Right now, it's Rich standing before you. Not Del. And he's asking you to forgive him."

Scott waited, barely breathing, his heart pounding like a drum inside him.

"Oh, God . . . ," Chris whispered. "Please help me."

Rich slowly lifted his hand. Couldn't lift his eyes. "I'm sorry, Chris."

"No." Chris lifted her hand as well. Held it out between them. "Don't you even say it—"

"I know I didn't touch you that night," Rich said to her. "But I let Del hurt you. I could have stopped him."

"Then why didn't you?"

Rich said nothing. Only barely shook his head.

"Don't tell me what you could have done." Chris growled the words.

"The truth is—both of you, hear me." Erin stayed close to Chris, glanced at Scott for a second. "The truth is, you did stop him, Rich. Del would have killed us both if you hadn't talked to him the way you did." She glanced again at Scott. Let her eyes linger on his. They seemed to sparkle in the faint light.

He blinked, then let her words replay in his mind. He studied the look in her eyes, the expression on her face, and saw only concern. He swallowed deeply and tried to comprehend her lack of fear. Of anger. It was impossible.

She smiled at him. Then turned her head when Rich spoke.

"I'm so sorry, Chris," he said. "Maybe I didn't hurt you that night, but I did hurt Erin. I can see what I did to her. And for that, I'm truly sorry. You've got to believe me, Chris. I am so sorry."

Tears flooded Chris's eyes.

*Lord God, I can't take this!* Scott wanted to pull Erin away, Erin and Chris both, and take them far away from this place, from this man, from this agony.

Erin gently rubbed Chris's shoulders and leaned in again, close to her ear. "It's all right, Chris. Please know that."

Scott grabbed the back of Erin's pew with both hands. *How can you say that? How is any of this "all right"?*

*Forgiveness.*

The word stunned him. His eyes quickly lifted to the illuminated cross above them all.

Even as they hurt Him, He forgave.

For a brief moment, his eyes pinched shut. *No. Lord, it's too much. To forgive . . .*

Chris barely turned her head toward Erin. "I know you've forgiven him, but you're so much stronger than I am. I can't do it."

"Just look at him," Erin whispered. "Look into his eyes. Start by trusting him."

"Trusting him? How am I supposed to trust him?"

Rich ran his hand through his thin hair. His other hand still gripped the back of the pew beside him. He stared at the floor. Then slowly met Chris's gaze. "I'm a changed man," he said to her. "And it all started that night when you talked to Matt before he died. What you said, how you reacted to how he hurt you . . . Chris, that changed my life."

"What I said?"

"You forgave him. And you helped him find peace with God. That . . ." Rich shook his head and looked down, then pulled a fist to his lips.

"Was it because Matt was a Marine?" Erin asked her. "We were wondering about that. Because he was in the gulf? You felt like you had that . . . bond with him?"

Chris swallowed. Slowly pressed her lips open. "Maybe. A little. I guess."

Rich gave Chris a watery smile. "I was in the navy. Back in the seventies." He let out a small laugh.

Chris's face softened as she almost smiled.

Rich again shook his head. "I know that doesn't mean anything, Chris. I'm sorry I said that."

"Can I trust you?"

The words startled Rich. Scott could tell since they startled him as well. He knew the expression on Rich's face mirrored his own. He watched the man, waiting for his response.

"I'm . . . a new man, Chris. Yes. You can trust me."

Chris gazed at Rich for a long time. Studied him, her eyes dark and hard, yet searching for anything they could recognize, anything they could make sense of.

In the silence of the moment, Scott allowed himself to really look at her. What he saw there, in her eyes, on her face, in the way she lived her life, intrigued him. So much contrast, yet so much the same. So much she kept hidden, yet so much of her heart lay open and bare.

Just who was this woman? What was she thinking? What would she say to the man standing before her?

Scott closed his eyes just long enough to silently whisper, *Lord God, please . . . help her.*

Chris turned her head, but not her eyes, toward Erin. "And that's the first step, Rinny?"

Erin squeezed Chris's shoulders. "I think it is. Try to trust him first, then try to forgive him."

Chris drew in a long, deep breath. Let it out in a rush. "I believe you're different. I mean, you even look different. And if you came here to hurt us again, you certainly had your chance."

Rich slowly nodded. "Yes, I certainly did."

"He didn't come here to hurt us." Erin glanced at Scott, her eyes soft as she smiled.

"That was why I came here. At first."

A cough spurted through Scott's lips.

Rich shook his head. "But that's not why I'm here now. All I know is that the good Lord was looking out for you both. That I know is the truth."

A few seconds passed before Chris said, "I can't argue with that." She stared at the floor.

Rich's eyebrows raised.

Scott felt his raise a bit as well.

"God has been looking out for us. For all of us." Chris lifted her gaze back to Rich. "And He brought you all this way. He has you here, right now, for a reason. He obviously cares about you." She suddenly let out a breath of laughter. "Of course, He cares about you. He loves you. Right, Rinny?"

Erin's entire face shone. "Yes, He does, Chris. Rich, God loves you very much."

"And He'll forgive you of everything you've ever done the second you ask Him to." Chris swallowed deeply. "So, I guess . . . I . . . have no choice."

"No," Rich said. "You do have a choice. I understand completely if you still hate me."

"I don't hate you."

"You don't have to forgive me."

"I know."

Rich's face fell.

Chris didn't say anything for a while.

Desperate impatience wormed its way through Scott's entire being.

Then, there it was. One simple word. "Okay."

Chris's broken voice barely carried the word to Scott's ears. Yet he heard it. He glanced at Rich. The man seemed to soften, as if a great weight had lifted from him. Scott glanced at Erin. Relief seemed to flow out of her. And not even a hint of tension remained in her at all.

Scott glanced at Chris. Saw . . . her eyes. Still bloodshot, still a bit swollen, so dark . . . she had turned to look at him. Directly at him. Their eyes locked on each other's for a long while. Scott didn't know what to say. What to think. His brain couldn't keep up with any of it. Yet, his heart had settled, and the look in Chris's eyes . . .

Her lips trembled as she smiled. Just a press of her lips. Her eyes, so dark, burning, yet so soft. She allowed the faint smile to soften her eyes. Then slowly turned them toward Erin. Her face and eyes held that gentle smile.

Erin blinked as tears flooded her eyes. She simply looked at Chris. She didn't say a word. Yet . . .

Two words filtered through Scott's soul. *Oh, Lord.*

At that moment, what was passing between the two women? What volumes were being spoken without one single word being said aloud?

He would never fully know. But he could imagine. And, for now, that was enough.

Chris turned to fix her gaze on Rich. Then drew in a deep breath. She held it a second, then slowly let it out. "Okay. Rich, if Erin has forgiven you . . . I forgive you too." She allowed a smile to carry her next words. "I forgive you, Rich. For all of it. Everything you did to me, or didn't do." She fell serious. "And for everything you did to Erin. I still hate what you did, but I don't hate you. I forgive you for it. For all of it."

The man stared at Chris. He didn't appear to be breathing. He only stared, then blinked, then slowly nodded, and then . . . he smiled.

"God will forgive you too," Chris said softly. "Just like He forgave Matt. And me. Just last month. No." She rubbed her nose, covering a smile. "Every minute. I really keep Him busy. He constantly forgives me. Every time I ask Him to. Which is pretty much all the time."

Gentle laughter worked its way up and out of all of them. Scott allowed his to calm him. And it did. His heart whispered grateful prayers to his Lord.

"Rich and I were talking about things. Before you two came in." Erin turned to Scott. Her eyes, her entire face, beamed with joy.

The sight stunned him. Her smile always did. But now . . .

Mouth ajar, he could only stare at her, could only soak in her beauty, the awesome wonder of her intoxicating smile. As she turned her gaze back to Rich, Scott closed his eyes, wanting to hold on to the sight of her smile for as long as he could.

"Rich wants to ask God to forgive him too," she said. "He wants us to help him know for sure that God has forgiven him for everything he's done."

"You can be sure," Chris said with a nod. "But I'm just learning this stuff myself. Erin will definitely have to be the one to help you. And . . . Scott." She gave him a sheepish grin.

Scott quickly returned it. The wonder of the moment was still too much to comprehend.

Erin reached to the pew rack for a Bible. Chris finally stepped away from her and sat in the pew in front of them. Erin sat. Rich sat across the aisle from them. Scott, the only one still standing, plopped down loudly in his pew. Too much. All of it. Still.

In his heart, only whispers. *Lord, I have no idea what just happened here. I can't believe any of this. But it's for real. My wife is going to lead this man to You. Straight to Your throne. And You will welcome him with open arms.*

Erin started to read from the Bible. The words soothed Scott's soul. But then she stopped and looked up. "Come and sit beside me," she said to Rich, "so you can also read the words."

Rich slowly crossed the aisle and sat beside Erin. And he smiled.

Between them, Scott gazed at Chris, who sat turned in the pew, resting her head in her arms over the back of the pew. She watched Erin and Rich for a second, then looked up at him. Directly at him. Gave him a small smile. She let it linger another long second.

*Yes, Lord. Oh, Lord God, this is for real. This is You. You are here.* He allowed every fiber of his being to relax. Breathed deeply. Gave Chris a bright smile.

*Lord Jesus, why did I ever doubt You? Why did I make this so difficult? For Erin. For Chris. For You! Chris is not dangerous. That is so ridiculous! She would never hurt Erin. She would never hurt anyone. Oh, God, why have I been such a jerk?*

He stared at the back of Erin's pew. Studied the long grainy swirls in the wood. The smooth, glossy surface.

*Lord Jesus, forgive me. Please. I've been such a fool. I've caused so much pain for Chris. I've made her life here so much more difficult. Oh, thank You, Lord, that she stayed. She didn't leave. She put up with me. She didn't want to leave. As hard as I made it for her. As stupid as I've been . . .*

Erin's voice. Then Rich's. Softly, they read aloud those soothing words.

*I'm about to gain a brother. Lord, this man is about to make the most important decision of his life! He's about to choose You! The angels are about to sing! But, You know it's true. If Chris would have stayed hard, she would have killed this man. No, not killed him outright, of course, and please forgive me for wanting to . . .* He barely grinned, then closed his eyes. *But, Lord, if Chris had refused to forgive him, he would have left. He would not have stayed to hear more about You.*

Too much. Too wonderful. He heard Rich reading Christ Jesus' own words. Words spoken out of love. Just for him.

Scott slowly blinked open his eyes, listening.

*He's the one, Lord. He's the one who tied her hands behind her! It's because of him the bootlace cut her so. Yet . . . she's leading him to You!*

He started to laugh, then quickly covered it with a cough. *Thank You, Lord. Oh, I can't believe all this. I can't believe any of this! It's too . . . amazing. Thank You, dear, blessed Lord. Thank—*

A loud noise startled him so much his heart almost exploded inside him. He spun around. A tall man stood behind him. Just a few feet away, hands stretched out, he clapped.

The smacks echoed across the empty room.

Clap.

Clap.

*Now who is this guy?*

The man moved closer. Scott started to get up, but felt Erin's hand on his arm. He turned quickly—saw unimaginable horror on her face. Scott's heart seized. He glanced at Chris. The same look poured from her eyes, filled her entire expression, then gave way to one of sheer terror.

The look on Chris's face sucked Scott's breath away.

Another loud clap. And the words, "Well, now. Isn't this nice."

Scott wanted to turn and look. But he could not take his eyes off his wife.

Rich was standing now. "So. You had to follow me."

"You didn't think I'd let you have all the fun alone, did you? And it looks like you're having lots of fun." Cruel laughter rumbled through the sanctuary.

Erin's jaw clenched as she swallowed. She continued to stare at the man. Her eyes, flooded with horror, had not yet even glanced Scott's way.

Enough. Scott quickly turned and stood, blocking his wife from the man's approach. He met the tall man's gaze.

They studied each other in silence for a second. Then the man nodded. "This is none of your concern, friend. Just sit back down."

Scott drew in a quick breath to respond—it froze in his throat as Erin's body pressed against him from behind. Her hands gripped his upper arms. A whisper in his ear. "Please, baby, don't push this man. Trust me."

The words fell heavily over him, quickly settling in his gut. His blood turned ice cold. Chills bolted through him.

The man smirked as he stared at Scott. "Is she yours?"

Erin's grip pulled down on his arms, as if she wanted him to sit, and to sit right now. Her touch short-circuited his brain, and he couldn't move or even think of a word to say.

"That's right, *baby*. You don't want to mess with me. Listen to your woman. You better just sit right back down."

The man had perfect hearing.

Still facing him, Scott slowly sat on the edge of the pew, his back to his wife, his arm out behind him, across the top of her pew. Erin eased her hands up to rest on his shoulders. He didn't take his eyes off the man, though everything within him screamed of his need to see his wife. To pick her up. To run with her from the room.

The man's gaze still raked over Scott. The longer it continued, the harder Scott's teeth ground.

"What do you want?" Rich almost shouted the words.

The man's gaze finally shifted. To Rich. After a deep sigh, the man leaned against the side of a pew a few rows away and crossed his arms over his chest.

Rich stood facing him, still waiting for an answer.

"Is this what you call finishing the job?"

"You need to leave, Del."

The word sliced Scott's soul. Of course. This was Del. No wonder Erin and Chris were terrified. Scott quickly turned to glance at his wife. Only concern remained in her eyes. None of the previous horror.

He looked at Chris. On her face, in her eyes, Scott still saw only fear. She looked so different, so overcome with it, Scott hardly recognized her.

"I knew you'd cave in, old buddy."

Del's words brought Scott's head back around.

"What, then. You came here to make sure I'd 'finish the job'? Why don't you just finish me, Del. That's what you really want, isn't it?"

Del's smirk widened into a full grin. "Oh, I'd love to kill you, Rich. But that's not what I really want. Not right now." His grin disappeared as his face hardened into stone. "Right now . . . I want her." He bore his gaze into Chris.

Breath burst out of Erin as she squeezed Scott's arm. He quickly looked at Chris.

Her face had turned cold. Not a trace of her previous terror remained. Muscles in her jaw rippled as her teeth ground.

"No," came from Rich. "Right now, this is between you and me, Del. Let's go outside and settle this. Just you and me. Man to man."

Scott turned in time to see Del reach behind him, back to the waistband of his jeans, and pull out a pistol. He held it in his hand. Studied it. Seemed to enjoy holding it. His eyes never left it as he said, "Did you bring your piece, Rich?"

"Into a church? Are you crazy?"

Del pointed the gun at Rich's chest. "Then sit down. And shut up."

Rich's face flushed crimson.

"Right now. Sit down. I'll deal with you later. I'll find you. I promise you. I'm gonna love shoveling dirt over your head."

Rich slowly lowered himself into the pew across the aisle from Scott.

Del swung the pistol and pointed it at Chris. Slowly pulled the hammer back with his thumb. The resulting click echoed across the room. "Let's go. You're coming with me."

"No, Del!" Erin's voice—immediately the gun pointed at her. Scott jumped to his feet, grabbed for the gun—

Del moved back, just out of Scott's reach. "NO! Shut up!" Violent curses ripped through the hall. He pointed the barrel at Scott's left ear.

"Sit back down. Right now. I'm only here for Chris." Del paused to let the words soak in.

They did.

"I don't care about your lovely wife. She is your wife, isn't she? Have you two 'tied the knot'?" The man suddenly roared with laughter. "Hey, Rich! You get it? Tied the knot! That's hilarious!"

Scott turned his head and gave Del a cold, furious glare.

"Sit down, please." Del's face hardened. "Right now."

With the gun pointed at his ear, Scott didn't think the words were a request. He lowered himself to the pew, then knelt beside it and reached over the back of Erin's pew to cover her with his arm.

"Touching." Again, Del laughed. "Get it? Touching. Hah! I crack myself up." He swung the gun back at Chris's face. "Coming, dear?"

She stared at him. Swallowed deeply. Blinked. Glanced at Erin and Scott.

*No, no, no!* Scott wanted to grab that gun and use it to blow off Del's head!

Erin slowly raised her hand toward Chris. Her eyes fixed on Erin's, Chris grabbed Erin's hand and squeezed it. Watching them, Scott could only imagine what flowed between them. Desperation flooded his soul. *Lord God, save us. We are all in Your hands.*

"Come on now, Christina. Time's a'wastin'."

"Del, stop this."

"Rich, just sit there and shut up! Or I swear I'll shoot you right here in this church."

Chris pulled her hand away from Erin's.

"That's it. Let's go."

She slowly stood. Stared at Erin. Then walked a step toward the man.

"Del!" Rich started to get up.

Del swung the pistol, cracked the butt against Rich's skull, then reached out and grabbed Chris. He spun her, then pushed her to the floor by the back of her neck.

*Lord!* Scott jumped to his feet as Erin screamed.

Holding the gun on them, Del pulled Chris up, then backward, down the aisle toward the swinging doors. "Don't get any ideas, lady," he said to her, "or I'll kill your friends. You know I'm not kidding." He pointed the gun at Scott, then Erin, then Rich, who sat holding his bleeding head. Back and forth the gun swung as he pulled Chris down the aisle toward the doors.

Chris reached up to push her hair from her face. "Last time I almost broke your nose," she said to Del. "That's got to have you a bit concerned."

Mouth gaping, Scott could not fathom the words.

Del laughed, then ground his teeth as he pushed Chris's head back down to the floor. "Just. Shut. Up." He let out a string of violent curses.

Rich stood and shouted, "Del! Let her go!"

"What are you gonna do, Rich. Try to follow me?" Del snorted. "That's a laugh. As soon as I turn off this street you won't have a clue where I went." He lifted Chris and continued to pull her backward by his grip on the back of her neck. "You never could track anything. Not even a squirrel. The navy let you down, buddy. Maybe you should've been a Marine."

Erin's breaths carried cries of terror. Scott watched Chris, saw her desperately trying to pull away from Del's hand, yet back-stepping with him. She tried to keep her face impassive, to not reveal her pain, or her fear.

As hard as she tried, Scott still saw both. Shouts of prayer ripped through his soul.

Almost to the double doors leading out to the foyer, Del pulled Chris back as Rich took another step forward.

Scott slowly stepped forward too, and felt Erin immediately step with him.

"Just stay put. All of you!" Del shouted the words as he backed Chris through the doors.

As soon as they swung shut, Rich sprinted toward them. Scott shouted to Erin, "Stay here!" as he followed Rich.

Both men hit the foyer doors as Chris and Del headed out the church entrance. But Chris suddenly fell backward. Grabbed Del by the knees. And held on until they both tumbled down the stairs, out of sight.

Rich shouted almost as loud as Scott did. They burst through the front doors and skidded to a stop—Chris lay crumpled on the front walk, Del beside her, to her right, the pistol still in his left hand. Both struggled to breathe, moved slowly, appeared dazed, maybe even badly hurt.

Rich jumped down the stairs and threw himself on top of Del. He grabbed the gun, trying to pull it out of Del's hand. They started to fight, rolling, cursing, clawing for the gun and each other's face.

Beside them, holding her shoulder, Chris struggled to stand.

Erin behind him—Scott quickly turned—her face deathly pale. She started for the stairs, shouting Chris's name, shouting, "No!" He grabbed her. She fought against him for a second, never meeting his gaze, staring down at the men. At Chris.

Holding her, Scott turned to look. Chris stumbled away from the men as they fought viciously. She stopped and leaned out over her knees, coughing, her breaths ragged. Yet, after another second, she looked up at Erin and Scott and actually . . . smiled.

Scott's heart swelled so quickly it almost burst. He eased his grip on his wife. They stood side by side, though Scott's arm still crossed her chest. She grabbed his arm. Held on to it.

Rich smacked Del's hand against the concrete until the gun popped free. Del flipped Rich then, and the two continued to fight.

Scott took a step toward the stairs, only to feel Erin pull him back. He turned, saw only concern in her eyes. He gave her a nod.

As they both watched, Chris walked a wide circle around the men, then struggled to bend over to pick up the gun.

Scott stepped toward the stairs. This time Erin stepped with him.

Chris glanced up at them again, standing there, the pistol in her hand, though she had yet to raise it. It hung down, pointed at the ground. She again gave Erin and Scott a weary smile.

Then she turned to the men. Stood there for a while, not moving, not saying a word.

Scott suddenly wanted to laugh. It felt so weird at that moment, but he couldn't help it. Watching Chris, it was as if she wanted to just stand there and let the two men fight. She could stop it at any moment—she held the gun. Scott knew she could use it. Would use it if necessary. Yet, she let them fight on. Let them wear each other down.

"What is she doing?" Erin said softly.

Scott only shook his head. And grinned.

A second later, grunting, Rich pulled away, but Del swung his fist out and caught Rich's jaw. Rich pulled away again, then popped his fist hard into Del's left shoulder. Scott thought the punch went wild, until he heard Del's groan.

"All right, you guys," came from Chris. "Cut it out." Her words sounded breathless. And incredibly weary.

Rich ventured a glance at her, only to have Del cuff him across the cheek.

"Knock it off, you two! I mean it!" Chris raised the pistol, popped out the magazine into the palm of her left hand, looked at it, then popped it back into place.

When the men still fought, she pulled back the pistol's top piece and let it slide back into place to chamber a round. That final click, as the hammer came back, caught the two men's full attention.

Chris stood there. Pointing the pistol. Scott wasn't sure if she aimed it at Del or Rich.

Rich struggled to push himself up, to disentangle his limbs from Del's. He glared at Del, then limped over to Chris. He stood there for a second, breathing heavily, mouth open and bloody. Then he said to her, softly, "Let me have it, Chris."

She looked up at him. Held the gun with both hands pointed at Del. She stared at Rich. After another few seconds, she blinked deeply, pulled the pistol up, released the hammer, spun the pistol in her hand, and gave it to him, butt first.

Del made a quick move to stand.

Rich kicked him back down, then asked Chris, "Is it loaded?"

"Fully."

Rich pointed the pistol at Del's chest.

The two men glared at each other. Del's upper lip curled into a vicious sneer. "You don't have it in you."

Rich spit blood into the grass. "Maybe I didn't yesterday. But now . . ." He held the gun steady in his hand, kept it pointed at Del's chest, then lifted his thumb and cranked the hammer back. "Let me just say, my friend, I'm not going to fire any warning shots."

Del didn't laugh. His teeth ground. Lines of blood trickled down his nose and the corner of his mouth.

Rich's expression did not change. Stony, deadly serious.

With a huff, Del fell back against the concrete and relaxed. After another few seconds, he winced, then reached up to rub his shoulder.

Chris stood at the bottom of the stairs leaning into the handrail, watching them. When Del relaxed, she slowly turned toward Scott and Erin and lifted her head to look up at them—her head quickly lowered as her eyes pinched shut.

Scott descended the stairs two at a time, Erin right behind him. He reached Chris and grabbed her arm to steady her as she swayed.

She didn't move her head, only her eyes to look up at him and smile. "Hey, you." She shifted her gaze to Erin. Tears welled in her eyes.

Erin pulled her close and held her tightly. Scott couldn't hear what she whispered into Chris's ear. But he saw Chris's smile.

Over his shoulder, Rich said to him, "You better call 9-1-1."

Instead of replying, for some reason, Scott lifted his eyes and peered across the street. And yes, sure enough, just as he thought, his sweet-little-old next-door neighbor, Mrs. Fiona Taylor, stood at the front window of her house, one hand on her hip, the other holding her brand-new cell phone against her ear, a scowl on her face, watching all of them even as Scott watched her. He wanted to laugh. No doubt the woman saw it all. No doubt she was calling every law enforcement establishment in the city.

Rich said over his shoulder, "Well, are you gonna call?"

"I think it's taken care of."

He gave Scott a puzzled look.

It didn't take long. Scott let his laughter surface as strains of several police sirens drifted toward them through Kimberley Square.

*** *** ***

"DON'T ARGUE WITH ME, CHRIS. Just sit. You are not all right." Erin pushed Chris into the examining room at the clinic as Scott prepared two ice packs.

"Rinny . . ." Chris sat on the padded table.

"Where do you hurt?" Erin reached into a drawer and pulled out two rubber gloves, a mini-light, and some alcohol pads. "Can you breathe all right? Take a deep breath." She pulled on each glove and flexed her hands.

Chris drew in a semi-deep breath, fully lacing it with teasing disgust.

Erin wanted to slap her. "Any pain in your ribs?"

"Nope."

She grunted. "Would you tell me if there was?" She grabbed the mini-light and shone it in Chris's eyes. "Why are your eyes so red? Did you hit your head at all?" Right. Left. Amid swollen blood vessels, both pupils worked fine.

"No, Rin. But I did . . . bite my tongue. See?" Chris stuck it out.

Erin looked, saw no blood—then knew she'd been had. "Oh, har har." She gave her a smirk, then palpated Chris's head as Scott sat behind Chris on the table.

"You guys, stop this. Really, I'm—" Chris gasped as Scott pressed the ice packs against the sides of her neck.

"Hold them in place, Scott." Erin said the words, then immediately cringed. What did she think her husband was going to do with them? She gave him an apologetic look. "Just be still, Chris. Don't move. Try to relax."

"You guys . . ."

"Are you always such a bad patient?" Scott asked over Chris's shoulder.

"You could have given me some kind of warning before you did that."

"Yeah, I know."

Chris closed her eyes and kept her face impassive, yet Erin knew the ice really had to hurt. "Just a little bit, yet. It'll numb." She couldn't hold back her anger any longer. Her voice climbed at least an octave. "Why did you do that? Did you trip? What were you thinking?" She tore open an alcohol pad and gently dabbed at a smudge of blood and mud on Chris's forehead. Noticed . . . Chris's hair looked—

"Jammed your shoulder again, didn't you," Scott said to Chris.

"What?" Erin pulled back to look into her eyes.

Chris pressed her lips into a firm line. "A little."

"Again? What—? Why is your hair singed?"

They both grinned at her.

"What am I missing here?" Erin threw the alcohol pad down on the table and crossed her arms over her chest. "What's the big joke?"

"No joke, Rin," Chris said. "It's just been one . . . unbelievable day."

"Unbelievable. Good word for it." Scott's eyes softened as he met his wife's gaze. "Velda's house caught fire when the power came back on."

Stunned, Erin's hands fell away from her chest. She could only stare.

"And Chris, here, needed to make sure Velda wasn't still in there. Even though men highly qualified in such matters were only seconds away."

"Well, yeah, Scott. Come on! Didn't you need to know too?"

"Of course, Chris, that's why I followed you in."

"Screaming at me the entire time, I might add."

"Well, I just wanted to let you know I was on my way."

"You didn't have to scream at me like that."

"I wasn't screaming at you. I was . . . passionately shouting."

"STOP IT!"

They stared at Erin. She stared at them.

"That sounded like a passionate shout."

"Yep, sure did. Here, hold these."

Dumbfounded, Erin waited. Chris reached up to hold her ice packs in place while Scott slid off the table and walked around to where Erin stood. He cradled her face in his hands, then kissed her tenderly on the lips. "Mmm." He kissed her again, let it linger, then pulled back and said, "She'll tell you all about it, sweetheart."

She wanted to ask him why his voice—Chris's too—sounded so scratchy and rough, yet his kiss sent tingles through her entire body, and the words wouldn't come.

His hands still caressed her face. "I need to go out and see what's become of our other . . . calamity." With that, Scott kissed her again, turned, and left the clinic.

Her lips tingling, her toes tingling, Erin could only gaze at her husband as he walked through the clinic and out the front door.

Chris started to lower the ice packs.

"Put them back."

She quickly obeyed.

Erin turned and again crossed her arms over her chest.

Chris blinked. "It's true, Rin. Velda's house burned down. But she's okay. We made sure of that. Ben said she was with Russell— that's her son, right?—that she was with Russell probably watching Oprah. Nothing to worry about. Except her poor house. Poor lady. She had some cool stuff. We should probably go on over there and see if we can . . ." Chris pulled the ice packs away again, acting as if she wanted to jump off the table.

And Chris would have jumped, if it wasn't for Erin standing in her way. "Don't you move. And put them back." Erin enunciated each word.

"Rinny—"

"You are not going anywhere. Put them back. And . . . be quiet for a second."

Again, Chris obeyed. Grinning.

Erin shook her head. Then rubbed her forehead. "You were what?" She gazed at Chris. "Running around in a burning house? You . . . and my husband?"

"More like crawling, Rin. The smoke was pretty thick."

"Smoke?"

"Lots of smoke."

"And you're *sure* Velda's all right?"

"Oh, yeah. We made sure."

"She was with Russell."

"Yep. That's what Ben said. Scott said he must have come out and got her since the storm was dragging on."

"When did you see Ben?"

"He was at the fire. After . . ."

Erin waited. "After what?"

"After Scott and I got back. I kind of . . . ran away. But he really ticked me off when he pushed me out the window, and then we fell off the porch roof and—"

"Chris."

"What, Rin?"

"What are you trying to do to me?"

"It's all true."

"I'm sure it is."

"Velda's fine, Rin. And . . . so am I."

"So you've told me."

"You don't believe me?"

"Right now, I . . ." Erin closed her eyes and continued rubbing her forehead. "I really don't know what to think right at the moment."

"Do you want to know what I think?"

Suddenly, she wanted to laugh. Wanted to smile. But she only sighed. Dropped her hand. Looked at Chris. "What. What do you think."

Chris slowly grinned. "I think, Rinny . . ."

As the pause dragged out, Erin wanted to strangle the woman. A Homer Simpson strangling his son, Bart, sort of strangle.

Chris still grinned. " . . . that I'm . . . really gonna like living here in Kimberley Square."

Erin's mouth fell open.

"And I think you've got an amazing husband—not that I want him, of course."

A laugh bubbled out of her.

"He'd do anything for you, Rinny. He really ... loves you. A lot."

Erin swallowed as her throat tightened.

"And, Rinny? Guess what."

She slowly shook her head. "What, Chris."

"So do I."

She couldn't think of a single word to say.

Chris lowered her hands, then left the ice packs on the table as she pushed herself off and stood in front of Erin. "Rinny, are you sure you're all right?"

"Yeah. I'm all right." Her voice cracked.

"Quite a shock, huh. Seeing Mutt and Jeff."

Laughter burst out of her.

Chris waited for Erin to look at her. It took a few seconds. "Rin, you are by far the best friend I've ever had. I mean it."

Erin's laughter gave way to a flood of tears.

"I would have died. Without you." Chris's smile trembled. "Thank you, Rinny. I mean it. For ... everything."

Erin shook her head. "You don't have to say that."

"I know. But I'm saying it. You and Scott ... everyone here in this place. You all literally saved my life. And you gave me a brand-new life all at the same time. I'll always owe you for everything you've done for me, Rinny. You never gave up on me. I'll always love you for that."

Her throat pinched shut as tears fell out her eyes, dripped down her cheeks.

Chris lifted her arms and wrapped them around Erin, then pulled her into a close embrace.

Erin tried not to sob as she held Chris as tight as she could. "I'll always love you too." She barely squeezed the words through her throat. "Always, Chris. I promise."

"You better, Rin. 'Cause you know what they say about a promise."

A breath of laughter rushed out of her. "I know, Chris."

"Okay. Just wanted to remind you."

Erin pushed away to gaze into Chris's eyes. She smiled at the tears she saw there. She pulled in a deep breath, slowly shook her head, and said, "But you've got to promise me something. Okay?"

"Anything, Rin."

"Please. Chris. No more craziness. Just be . . . boring. Okay? I like boring. I'm boring. Can you just be . . . boring for a while?"

Laughter played out in Chris's weary eyes. "Sure, Rin. I actually had that in mind."

"How about for the next fifty or so years. Okay?"

Chris nodded as she said, "Okay, Rin. Boring. Fifty years. It's a deal."

# FOURTEEN

CHRIS LEANED BACK IN HER chair and gazed out across the massive dining room table littered with dirty plates, empty glasses, leftover roast beef, carrots, baked potatoes, heat-and-serve rolls . . . so much food. She could hardly breathe. She certainly didn't need that piece of pecan pie.

So many empty plates, so many people, her new family, sitting around the table with her. Laughter played out on everyone's face, from tiniest Kayley to Big Benjamin Connelly. Everyone moaned about how much food they had eaten. Everyone raved about the pecan pie.

So many friends. It didn't seem possible. After all her years of solitude, of pushing people away, here she sat in a roomful of people who really loved her. People she really loved. It wasn't possible. Yet, here she was.

Kimberley Square, Portland, Oregon. A million miles—no, light-years—away from anywhere she dreamed she would be.

Raucous laughter surrounded her, breaking her out of her daze. One by one, heaving great sighs, her friends slowly stood, tossed their napkins on the table, then ambled in several directions. Finishing her milk, Chris barely smiled, watching the men congregate in the living room, Ben to sit in his recliner. The women hung around the table gathering up plates, talking about such things as the sale at Oshkosh B'Gosh and the fact that Kayley's first baby tooth popped up in her mouth the exact same day her big sister lost her tooth in her apple.

Overwhelming. All of it. Chris still smiled. She let out her own deep sigh, then stood to help gather plates to lug to the kitchen.

"Oh, no you don't," came quickly from Sonya. "Christina, you just go on now. Sit right back down there and let us get these. You've already done your share of dishes in this house. Today, I think it's Erin's turn. Don't you?"

Chris laughed aloud, remembering how long it took her dishpan hands to heal.

"How about another piece of pie. You want another piece of pie?"

She almost groaned. "Oh, no, Sonya. I couldn't eat another bite."

"I'll send the rest of it over with you and Capriella. How's that sound?" Sonya gave Chris a wink as Cappy leaned in to tell Sonya she liked that idea quite well.

"Me too," Chris said. "Thanks, Sonya."

She sat back down at the table, slouched in her chair, and eased her head back to rest on the top of it. She watched the men in the living room and the women moving back and forth from the dining room to the kitchen. Just sat and watched. Until Scott walked up carrying a colorful box in his hands. Chris quickly sat up.

"This is for you," he said through a blushing smile. "Thought you'd like it."

Chris reached up and accepted the box, not sure of what else to say except, "Thanks."

"No problemo, *señorita*." Scott smiled another second, then turned and walked back toward Ben and the guys.

Chris stared at the box in her hands. Had Scott just given her a present? She carefully lifted the lid on the box. Sifted through the tissue paper. Then lifted out four books, all hardbacks . . . Nevada Barr. The Anna Pigeon Mysteries.

Her mouth fell open.

All of them were first-edition hardbacks. With immaculate dustcovers. They looked like they had never even been opened.

She lifted her eyes toward the living room, saw Scott talking to Andy, wasn't surprised that he didn't turn to look at her. Was almost glad he didn't. She didn't want him to see her tears.

She barely turned her head and glanced into the kitchen. Saw Erin looking at her. Grinning at her. Chris blinked away her tears and returned Erin's grin, then looked back down at the books in her hand.

*Track of the Cat.* Anna's first adventure in the Guadalupe Mountains of Texas.

*Superior Death.* Her second adventure, up in Lake Superior.

*Ill Wind.* Her third, this one in Mesa Verde.

And Anna's newest adventure. Chris hadn't read this one yet. She read the title. Laughed aloud. Hoped no one heard her. Hoped no one saw how her eyes bulged.

Anna Pigeon's fourth mystery adventure was called *Firestorm*.

Chris could only laugh. Sounded too much like her own latest adventure.

Inside the book's front flap, she found a note. She slowly opened it and saw such terrible handwriting she wondered if she could even read it.

What was it about doctors and their handwriting?

She struggled through it. And was blown away by what she read. *I know I'm the last one to say it to you, but I'd like to say it now. Welcome home, Chris.*

She looked up. The living room shimmered through her tears. The kitchen too. She wiped her eyes, glanced back down at the note in her hand, and let her eyes close.

Peace, then a simple prayer whispered through her. She savored the words, knowing her Lord would hear. Knowing He'd be pleased with her prayer. Knowing He was the One who had brought her here.

*Thank You, Lord Jesus, for this place. For these people. Thank You, so much. For the first time in my life, Lord, I really do feel like . . . I'm home.*

# Read an excerpt from Book 3 of the Homeland Heroes series

# ONE

**May 1996**

*I DON'T THINK I CAN be a Christian anymore.*

The words sliced Chris McIntyre's heart. The Bible in her hands shook.

*I'm sorry, Lord. Rinny said to take it slow, but I can't get away from it. I mean, it says it again, right here: If I don't forgive others, You won't forgive me. Jesus, You said it so many times, in so many different ways. In Your prayers. In Your teachings. You said, "If you don't forgive . . ."*

With Erin's help, Chris had forgiven Rich. With prayer and the passage of time, she had even forgiven Del. But Del was a moron. Sometimes it was easier to forgive morons.

She had even forgiven herself.

It was so much harder to forgive the one she had dared to love, the one whose love for her had caused so much pain.

*He did love me once, didn't he? When I was young?*

The memory of that day returned to haunt her, the day she had climbed up on her father's lap and leaned against his chest and rested her head against his shoulder. His strong arms encircled her and tenderly pulled her against him. He spoke soft words in her ear, words she would always treasure. His voice, she would never forget: "You're a good girl, Chrissy. You're a good girl."

*But, Lord! What did I do? Did I suddenly turn bad? Did I cause him that much grief that he grew to hate me?*

Only hate could drive a father to beat his child so viciously.

Chris jumped off her bed and tossed her Bible on the nightstand. She quickly headed for the kitchen, running her fingers through her hair as she walked, as she let out a long, deep breath.

*Later, Lord. Later.*

She grabbed the gallon of milk out of the refrigerator and poured herself a glassful and then hurriedly lifted the glass for a long drink. She closed her eyes as the milk left a cool, soothing trail from her throat to her stomach. She waited another second, hoping it would soothe the burn there.

If the milk didn't work, she knew something that would. It had been months since she'd taken her last drink of Jack Daniel's whiskey, since that night at Dandy's Pub, the night that jerk pushed Erin down, the night Chris, for the first time in her life, cried out to Jesus for help.

Her eyes closed as she remembered that night, the night Erin would not let her leave, the night the Lord Jesus Christ heard her cry.

*Please hear me again, now. I don't want to hurt You. Help me know what to do.*

Well, that was a dumb prayer. She knew exactly what he wanted her to do. The question was, would she do it?

*Lord Jesus, I know You're asking me to forgive my dad. If I refuse to forgive him, how can I expect You to help me forget? I know it's true. I need to forgive him.*

She took another long drink of milk, swallowed, and slowly opened her eyes and blinked.

*But there is no way.*

Her throat tightened, started to ache.

*I'm sorry, Lord, but there is no way I can ever forgive my dad. If You know anything about me, You know I can't.*

Tears burned her eyes.

*And if You know me, You know that isn't true. It's not that I can't forgive him, it's that I* won't. *Ever.*

She turned, grabbed her keys, and left the apartment, slamming the door behind her, leaving her jacket hanging on its peg, her half-empty glass and the gallon of milk on the counter.

✮ ✮ ✮

FROM INSIDE THE KIMBERLEY STREET Medical Clinic, Erin Mathis heard the door of the apartment above her slam. Chris and Cappy's apartment. One of them stomped down the outside stairs. Angry stomps. She hoped it was Cappy.

Past the front windows of the clinic, Chris McIntyre, Erin's dearest friend, made her way down the long porch. Erin held her breath for a second, hoping Chris would stop at the clinic's door and peek her head inside. Just to say a quick hello.

The door didn't open.

More angry stomps.

Erin peered out the big front window and waited. Chris, head lowered against the spring rain, walked down the sidewalk, down Kimberley Street, probably toward the new gymnasium, on her way to work.

With a deep sigh, Erin relaxed in her chair and rubbed the back of her neck. She had never felt so bloated, so positively monstrous. Her weight gain, her bulging belly, her increasing impatience, being pregnant so long, so ready to be over and done with it—

"Are you all right?" Hot breath tickled her ear.

She smiled at her husband's words and then squirmed as his lips nibbled her earlobe.

"Hold still. You taste good."

His hands gently massaged her shoulders as his lips found the side of her neck. Erin squelched her immediate desire to hum with pure delight. Instead, she asked him, "Aren't you supposed to be at the hospital?"

"Yes." More nibbling. "Just wanted a taste before I left."

"You're getting more than a taste." She turned to face him, gazed into his light brown eyes, watched the light dance in them.

"You are so beautiful."

She grunted. "Please. I look like I swallowed a beach ball."

Her husband grinned. "Three more weeks, love."

"Two weeks, four days, and hopefully not a minute more."

He laughed.

"Don't laugh! You did this to me."

"I'll make it up to you first chance I get."

"You better."

He knelt in front of her and gently placed his hands on her protruding abdomen and leaned in to kiss it. "Hello there, little babe. Daddy can't wait to see you. You be good for Mommy today. Try to stay off her bladder, okay? And don't kick too hard." He looked up with laughter playing in his eyes.

Erin could only smile.

Standing, Scott returned her smile for a few seconds and then moved in to kiss her lips. He pushed back her hair and cupped her cheeks in his hands.

"You're gonna be late." Barely a whisper.

Another kiss, this one deeper, lingering. When he kissed her like this, what choice did she have? She could only fall headlong into the joy of his love, the joy of sharing life with her true soul mate, of being Mrs. Scott Mathis. She savored the overwhelming gratitude in her heart to the one who had saved them and brought them together.

Scott slowly pulled away. "Okay, you're right. Gotta go. But I'll be home around three." He traced the backs of his fingers down her cheek, touched the tip of her nose, and then turned, wrapped his jacket around himself, and headed for the front door.

Still basking in the moment, Erin's lips and cheek tingled. "We'll be waiting." She rubbed her belly with one hand and returned his wave with the other as he pulled the clinic's door closed behind him. His Mustang roared to life and carried him away.

"We'll be waiting, love," Erin whispered into the silence, still rubbing her belly. But then, just for a second, a wave of sadness swept over her. She sighed deeply, shook her head, and returned to her insurance paperwork.

She couldn't concentrate; she slowly looked up. Fat drops of rain splashed off the porch railing, slapped against the leaves of the azalea bush in the front yard.

*Father? I'm worried about Chris. Is she going to be all right?*

Constant, relentless splashes of rain.

*She wants so much to learn about you, to follow Your Son. She's really struggling right now, and I don't know how to help her.*

Tears blurred the splashes of rain. Erin made no effort to blink them away.

*I can only pretend to imagine what she's facing, what she's been through. Only You can help her find a way . . . to forgive her dad.*

Bitter memories flooded her mind, horrible things she had seen, things she had heard. The few things Chris had told her.

*Please help her, Father. Help her once and for all to put everything behind her. Please free her from all of it. For the first time in her life, Lord, please help her to be free.*

★★★

WATER COURSED DOWN HER FACE and dripped off her chin, dripped from her drenched hair to the back of her shirt. It seeped through to her skin, chilled her to the bone.

Stupid. Leaving the apartment without her jacket.

Water dripped off her nose and landed at her feet. She glanced down at her sneakers and wiped them on the mat just inside the door of the new Kimberley Street gymnasium.

The mat had been Isaiah's idea, and it was a good one. The new floor in the gym had fit and settled well, and though it was old and scuffed and second-hand, it suited their needs and budget perfectly. Donated by a local middle school, it had taken three days and the help of fifteen volunteers from the church to lay it out. And, so far, there was only one slightly dead spot, over in the far corner, about twenty feet from the basket.

Alaina had found it.

Chris wiped her face with her hand and smiled.

After the floor had been laid and sealed, she told nine-year-old Alaina Walker and her two nine-year-old friends, Jazzy Sadler and Jen White, to dribble their basketballs over every inch of the floor. Chris had followed behind them, dribbling her own. Every time they found a squishy spot in the floor, Chris would mark the spot with a masking tape X to keep track of it and also keep score. The one who found the most squishy spots won a Pepsi. That was the deal.

It took almost a half hour for the four of them to dribble their basketballs over every inch of the new floor. Right after that, Alaina sipped her ice cold Pepsi as Chris whispered a heartfelt prayer of thanks. Finishing the floor and finding it good-to-go had been the biggest and most rewarding accomplishment of the warehouse-to-gymnasium conversion project.

Seeing Alaina share her Pepsi with Jazzy and Jen had been, for Chris, the sweetest moment of all.

Pushing back her wet hair from her forehead, Chris drew in a deep breath and let it out slowly.

So much had happened in the last five months. She had been ready to end it all, but then, drunk and passed out on her couch, she heard a knock at her door. That moment changed everything. At this moment, standing in this place, off Kimberley Street in Portland, Oregon . . . all of it still seemed like a dream.

She was home. The place had become her own: Kimberley Square. And this converted old warehouse, the smell of it, the cavernous depths, the ringing echoes of laughter and bouncing basketballs, had become her own too.

Alaina.

Her smile faded as her heart sank. She turned and walked toward the office.

Something was wrong with Alaina. All this week, especially, she seemed down, quiet. Even Jazzy seemed concerned.

Chris drew in another long breath to calm the ache in her stomach. She unlocked the office door and walked in, flipped on the light, and tossed her keys on the desk. She walked over to a rack of basketballs and picked one up, squeezing it in her hands.

Her stomach burned. She closed her eyes.

Of all the kids in the neighborhood, why Alaina? Jazzy's parents were the best. Isaiah Sadler, Chris's good friend and coworker—and Jazzy's grandpa—had seen to that. Jen White's parents were the best too. Every Sunday they sat together as a family, all six of them, up front in the Kimberley Street Community Church.

Alaina had come to church once or twice with her mother, never with her father.

Chris slammed the basketball back down on the rack.

She had seen the look in Alaina's mother's eyes: fear. The haunted look of shame. She knew that look, knew it well. She had seen it in her own family's eyes, in her aunts' and in her uncles', even some of her cousins' eyes. Long ago she had turned to them for help, and they had all given her that look and then all but turned their backs on her. They knew what was going on, what she was going through, but they were too afraid to stand up to Donovan McIntyre. They were all too afraid to do anything about it.

"I'm not too afraid," Chris whispered aloud. "God, please, when Alaina comes in today, please let her be all right." She turned and picked up one of the towels on the shelf by her desk, slowly wiped her face and hands with it, and then tried to squeeze some of the water from her hair.

*Please, God. That's all I ask. Please just let her be all right.*

✦✦✦

SOME PRAYERS GOD SEEMED TO answer quickly. Some he didn't seem to answer at all. And some prayers . . . some prayers Chris wished she had never prayed. Some things just played out the way they played out though she didn't doubt for one second God still knew what he was doing.

At least, in this case, she hoped he knew what he was doing.

At that moment, Alaina Walker looked worse than ever, and the ache in Chris's stomach spread up the back of her neck to radiate through her entire head.

The child didn't smile. Her normally bright blue eyes were sullen and dark. She didn't want to play with her friends. Jazzy sat on the floor beside her, leaning back against the wall, just sitting there, both of them watching the others shoot baskets and goof around.

A tiny smile. Alaina's only response as Kelly's basketball wedged itself between the backboard and the rim. A few of the older boys tried to jump up to dislodge it, but they were about a foot too short. Kelly, red faced and giggling, asked Chris for a broom or something like that, something long enough to knock it free. But Lissa had saved the day. With a squeal, she launched her own basketball straight up with enough force to nudge Kelly's free, and not only free, but right into the hoop. Loud joyous laughter echoed across the big room.

Alaina only faintly smiled.

Chris turned to find the one other adult in the room, Kay Valleri, gave her a quick nod, then hurried to the gym's double doors and pushed herself through. Outside, the heavy cool air comforted her and filled her lungs as she drew it in as deeply as she could.

Maybe Alaina was just sick.

Chris almost laughed. Of course, that was it. There was nothing happening at home; the girl was just sick, and Chris was just overreacting. Yes, the signs were there, but did that mean Alaina was in danger?

Only one way to find out.

Her teeth clenched as she drew in one more deep breath. She turned and headed back inside the gym. She smiled at Kay Valleri.

"Are you all right?" Kay's eyes narrowed.

"Um . . . yeah." Chris glanced at her feet. "Needed some fresh air." She tried to give Kay another smile. "I'm glad you're here. Thanks for your help."

"Well, you can't be here every minute, you know." Kay patted Chris's shoulder. "And you can't have all the fun. You've got to share some of it with the rest of us."

*Fun?* Chris held back a laugh. *Fun?* Yes, most of the time it was fun. Five and a half days a week she enjoyed supervising the gym's activities, watching the kids and cleaning up after them, watching the adults too, sometimes even refereeing their pickup games. But at that moment, what she felt in her stomach and head and heart, she couldn't share with anyone. No one else could understand.

"Why don't you head on home?" Kay said. "I'll keep an eye on things."

Chris glanced at the clock on the wall across the gym. It was almost lunch time. Her work week was almost complete. "Yeah, I think I will. Thanks, Kay. I mean it."

"I know you do. And you're very welcome. See you at church tomorrow."

"Yeah, okay. See ya, lady." Chris squeezed Kay's shoulder then turned for her office to grab her keys. She found them where she had tossed them although they were buried under some papers. She picked up the papers and looked them over. Two of the children had returned their parental permission forms.

Her eyes shifted to the small filing cabinet by her desk. She sat in her chair, unlocked the cabinet, and pulled out Alaina Walker's parental permission form.

It had been signed the very day Chris sent it home with Alaina, signed in elegant script by her mother, Laurie. No serious medical conditions were listed. Alaina did not suffer from allergies or asthma. Chris studied the home address listed: Cameron Street, two blocks north of Kimberley, close to the abandoned lot where Chris first saw the blonde-haired, blue-eyed nine-year-old, where Chris stood and watched the girl dribble a basketball in a figure eight pattern around those tiny, worn-out high tops on the girl's feet.

She memorized the address, just in case, and then refiled the form and locked the cabinet. She stood and left her office, heading for Alaina and Jazzy to find out for herself if Alaina was sick or hurt or what.

She stopped and stared and bit back a curse.

Jazzy stood out on the court, laughing and playing Horse with her friends.

Alaina Walker was gone.

✳✳✳

TEARING LETTUCE FOR A SALAD, Erin glanced at the clock on her kitchen wall. Again. It was about that time, but she tried not to worry. She had set out two salad plates and made two turkey and Swiss sandwiches. She would wait to pour two tall glasses of milk. There was, of course, no guarantee Chris would stop by for lunch.

But Erin could hope.

So many hopeful prayers lately. So much to talk about, so much to share. Since becoming a Christian four months ago, Chris had read most of the New Testament and asked most of the important questions a new believer needed to ask. Erin treasured every opportunity to guide Chris further into her faith. Their friendship had been born in a time of fear and war, had outlasted years of silence, and eventually blossomed into something pure and sweet, something sent from the Lord Jesus Christ Himself, a priceless gift, wrapped up in His love, because of His love.

*And your obedience.*

She stopped tearing lettuce. Her eyes fell closed. *Thank You, Lord.*

She wasn't going to cry again, was she?

Gentle laughter worked its way up from her bulging belly. She tore the last of the lettuce and reached for a paring knife to slice up the tomatoes.

A few faint knocks on the front door startled her. She wiped her hands on a towel and turned to see Chris McIntyre leaning around the half-open door. Erin grinned. "Hey you."

A weary smile softened Chris's face. "Hey you too."

"Are you coming in?"

Chris stepped the rest of the way around the door, pushed it closed, turned, and kicked off her shoes.

"You don't have to do that."

She dismissed Erin's statement with a wave.

"Hungry?"

Chris's smile brightened.

"I just have to slice up some tomatoes for the salad. Go ahead and get out the dressing you'd like." Erin turned and picked up the knife. "Grab the Thousand Island for me, will ya?"

"Sure."

She quickly sliced up two tomatoes and sprinkled herb croutons on both salads.

Chris moved in beside her. "How are you feeling?"

"Pregnant. You?"

Chris let out a breath of laughter.

Grinning, Erin grabbed the salads and carried them to the table. Chris carried the sandwiches. Then she turned to pull the gallon of milk from the refrigerator. She filled the glasses Erin had left on the counter and brought them to the table. Erin eased herself down into the chair, breathed a deep sigh.

Chris sat beside her, giving her a sheepish look. "Are you sure you're all right?"

Erin pressed her lips. "I feel like I've lost my 'glow.'"

"Nah." Chris lifted her glass of milk for a quick sip. "I'd say you're just ready for the next step."

"I want to hold her. So much, Chris, I can hardly stand it."

"I know. I can see it in your eyes. You have definitely not lost your 'glow.'"

Erin's smile came easily.

"Wanna pray?"

She nodded and gave thanks for the food. When she said, "Amen," she started to pick up her sandwich but waited another second as her heart gave thanks for the friend sitting beside her.

Chris poured Hidden Valley Ranch dressing on her salad. Then she picked up her sandwich for a bite. Erin took a bite of her own sandwich and dribbled Thousand Island on her salad as she chewed. She kept glancing at Chris, her heart growing increasingly concerned. After a few bites of salad, she couldn't take the silence any longer. She swallowed and said, "You're not alright."

Chris's dark eyes flickered. "What?"

"What's wrong?"

Chris held her gaze on Erin's for another second and then looked down at her sandwich. It took a long while for her to answer. She swallowed a drink of milk and wiped her mouth with a napkin. "Rinny, what do you know about Alaina's dad?"

The question took Erin completely by surprise. "Alaina Walker?"

"Yeah. Do you know her dad? Or her mom very well?"

She shook her head. "No, not really. Why?"

"Her mom's name is Laurie, isn't it?"

"I think so." Erin had only met the woman once, maybe twice, at church.

"Do you know her dad's name?"

Where was this going? "No, I've never met him."

Chris stared at her glass of milk.

"Why do you ask? Is something wrong?"

"I don't know."

Erin put down her fork and wiped her mouth. "Chris, what is it?"

"I'm hoping it's nothing."

Silence fell heavily. Erin struggled with the moment.

Chris picked up her fork and stabbed it into her salad. Except for crunching croutons, the silence lingered.

Erin swallowed a drink of milk.

Chris finished chewing, swallowed, let out a sigh, and then pushed her half-eaten salad and sandwich away. "I'm sorry, Rinny. It's really good but . . . I'm not hungry."

"That's okay." Erin glanced at her own half-eaten sandwich. Maybe later, after her sudden queasiness eased, she would be able to finish it. It would keep until then. She looked at Chris. "You want a cup of tea?"

Chris's head lifted as her eyes found Erin's. They seemed to soften as she barely smiled. "Yeah. That sounds good. But sit still. I'll get it." She pushed away from the table and carried her lunch into the kitchen.

A prayer for guidance whispered up from Erin's soul.

In the kitchen, Chris tore open two packets of peppermint tea as the water in the kettle started to boil. A minute later, she carried the steaming mugs of sweet-smelling tea to the table.

"Thanks, girl," Erin said as she reached for her glass of milk. She tilted the glass and poured a few drops into her tea. Then she tried to restrain her smile as Chris did the same thing. She lifted the mug for a sip. Perfectly sweetened, the warmth of the mint lingered on her lips and tongue. She hummed.

Chris still stirred her tea. She gazed into the swirling liquid, but had yet to take a sip.

"If you tell me, maybe I can help."

The words brought a faint smile to Chris's face. But she didn't look up from her tea.

"Is something wrong with Alaina?"

Chris sighed deeply. "I . . . I don't know. I think she may be hurt. I just have this feeling . . ." More stirring. "You're gonna laugh at me. You're gonna think I'm crazy." She finally stopped stirring and pulled out her spoon. She watched a drop of tea fall off it into her mug, then licked it and placed it on the table beside her glass of milk. "I think, Rinny . . . I think she's being hurt at home. By her dad."

Erin's jaw dropped.

"I don't know for sure, but . . . I'm afraid for her. I can't explain to you why I'm afraid. I just am."

The queasiness in Erin's stomach sharpened. "Have you talked to her?"

"Not really. I've just seen it in her." Chris finally picked up her mug for a sip. She swallowed and lowered it back to the table still not look at Erin. "She's been . . . different lately. She's been getting winded, like she can't breathe that well. And the past few days she's been holding her arm close, like she's trying to protect her side. She's been looking . . . bad, Rinny. She's worn-out. I can see it. Her eyes are sad."

Erin lifted her mug but did not take a sip. It shook in her hands.

"I've been seeing it for a few weeks now. And that one time, that one Sunday when Alaina came to church with her mom . . ."

Erin waited. Steam from her mug carried the tea's sweet fragrance. She took a small sip, still waiting, praying for words to say.

"I saw it in her mom's eyes that day. There's something going on. I'm sure of it."

Erin lowered her mug. "I don't know what to say, Chris. I mean, I haven't seen Alaina since the day we opened the gym. And she seemed all right then. I've met Alaina's mom, but I have no idea what her dad is like."

"Does she have other family?" Those dark eyes finally looked Erin's way.

"She has an older sister."

"No. Does she have a grandma or grandpa that lives around here? Maybe some aunts or uncles?"

Erin shook her head. "I don't know. I'm sorry. I wish I could be more help."

Chris bit her lip for a second. "She has a sister?"

"Yes, Meghan."

"How old is she?"

"I'm not sure. She's probably in her teens. I haven't seen her in years. I first met her and Alaina at a Vacation Bible School at the church."

"When was this?"

"Oh my." Erin tried to think back. "Probably three years ago. At least. Meghan only came that one summer, but Alaina's been coming every summer since then. That's really the only way I know her. Except for when I used to see her playing in the lot. And the time we put up the hoop for her."

Chris's face hardened as she looked away. "And you've never met her dad. You don't even know what he does? Where he works?"

"No. I'm sorry."

Chris pushed away from the table and walked a few steps toward the living room. She ran her fingers through her hair. Then turned back toward Erin. "I'm sorry too, Rinny. But I can't let this go."

The expression on Chris's face tore at Erin's heart. "What can I do? How can I help?"

Chris's eyes narrowed and turned ice cold. "No, Erin. You are not coming with me."

"What? With you where?"

Those eyes suddenly widened and glanced around the room toward the door.

"Oh . . . no." Grunting with the effort, Erin forced herself to her feet.

Chris took a step closer. "Rinny, don't—"

"Are you thinking about going over there? To see Alaina's dad?"

"Well, yeah. I need to know if she's all right."

Erin gripped the back of Chris's chair. "I know you do, but does that mean you have to go over there right now?"

"Maybe it does."

Erin shook her head. "No, I don't think so. I mean, if you suspect something's wrong, let's call the police. Or Ben." She glanced at the phone for effect. "Let's call Ben and Sonya. Right now. They may know Alaina's father. Actually, I'm sure they do. They'll be able to help us know what to do."

"I am not calling Ben." Chris's face hardened with every word.

"Chris, come on."

"No, Rin. I'm not calling anyone until I know more. No one will believe me anyway. No one will believe me or do anything about it unless there's proof."

The words stunned Erin. "How can you say that?"

"Because I know, okay? No one will do anything for her unless she ends up in the hospital or something."

Erin could only stare.

Chris turned away and walked a few steps into the living room. "Look, Erin, I'm sorry about all this. I know you must think I'm crazy."

Erin moved closer. "I don't like what you're saying, Chris. Not one bit. I don't think you're crazy. If you think Alaina is being hurt, I believe you."

As Chris slowly turned back around, her mouth fell open and her eyes widened.

"Of course I believe you, and Ben will believe you too. He will do anything he can to help you."

"No." Chris raised her hand as her head shook. "Rinny, this is crazy! I'm not going to call Ben or the police and accuse a man I've never met unless I know for sure. I shouldn't have said anything to you. I should have gone over there before coming here."

Erin closed her eyes and prayed for patience.

"This is no big deal. I'll just go over there and ask to see her. I'll take a look around and see what I see. I'm sure she's all right. I'm sure I'm just being stupid. I mean, maybe she has a cold or something. Maybe she's just sick."

Erin sat in Chris's chair. She let out a deep breath and pressed her lips into a firm line. "But what if you're right? What if she's not sick?"

Chris sat again at the table and gave Erin a long look. Tears slowly lined her dark eyes.

"Listen, try not to worry. Let's call Ben and Sonya. Let's talk to them before you go."

Chris wiped her hand over her eyes. "Rin, it'll take me ten minutes. I'll just go over there, ask to see Alaina, ask her if she's all right, and then we'll know."

*Those dark eyes . . . such concern, such stubbornness.* "I want to come with you."

A laugh. "There is no way you're coming with me, Rinny. Absolutely not. Nuh-uh. No way." Another laugh. "Oh man, if you came with me . . . Scott would kill me."

Erin's smile wavered.

Chris patted Erin's hand. "Don't worry. Please? I know I'm just overreacting. I'm sure she's fine."

Erin swallowed deeply, grabbed Chris's hand, and squeezed it.

"Her dad may be the biggest sweetheart of all. A big teddy bear."

"And . . . he may not."

"Yeah, I know."

"You have no idea what you'll find."

"It'll be okay."

"I still think we should call Ben."

"After I come back. I promise. If I find anything out, I'll talk to Ben right away, and then we'll call the police."

Erin held on to Chris's hand, almost afraid to let it go. "Promise me? Please?"

"I promise. As soon as I come back."

"Don't do anything . . . heroic."

A soft giggle. "No way."

"I know you, Chris. So promise me: nothing heroic."

"Come on, Rinny. It'll be all right."

Erin lifted her right eyebrow as far as she could.

"Okay, okay. I promise. Nothing heroic."

But the words did little to ease the concern growing in Erin's soul.

# Book One in the Homeland Heroes Series

## Wounded Healer

*Donna Fleisher*

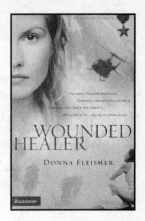

*Flooded with panic, two words burst through Erin's mind: GET HELP. She ran for the door, but someone grabbed her, twisted her arm behind her. Erin's shriek was smothered by a cold, clammy hand.*

*"Shhh"—Breath tickled her ear— "Just take it easy ..."*

Surrounded by the oppressive sand, heat, and tension of Operation Desert Storm, soldiers Erin Grayson and Christina McIntyre shared a special bond. But when an ugly secret from Chris's past shattered their friendship, they went their separate ways without even a good-bye.

Four years have gone by since that day in the desert, but Chris has spent her entire life running from the past, hiding her deepest secrets from those who care for her most. And now tragedy has ripped apart her life. She sees no hope in tomorrow.

Overcoming her own anger and doubt, Erin rushes to Chris's Colorado cabin. When Chris's fear of God and Erin's faith in him collide, they are involved in a different kind of war that only one of them can win. As Chris wrestles with grief, fear, and ghosts from the past, Erin fights to pull her from the brink of self-destruction. She will not lose Chris again. Chris's life is at stake ... as well as her soul.

Softcover: 0-310-26394-8

*Pick up a copy today at your favorite bookstore!*

**ZONDERVAN**™

GRAND RAPIDS, MICHIGAN 49530 USA

WWW.ZONDERVAN.COM

We want to hear from you. Please send your comments about this book to us in care of zreview@zondervan.com. Thank you.

# ZONDERVAN™

GRAND RAPIDS, MICHIGAN 49530 USA

WWW.ZONDERVAN.COM